Early Praise for Über Alles

"*Über Alles* is a well-constructed novel focused upon one of the pivotal eras of human history. It succeeds both as an engaging romantic tale and as a solid look back at World War II. Readers will be well rewarded."

—Gregory Coleman, President, BuzzFeed;
former president, *Reader's Digest*

". . . moves along with a narrative authority that allows the reader to focus on and thoroughly enjoy the story and the characters . . . the narrative flow is strong, clear, and vivid . . ."

—T. Chandler Hardwick, Headmaster
(retired) of Blair Academy, Blairstown, NJ

" . . . I found it impossible to put down, reading 100 pages a sitting . . ."

—Arnold Koch, journalist, *Melrose Free Press,
JazFax, Boston Business Journal, AdWeek*

"Robert Neff's excellent grasp of and perspective on historical events and musical genres and his skillful ability to weave the conflicts of individual lives results in a spellbinding novel which I could not put down . . ."

—Melva Cummings, musician/teacher, NJ

" . . . an absolutely riveting account of the lives of two musical artists . . . in that decade when the Nazis sought to eradicate anyone they deemed racially impure or sexually deviant. . . . You won't be able to put it down. . . ."

—Maestro George Marriner Maull,
Artistic Director, The Discovery Orchestra

"It's seriously fantastic!! A truly gripping novel that brings together romance, art, history, and intrigue."

—Victoria Bailey, Executive Director,
High Net Worth Clientele, Morgan Stanley

"As a student of WWII history, I was impressed with the personal insights about key events in the Nazi rise. In the end, this wonderful novel, through its female protagonist, left me with a haunting plea which is timeless: *I want the ability to be just a little different, so long as I am honest, hard-working, and law-abiding. I don't want a tone-deaf government minister telling me what songs to sing or what ancestors my companion must have. Am I unreasonable?*"

—Ret. Major Jason Howk, author and lecturer, NC

"Some books . . . really bring you into the time, the place, the smells, the sounds, the sweat, and the 'reality' of the scene being painted for you. I could see the scenes vividly, and I could really feel what the characters felt, hear the music and the shots, see the responses, and understand the emotion . . . I liked being a part of it. Being a man, I liked being hero, brother in spirit, father, or villain depending on where I was in the book, and, having spent years in national defense, I can appreciate war and what it does to people."

—John Wiles, professional hunter; managing partner, B&W Sporting
LLC; founder: Pinehurst Gun Club

". . . kept me engaged—always had me wondering where it would lead next—neither predictable nor overtly twisted. Perfect. My best read in three years. . ."

—Dr. Dennis Stark, academic and biomedical professional,
Cap d'Antibes, France

"Set in dark times, but light enough for a good summer read, Robert Neff plants his characters firmly in a complex historical context where victims and persecutors alike are presented, first and foremost, as human beings. Music of all varieties deftly carries the novel forward. *Über Alles* is a love story, history, and suspense tale all rolled into one well-written—and often spellbinding—novel."

—Katherine Anderson, development professional, Ithaca, New York

" . . . a fresh, informative, and compelling tale from an era which still fascinates readers to this day. An epic and gripping story, it has all the ingredients for a captivating movie or television series. You will savor this excellent read."

—Jack Counihan, marketing executive, *Newsweek,*
The Wall Street Journal, Sports Illustrated

"Robert Neff explodes onto the scene with his first historical novel. The treachery of the Third Reich and bits of nearly forgotten history unfold through vividly written characters and relationships. The love between a half-Jewish piano player and a Wehrmacht general's half-Jewish daughter sets the theme in 1938 Germany. Neff's fictional characters are real in every other sense, and the story of Hitler's city for the Jews, Theresienstadt, evokes needless suffering, loss, and the strength of the human spirit. Love drives a story that confronts a history we must never forget: Neff has brought a slice of that history alive in this page-turner."

—Richard Pabst, CIA officer (Ret.)

" . . . *Über Alles* weaves aspects of WWII into a beautiful fictional story about a place that you rarely have heard of before . . . Theresienstadt . . . the persecution of homosexuals under Nazi rule, and more . . . This story stays with you and is highly recommended for serious readers."

—Lindy Bolling, President, The Rapid Reader Book Club, Michigan

"Authenticity illuminates every page . . . These are not action figure stereotypes, but individuals . . . intellectually and emotionally alive . . . good people sucked into the whirlwind . . . Even the bad guys have a backstory . . . that rings true."

—Richard Hinson, retired international executive, Genentech, Roche
Pharmaceuticals, BristolMeyersSquibb

"Well-drawn characters, realistic dialogue, insightful historical background combined with the factual events and places . . . a page-turning novel that one wants to finish but hates to end. I felt the fear, the joy, the terror, and the relief of the characters and realized once again how lucky we are to be born in this time and place and not in the time of Hitler's reign."

—Kathy Knight, community activist, Rivas, Nicaragua

ÜBER ALLES

*A Novel of Love, Loyalty,
and Political Intrigue
in World War II*

Robert Arthur Neff

OLD STONE PRESS
www.oldstonepress.com

Über Alles

Published by Old Stone Press
an imprint of J. H. Clark & Associates, Inc.
Louisville, Kentucky 40207 USA
www.oldstonepress.com
© 2016, Robert Arthur Neff

All rights reserved.

For information about special discounts for bulk purchases or autographed copies of this book, please contact Old Stone Press at john@oldstonepress.com or the author at princetoneff@aol.com.

This is a work of fiction. Names, characters, businesses, places, events and incidents are either the products of the author's imagination or used in a fictitious manner. Any resemblance to actual persons, living or dead, or actual events is purely coincidental.

Über Alles
Library of Congress Control Number: 2016908559
ISBN: 978-1-938462-26-9 (Hardcover)
978-1-938462-25-2 (Paperback)
978-1-938462-27-6 (eBook)

Published in the United States

FOREWORD

EVENTS LEADING TO World War II in Europe and the conflict of nations that ensued have been documented more completely than those of any similar period in world history. There are literally warehouses crammed with documents, correspondence, diaries, photographs, motion picture footage, and data. Textbooks written by meticulous researchers have traced the movements of military units from both sides. They describe the composition of the forces, the military leaders, their armaments, and even the weather conditions of every hour of the vast conflict. *Über Alles* does not attempt to enlarge upon that body of information.

Instead, this story goes beneath the intensity of the political and military storms that were raging. Documentary history easily loses sight of the fact that more mundane human activity continues to play out. Most people continue to nourish their careers, fall in love, conduct business, tend to their illnesses, and raise their families even as military machines cross the landscape and traditional boundaries disappear.

Many ordinary citizens failed to grasp—or were unwilling to acknowledge—the nefarious agenda of the National Socialists (Nazis) until it was too late to oppose it effectively. Truly, in its earliest manifestations, the Nazi leadership was successful in restoring some of Germany's lost pride, and it earned tacit approval from many who were non-political but had enormous love for the traditions and values of their homeland. Thus it was that not enough warning flags were raised within Germany or at the highest levels in neighboring nations until the Nazi movement had advanced beyond the point where it could be intercepted.

Germany in 1938 aggregated many substrata. The old military professionals did not share the same goals as the new political leaders.

Many Jewish groups recognized that they were scapegoats for the nation's recent economic shortcomings, but at the same time they welcomed the return of a more stable national economy and the emergence of technological advancements, both of which initially resuscitated the nation's business climate. Smaller minority groupings—Gypsies, artists, and homosexuals—knew that they were disparaged, but they did not anticipate the extreme danger that was descending upon them.

Über Alles revisits the troubled landscape of Western Europe on the eve of World War II and imagines several people whose lives were disrupted and whose dreams were extinguished during the following years, even though they considered themselves to be living apart from the political conflicts of their time. They are not real people, although they *could* have been. Their stories are interwoven with real historical events and personalities of that period. Because "non-involvement" frequently gives permission to malevolence in our society, this story might be translated to a number of other historical times and venues. We have a discouraging habit of forgetting our errors of omission, which may eventually condemn us to repeating them.

Munich, the 29th of September 1938.

Signatures of Adolph Hitler, British Prime Minister Neville Chamberlain, French Prime Minister Edouard Daladier and Italian Dictator Benito Mussolini on the 1938 Munich Pact, which appeased the Nazis and allowed them to begin their takeover of Europe without opposition.

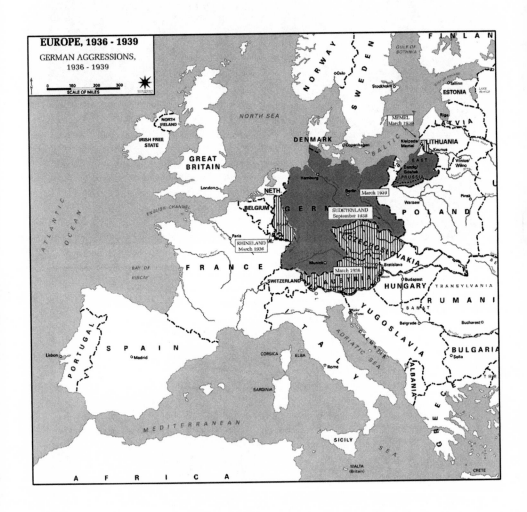

Iceland
(British occupied)

Faroe Islands
(British occupied)

Finland

Finnish
Military
Admin.

Reichs-
kommissariat
Norwegen

Sweden

Reichs-
kommissariat
Ostland

Soviet Union

Denmark

Ireland

United
Kingdom

RK
Nieder-
lande

Under
Military
Admin.

German Reich

Bohemia
Moravia

General
Goverment

Slovakia

Hungary

Reichs-
kommissariat
Ukraine

Under Military
Administration

Zone occupée
(Under Military Admin.)

Vichy
France

Zone libre

Monaco

San
Marino

Inde-
pendent
State of
Croatia

Romania

Under
Military
Admin.

Bulgaria

Turkey

Portugal

Andorra

Vatican
City

Albania
(Italy)

Spain

Italy

Italian
Military
Admin.

Dodecanese
(Italy)

Syria
(Free France)
(From July 1941)

Iraq
(Br.-oc.)

Tangier

Morocco
(Spain)

Morocco
(Vichy France)

Algeria (Vichy France)

Tunisia
(Vichy
France)

Malta
(Britain)

Montenegro
(Italy)

Cyprus
(Britain)

Trans-
Jordan
(Britain)

Saudi
Arabia

**Europe at the height of
German expansion, 1941-1942**

■ Nazi Germany*

■ Areas under German
occupation

■ German allies*, co-belligerents,
and puppet states*

□ Nominally unoccupied

■ Allied-held areas

■ Retaken during Soviet 1941-
1942 winter-offensive

■ Neutral countries

* Including annexed and
occupied territories

PROLOGUE

T WO MEN FACED one another near the entry door of a well-kept farmhouse about four kilometers from the town limits of Forst, Germany, on a raw afternoon in the early winter of 1939. The older man wore the comfortable weekend garb of a successful farmer, topped by an oatmeal-colored, hand-knitted woolen sweater. The younger man was resplendent in the dress uniform of a Gestapo lieutenant colonel, complete with four rows of multicolored decorations and campaign ribbons. The two had never met before that afternoon, but each had known the other's name and had anticipated such a confrontation.

Their dialogue lasted only a few minutes and was conducted in low tones, but something in their respective postures conveyed growing tension and irritation. Abruptly and without apparent warning, the Nazi officer drew a Mauser Schnellfeuer pistol from his formal gun belt and pointed it directly at the unflinching farmer.

"You are a stupid and insulting peasant!" he shouted. "An officer of the Third Reich need not tolerate such offensive insults!"

The distinctive crack of an exploding shellcase echoed briefly off the walls of the isolated farm's structures as a small lead projectile was propelled forward to a muzzle velocity of nearly 800 meters per second. Instantaneously, it shattered protective skull bones, jelled the cerebellum's intelligence center, and lodged in the sutura coronalis bones of its intended victim. Death was immediate.

If that bullet had not reached and destroyed its target, the life of one Dieter Meister would have been short and unremarkable, and the story related in *Über Alles* could never have been written.

CHAPTER ONE
43 Eaton Place, London – March 1943

THE ENVELOPE

A WEATHERED WOMAN SAT in a quiet corner of the reading parlor of a well-appointed London house, encircling a steaming cup of tea with both hands as if to extract all of its available warmth. Harbingers of spring were everywhere outside the curtained window, but her coloring and demeanor remained those of deep winter. Her hands were steady and appeared unusually strong, especially for one in her late sixties, and her eyes were penetrating blue, suggesting intelligence and determination.

An overstuffed, sealed diplomatic envelope secured with a red ribbon lay unopened on the small table beside her chair. She had attempted to trace the path of the envelope and its contents by reading backward from the last name—hers—through those in three prior addressee blocks. A wide black grease pencil had been applied heavily to obscure each of those names, leaving only hers legible, but close examination had allowed her to trace the indentations of some of the blackened letters.

Immediately preceding her name was apparently that of Wladyslaw Raczkiewicz, Poland's president-in-exile, who normally resided at 43 Eaton Place. She had been called by his aide, who told her that a diplomatic packet was being held for her at the presidential residence, and who invited her to retrieve it at her earliest convenience. So, that step in the progression was really not unexpected.

For now, she was most curious about the first sender in the sequence. The earliest-entered name had not been printed with sufficient pressure to stand out easily, but, by holding the envelope at a precise angle to the light and studying it at length, she concluded that it read "Giznad Asle." That brought a faint smile to her lips. She did not try to decipher the intermediate smudged name; there would be time for that later.

She believed that the envelope should be opened immediately and its contents considered carefully. It had already been over a week since the call from a Prague hotel alerted her to its existence. There would be unexpected disclosures inside, and it probably contained answers to some of the obscured events of the last five years. "Giznad Asle" was not the name of a real person but was instead a clue to the originator of the enigmatic envelope. The name "Elsa Danzig" had been reversed intentionally to "Giznad Asle" when it was lightly printed on the origination line. That was a frequently employed attempt at gallows humor within Poland's intelligence organization—the Stuzba Wywiadu Wojskowego, or SWW. It was, in itself, a form of professional greeting to the old woman from a female compatriot somewhere near Prague.

"Ah, yes—my brilliant and courageous Elsa. You are back out there in harm's way, even though our army struck its colors within three weeks and our navy steamed immediately for the security of England. How painfully ironic." The blue eyes closed momentarily, and in her imagination she pictured a diminutive woman—now about age thirty-two—with a chameleon's ability to blend and disappear into insignificance. Elsa had begun the chain of helping hands that moved the bulging envelope from German-occupied Czechoslovakia to her side in wartime London.

So, the burden had now shifted squarely onto her, she mused. As much as she would prefer to involve herself exclusively in helping to plan the future of her occupied country, there were too many personal issues from the past that must be sorted out and passed along. This envelope might be the figurative Rosetta Stone for several people dear to her—it could even enrich her own remaining time, or at least satisfy her compulsion to fix and repair nearly everything requiring attention. And so, with an audible sigh, she set aside her teacup and untied the red ribbon, then sliced neatly through the envelope's seal, using a menacing blade which she had extracted silently from the handle of her worn handbag. With steel-rimmed reading glasses straddling the bridge of her broad nose, she readied herself to begin assessing the envelope's contents.

CHAPTER TWO

Carinhall, Near Berlin – March 1943

TWO TIRED WARRIORS

CARINHALL WAS TRULY one of the most lavish homes anywhere in Europe, filled with famous paintings, priceless artifacts, and all of the trappings of the wealthiest man in the Third Reich. Never mind that the house and its contents were all stolen from victims of the Nazi regime; he was held in awe by most of his countrymen. His name was Hermann Göring, and he had been designated personally by Adolf Hitler as the second most powerful man in his government—the one named to succeed the führer, should he not be able to continue his command.

Through the first three years of the war that was irreversibly spreading across the Continent, Göring had seemed capable of achieving any objective assigned to him, but as 1943 ground along, there were cracks in the Master Plan for European conquest, and Göring had increasingly pulled back from personal direction of campaigns. He had known that the führer's attack upon the Soviet Union, to the east, was much riskier than the easy conquests of Poland, France, and the Low Countries had been. Logistical distances would be dramatically greater, and the cruel winter weather that had once defeated Napoleon might be equally daunting for the swift German armies and the *Luftwaffe* providing air cover above them. And finally, there were the fierce and fearless enemy troops of Russia—waves of men with nothing better to do than rush forward and die for their homeland. Göring knew that Germany's troops were tiring—even in victory—and he wished that he could persuade the führer to pause and consolidate.

He had just received disquieting news that again demonstrated the immoral ferocity of this enemy. German forces in Poland's Katyn Forest had reportedly found the bodies of thousands of Polish military officers, all thrown ingloriously into shallow trenches after being murdered. Those first secret accounts seemed to suggest that the entire officer cadre of Poland had been wiped out in one treacherous move. The Western Allies, led by Britain and the United States, would reflexively ascribe the evil deed to occupying German forces. They would be entirely unwilling to consider that it might have been an execution ordered by Soviet leadership in the Kremlin, for fear of offending their Eastern ally. But of course those Western Allies would know, as Göring did already, that Joseph Stalin had ordered the massacre.

Göring had reached out swiftly to exiled President Wladyslaw Raczliewicz in London through a neutral intermediary, because he wished to assure the Polish president that, even though Germany occupied large portions of his homeland, such a slaughter would be unthinkable to Germany's professional Wehrmacht officers. He had presented persuasive evidence identifying the true culprit, and somewhat to his surprise he had received an immediate acknowledgment from President Raczliewicz that Polish loyalists on the scene confirmed the authorship of the mass murder. Göring was pleased by this acknowledgment; he felt that it would make daily life much less dangerous for occupying German personnel. They would not be shot or firebombed from the shadows by outraged friends and relatives of the murdered Polish officers, because those people knew well that being occupied by Germany was considerably less onerous than being occupied by savage Russians.

Wehrmacht General Otto von Seigler was to be the dinner guest of Emmy and Hermann Göring that evening. It was a long-standing friendship that had survived serious political strains. Hermann had protected his friend, and Emmy had spread her maternal cloak over von Seigler's talented daughter, both of whom had come under Gestapo suspicion after an unsuccessful attempt upon the führer's life in 1938. Otto von Seigler had validated Hermann's judgment many times over by providing brilliant planning for Germany's swift and relatively bloodless conquest of Poland in September 1939. Both men were now veterans of two wars, and they shared a weariness that could be articulated only to the closest and most trustworthy friends.

A telephone from the main entrance to Carinhall—nearly a mile from the great house—informed Göring that General von Seigler's car had just passed the control point. Hermann stoked the logs in the massive hearth to coax more warmth into the cool March evening, and Emmy rang for their servers to bring the libations and hors d'oeuvres that the oversized reichsmarschall loved to savor during informal conversations. Minutes later, the two military professionals met with a backslapping embrace, totally ignoring the requisite greeting of "Heil Hitler." Then Otto kissed Emmy on both cheeks and asked if he would be seeing their five-year-old daughter, Edda, that evening.

"If you want to, then surely you shall see her!" the pleased mother replied, and she motioned to the server, who turned quickly to fetch the youngster from some hidden corner of the great house. The three old friends stood silently for just a moment—a silence which conveyed all of the pressures and uncertainties of wartime leaders—and then, as if on cue, they burst into laughter over nothing except their happiness when anticipating an evening of civility and trust.

At the end of a long and excellent dinner, featuring game birds which the reichsmarschall had personally bagged on his estate, Emmy bade them both *gute Nacht*, planted a warm kiss on her husband's broad forehead, and summoned a server to bring a bottle of fifty-year-old brandy to a small table nestled between two fashionably worn leather chairs near the banked fire. It was her invitation for the two old warriors to enjoy a private conversation and treat with issues not vented in public. Emmy had developed a delicate feel for the nuances of wartime politics, which served her famous husband well, even as his value to the führer commenced to fade.

General von Seigler began. "Hermann, once again I need a favor from you—one which must go no further than the two of us. Well, the three of us, because Emmy should know as well. May I speak freely?"

"I believe you already have," was the good-humored reply. Then the larger man leaned forward and, with a much more serious face, inquired, "What do you need, Otto? It is far too late in the game for me to be coy about such things."

"I have heard that you and President Raczkiewicz have opened a behind-the-scenes channel in the aftermath of that reported massacre of Polish officers in Katyn Woods, and that he understands the Soviets committed the murders with no knowledge of our people. No—don't comment—just hear me out. I have that knowledge on good authority and approve of what you did, wholeheartedly. It could save the lives and limbs of many young Germans within Poland and may someday serve as the basis for greater rapport between the German and Polish peoples.

"My request is to use your informal communications channel to transmit some written materials to a female member of Raczkiewicz's Polish government-in-exile in London. She is a veteran SWW person, but what I am sending has *no* espionage importance—it is of a personal nature. You see, Hermann—that woman in London is Lilka Rudovska, the mother of my daughter, Sofie, whom you and Emmy know. The materials are a memoir composed at Theresienstadt by my daughter's musician gentleman friend, who by now is probably dead. He recently got the memoir into the hands of Czech Gypsies and a young Polish woman named Elsa, who believed that I could use my offices to deliver them intact to my daughter. I know it is complex, but . . . "

"Where *is* your daughter, Otto? At one time her whereabouts baffled our friend Herr Himmler, who thought that she and a Jewish companion might tie you to the Oster thing. They gave the slip to some experienced people."

"Hermann, it is that same fellow! He has written to her—from Theresienstadt—you know. I'm not sure where she is, but I believe that her mother does know. If I can get the packet to London, I will have done my best to carry out his last wishes—and perhaps to give closure to my daughter."

"Theresienstadt, you say. Do you know that it has been dubbed 'The Village That Hitler Gave to The Jews'? It is a fascinating story, Otto. Do you know much about Theresienstadt? How can I be sure that I am not transmitting a lot of anti-Nazi propaganda to someone in London who will use it to paint us as cruel oppressors? If I agree to help you—and I'm not saying I will—it can only be with the assurance that whatever the fellow has written doesn't embarrass us. Are you certain of that, Otto?"

"Perhaps. I don't know much about Theresienstadt—what is its significance? I thought it was just a processing area for Czechs being detained. Is there something more?"

"Theresienstadt is used to show the world that we are doing our best to give a full range of artistic opportunity to those who are temporarily removed from the streets. It is home to many fine musicians, members of classical orchestras, choirs, even contemporary 'jazz' players. *That* stuff can't even be performed in our own taverns any more, but at Theresienstadt there is a full program of 'hot' music—like in Paris, Otto! Like in Paris!! And there are poets and writers there, too. The only difference is that the residents are all Jews and Gypsies and homosexuals, whom the Reich has temporarily removed from our occupied cities until sound government and vibrant commerce can be established firmly. You said your daughter's friend is a musician, no? And a Jew, too. If he was in Czechoslovakia, I am not surprised that he is in Theresienstadt. So, what is the problem, Otto?"

"The problem is that they were in love. And the problem is exacerbated because people die in Theresienstadt with great regularity, despite its fabricated reputation for artistic brilliance. And the problem is that the young man had been in Theresienstadt for over three years and wished to send a sort of 'last testament' to his lover before he became one of those attrition statistics we lock into our Gestapo safes. That is the problem, Hermann. I will understand fully if you decide that it is too risky a favor to implement, but I give you my word that this is not some nefarious plan to disclose anti-Nazi materials to the world. My daughter is, above all—*über alles*—a proud daughter of Germany."

"Have you brought the packet with you this evening?"

"I have."

"Then please leave it with me."

CHAPTER THREE

Salbris, Département Loir-et-Cher, Occupied France March 1943

A LETTER FROM THE HEART

A SNIFTER OF COGNAC was perched on the edge of a small writing desk, which was illuminated by bright sunlight streaming in from the walled garden on the south exposure of the small stucco residence. In earlier years, it could have been a poster intended to lure tourists away from the major cities and into the friendlier countryside of central France. Even during wartime in German-occupied France, Salbris was very little changed, except for a contingent of German military housed in L'Hotel de Valaudran, which was their departmental headquarters.

Outside the window, a young woman sat on the garden bench reading what appeared to be a letter. Letters were rare in Salbris in the spring of 1943, because the French postal system had crumbled much as the national army had done. She finished reading and held the sheets of paper quietly in her lap, then, after a few minutes, she unfolded the pages and reread them. There were tears brimming from the corners of her large eyes, yet she made no move to dry them as they trickled down the sides of her comely face. Clearly, the letter had evoked memories of places and faces taken from her during the four years of European fighting. Finally, she dabbed at her eyes with the hem of her white apron and stuffed the folded letter inside her waistband. When she stood, her head was held high and she walked purposefully into the house and to the waiting cognac glass. After it had been emptied, refilled, and emptied a second time, the young woman spread a sheet of writing vellum atop her desk and began—slowly—to write.

Salbris, France, March '43
My dearest Stéphane,

Your welcome letter was delivered to me today. What a pleasant surprise! I had been told that Portuguese fishermen organized a cross-Channel mail carriage between England and France but was not aware how efficient it has become. Now I have decided to send this reply through the same conduit. The French international mails are very unreliable and local service only a bit better.

Your decision to remain in England after war broke out certainly did make sense to me, Stéphane. I understand that you worried that you might be impressed into Mussolini's army if you went back to occupied territory, because your father served there and that would obligate you, too. Reinhardt was not as comfortable as I was with your decision. He wanted to be in Paris again, and he is arrogant enough to believe that the war affects only others.

At first I thought he was being totally insane—especially because he is Romani and his people are vilified by Goebbels and the other Nazis who want to obliterate them. But his notoriety and popularity have attracted a "protector," and thus far his life has been unaffected and his work remains lucrative. The new group he has assembled—in your absence—is not so creative, and, because I was your protégé, my participation has been reduced to a few scraps of work.

I have been living in a little holiday cottage he owns in this pretty town south from Paris. He and Naguine share a fancy Paris duplex on the Champs and they rarely visit Salbris. But now they have decided to be married down here next month, and I won't be comfortable remaining where I am— even though they insist it won't inconvenience them and that I'm welcome to stay.

And so, my dear Stéphane, I am looking to you once again for direction.

I have heard that you are the lynchpin of Arthur Young's Orchestra at Hackett's-in-Picadilly, and I am ready to abandon

France and pursue my life and career in England. I have been deprived of the three persons who should be closest to me. Both parents are in sensitive positions and on opposite sides of this war. And my loving Dieter has been rotting in Theresienstadt for more than three years and may never return.

I am more depressed with each boring day, and I know that I am drinking to excess and behaving badly because of it. A chance to resume singing and working with you could change things for the better. Thank you for thinking of me.

Your Sophia

CHAPTER FOUR

43 Eaton Place, London – March 1943

A MESSAGE FROM BEHIND THE WALLS

Lilka Rudovska locked the blade back into her purse handle, thinking how long she had owned the menacing thing and grateful that she had never used it for any task other than opening letters and coring fruit. The SWW had trained its people—even women—in defensive maneuvers, and had provided them with hardware, like the purse, which might someday purchase the extra time needed to step away from danger. "Thrust upward using both hands and try to enter your opponent's dorsal below the rib cage" had been the instruction when she was trained with the blade. She wondered if she could really execute the move on a live person, as opposed to the stuffed dummies of training school. The whole thought process was only another way to put off examining the envelope's contents, and so she set the purse aside and retrieved the package one more time.

Sliding her hand inside, Lilka extracted the contents. The larger portion was tied elaborately with cords, encircling a thick pile of pages in ordinates and abscissas of strings, which were knotted at dozens of juncture points. She thought that it looked like the product of some ancient, dementia-stricken hoarder of trivia, rather than a communication from a man in his thirties. Atop that was a letter, folded neatly and held closed by what appeared to be candle wax dripped along the overlap. The letter had the name "Sofie" written on the outside. Oddly, all of the contents seemed to be hand-written on the backs of sheets of music.

She had known since the telephone call from Prague that a package intended for Sofie had been smuggled out of Theresienstadt, and Elsa had found an intermediary to get it to Lilka in London. Sofie had made the choice to return to France three years ago, while she had the option of remaining in England, farther from the conflagration. Lilka wondered whether she, as a good mother, should respect her daughter's privacy and get the unopened contents to her in France, or should she serve as a filter to make certain the contents could not hurt her daughter? By slitting the outer envelope and extracting the two items, she had partially answered her own conundrum, but now she must decide whether to go further and read the letter. Forty years of gathering and analyzing intelligence left her no choice. The blade was again unsheathed, and it travelled neatly along the candle-waxed seam, allowing her to read Dieter Meister's penned message to Sofie von Seigler.

Theresienstadt, Friday, 5 March 1943
My incredible, unforgettable Sofie,

They say that there are only two ways for a Jew to leave Theresienstadt—on a train to the East, or in a plain pine box. For three years, I have watched many departures and, so far as I know, all have been thus. Jura and I have considered this dilemma, and tonight we will be able to test another alternative for departure.

Unfortunately, only one of us can attempt this trip. It would be much too arduous for Jura's diminished strength; he has consumption, as do so many others here. In addition, he is one of the few physicians remaining, and he believes that it is his obligation to attend to those who can benefit from his skills—even though he is not officially permitted any medicines or surgical instruments. I hope that no one will think me selfish for being the one leaving.

During our time here, Jura and I have been inseparable. Our captors have made it so—but that has been one aspect of the internment that I would not wish to change. He is certainly the finest man I have ever known. He thinks constantly of others, and he will spare no effort to cure their ills or alleviate their pain. He has inspired me to stay as healthy as possible—

both my body and my mind—so that if there is the opportunity to start over somewhere, I shall be prepared to do so.

Life in Prague quickly became flat without you, and the determined meddling of Jurgen Deitz eventually threatened everyone at the clinic and caused it to disband. But you shall learn more of that later. During my years at Theresienstadt, I have concentrated upon two time-consuming activities, and both have helped me to avoid the sorry fate of others here. The first involves my musical performance capability. Our camp overseer, Dr. Siegfried Seidl, an SS-Hauptsturmführer, has assembled fine musicians from all over the occupied areas of Austria and Czechoslovakia, and we practice and perform together constantly. Of course, it is all a sham to create the image of a cultural Mecca for Jews, or something like that. Never mind the façade, we do learn from one another, and it is far preferable to splitting mica—the full-time occupation for everyone here except the artistic residents. (That is what I am considered to be.)

My second pastime has been creating a written history of ourselves—you and me and our immediate families—drawing upon things learned from you, Jura, Lilka, and others who you will recognize. I want you to have it, for whatever use you feel is appropriate.

Above all things, I want to state to anyone who reads the account that we continued to be human in bad times. We loved, laughed, refined our art, cared for one another, and planned for better times. It is all set out on the backs of the music sheets that accompany this letter—which may be my last letter, who knows? Please think of me lovingly as you read it.

If tomorrow I am outside these walls and a fugitive, I do have a plan. But I am not at liberty to tell you more now, because it could endanger others and also facilitate my recapture if this falls into unfriendly hands. When it is safe to do so, I will send some notice of myself to London, as I have this package. Meanwhile, I hope you will read "our story" and understand that you will forever be my only true love.

Über Alles, your devoted Dieter

Lilka closed the letter and placed it upon the larger, tied bundle of papers. Her emotions were confused; she was torn between happiness that her daughter had so devoted a person sharing some of her life, but simultaneously she was profoundly sad that they had been driven so far from one another that only an illicit document passed through secret hands could provide Sofie with a greeting. No, it was not even a greeting for certain; it could easily be a farewell, composed by Dieter in his last hours. It reminded her of Sydney Carton awaiting the executioner's blade at the conclusion of *A Tale of Two Cities*—she had always considered that to be the very saddest of circumstances.

There was, of course, the much more practical question of the danger which this document might represent for its possessor. Not here in England, she thought, but in a German-occupied country, it would likely condemn one to imprisonment to be in possession of a communication emanating from inside a detention camp and describing its horrors. If the author were dead, it could be an indictment of his jailers—and if he had escaped successfully, it would be an embarrassment. Even though Salbris was well removed from most of the war's consequences in France, it was nevertheless under the German thumb, and some minor official seeking recognition could be expected to claim that he had uncovered a great plot if he found such a document in a citizen's possession.

"I believe that I must read it rather than sending it unread to Sofie," she said to herself. "It could be totally harmless, but if not—and I had failed to intercept it . . . " Certainly this residence was not the place to begin her review, so she replaced both pieces in their original diplomatic envelope and departed the building with a wave of appreciation to the aide who had contacted her. As she walked the short distance to her rented flat, Lilka was surprised that she was nearly overcome with anticipation. She admonished herself for being a voyeur but walked more briskly than usual to avoid losing any time before beginning her reading.

And so, on that March 1943 evening in wartime London, a story compiled over a three-year period on pilfered music sheets in the dampness of the Theresienstadt concentration camp was opened and read for the first time.

Friday, March 5th 1943

This will be the final entry in my account of the years since I met you, Sofie. If things go as I wish, I shall begin March 6 outside the walls of this fortress, beside the grimy river to which Theresienstadt's waste and garbage are directed.

I hope that I shall be able to stand after having my legs folded closely against my body for three hours or more. I hope that breathing through my air tube in short, shallow gulps of outside air, I shall be able to retain consciousness. I hope that the cold March night won't produce hypothermia inside my capsule. I hope that the stench of fresh guts sharing my small space won't cause me to retch and choke myself to death. I hope that, when I finally stand by the river, I shall be able to filch a cigarette and a light from whoever has extracted me from my chrysalis. If so I shall enjoy a slow, deliberate smoke before beginning a new life.

Dr. Juraslav Havlik will not get to read this account in its final form. We both know that his consumption has advanced past hope of recovery, particularly within the dank chambers of our prison. I am pleased that he was able to listen as I read my daily entries into the story, and I thank him for insights he provided

CHAPTER FIVE
Berlin – Early Summer 1938

DIETER MEISTER
[From Dieter's Journal]

*I*n any other setting, the Bösendorfer Imperial concert grand piano would have seemed too opulent, but in the house at 80 Wilhelmstrasse, anything smaller would have been trivial. With eight full octaves and ninety-seven keys, the outsized instrument could produce resonant explosions of sound to fill the great reception gallery, while its treble keys were capable of crystal-clear notes suggesting a toast with delicate cordial glasses. A week earlier, when I had finished an evening of playing party songs on the painted upright in the Fischerstube—my pedestrian but profitable night job—an aide to General Otto von Seigler had approached me and asked if I also tuned pianos.

During those sad days in the early summer of 1938, I would gladly have accepted extra work cleaning tuba spit valves, but I was actually competent at tuning pianos—or any instruments where my gift of perfect pitch could help me to sort out nuances which most ears could not resolve. I'm certain that I smiled condescendingly at the young lieutenant, assuring him that he was speaking with the finest piano tuner in the city. I was expecting a 10 RM visit to the officers' barracks where a dead keyboard was missing some working keys and first aid was needed before another raucous military songfest. Instead, he handed me one of the General's engraved personal calling cards, on which he had written a private telephone number and the virtual summons to appear with my tuning kit after the lunch hour of the appointed day.

There was no discussion of my rates and no request for references, just an address in the finest part of the city and a telephone to be called before arriving. I wondered whether the General or his aide knew I was Jewish. Normally, Jews weren't welcomed anywhere near Wilhelmstrasse unless they were renowned cooks, art critics, or concubines. But piano tuners? Impossible. So my blonde hair, blue eyes, and innocuous name, Dieter Meister, hadn't sent a disqualifying message, and perhaps General von Seigler's fondness for American-style jazz had earned me the presumption of competence. Sometimes it is better not to question good fortune by analyzing its motive; just accept it with an enigmatic smile and the hope that it marks the beginning of better times.

For my visit, I dressed well, but not so much as to suggest that the engagement was somehow above me. A barmaid from the Fischerstube called the number on my behalf and said, "Herr Meister will arrive at approximately 2 p.m. after completing his assignment at the Music Hall." I thought that was a nice touch. My tuning instruments were packed in a salesman's black leather sample case, which I regularly polished. It was heavy enough that I should have taken a taxi from my rented room, but to economize, I walked, pulling the bag on its wheels, for nearly three miles before flagging a cab to take me the last quarter mile. It would be better to arrive that way. At 2:05, I rang the bell at the gated entrance to #80. The same grim aide opened the door and motioned me inside.

After navigating through an entry foyer, a long portrait corridor, and a small smoking parlor, we entered the great reception gallery, where beautiful woods, imported fabrics, and oil paintings depicting battle scenes vied for every visitor's attention. Then I saw the Bösendorfer—regal even in this room—beckoning me to approach and become acquainted. The lieutenant said something, but my attention had been captured by the elegant, oversized piano. So he raised his voice and repeated himself. How long would I require to tune the piano, and what might I require to be comfortable during that time?

I knew that I wanted to maximize my opportunity to explore the piano, so I launched into a wordy explanation. I described how I would initially play some scales and arpeggios to evaluate, and following that, I would be removing the music rack to gain access to the piano's 249 tuning pins. Then I would make certain that A-4—the A above middle C—was set at correct pitch, and proceed to . . . He held up his hand and repeated, "How long?" Could I have until six p.m.? And could I request that no one play a radio within my hearing? And might the door be closed to discourage visitors? And could I return in a few days to adjust my work after the first tuning had settled?

"You will be alone in the house until six. I will return then to pay you and see you out. Tea and cakes are on the table by the window. Call the number you have if you need anything before six." He nodded stiffly and departed through the three-meter-high double doors, which he closed quietly. I was alone with the finest piano I had ever seen, in a setting I could scarcely absorb. I removed my coat and sat on the bench, hardly daring to touch the overlong keyboard. But of course I did. Beginning my evaluation—testing the piano's limits and characteristics—I chose scraps of Schubert and Bach—compositions learned for recitals in my youth. Then I shifted to the "stride" jazz style of my favorite American Negro pianists, who rarely got to perform on grand pianos. It sounded particularly melodic on this one. After ten minutes I was able to identify those notes that had wandered furthest from tune, and I began my labor. It certainly was not a neglected instrument, and I knew I would have more than enough time to complete the initial tuning.

At about four thirty, I removed my red velvet muting ribbon from the strings and replaced the sliding music rack into its track. The Bösendorfer was ready to be tested. Again I launched into the classics from my youth, composed by some of the great Viennese musicians who had first patronized Ignaz Bösendorfer and his son, Ludwig, the designer of their signature instrument. I imagined that I was alone in a great concert hall, seated at this piano with ample time to enjoy the experience. It seemed to add to my own proficiency, and I felt giddy as my hands swept easily over the expanse of ivory keys.

Thinking back now, I can't recall what it was that caused me to look up—perhaps some small sound which penetrated through the larger tones of the piano—but more likely, that atavistic instinct which often alerts us to unseen eyes. Whatever the trigger, my attention shifted from music to an indistinct form in the corner of the room, partially concealed behind a massive velvet drapery. I had stopped playing, and the sound of silence replaced the musical fragments which had filled the gallery moments before; then total silence was broken by light laughter. The voice was that of a young woman, who stepped confidently from her concealment and said, "You play very nicely; I have been listening."

"And so you have," I retorted, "and for whom have I had the pleasure of playing?" By now I could see that she was tall, probably in her early twenties, and endowed with the largest of brown eyes, framed with the longest lashes one would dare request of any wish-granting fairy. Her clothing was simple but expensive-looking, and there was just a suggestion of a well-formed body beneath. She moved a few paces toward me and displayed a smile that rivaled her eyes. "I'm Sofie—and that is my piano," she offered, adding, "but I can't play so well as you do." She seemed to sense that her short introduction wasn't adequate and, after pausing, she continued. "This is also my house—where I live when I'm home from university. I was supposed to come tomorrow but caught a ride earlier with friends. My father will be surprised."

"As am I," I smiled. " I was retained to tune your wonderful piano and told that I would be here quite alone until six o'clock. But, Sofie from the university, I have finished tuning and have unintentionally played a short concert for you. Why don't you sit and play something for me so that I may judge my tuning work?" I thought as I said it that I was being much too familiar with the daughter of a general who lived in a palace, and I wished instantly that I could retract the errant words. But they were already out— and I may already have squandered my potential job as regular tuner for the Bösendorfer.

"Do you know Josephine Baker, the Negress chanteuse?" she asked, totally ignoring my gaffe.

"I know her work, if that is your question, but I surely don't know her. She is from America but lives and performs here—mostly in France. She is—"

"She is sensational," Sofie interrupted. "She sings the best songs and dances like a great cat and wears costumes which can't be described in good circles. Besides, she really has a German father; did you know that? Her mother worked for a German family in America and bedded her employer. That's why she likes Europe, I think. Can you play any of the songs she does? I won't play piano for you because you are too good at it, but I can sing Josephine Baker songs as she does. Play something à la Baker—please."

Her enthused chatter deserved some appropriate response. I remembered having listened to a recording of the sinuous Creole delivering a purring rendition of "Sleepy Time Gal" and knew I could improvise my way through it, so I started slowly and deliberately, imitating her pace. It seemed to matter a lot to me that I do it well, and so I concentrated on achieving Bakeresque insouciance as I created the familiar melody line. When I looked up to see whether I was earning Sofie's approval, she was gone!

Then, in the manner of her earlier appearance, Sofie "materialized" in the dark corner, now moving with the sullen slither of Josephine Baker, and wearing only the scantiest of silken undergarments, which clung to her body miraculously. She stopped in the middle of the room and began delivering the lyrics to the song I was, by now, playing unconsciously, never diverting her eyes from mine or exhibiting any level of the discomfort which was washing over me in waves. She caressed each note and formed each word perfectly, always faithful to the naughty persona of Josephine Baker. Soon I had totally lost control of the situation as well as any notion of the passage of time. If it was nearing six o'clock, I was a dead man, and I had just enough good sense remaining to glance furtively at my watch as she finished "a stay at home, play at home, eight o'clock sleepy-time gaaal."

It was 5:40. I was sweating like a long-distance runner. Sofie was delivering a demure bow in my direction, and her movement exposed one perky breast. She put her index finger into her puckered mouth in a mock expression of surprise, using those huge eyes to poke fun at her "audience." Then she retreated into that dark corner (and hopefully to the discarded clothing), pausing for one last Josephine wink over her shoulder. I breathed deeply for several seconds and then began packing my instrument bag. At precisely six, I heard hard-nail boots approaching through the hallway, as the lieutenant came to pay me and see me to the door. Walking by his side, a fully clothed Sofie glanced at me as if seeing me for the first time. "I trust that you have done a satisfactory tuning of my piano," she said. "Klaus has a bank draft for your work. When I have practiced my lessons, Klaus will contact you to arrange for a second tuning. Danke."

As I passed her to leave the grand room, following the impassive Klaus, she gave me one last glance with those incredible eyes and, in a voice too low for the officer to overhear, she said, "Please brush up on some more

Josephine Baker tunes before you return, *Judendeutscher.*"

The next two weeks were a curious time for me. First of all, I found myself thinking of Sofie all too often. For over two years, I had shared a rented room with Miguel, the handsome Portuguese manager of the Fischerstube, and on the occasions when I did pause to entertain romantic thoughts, they were of Miguel. We usually passed our leisure time together listening to classical music or jazz on Miguel's Grundig, and we enjoyed long walks together by the river when the weather was pleasant. I was accustomed to telling Miguel about everything of interest that happened in my life, but I realized that I had omitted *any* mention of my visit to Wilhelmstrasse or my encounter with Sofie. Why wasn't I candid about those events with him?

Then there were those last muttered words from Sofie, intended only for my ears. *Judendeutscher* was a Yiddish term for German Jews. It wasn't pejorative, but in the tense climate of that year, it was dangerous to be thus identified, particularly by the daughter of a general living on Wilhelmstrasse. And how had she even suspected? It was *she* who had been mostly unclothed, not I. Was I being lured to an entrapment? If that were the motive, she could as easily have told Lieutenant Klaus that I had assaulted her, and I would by now have been arrested and charged. No, I was missing something—and I was constantly surprising myself with mental pictures of the ersatz Josephine Baker cleverly exposing just enough of herself to ruin my concentration and then disappearing like a puff of cigarette smoke. Damn her for entering my mind!

Twice during that period, I saw her father at the Fischerstube. He usually entered with his cadre of young officers, and they sat drinking beer from tall pitchers at a table far from the piano. They were quiet for Nazis, and instead of shouting their food and drink requests across the cellar, they raised their hands and summoned barmaids to come and write their orders. I thought about acknowledging him once when he seemed to be listening as I played but thought better of it and concentrated upon the songs popular to patriotic Deutche. Lieutenant Klaus dutifully placed tips from their table into my cigar box as the group departed, but there was no hint of recognition when he did so. It was as if I were totally invisible to all of them; perhaps that is the posture which piano men should assume. Perhaps the entire tuning episode had been accidental, and I had imagined it to be more than it was.

I was deep into this thought process when Greta, their server, touched my shoulder to get my attention. "Dieter . . . Dieter! Dieter, hey—are you sleeping with your eyes open?" she demanded. "The *boche* left this on my tray for you, piano man." My name was printed on a small envelope, which bore an engraved regimental seal in the corner. She stood by my side, obviously waiting to see the contents when I opened it, so I stuffed it into my pocket as casually as I could and smiled at her. "Probably fifty thousand RM from the führer if I'll go to Berchtesgaden and play for him," I jested, but I could see that my levity only raised her curiosity. I picked a crumpled bill from my cigar box and handed it to her. "Thanks, Greta. I must get back to work. It's too quiet in here tonight." She nodded, and I wondered if she was thinking that I was a Gestapo snitch or worse, getting money for information from the officers. At least she didn't know I was a Jew, I thought to myself. I had never revealed that to *anyone* at the Fischerstube—except, of course, Miguel, with whom I shared secrets . . . but not the one currently troubling me.

"Herr Meister, Your services will be needed on Saturday at two in the afternoon when we will be hosting senior Luftwaffe officers and their wives at 80 Wilhelmstrasse. Our guest of honor will be the aviator, Charles Lindbergh. Accordingly, please include American selections and traditional German tea melodies. You may leave when dinner is announced. The house is available on Friday evening if you wish to practice. The contents of this letter are strictly confidential.

Cordially,
Sofie von Seigler."

I stared at the note and re-read it several times. It was not an invitation, but rather an order to appear and perform. Sofie apparently served as her father's social aide—or perhaps even as his hostess—and she was empowered to organize this important soirée with one of the most famous men of our time. I knew that Mr. and Mrs. Lindbergh had left

America to escape the notoriety of their son's kidnapping and death, which had become smothering for them. Seeking privacy, they had resided for a while in Britain, and then, more recently, in France. Of late, there had been talk of their possible move to Germany, as the famous flyer became more and more interested in the progress being made by our aircraft manufacturers. Our newspapers and periodicals had been very friendly to the "Lone Eagle," and photographs of him in the company of Air Minister Göring had appeared frequently.

I was both excited and depressed by the fact that I would have this chance to observe history from the vantage point of a piano bench—excited to see a few of the most famous faces of our time, but depressed because I knew I could tell no one. I was also strangely elated to have a note from Sofie in my pocket, and to be certain that she actually knew my name. And I was depressed because I knew I would fabricate some lie for Miguel about my time commitments on Friday and Saturday and the reason for pressing my best, and only, dark suit. I realized that I had already decided to visit the house on Friday evening, even though I could as easily compile and practice my selections at the Fischerstube. That was one more confusing aspect of this unlikely situation.

On Friday, I went to Wilhelmstrasse only after visiting an excellent tonsorial parlor, where my beard was trimmed and my neglected hair well cut by a professional, who talked incessantly about the need for more frequent attention for such luxuriant locks. I assured him that I would return soon, then looked one more time into the hand-held mirror he had provided. It was a satisfying image, and I departed brimming with confidence as well as considerable anticipation. I had told Miguel only that I had been hired for a private party, even though he stood poised to receive more detail. All I could muster was, "rich people."

Sofie greeted me at the entry to #80, and she seemed to appraise my enhanced appearance with a slight nod of approval. "The reception is not until tomorrow, Herr Meister—tonight there are only two of us. Did you forget?" I had anticipated such a teasing comment, thus had my response well phrased. "Miss Sofie, if one is to perform in dress clothing, one must rehearse in the same fashion. It can be decidedly different, you know, and I certainly wish to add to the success of your father's reception tomorrow."

She did not comment, so I continued with a thought that had puzzled me. "Naturally, I am quite flattered to have been chosen, but do you know why he selected *me*? Surely there are many other fine musicians available whose names would be better known to his guests. Can you help me to understand the choice?"

"You are a very intelligent man, Herr Meister, but, like many other men, you don't always see what you look at. When my father and his staff enter the Fischerstube, you all scurry about. The word passes quickly—a general officer is in the house! Be attentive!! He drops by about twice in a fortnight, no? But you do not see the tangle of university students who come through your doors frequently and fill the back tables. So, you do not see me at all, though I am there often. We wear no braid and order no cognac and leave only coins for tips—and so we are invisible."

"But . . . I don't understand your point. What does it have to do with his selection of a pianist?"

"You are *still* being obtuse, Herr Meister. Why is it *his* choice and *his* party? I am my father's hostess, and he places full confidence in my selection of the flowers, the seating arrangements, the caterer—and the goddamned piano player! You are here because I have come by to listen dozens of evenings, and because I have said, 'Father, I am having the piano man we enjoy at the Fischerstube. He can keep the party light and can integrate music of the best contemporary American composers with the cast-iron German klunkers your guests feel they must enjoy.' You are coming here tomorrow because I want you here, and you are here tonight because you wanted to see me again. No?"

I had rehearsed no response for this onslaught and could summon only a shy smile as I said, "Yes." It was only then that I realized I had not even brought my tuning case, and that I must appear as a total tyro to one so obviously sophisticated. Sofie—*sofie-sticated*—it teased me for a moment, and then I fixed on those incredible eyes and ventured forward with the suggestion that we might leave the foyer and take a look at the arrangement in the reception hall. "I must decide how far raised the piano top should be. We don't want to compete with the conversation of *your* guests. Show me where I shall be seated."

"My father may ask me to sing," she offered. "Sometimes he believes that puts people at ease, and it allows him to embrace his daughter proudly and let guests see that he is also a warm family man. Many of our foreign visitors have the impression that Nazi leaders are heartless, and father likes to disabuse them of that notion. I am a wonderful shill in that game—although he really *is* a kind and considerate father, you know."

"I know that he is not rude in public and that he tips generously. I can also see that he has raised a daughter with aesthetic appreciation and good taste . . . "

"And intriguing breasts, I would imagine, judging from your glances in that direction. Ah, but I was totally unfair on your first visit, with my Naughty Josephine rendition. Sometimes I like to make people a bit uneasy so that I can judge them with their composure rattled. Forgive me. I was playing a game at your expense and you did nothing to deserve that. Let's sit on the divans and have a glass of Father's best cognac and talk for a few minutes."

The next two hours rival any other similar period in my life for the pure pleasure of discovery and enjoyment of another person they provided. We were two young adults lounging on priceless furnishings and sipping very old brandy from oversized snifters. We were two trains pausing momentarily on some lonely trestle before we proceeded to different destinations. We were close friends who had not yet met one another.

Sofie knew much more about me than I had imagined. During her visits to my workplace, she had chatted with my co-workers and learned of my education and my modest circumstances. She had listened carefully to the melodies I favored and the styles I imitated. Apparently she also found me attractive, because she said she had peeled my photograph from the Fischerstube billboard outside the entrance and taken it to her room at Humboldt University, where it now rested on a bookcase—in its own frame.

When it seemed safe to inquire, I asked about the absence of a mother in the vast house, and for the first time I saw the splendid eyes of Sofie von Seigler cloud over with sadness and the hint of a gathering tear. "I really should not speak of her," she said, "because it could be a point of vulnerability which we all may regret someday." Having delivered that caveat, Sofie stretched her long legs over the end of her divan and launched *into a story that both amused and troubled her. After I had departed and returned to my flat, I created this account of our conversation, so that I might always retrieve it . . .*

CHAPTER SIX
Berlin – Summer 1938

A CONVERSATION WITH SOFIE
[From Dieter's Journal]

"*I was born in Krakow, on the Vistula River, in 1915. Father had been posted there as a part of the contingent working with Józef Piłsudski to drive the Russians from the Polish Kingdom and thus secure a tripartite alliance among Germany, Austria-Hungary and Poland. He was only twenty-four—three years out of Offizierschule—but already attracting serious consideration for higher responsibility. He had been top student in his Order and was Company Commander of his graduating class. You may recall that The Imperial German High Command wished to neutralize Poland, and, to achieve that, they dispatched a strategic team to coordinate directly with Piłsudski and his Socialist Party.*

"*In some ways it was surreal, because Europe was already becoming embroiled in an unforgiving war, with many strained alliances and incredible subterfuge. Father knew much about Polish history and even had a working knowledge of the language. So, he was attached to the staff of General Wertz and assigned to interact with leading Polish banks and the Polish Finance Ministry. He later said that he was functioning more like a businessman than a soldier during those years, and I truly believe that he was apologetic toward many of his military contemporaries who were seeing a harsher face of warfare and living by the creed of von Clausewitz.*

"*Despite Father's grasp of their language, his Polish hosts insisted that an interpreter be assigned to the young Kapitän von Seigler, to redact his correspondence and keep his appointments ledger. Lilka Rudovska was* undoubtedly also a spy, using her excellent command of the German language to gather snippets of conversation wherever she accompanied the young officer. But, at age forty, she hardly looked the part and managed always to disappear into the background when her services weren't being specifically utilized. She was his shadow and initially, at least, an annoyance to Father.

"He later said that he scarcely acknowledged Lilka during the first month, when she was occupying a small desk in his outer office. Often he left for appointments without even bothering to inform her of his departure or plans to return. That changed abruptly one Saturday evening when Father, in mufti, entered a local tavern to dine alone. He probably consumed too much Slivovitz and departed the establishment after dark, weaving in the general direction of his quarters. As he entered a passageway in Stare Miasto—the Old City—four men surrounded him and commenced beating him severely.

"Whether they might have killed him or merely stolen his valuables is unclear, but his situation was helpless until a loud female voice commanded the men to stop. The command was delivered in Yiddish! The aggressors apparently recognized the intervener and obeyed instantly, melting away into the shadows beyond the passageway from which they had come, leaving their victim alone on the cobblestones.

"Of course, you have guessed that the rescuer was Lilka—and Father realized at once that the quiet woman had a portfolio much more weighty than that of a mere interpreter. He also knew that the decisive command had been delivered neither in German nor in Polish, but in the "language of intrigue" in that city at that time. So, who was the nearly invisible woman sitting outside his office, performing ministerial tasks? And how did she happen by at such an opportune moment? And how did she know to shout at his assailants in Yiddish? And why did they desist immediately without protest or question? It was too complex for a smart but inebriated young officer so far from home. So, he allowed himself to drift into sleep, partly induced by Slivovitz and partly as a result of having absorbed a painful beating.

"Father revived in distinct stages: first he heard birds, then squinted at painful daylight, then ran his tongue slowly over coated teeth and a swollen upper lip, and finally inventoried mentally each aching member of his body.

He felt dreadful, but at the same time, he was comfortable in what seemed to be a featherbed covered with scented linens.

"A voice interrupted his musings. 'Ah! You are finally awake, Kapitän von Seigler. Guten tag!'

"'Lilka??? You are here? You were . . .'

"'I was nearby when those felons decided to crack your skull and steal your money. They knew you were German staff, and they dislike Piłsudski's collaboration with Germany.'

"'You told them to stop, and . . .'

"'They know me and they know that I am from the Party headquarters. It would be serious trouble for them if they were identified attacking you.'

"'And you shouted in the Jew language!'

"'Yes—they are Jews. So am I. We live in the same neighborhood.'

"'Ah, yes! The tribe of Lechitians, I think.'

"From that day, Lilka and Father became closer, she assisting his career and he spending frequent evenings relaxed in her flat near his office. Neither knew exactly when the relationship became romantic, perhaps because of the unlikely pairing of a young German military professional with an older Polish secretary who was also Jewish. Nevertheless, they were comfortable and content passing evenings together, neither making unreasonable demands upon the other.

"Lilka's pregnancy came as a surprise to Otto. He was cross at her for a few days but then accepted the fact that he was an equal partner in creating the new citizen forming inside her. Both knew that, in time, he would be transferred to another theater in the growing European conflict. They agreed that they should marry before that happened so that his officer's benefits would be available to Mother and to me.

"And so it was that they stood before the Civil Magistrate in Krakow's City Hall and became man and wife, three months prior to the day when I was born into the war-wracked world of 1915. They spent another six weeks together after Mother delivered, but then Father was ordered to a staff position in Berlin. My mother and I remained amid the growing tumult of Poland. Both my parents knew there was little chance that they would be together again during wartime, but they resolved to communicate as often as possible and to work together to provide a stable, loving foundation for me.

"Mother proved to be a resourceful survivor over the succeeding four years, no matter which combatant's flag flew over the Great Square or which Polish partisans were in the ascendancy. She did nothing to contradict the rumor that she was a war widow with a child, and she accepted gratefully any assistance that status precipitated upon us.

"I was apparently a cheerful and intelligent child who loved the great music which still lingered in Krakow, and from an early age I navigated well among the German, Polish, and Russian language conversations which surrounded us.

"My father's career seemed charmed, as he passed unscathed through various combat zones and earned high praise for his leadership qualities and commonsense solutions to problems. He was able to send funds regularly to Krakow, and he waited with keen anticipation for each bit of news of Mother and me. However, this dedication in no way inhibited a series of dalliances which came easily to a handsome young officer during times when much of the world was 'living for the moment.' As hostilities wound down toward an armistice, Otto and Lilka made their way to Prague, where each had friends and where they could again contemplate whatever future might be ahead for them.

"They never stopped being devoted friends, but whatever romantic love had once moved them had apparently been dampened during the long absence. Father sensed that he now had a significant role to play in the reconstruction of postwar Germany, and Mother had become the object of affection of an affluent Jewish hotelkeeper in Krakow. Otto agreed that—for now—it would be unfair to uproot me from familiar surroundings in Krakow, but both acknowledged that I should visit Berlin at regular intervals. And so it was that, six years after their lives first came together, two survivors of the Great War set off in different directions, still linked by their shared devotion to me.

"Father never remarried, and, like Mother (and thousands of displaced people in those troubled times), he encouraged the notion that his spouse had somehow been a casualty of war. However, by 1931, the landscape of Germany was again revitalizing, and he was aware that I would soon reach my sixteenth birthday in a country now lagging behind much of postwar Europe. We had seen one another infrequently since his departure from Krakow—usually in crowded railroad waiting rooms where Mother had arranged to meet him. By then, I was corresponding regularly with my father in German, and our monthly exchanges were affectionate and often accompanied by recent photographs.

"At sixteen, I was fully ten centimeters taller than Mother, and the photos I mailed revealed long, dark hair gathered into a bun, athletic shoulders, and, of course, my unusual eyes! Father decided that he could wait no longer to suggest that his only child join him in Germany to continue studies in an excellent school where he believed I would thrive. This was certainly not a suggestion to be conveyed in a letter, but rather one to be advanced personally with my mother and me. Otto believed that the venue for his proposition should be somewhere enticing in Germany, and accordingly he dispatched first-class, round-trip rail passage, inviting us to holiday with him in the spa town of Bad Nauheim, where there would be park-like surroundings and classical music to embellish the 'seduction.'

"He did not realize that, at sixteen, I was more than ready to explore a new lifestyle. I wanted to escape from the closed Jewish community of Krakow as well as the strict rules imposed by Liv Zimmerman, Mother's patron and companion. I suspected (from our correspondence) that Father favored the educational opportunities in Germany, but, even more, that he wanted to know the young woman his daughter had become. As a result, we traveled to Bad Nauheim. I was eager to persuade Mother to allow me to matriculate at a German school convenient to Father's home.

"During the initial two days of our family vacation, there was no mention of the subject, but, on the third evening, a group of young Humboldt University students were seated near us during dinner, and soon everyone was engaged in lively conversation. The students were attractive and articulate, and they described their University experience with superlatives. Father must have feared that his "shills" might actually go too far and reveal inadvertently that their presence in the restaurant that evening was contrived, but the deception wasn't detected and it had the desired result. I was enchanted and soon asked whether we could accept the invitation of one student to visit the University when we were in Berlin a few days later. And thus, the trap was closed, and my move from Poland to Germany at age sixteen became reality."

When she had concluded her story, Sofie looked up for the first time and smiled as if she had been relieved of a burden. "Dieter," she began, "we are much alike. We are Jews by birth, but not integrated into any Jewish community. We are young, artistic, and being swept along on a wave of historical change that could threaten our future happiness. We can't even be ourselves with those we see each day, and so we don't form many close friendships. I was drawn to you because I saw such beautiful talent and energy in a place where many of us go to escape for a few hours.

"I have the advantage of my father's position and affluence, but that doesn't permit me to be truthful about many of the important facts of my life. Even Father must proceed with caution and preserve the deception of a missing wife and surviving daughter. When Miguel, the manager at the Fischerstube, told me you are a Jew, I knew that it was supposed to deflect my possible interest. He could not have known that it actually added to the intrigue."

"Miguel told you . . . "

"Yes. I said that my friends and I were interested in the good-looking young piano man, and he said that we should keep our distance because socializing with Jews could result in our interrogation."

I was stunned but tried not to reveal it. For weeks I had been chastening myself for keeping my roommate uninformed about the whole matter of Sofie, and at the same time, he was taking pains to discourage Sofie from coming into contact with me. The irony of this double deception seemed to me like some Greek tragedy or Wagnerian opera.

"Sofie . . . Miguel and I share a flat . . . well, and a bedroom . . . "

"I know," she smiled, "and here you are with me!"

German men are seldom moved to tears, but in the quiet moment which followed, I buried my head into the soft pillow below her shoulder and squeezed my lips together hard, still not quite controlling the wayward tear which escaped and slid down my cheek. The moment passed quickly, and I laughed more than I needed to in order to assure both of us that I considered my reaction to be comical.

Sofie fixed her eyes upon mine, then she pulled me into a lingering kiss. I had all but forgotten how soft and flavorful a woman's kiss could be, but I knew instinctively that this woman was truly special.

"Sofie—I must leave—now. I'm confused and need a little time alone. You must not . . . you are not being rejected. I've thought about you constantly since Josephine Baker captured my fancy, but I must understand *how that can be possible with the Dieter I have been. I've overlooked some part of myself and it is now talking to me as never before . . . give me time to listen to the message."*

She smiled. "We are all complex mixtures. Tomorrow, I shall be Helen Morgan—you know her? We are going to perform Gershwin—a superbly talented American Jew, who has just died in his thirties—and I will sit atop the Bösendorfer and sing 'The Man I Love' to every man at our soirée. It can be our joke on all of Wilhelmstrasse, okay? Can you be my partner in that? Perhaps it will help you to discover more of yourself to be sharing a laugh that only we understand. Kiss me goodnight and go home to Miguel, my beautiful Dieter."

CHAPTER SEVEN
Berlin – Summer 1938

A GRAND RECEPTION
[From Dieter's Journal]

*S*ofie's selection was, indeed, an inside joke. The brothers Gershwin had composed the song as a part of their anti-military musical entitled *Strike Up The Band*, but then they had dropped it from the score after the production opened in New York. The flamboyant singer Helen Morgan then recognized its potential and soon made "The Man I Love" her signature piece. I was certain that versatile, uninhibited Sofie could give a credible imitation of Miss Morgan, just as she had captured Josephine Baker. I was not to be disappointed.

On Saturday evening, I dressed and groomed myself carefully, knowing that the guest list for the gathering at 80 Wilhelmstrasse included many prominent military and political figures. Among the most celebrated would be the recently anointed First Reichsmarschall of the Luftwaffe, Hermann Göring, together with his second wife, Emmy, who had recently given birth to their first child, a daughter named Edda. Göring had been commander of "Red Baron" von Richthofen's famous Jagdgeschwader 1 Squadron during the Great War; he was personally credited with twenty-two kills. More recently, his Condor Legion had gone to Spain during that country's civil war to assist the Nationalists. He was the country's leading advocate for air supremacy, and I assumed that posture had attracted Charles Lindbergh to him.

Göring's growing personal popularity had allowed him to lead a group of officers who had forced both War Minister von Blomberg and Army

Commander von Fritsch from office. The press portrayed him as a dynamic figure with a key role to play in the führer's strategy to annex Austria and extend German control beyond its postwar political borders. His roly-poly figure and elaborate uniforms, resplendent with colorful ribbons and medals, made the man look bigger than life, but also a little foolish, in my opinion. And tonight I was actually going to see this icon! I had read that Göring's family contained several Jews, and for that reason it pleased me that he had now assumed such a prominent position in the military as well as in the new government. Perhaps this fact alone would make it more comfortable for people like me.

As you can imagine, I arrived at Sofie's house brimming with excitement and expectation. It was still over an hour until the first guests would appear, thus I had time to admire the tasteful floral arrangements and discreet pictorial displays honoring Lindbergh and his wife, Anne Morrow. As I was examining a historic photo from his 1927 trans-Atlantic exploit, a deep voice intruded upon my thoughts. "Herr Meister, I do not believe that we have been introduced formally—but perhaps you have seen me at your tavern."

Without looking, I knew that General Otto von Seigler was standing behind me, and I tried to turn toward him with confidence and assurance. "Of course, General, we all know when you and your staff pay us a visit, and we are gratified that you appear to enjoy the Fischerstube." I extended my hand, which was immediately captured in his strong grip.

"I understand that Sofie has told you something of tonight's gathering—the distinguished countrymen who are joining us and our famous American guests. No part of this is to be discussed with others. Do you understand?"

"Of course, sir."

"Good. Good. You are here because Sofie has selected you, and I trust her judgment in such matters. Please do not give either of us any reason to regret her choice. I intend to invite her to sing one of her songs for our guests, and I assume that you will accompany her. Please remember that it is *her* talent on display, not your own. Correct?"

"Of course, sir."

"Good! Enjoy yourself, but speak only to Sofie, Lieutenant Kolb, or me if you have questions. And you will be free to depart when dinner is announced. Lieutenant Kolb will have an envelope with your professional fee, and a driver will return you to your flat."

Why my "flat"? I thought. Could von Seigler actually know—or care—where a piano tuner lives? Is the Gestapo so thorough in protecting key government figures? Or had Sofie told her father more about me than she had indicated? It troubled me, yet I liked the General and truly fancied his stunning, talented daughter. Perhaps my imagination was taking liberties with my normal good sense. *Relax and think about the music you intend to play, Dieter!*

Guests began to drift into the great room a fashionable few minutes after the time of their invitation, and, from the insignia, it was clear that arrivals were generally in inverse order of rank. Forty minutes after the younger officers and their nervous ladies plucked the first hors d'oeuvres from silver trays, the room began to electrify with gray heads in elaborate uniforms and elegantly dressed women wearing sparkling jewelry.

I did not see Göring enter, but I became aware of a knot of admirers greeting Emmy Göring and asking about her new daughter. Emmy was glowing and confident; I could imagine how she might have helped her war hero husband recover from the sadness of his first wife's passing. Then a burst of spontaneous applause announced Göring, who abbreviated an imitation of the Nazi salute and began a circuit of air kisses to the ladies and hearty embraces of their escorts. He was exactly as newspaper photos captured him—broad, powerful body and high, Slavic cheekbones. Tanned skin and elegant, wavy blond hair. A perpetual, broad smile seemed to lead him through the admiring crowd until he arrived at the center of the room and raised his glass to toast the nation, its leader, and our host and hostess. Even this anonymous Jewish piano man was moved by Göring's charisma!

Von Seigler and Sofie nodded condescendingly, then Otto von Seigler thanked Reichsmarschall Göring and continued, "As most of you know, we are being honored tonight with a visit from Charles A. Lindbergh and his wife, Anne. They are world famous but not totally comfortable with excessive attention or praise. They use neither tobacco nor spirits, and so I must ask you to be moderate in your use of either in their presence. They have departed America to seek more privacy and perhaps greater *sophistication of taste—so we will not disappoint them.*

"Reichsmarschall Göring assures me that Mr. Lindbergh speaks our language adequately, but I hope that those of you who can converse in English will do so around them. Mrs. Lindbergh—Anne—also speaks Spanish fluently from her years in Mexico, so those among you who were with Reichsmarschall Göring in the Condor Legion in Spain may wish to say a few words in el Español. We are told that she enjoys practicing.

"Now, I am informed that their car is en route and will arrive shortly. I will alert you just before they enter the room, and we will welcome them with polite applause. Reichsmarschall Göring will extend a brief greeting, and we will all show them how a superior civilization enjoys itself and entertains its friends. Questions?"

There were, of course, no questions, but I detected a shifting of positions by several of the younger attendees who wanted to be nearer the great entry doors directly across from me. Sofie motioned for me to resume playing, and—for some unaccountable reason—I launched into "Lili Marleen, das Madchen unter den Lateran," the song popular among military men about a girl waiting under a lantern. Soon several glasses were raised and heads swayed as many of the guests sang the lyrics.

General von Seigler quieted the room with three quick claps of his large hands, and two footmen opened the tall doors, with one announcing in perfect English, "Mr. Charles Augustus Lindbergh and Mrs. Anne Morrow Lindbergh from the United States of America." Heads craned for a glimpse of one of the most famous men of our time, and enthusiastic applause continued until the guest raised both arms, palms facing outward, and slowly lowered them as if he were embracing everyone in the vast room.

Göring's firm voice began, "My dear friends Charles and Anne, it is a great pleasure to be in your company again. Germany values your friendship, and we are flattered that you have come here to get to know us better. I warn you that I intend to ask too many questions about aviation, because I am committed to creating the world's finest aircraft and training the world's best pilots here in Germany. The evening is yours—please enjoy the home of Otto and Sofie von Seigler and the company of many German admirers."

I watched Lindbergh and could see that he noted the warmth of the greeting. He was much taller than I had anticipated—at least 1.85 meters, I judged—and I wondered how he could have been confined in a small, crowded airplane cockpit for nearly 27 hours without going crazy. Even though his epic solo flight had occurred eleven years earlier, and he was now thirty-six years of age, he still looked boyish, with tousled hair and a lean figure. His blue suit was very simple, with an anonymous necktie (slightly crooked) and a simple red, white, and blue button in his lapel. His smile seemed genuine, and he took in the entire room with a slow, searching arc, almost like a cautious flyer checking his surroundings one last time before descending to land. Then he raised his voice just enough to be heard by a respectfully quiet gathering.

"My wife and I are pleased to be in Germany once again. Reichsmarschall Göring earlier honored us with your Service Cross of the German Eagle, and we are, frankly, awed by the progress which Germany has made in one of my primary interest areas—aviation. As you know, in addition to my overly reported solo flight to Le Bourget, France, I have flown the mail to many cities in my own country and—with my adventurous wife, who is becoming a competent pilot—have visited many important cities in America and across Europe. We believe that aviation will offer new dimensions to personal travel and to commerce, and we hope passionately that your progress and ours will be devoted to those ends and not to a new form of destruction. Let's get on with this fabulous evening our hosts have arranged. Thank you, Hermann, Emmy, Otto, and Sofie; you are more than generous in welcoming us to Germany."

I wondered how often he had extended thanks in new places since spanning the Atlantic. Certainly many, many more times than he had envisioned when he set out to win the $25,000 prize offered by New York hotelier Raymond Orteig to the first adventurer to cross the Atlantic alone in a flying machine. And, if he indeed chose Germany as his new residence, how many millions of people around the globe might conclude that my country had now been recognized as the postwar leader of Europe? Lindbergh's actions could, indeed, change history.

At precisely 9:00 p.m., General von Seigler tapped his champagne flute with a knife to quiet the room. Then he announced that, shortly, dinner would be served in the grand dining salon, pointing past my Bösendorfer toward another set of tall doors. He continued, "I must thank my lovely Sofie for allowing me to appear as the gracious host. She has arranged this evening for me, as she has done for several years. Of course, nothing comes without a price tag, and in this case, it is Sofie's desire to show us all her progress as a musician and chanteuse. Please join a very proud father in encouraging a pre-dinner song from our hostess, Fräulein Sofie von Seigler."

She stepped from that same hidden corner where I had first seen her, wearing a simple black sheath, walked confidently to the piano, then lifted herself effortlessly to a sitting position atop the now-closed Bösendorfer. She crossed one leg over the other and smoothed the black fabric slowly, so that the lines of her long, graceful legs were unmistakably clear. Then Sofie leaned on one hand while extending the other toward Hermann Göring, who for once seemed uneasy with attention.

"As you all know, American jazz and the American musical theatre have captured us as no army ever could. Their composers are giving us melodies for dancing and singing—and none can surpass the beautiful compositions of the brothers Gershwin. Mr. and Mrs. Lindbergh, may I offer this Gershwin gem to you . . . "

Sofie was Helen Morgan, pouring out her heart to someone she was yet to meet, yet was certain would come along. "The Man I Love" was a nicely contained melody, with no great leaps to trip the singer or lure her off key, and Sofie stayed well within herself but extracted all of the poignant message in a velvety voice which oozed sensuality to every man who imagined that she was singing only to him. I was one of those on that night—perhaps the only one who correctly imagined that exclusivity.

The guests were lavish in their show of appreciation, and they applauded with enthusiasm at the conclusion. Sofie leapt from the piano and planted a kiss on her father's cheek, then gave him an affectionate hug that said to everyone that he was a general—but one with the warmest of parental instincts. Lindbergh seemed especially pleased with the rendition and thanked Sofie for all the care that had gone into their evening.

And, with that, Otto and Sofie led their guests past the Bösendorfer (and its invisible attendant), through the doors to the dining salon. When the last junior officer had departed and I stood alone, Lt. Klaus Kolb entered and in his usual colorless way pressed an envelope into my hand, clicking his heels. "Your car is awaiting—now. Guten abend, Herr Meister." I had been dismissed.

CHAPTER EIGHT

Lilkahaus, Near Berlin - Summer 1938

NEW AWAKENING

[From Dieter's Journal]

I departed 80 Wilhelmstrasse through the service door and walked toward a Mercedes staff car with its lights on and engine purring. Behind me there were sounds of voices, laughter, and food being served. I even imagined that I could hear Sofie's voice through the din, but of course that would have been impossible. For the first time, I glanced inside the envelope Lt. Kolb had given me and realized that, in less than three hours, I had earned more than a month's wages and tips. Could I offer any reasonable explanation to Miguel, or should I add this evening to the catalogue of secrets I now kept from my closest friend? I decided to keep my own counsel, at least until I understood better myself. There would be time for an intimate chat with Miguel—but later.

The trip home would give me the chance to compose a proper note of thanks, and tomorrow I could transcribe and deliver it. Let me see: Do I address it to *General and Fräulein von Seigler?* Or to *Fr. Sofie von Seigler and General Otto . . . ?* I settled upon that, then continued, *Thank you for allowing . . .* No. *—selecting me to work . . .* No. *—to provide background music for your guests. I hope . . .* No. *—trust that you . . .* No. *I will be . . .* No. *I would be pleased to . . .* Where were we? Certainly *not* nearing my neighborhood.

I tapped on the driver's glass partition and said, "This isn't the way . . . " He looked at me in his mirror and said, "I am familiar with the route, sir. Please sit back and we shall arrive in about thirty minutes."

Through the window I saw a road sign indicating that we were proceeding in the direction of Grosser Müggelsee, the large lake area where wealthy Berliners went to escape during hot summer weekends, and also the location of Reichsmarschall Göring's lavish hunting lodge Carinhall. It had been profiled often in popular magazines and was generally considered an accent piece for the flamboyant Göring. For a fleeting moment, I had a vision of the overweight Reichsmarschall pursuing me like game on his private tract, with his carved shotgun firing off buckshot. Ach—Juden und hunds!!! Such good sport. No, it must be a mistake that I was being driven away from the city. Or . . . ?

Soon we were passing through a pristine pine forest, which offered occasional peeks at a moonlit lake surface beyond. Probably Grosser Müggelsee. And I could see lights from a few Alpine-style lodges tucked into spruce groves. My driver turned off the road into one of these—a long, winding driveway with a small entry marker identifying it as Lilkahaus. The entry lights of the vaulted wooden lodge were turned on, and through a window I could see a log glowing on the stone hearth. Yet, there were no signs of people inside. What was I expecting? Some Hansel und Gretel denizen of the woods waiting to fry me and feed me to domestic pets? It was an empty house that had been prepared to receive me, and I had no choice but to proceed inside and learn more.

My driver opened the door and handed me the key he had used. Then he pointed to a single place setting on a small table near the warm fire. He told me that I would find dinner prepared inside the black iron oven in the adjacent kitchen and, with a rare smile, bade me a good evening and departed. I was alone with a good-smelling venison stew, a loaf of brown bread, and a bottle of rich red Rhine wine, already opened and breathing. I concluded easily that there was little chance I was being poisoned, and by now my appetite was ravenous, so I spooned out a generous plate of the savory stew, poured a full glass of wine, and sat back to enjoy my dinner and speculate about the events of the evening.

On a full belly, I considered my circumstances. It seemed probable that this lodge belonged to General von Seigler; there were several framed photos of the young Sofie on tables around the room. And, of course, Lilkahaus

incorporated the name of Sofie's Polish mother. I wondered if she had ever seen the retreat or even knew of its existence. Perhaps it was Otto's quiet way of reminding himself of the unusual woman he had known and loved so long ago, who had provided him the daughter he now adored. Somehow, it reminded me of a man who secretly carves the name of a long-ago lover into a tree where only he knows it exists. I wondered if their affection had been greater and endured longer than Sofie had indicated in our late-evening conversation at Wilhelmstrasse. One thing seemed abundantly clear—I was not going to be returning to my room that evening because someone did not want me to do so.

I had no reason to try running away from the lodge, and so I folded myself into a deep, worn leather chair by the fire and finished the bottle of excellent wine my host had provided. If there is a better soporific combination than red wine and a wood fire, I have not encountered it. Even my intense curiosity could not stop me from relaxing into a warm, deep sleep.

If my falling asleep had been pleasant, my waking was even more so. Soft hands braced my head and softer lips touched my brow gently. "Dieter—are you in there?" I opened my eyes and saw hers only a few centimeters away. "You were excellent tonight, you know. All through dinner, people came to my table to tell me they loved our song. I had to thank you, and I couldn't send you away hungry—so you got to enjoy venison stew and Father's best Schloss-Johannisberger in my secret retreat. Are you angry that I have abducted you?"

"Sofie, I . . . no, I'm not angry. I'm more confused than anything, and probably somewhat frightened, to be truthful. Can you understand that a musician of modest talent who shares a room with a tavern manager and owns one suit doesn't often play for the most famous personalities of his time and then get wakened by one of the most fascinating women he has known?"

"I suppose not," she returned, "but remember that everyone tonight was in new territory. Göring was winning the approval of Lindbergh; Father was seeking Göring's favor; I was trying to please Father . . . and you were about to become my lover."

My heart stopped. Even though I knew it hadn't been necessary to drive 45 kilometers to eat dinner, I had managed to sublimate any notion that Sofie and I could be about to embark upon a romantic involvement. I had slept with a few women when I was a student, but it had all been mechanical until I encountered the mysteries of Miguel do Nacimiento, and that was when I first understood who I was. Sofie *knew* most of that but seemed to pay it no attention at all. I looked to see if she was laughing at my dilemma but saw only the incredible eyes awaiting my response.

I said, "Sofie—I believe that you perceive that I adore you. But you also know that I have had a homosexual lover for two years. If I reject you now, you will resent me. But, if I accept, it could result in an even more hurtful form of rejection. Do you understand my confusion?"

She smiled and responded, "Dieter, I know the talented, sensitive, and romantic musician you are, and I know myself even better. I truly hate to fail when I want something. If that were not the case, I would be working in a musty office in Krakow and listening to short-wave broadcasts in a tiny bedroom. I don't believe that you will walk away."

She pushed the straps of her evening gown over the ends of her broad shoulders and along her arms, finally allowing the garment to slide down her body until it gathered by her ankles. I was startled that she was wearing nothing more, then I shamelessly let my gaze travel leisurely upward from the long, defined legs to the creamy abdomen and on to the full, cantilevered breasts, finally staring directly into the humor-filled eyes of the luxuriant Sofie.

"I believe this will be easier than I had imagined," I said, and we gathered ourselves together in front of the dwindling fire, allowing all of our curiosity, excitement, and sensuality to move us along without hesitation. To say merely that Sofie was magnificent would be an injustice. To imagine that any woman could ever be more desirable to me would be absolute folly.

During the following days, Sofie and her student companions came with greater frequency to the Fischerstube, and they appeared to migrate from the shadows at the back of the cellar to occupy the more visible tables. Several times they led Sofie to the piano and demanded that she sing for them. We seemed always to be in harmony as she willingly filled their requests, with forays into the mannerisms of the unique song stylists of the moment. When she did so, it seemed to me that she was able to transpose her total personality into that of each imitated entertainer. I found myself wondering whether it was Sofie or Helen Morgan or even Josephine Baker who passed intimate hours with me at Lilkahaus.

One evening she lingered after her friends and told me that a car would be awaiting me after closing to transport me back to the lakeside retreat. It wasn't a question inquiring whether I cared to join her but a simple statement that didn't invite contradiction. Excitement surged through all of my senses for the balance of my Fischerstube responsibilities, and after closing I hurried to the car parked across from the entrance.

As previously, there was a welcoming fire burning, but this time, late dinner for two was graciously arrayed by the hearth, and a smiling Sofie took my hands at the door in a warm greeting, then placed a piquant kiss squarely on my lips. "I hope I'm not being silly, Dieter," she began, "but since our night together here, thoughts of you have cropped up at the most inconvenient times, so I must sit alone with you and try to understand what it all means. Do you understand at all? Perhaps we were both fueled by the exhilaration of that extraordinary evening on Wilhelmstrasse, or possibly there were *two* very unique shared experiences that night. Can you . . . do you know what I'm trying to say? I think that it is terribly important that we probe deeply into ourselves—beyond fleeting emotions and the excitement of newness—to our core needs. I am very vulnerable, Dieter; even though you may see me as composed and impregnable, I am vulnerable to being hurt because this wonderful Third Reich has built a barrier between me and the two people I most love in the world. I am afraid to become emotionally attached to anyone now, lest another wall go up. And damn you for coming to tune my piano with all your sincerity and humor and warmth. And damn you, too, for disarming me and taking my breath away with your uncomplicated approach to intimacy. Do you understand . . . do you?"

I laughed, even though it was totally inappropriate in the face of her confusion. "My Sofie, I haven't been able to decide whether I made love to Helen Morgan or Sofie von Seigler, and I imagine that some of the same questions are vexing each of us. But, if I assume, for the sake of argument, that there was no element of method acting in you, and that only Sofie was next to me by the fire, I then must move to even more complex considerations. Am I truly capable of reviving such intense feelings with a woman? And, if the answer to that is 'yes,' is it fair in these times to allow a general's beloved daughter to risk a relationship with a Jewish piano jockey from a local pub? If I care for you this much, should I not walk away rather than trysting at Lilkahaus? What course is the truest expression of affection, Sofie?"

"You are amazing!" she brightened. "I'm not even sure how much of me was Josephine Baker or Helen Morgan when I copied them, but I am sure that I wanted each of them to be at her best for you. It was your approval I needed. Perhaps I wasn't totally certain that a university student named Sofie could carry enough cachet to hold your interest, and so I added the flavor of more-intriguing women to make myself more secure.

"Now—what was your other issue? Oh, yes—am I endangered because I am spending intimate hours with a working musician who is a Jew? Of course I am! Otherwise, we would be dining together in a fine restaurant in Berlin. Some say that an element of danger enhances the intensity of love. You know—harder breathing, more tears and explosive orgasms. Ah, I have shocked you! Dear Dieter, my father will *always* protect me, and whatever transpires will be rewritten to portray me as the innocent and you as the moral transgressor. You may—and should—worry about yourself, but not about me. I can't help you with that consideration, and, if the circumstances of these times are inhibiting for you, I shall truly understand and even applaud your retreating to a safer place. Thank you for listening to my silly selfishness. I needed to put those thoughts into the open, but now I want to be here with you away from that complicated world we both inhabit. Perhaps you will dine with Marlene Dietrich tonight if I can get my throat into a husky pitch. I hear she is an intense lover."

CHAPTER NINE

Berlin - Autumn 1938

EMERGING CONFLICTS

[From Dieter's Journal]

*A*nd so it was that two young Germans embarked upon a secret romance, requited at odd times and in hidden corners, but growing in intensity and commitment with each repetition. Sofie's free spirit soared in the warmth of my affection, and my heterosexual component quickly eclipsed all other romantic inclinations as I marveled at the extraordinary woman who had earned my devotion.

I scarcely noticed the increasing hostility toward Jews that was spreading throughout the country in 1938. When Jewish men were commanded to register with the government, I conveniently neglected to do so, and I avoided Jewish friends and contacts, preferring the company of Sofie's university contemporaries, with whom I blended easily. Only Miguel ever commented upon the situation. He knew, of course, that I was not an Aryan, and he was certainly aware that I was no longer his loving companion. We still spoke freely of most events in our lives, and gradually he learned of my involvement with a young woman, although I was careful not to name her or to reveal that she was from a prominent family. But, Miguel was no fool and could observe the popular student who sang to my accompaniment in the Fischerstube; he surely perceived the growing closeness between us.

One evening as we strolled by the river, Miguel focused his remarks upon Sofie, without using her name. "She speaks Polish—the girl who sings with you. Did you know that?"

"She is a student. She may know many languages, but I have never heard her converse in Polish. What does it matter, Miguel?"

"Polish people with any Jewish relatives are being viewed very negatively. There is talk of deporting them forcibly to Poland. I just wondered if your friend might be in any danger of being sent to the East."

"I am sure she is German," I noted. "There is nothing Polish in her manner, and I know that she has attended schools near Berlin for many years—she has referred to them in chatter with her friends. Why would you think otherwise?"

"Someone complimented her on her Polish and said that it was like the more-refined speech pattern of the Krakow region. She acknowledged that it was an astute observation, so I believe that it was a correct one."

"Well, Miguel, I would be totally surprised to learn that she is Polish, and I certainly don't think she is a Jew—so the initiative to repatriate Polish Jews has nothing to do with her."

"I guess you'd know if she was a Jew," he mused. My mind was tracing the threads of my knowledge of Sofie, because I sensed that Miguel's questions were not launched accidentally, and I was determined never to allow our closeness to put her in danger. Finally, I felt the need to respond in a way that would end the conjecture.

"I don't think that students are the focus of this initiative; they are looking at merchants, money lenders, and political agitators. Minister Goebbels is always identifying those Jews as the enemies of our New Order, and if someone is thinking of sending Polish Jews out of Germany, it will be they who are leaving."

"Perhaps," he commented, leaving it clear that there was still a question in his mind. There were questions in my mind, too, but they were growing concerns about the mood of my roommate and incipient doubts about the wisdom of letting him know anything more about my life outside the workplace. There would be no further commentary from me about the Jewish Problem or the national measures being formulated to deal with it. There would be no additional mention of Sofie or conjecture about her origins. It was going to be the beginning of a strained relationship—one which I should try to leave as soon as a convenient alternative presented itself.

When Sofie and I next stole an evening together, I reviewed this conversation and she quickly sensed my concern. I could see that the subject matter was familiar to her and then learned that she and her father had spent time exploring possible implications for them. "This may all be part of an effort by Minister Goebbels to regain the führer's favor. You know that he—Goebbels—apparently made a fool of himself pursuing that Czech actress, Lída Baarová. Hitler does not approve of public scandal, and little Herr Goebbels fawning over a beautiful, taller woman was the antithesis of the image our government is attempting to project across Europe. Father feels that Goebbels may undertake some dramatic move to revive his persona—to show everyone that he wields enormous power and must not be ignored. Right now it is Polish Jews in his crosshairs.

"The larger problem may be with the Polish government, which has said that Poles who have emigrated to Germany may not repatriate to Poland. So, we could end this with Goebbels sending Jews back to Poland and Poland refusing them entry."

"Could you possibly be at risk in this?" I queried. "What do your birth certificate and your passport say?"

"I have official government papers showing that I am a German, born to a military officer serving outside the country. Like the führer himself, I have been confirmed in the Holy Roman Catholic Church. My mother is mentioned only by name in my papers, and she is listed as 'missing'— nothing more."

Looking back later, this was the critical point in my life and in our relationship where I first understood that it would not be possible for me to just stand beside the river of German history watching events unfold without becoming a part of them. I'm certain that many of my countrymen had similar epiphanies, and the choices we were offered were not always clear ones. Our new leadership and the plaudits rained down upon them by their propagandists had initially been easy to accept, but our individual experiences were becoming increasingly disturbing and no amount of rationalizing could reconcile them.

I paused at my own Rubicon to consider whether I would have the courage needed to set an independent course or if uncomplaining acceptance might be more prudent. Subsequent events would dictate my decision.

Not long after we had that conversation, the scenario about which Sofie had speculated actually began to materialize. Propaganda Minister Goebbels ordered that all of the undocumented Polish Jews residing in Germany would have to depart from the country not later than October 31, 1938. I heard from Miguel and some of his knowledgeable friends that more than twelve thousand people could be affected by that order, and I wondered where they would go. A few months earlier, Poland's government had announced that the citizenship of any who had resided outside their country for five years or more had been revoked, so many of those being ordered out of Germany would not be allowed to return to live in Poland.

I watched Polish men leaving their jobs in order to register themselves and their families for the trains being prepared to carry them east, and I saw many postings for furniture and belongings for sale by people anticipating their forced exodus. They were trying to wring a few RM from the things they owned and would have to leave behind. It was pitiful, but it would get worse. Much worse. By the end of October, thousands of those Polish Jews had been dumped at the border, near the Polish town of Zbąszyń. The nights were getting cold, and even those with a little money couldn't find much food to purchase. A catastrophic situation had been created, intentionally, and much of Germany sat back to watch it simmer, awaiting an inevitable explosion.

Eventually, it was a Polish family named Grynszpan, who had been living in Hanover for many years, who unknowingly ignited the fuse. In miserable conditions, hopelessly stranded near the border, the Grynszpan's daughter sent a message to her seventeen-year-old brother, Herschel, who was living illegally with an uncle in Paris, begging his help to get money to them so they could buy food. It was said that he received her communication on November 3 and took what little money he had and purchased a pistol. On November 7, he entered the German Embassy in Paris, seeking the Ambassador, where he demanded that the matter be heard and considered without delay. Out of frustration and desperation when his plea received no attention, he shot and fatally wounded a minor *diplomat named Ernst vom Rath.*

Two days later, Minister Goebbels delivered a passionate speech in Munich, relayed throughout the nation, announcing vom Rath's death and urging Germans to force Jews to atone for such criminal behavior. Bands of marauders, encouraged by their country's leadership, quickly fanned out through Jewish neighborhoods in Germany and Austria, where they smashed windows, burned temples, and pillaged homes—all without any intervention by police and military forces, who had been ordered to stand down during the unruly demonstrations. The sound of shattering glass filled the night, as did the screams of whole families being assaulted. The night became known as Kristallnacht because of those sounds, which continued on into November 10 and marked the end of any pretense that Jews could survive under Nazi domination. It also signaled to me that my life could be on a collision course with disaster, even though I was merely a musician with no political affiliations.

The Fischerstube was temporarily closed. Even though it had no Jewish connection and was geographically remote from any restaurants or shoppes favored by Jews, its large plate-glass entry window at street level was too tempting once the rioting took on a momentum of its own. A single brick hurled from a passing vehicle shattered the ornate glass and distributed shards downward through the stairway from the street level. Miguel gave me the bad news after we had reported for work. "We will be unemployed for a while. Every glass cutter in the city has weeks of orders to fill, and most Jews have not even addressed their damage—the demand is all coming from German shops and stores."

"But couldn't we put some wooden boards over the opening temporarily and get back in business?" I asked.

"Of course," he responded, "but the problem is more than one of broken glass. There are hundreds of police, Gestapo, and black shirts visiting gatherings of people and checking their documents. Even those with perfect papers are afraid they might be detained on some technicality by a badge-heavy martinet seeking to gain favor with his superior. You can hear it— 'Look at me! I have found a Jew!' And, you see, where Jews really have fled or been carted off, it is now open season on their unguarded possessions. All these roving heroes are looking to capture someone's silver service or Rosenthal Chinaware or other 'abandoned' valuables.

"They are indiscriminate. I have seen chairs, tables, rugs, and bags of clothing being toted away from private homes. In a few days, even the light fixtures and cabinets will have been stripped away, so the owners will return to nothing—if they return at all. My guess is that we will never see many of these Jews again."

Miguel spoke without any of the passion or fear I was already experiencing, perhaps because he was a Catholic from Portugal who had no part in this internecine German madness. Or, I thought, maybe he had his own animosity toward Jews, and particularly Polish Jews, which allowed him to accept what was now turning into a national explosion of hatred.

Without thinking about it, I asked him, "Miguel—what is your feeling about this assault on a group of people? Does it trouble you that the same anger being visited upon a calloused, cheating pawnshop owner may also reach out and hurt—"

"A beautiful young woman attending Humboldt University?" he completed my sentence and my thought. "I know that the bounty for turning in one is exactly the same as that for the other. Each is like a unit of credit, with no regard for affiliations or behavior. They're not comparing Good Jews to Bad Jews or Desirable Poles vs. Disposable Poles. This pits friends against friends across the city. Everyone jumps on the Jews to get some kind of immunity from the wave of hatred."

"At the expense of others!" I added.

"You get it," Miguel continued. "Until this is completed, there will be selfish actions taken by people who are buying insurance for themselves by becoming informers. That's what the Nazis always wanted—loyalty to the State, not to friends, family, religion, or any other concept. Even love will bend to self-interest."

"So, Miguel, you would turn me in as a Jew to save your own skin? Is that what you're saying? Is that how you would dismiss our two years together?"

"Ah, Dieter," he responded, "Isn't that about what you have done to me? But, not even to avoid arrest and maltreatment by the authorities, but only to romance some schoolgirl!"

So, there it was—a hurt former lover, weighing his available weapons of revenge. It was frightening for me, because he also had the ability to inflict harm upon Sofie. I had never before felt so vulnerable, and with that realization I knew that I was becoming angry. I wondered if I could ever preempt my own disclosure and punishment by removing Miguel from the equation entirely. It was one of those fanciful scenarios we all entertain at times, but which rarely find their way to execution. When civilized people did take such drastic actions, it was *not* usually for their own benefit, but rather to protect a loved third party. I didn't want to follow the thought further, so I said to Miguel, "Let's walk back to the room and relax together."

CHAPTER TEN

Rahnsdorf – Autumn 1938

DRAWN INTO EVENTS

[From Dieter's Journal]

*H*umboldt University suspended classes temporarily and students were directed not to congregate in groups larger than four persons. Of course, everyone knew that academe traditionally spawned rebellious activities by indignant young men and women. The leadership did not want the foreign press to take films of student protests. The story they wanted to be reported to the world was already out there: German citizens had reacted spontaneously to a cold-blooded murder and directed their anger toward a foreign clique which had caused this detour in their nation's postwar revival. National police had been mobilized swiftly to avoid rioting, but it had taken days to stamp out all the embers of antisocial behavior. There would be no student protests of the police actions!

I wondered about Sofie's whereabouts, although I was relatively certain that she would be well protected. After debating with myself, I called the private telephone number I still retained in my wallet. The voice that answered asked simply that I state my business, without any clue as to its location. I hesitated, then said, "I was given this contact number for Fräulein Sofie—would it be possible to speak with her?"

"Give me your name and telephone number and we will inquire whether she wishes to return the call," came the curt reply.

"Just tell her that we have found some music sheets at the Fischerstube which we believe are hers. Our piano tuner will be holding them if she comes by. We are closed for normal business today, but he is tuning the piano this afternoon. *Danke schön.*" I hung up the receiver before any further question could be put to me; it was enough information for her to act upon if she got the message and was free to leave home.

For the next two hours, I sat alone in the tavern. My kitchen key had served to gain entry, and inside there was electric service but no heat, although the day was mild for November. I resolved to tune the piano, just in case my cryptic message precipitated a visit by others to the Fischerstube. I even had the "cheat sheets" from "The Man I Love"—left from the Lindbergh evening—on which I had printed *Sofie von Seigler* neatly on the face page, to cover the possibility of that canard being tested. Now, I waited—and wondered if Sofie and I would ever again share our lives in the same way in the intrigue-laden city.

A noise from the kitchen startled me momentarily, but I concluded quickly that Sofie had chosen not to draw attention by knocking at the boarded entry. Clever girl! She had been in the tavern often and knew of the service entry off the alley. "Sofie—come here," I called. "I'm tuning the upright. Perhaps we will be able to open again by the weekend."

Klaus Kolb stood in the doorway, impassive as always, and motioned for me to follow him. I had to assume that it was a friendly gesture—otherwise no good Wehrmacht lieutenant would pass up a chance to knock a civilian on the head. And so I closed the piano, gathered the sheet music, and walked toward him, with no words from either of us. In a moment we were inside a small military car in the alley, and Klaus was wasting no time getting away from the Fischerstube and onto a major artery leading away from the center of the city.

It was not the direction of *Lilkahaus* or the lake area generally, but rather, after a silent, twenty-minute journey, we entered a small residential suburb with modest but well-kept private houses—the kind of neighborhood where one would expect to find a factory foreman's home or a dressmaker's business. He drew up beside one such house, distinguished only by a well-trimmed hedge and two street lanterns, and he handed me a valise and key, saying, "Front door."

It took only seconds to enter, and I saw no observers who might have noticed the gray car arrive and depart. Once inside, I looked about and saw comfortable furnishings and a well-appointed room. With no guidance at all, I decided to sit and read any book or newspaper I could find. *Look as if you belong here!* I told myself.

The shrill double ring of a telephone interrupted whatever thought process I was developing, and I picked up the receiver and uttered a totally impersonal, *"Ja?"* Sofie's voice, in near-whispered tones, responded, "Good. You are there. Don't leave the house or stand near the windows. There should be cheese and meat in the fridge, bread and beer in the larder. Leave a candle burning, and get some sleep. I will try to join you later, *schotze."*

Despite her use of that endearing term, Sofie was clearly not herself, and I tried to revisit her precise words to understand better the concerns I sensed in her furtive message. She seemed relieved that I had arrived safely, so perhaps the drive had been dangerous. Then, if I had to stay hidden within the house, that suggested someone hostile might be outside. She had said she would *try* to join me, so I concluded that she was not entirely free to move about.

I found the food and picked at it for a few minutes while I considered my options. Sleeping in a bed with an attendant candle seemed to maximize my vulnerability, so I arranged pillows to suggest a sleeping form in the bedroom. Then I found a deep chair in a distant corner of the library where I could doze and not be seen easily.

Being awakened from a sound sleep in unfamiliar surroundings can lead to moments of panic, as one tries to recall where he is and why he is there, and then to review what has awakened him. The sound of muffled voices had intruded upon my pleasant dream of an evening at *Lilkahaus,* and the great chair into which I had burrowed refreshed my memory of my current location. Now I was focusing with a clearer mind, and I reckoned that it was two or three o'clock in the morning and that the voices I heard were male.

"They are not here!" one declared. "Someone must have alerted them—they even left a decoyed bed, but no bags or clothes in the room."

"There are dishes in the sink and two empty beer bottles on the counter," came the reply. I was grateful that the beverage had been so tasty that I had consumed two bottles, adding to their assumption that "they" had been here and departed.

"Should we search further or contact Central Control so they can widen the effort?" asked voice number one. "Perhaps they can put some cars in the streets near here and intercept their flight. Someone is protecting them and likely is using the dark hours to move them from the city. Frau Hildemann reported that a car stopped briefly at about 10 p.m. and that the house lights were extinguished before midnight. Our people were able to put surveillance onto the block less than an hour after her call, and they say no one has entered or departed since then."

"Jews are furtive and they can appear and disappear as Gypsies do!" the deeper second voice laughed. "This is why the country must rid itself of that element so that our dealings can be more transparent and honorable!"

"What about their things? Houses, jewelry, small businesses? They will all be left behind, won't they? Who gets them when the Jews are gone back to Poland?"

"Government will see that we all get a share. Can you imagine how many treasures are concealed in the walls and under the floorboards of all those Jew houses? Those people save and collect and save and hoard—even a small shopkeeper may have extensive riches squirreled away. We will all benefit from their departure."

"Who were the Jews in this house?" asked the deep voice.

"This was just a place that Jews who broke the law could hide in for a day or two, until transportation out of the city—or even out of the country—could be arranged. It has been watched for several weeks. But, they are so very sly, and, once again, their spy system seems to have sent a warning before our sweep could react to a tip from a cooperating citizen."

I breathed as little as possible and moved no muscles at all as the two eased past my chair toward the front entry. They were still chatting as they descended from the doorway to the street, but I maintained my silence in case some "sleeper" had remained behind to snare a cagy Jew with the good sense to hide. I wondered whether Sofie's call to me had been part of a trap or whether she had been overheard. Or, perhaps she was still planning to arrive at the house, in which case she could be in danger for hiding a Jew, even if they didn't know about Lilka.

Since I could resolve none of this, my only course for now was to get away from here and avoid my friends and usual places until I could devise a workable plan to get to a safer location. It is extra challenging to get away when you don't know your starting point, so I left my hiding place and returned quietly to the telephone, hoping to find something that would *identify my location. There was nothing.*

Finally I saw the six digits on the telephone dial itself and concluded they were my best resource. Taking the handset off its carriage, I began banging on the cradle to attract the attention of an operator. When one finally said, "Operator," and asked if she could help me, I shouted, "This is 62-63-66, and we have a serious kitchen fire. Please send help!" Then, before she could ask details, I let out a convincing shriek and slammed the handset down on the cradle. I was hoping that the number would be sufficient information to identify an address and that a major distraction would begin soon.

Then I lighted the gas burners on the stove top and covered them with papers, pillows, boxes and the grease can I had found beneath the sink, and in no time I had a kitchen fire worthy of my call. I opened the front door a crack to increase the draft and headed for the rear exit through the attached garage. Emergency sirens pulsed in the distance, and I could see that flames were licking the kitchen ceiling, while the grease belched black smoke into the room. I was actually quite proud of my improvised device for covering my departure and waited in the shadow of the garage for the neighborhood crowd this event should attract shortly.

Something was wrong. What was it? What had I forgotten? My mind raced backward through the events of the past few hours. The unexpected appearance of Kolb at the Fischerstube; the swift ride to this neighborhood; the whispered call from Sofie; the dinner; the late visitors. Kolb. The key and the valise! Had I left the valise in the car? No—I had carried it to the door and opened the door with the key. I had pocketed the key, then inspected my surroundings and nibbled at the food I had located. By then, the valise had completely dropped from my purview. From that point forward, it hadn't entered my mind. It could be anywhere in the burning building, and its contents could be anything. Because it could implicate others, I decided that I must try to find it in the two or three minutes I reckoned remained before the sirens turned a nearby corner and trapped me inside.

I no longer had the option of keeping the house dark, so I turned on the overhead lights in each room I had visited. My circuit was nearly complete and my allocated time nearly exhausted when I saw the corner of the valise protruding from the partly open bathroom door. Of course—I had planned to examine the valise contents while in every German man's favorite reading room but had never gotten back there, favoring a comfortable sleep in the library chair. How fortunate that my guests had also passed up the WC! Seizing the handle, I bolted toward the garage door as the blinking lights from the fire squadron began reflecting on trees and two units came into sight.

Small knots of people had gathered, and I was able to insinuate myself into one group of four who pointed at the growing conflagration with concern and urged, "Hurry!" to the Feuerwehrleute. I joined them in their useless pointing and urging, trying my best to appear as another excited neighbor. The valise between my feet was incongruous, but no one seemed to notice it or me. As I had hoped, we were all ordered to retreat so that they could move in their equipment and fight the flames. I was happy to obey, slipping around a corner and walking away at an unhurried pace for several blocks until I arrived at the nearest bus stop, where I might finally pinpoint my location and consider my alternatives for preserving short-term freedom.

The shelter was identified by a small white-on-black sign reading RAHNSDORF and a map with an arrow telling me, You Are Here. Here appeared to be three or four kilometers southeast from the edge of the central city. Two colored bus route lines intersected at Here in RAHNSDORF, and I traced each, hoping to generate a viable plan for disappearing into the background of the troubled region. Running my finger along the Red Line, I repeated the name of each indicated stop until I arrived at one with a white circle labeled HUMBOLDT UNIVERSITY on a boulevard named Dorotheenstrasse. It looked as if the distance from RAHNSDORF could be five or six kilometers. Sofie was enrolled in the Institut für deutsche Literatur, a college within Humboldt University. It supplied many of the young revelers who regularly sipped beer and sang songs at the Fischerstube. That would be my destination, once the northbound Red Line bus finally made its way to Here. Meanwhile, I settled in the shadows on the kiosk's hard bench and waited.

As I climbed into the bus, I glanced quickly at the fire-pink sky behind me and the yellow portent of dawn ahead. Sitting with the valise between my feet, I was, for now, indistinguishable from the hundreds of others headed toward

their jobs and other early destinations through the fresh November morning.

My age and appearance were similar to those of Sofie's school companions, so I believed I could blend and possibly learn more about current conditions in the city. Perhaps there would even be threads leading to Sofie. She was popular, and anything affecting her might be noticed and discussed in the coffeehouses of Humboldt. At least it would be preferable to standing in the public square of Rahnsdorf until some patriot dispatched police to interrogate the stranger.

I saw a discarded newspaper wedged between seats and extracted it. The headline blared that Hershel Grynszpan had now been named as the Polish Jew who had assassinated diplomat Ernst vom Rath in Paris. The sub-caption told that outraged citizens throughout Germany and Austria had vented their anger over the cowardly killing. Authorities now controlled the spontaneous violence but, in response to citizen demands, were taking new steps to purge undesirables from their subversive cells in our cities. A final paragraph urged vigilance from all loyal Germans and listed a telephone number where they could report suspicious persons or behavior so that they could be investigated promptly. There were hints that such public-spirited alertness would be duly noted and rewarded. I wondered whether the sharp-eyed Frau Hildemann back in Rahnsdorf might soon be enjoying an extra ration of sausages as she peered out at the slightly charred home visible from her window. *Reichspogromnacht* had forever damaged the trust of one neighbor for another, of one friend for another—perhaps even of one lover for another.

As I re-folded the paper to put it back in the same crease between seats, a small article on an inside page caught my eye: *Oster Conspiracy Against Führer Exposed.* The short account said that the Gestapo had uncovered and prevented a conspiracy to attack the Reich Chancellery in September. Lieutenant Colonel Hans Oster of the German Office of Military Intelligence was identified as the ringleader, and it was alleged that the objective of Oster and his co-conspirators was to take the life of Hitler during the assault. Oster was now awaiting military court-martial. His commanding officer, General Otto von Seigler, was being interrogated to determine how such subversion could occur within the elite Wehrmacht command.

My hand was shaking as I pushed the offending pages deep into the recess between seats.

CHAPTER ELEVEN
Humboldt University - Autumn 1938

A NEAR MISS
[From Dieter's Journal]

*A*t the Humboldt University bus kiosk, I was one of several indistinguishable young people dismounting from the Red Bus, and not even the only one carrying a valise or similar tote. We moved together through an ancient gate and onto a tree-sheltered quadrangle, ringed with granite buildings, where the knot of newly arrived people commenced to separate and move in many directions. Some hurried deliberately toward the gray structures, but an equal number seemed to gravitate toward small groups, where there was animated chatting in progress. I stepped inside a bookstall not far from the kiosk and purchased a small notebook, a pencil, and a used textbook on the Franco-Prussian War. *Now*, I thought, *I really look like I belong*, and so I crossed the open grass toward a popular-appearing coffeehouse, where about two dozen similarly indistinguishable young adults were draped over chairs, benches, and tables. Tossing my valise onto a bench, I added my body to the accumulation, opened my newly acquired text, and began examining the photos of military leaders that filled the center pages.

After a few moments of this deception, I attempted to discover the contents of the elegant valise but soon realized that its hasp was secure. Trying to force it open in a public place would surely draw unwanted attention to me, so I abandoned the effort and resumed my mock reading.

Conversations around me—of which I could distinguish only disconnected fragments—seemed largely concerned with a newly imposed curfew and with the absence from classes of some classmates. The name of Herr Goebbels was interspersed liberally, and it appeared always to be accompanied by small facial distortions of dislike. Apparently the Minister was viewed as vain and power-driven. I wondered why the politically acute Herr Hitler would risk diminishing his own popularity by allowing Goebbels to remain so visible a part of the führer's inner circle. I concluded that he must be an efficient contributor to the Nazi program and too valuable to discipline publicly.

It was easy to imagine Sofie sitting at this very spot, chatting and laughing and popular with contemporaries. The setting permitted me to gaze over dozens of faces, and I set about searching for one that was familiar. An hour passed, and then another drifted by. Students came and departed, with any one easily replaced in kind by another. Same clothing, same casual manner, and same punctuations of laughter amid serious conversations. Finally, I concluded that, by remaining too long in one location, I was actually standing out from the others. and so I gathered my book, pad, and valise and wandered off toward the next gathering, a few hundred meters deeper into the heart of the university.

Once I thought I heard the distinct tones of Polish conversation, and I eased forward toward the source, only to have that small clot of friends dissolve. Had I heard the name *Sofie*? Or did my mind only create it from my thoughts? I was trying much too hard to stumble upon a link, and I wondered whether insinuating myself into the university was really as good an idea as it had seemed initially.

"Are you Dieter?" the disembodied voice queried. "Dieter, the piano man?" It came from a young woman who looked vaguely familiar. I had looked up automatically at the mention of my name, and now I was fixed squarely upon her eyes. Some response was due and necessary.

"How do you know Dieter?" was the best diversionary response I could marshal, although it seemed instantly to sound foolish.

"Yes, you *are* Dieter, from the Fischerstube! You play piano and accompany our songs, no?"

"Do you visit the Fischerstube often?" It was another non sequitur, but an attempt to gain information without volunteering any.

"Yes, yes—you are Dieter. I have been there many times, and my friends all like you. Are you also studying at the university?"

"I'm here to meet a friend—er, friends—some of the same students you know, perhaps. Do you know Sofie, who sings so well when she visits our cellar? Sofie—a tall girl with attractive eyes? She favors songs by Mable Mercer and Helen Morgan and Josephine Baker. Do you know her?"

"Yes, of course. She is quite popular, and her father is an important officer in the military hierarchy, so everyone knows Sofie. Why do you ask about her?"

Was I being examined by yet another citizen informant? Was there already a net spread for anyone mentioning Sofie von Seigler? "I was hoping she is planning to favor us with a visit soon—it is always lively when Sofie sings popular jazz songs—and, of course, the tips are more generous when our patrons are having a good time. So . . . can you tell me whether we can look forward to a profitable evening anytime soon?"

The girl turned away without answering, and in a moment she was gone. Was there sadness in her expression? Was there fear? Had she seen something or someone I had missed? Was there suspicion of Dieter the Piano Man, here to ask questions? I couldn't read the signs, but I was certain she had become uncomfortable with the conversation and wanted no more of me as her companion on the Humboldt campus. After a few moments, I gathered my things and walked in the direction she had taken. The route took me toward a shaded passageway between two centuries-old granite buildings near the core of the university.

As I entered the man-made canyon, a surprisingly strong hand gripped my forearm and guided me into a recessed stone doorway. The young woman from the campus was no longer engaging in idle chatter. "Dieter," she began, "We were told an hour ago that you had been trapped in a house fire, where you were hiding from the authorities. Some said you were dead; others that you were taken away to a work unit for Jews. I am bewildered to see you on this campus and in apparently good condition. Sofie is very saddened by the rumors—you know, of course, that she cares about you—and she has some notion that your involvement with her has put you in danger."

I dropped my earlier attempt to be non-specific. "Do you know where I can find Sofie now?" I asked. "She must understand that I am neither charred nor chained. Can you help me . . ." I did not know a name for the girl before me.

"Giesela," she finished my unfinished sentence. "I am Giesela Hoff, and you can trust me. Sofie and I have been friends for years, and I have sensed her warm feelings for you, although we have not spoken openly about the subject. You must follow me now to my flat near the campus—you should not remain in the open."

She jotted an address on my pad and pointed in the direction of a nearby avenue with streetcar tracks running in both directions through its center island. "It is about half a kilometer to your right down that street, across from a brown sandstone library building, which is easy to identify. Enter the main doorway of my building and go to Apartment 2E, on the second floor. The door will be unlocked; I'll join you there as soon as I can. Don't walk with me now—wait five minutes so that I can unlock the door and leave the building before you arrive. I'll try to find Sofie."

Giesela seemed capable and certainly in command. What were my options? Should I wait a few minutes and go in the opposite direction as swiftly as possible to avoid entrapment? Or should I trust a total stranger who had at least some knowledge of Sofie and me? I searched my memory but could not recall any mention of a friend named Giesela Hoff in my conversations with Sofie, nor could I place her among the students with whom I had socialized at the Fischerstube. She certainly looked much like the students I did know, and Giesela, unlike Sofie, was not a young woman whose appearance instantly grabbed and held one's attention. Even now, as I reviewed the events of the past hour, I could scarcely summon an accurate recollection of Giesela. Her height was ordinary; she was neither slim nor voluptuous; her hair was a nondescript color, and I could not remember the color of her eyes. She was simply ordinary.

Could she really be a close friend of the flamboyant Sofie? Or should I be wary of someone who took my arm in a dark passageway and directed me to a second-floor dwelling nearby? I walked to the indicated street and sat on the first park bench I found, near a concentration of lower-form school children who were clapping in unison and singing a song which their teacher was leading:

Our noble führer
Shows the way
To make the most
Of every day
Ja - Ja Ja Ja Ja

To be your best
At work and play
Stop and think
What He would say.

Ja - Ja Ja Ja Ja

It reminded me how omnipresent our government had become in directing our private lives, and that, in turn, convinced me that I must proceed with caution before trusting Giesela or anyone else. I decided to observe Giesela's apartment building as discreetly as possible before risking my safety. To do this, I walked briskly to the brown library building and entered its main reading room without even glancing at the apartments across the broad avenue. Once inside, I climbed a stairway to the second floor, where a series of bays faced the street through tall windows that admitted sunlight but filtered out the street noises below. Now I was in position to observe the main door to which I had been directed, but of course I had no idea what I was looking for. Perhaps just some assurance that it was really a student residence, with normal-looking people coming and going, unimpeded by police or others.

A half hour of this vigil yielded nothing. No cordons of police surrounded the block and no brown shirts lurked in nearby doorways. The people coming and departing through the principal entry looked like most of those strewn across the campus. They carried books and moved purposefully in groups, chatting amiably, and seemingly oblivious to their surroundings. It appeared that Giesela's apartment building might indeed be a safe place, and, hopefully, one blessed with cheese and brown bread. However, a final nod to caution convinced me to circle the block on which the apartment building was constructed and to search for a service entrance not visible from the front. I found one within minutes and stood by the door until a deliveryman exited, then admitted myself as the door eased back into its locked position and the man departed from view.

Instead of going directly to Apartment 2E, I climbed the rear staircase to the third floor and moved along the longitudinal hallway to its midpoint, where I found a doorway marked 3E. Knocking on that door produced no immediate response, so I listened quietly for a moment, then knocked more vigorously. A small viewing pane slid open and a single eye glared out at me.

"Is this the apartment of Fräulein Hoff?" I asked in my most ingratiating tone, even smiling at the single eye on the other side of the barrier. No answer. "I am a friend of the student—Giesela—and I believe that she lives in this building. Do you know her?" Again no reaction or response.

Then the small opening snapped shut and I heard an expletive followed by the word *trash* as the person on the other side walked away from his side of the door. What should I make of this encounter? And what should I do next? I was still pondering my options at the doorway when I heard shouting on the telephone from inside 3E. "He was here! At my door—yes!! He asked for Giesela. No—I told him nothing. What is going on? No one prepared me for this—I thought he had been directed to 2E to wait, and we could proceed there. I am watching the street from my window, but I have not seen him walk out from the building. What do you want me to do? . . . And the same to you; this was not *my* error." Then, the sound of a telephone receiver being replaced angrily. I knew I must get to the service door and leave the area at once.

Again I was the beneficiary of good luck; at the service door, several white porter's jackets were hanging from the hall tree, and I was able to slip into one and depart without encountering anyone. Moving back toward the central campus at a quick pace, I discarded the purloined coat into a trash bin as soon as I was out of sight from anyone inside Giesela's apartment building; then I reverted to being the anonymous student moving within constantly fluctuating groups, with no notion of what my next destination should be. Obviously the campus was no longer the best place to be, and I decided to get on a bus—any bus—and then to switch from line to line randomly until I arrived at a railroad station. Surely most intra-city buses eventually intersected with railroad depots, didn't they?

For the first time that day, I was able to pause and try to make sense of the contradictory events that had piled one upon the other, beginning the previous evening. Sofie had directed me to the house in Rahnsdorf, and I was certain she would not have betrayed me, so someone knew about her direction to me, and that knowledge had resulted in Sofie's never arriving. The house was being observed by a government snitch, which meant it was already a known destination for people attempting to flee . . . from what? Was it all part of the strategy to send Jews away? Would an obscure young Jew merit so much attention by himself, or only because of others with whom he was associated? Of course—I was only pertinent because of my association with the daughter of a prominent Wehrmacht general. But who even knew the extent of our involvement?

Outside the clouded window of the bus, I watched the neon signs materialize, then disappear, as we plied our desultory way through a neighborhood totally unfamiliar to me. It was a section with shops and massage parlors, barbers and butchers, used-clothing shops and pawnshops. The people on the sidewalk looked grey and muted without the colored scarves and tweed jackets of the university denizens. I wondered if they were Jews, worrying about recent events and pondering their futures, much as I was. I looked for a synagogue—or a Christian church—to see if I could fix upon the identity of the neighborhood. And here I was, still schlepping an unopened valise without anything in my audibly complaining stomach.

A public bathhouse appeared outside the right window as the bus ground to a noisy stop. Looking across the aisle, I could see a tiny restaurant through the left window offering a kielbasa-and-sauerkraut special to early diners on its outdoor chalkboard. This was as good a corner as any to dismount from the Blue Line Bus; both establishments offered welcome diversion. Even though I was intensely hungry, I decided to go first to the bathhouse, where I could pry open the locked clasp of the valise and examine its contents in the privacy of my own compartment, then wash and relax for an hour before attacking the kielbasa at the nearby diner. I was pleased with the prospects of the next two or three hours and entered the Fremd Bathhouse. It was prophetic: fremd = stranger, or guest.

CHAPTER TWELVE

Berlin – Autumn 1938

PERSONAL REFLECTIONS

[From Dieter's Journal]

Opening the valise proved more difficult than I had anticipated. I carried a pocketknife but found the reinforced latch strap very resistant to cutting and the brass hardware too sturdy to pry apart. I was making a mess of the good-quality piece until finally I resolved to just slit the side neatly and empty the contents on the floor of my stall. The first item I could extract was an envelope, sealed and with a notation—*Please Read*—written in Sofie's meticulous hand. It said:

> *Corporal Meister,*
>
> *Father has been seriously debilitated as a result of a tainted Oyster, and he remains confined at Grosser Müggelsee. I may not be able to join you for dinner as planned if his condition deteriorates further, but in any event, I am still going to meet Mother in Prague on the weekend. Your uniform needed cleaning and pressing, so I have attended to that. Until I see you, I send a kiss.*
>
> *Your Josephine*

My uniform? *What uniform???* I pulled at the fabric inside and eased it through the long slit made with my pocketknife. First, the jacket and then the trousers of a Wehrmacht corporal materialized on the floor. The jacket bore the name *MEISTER* on a tag above the breast pocket, and on the other side there were three campaign ribbons and a cavalry badge. Mining further into the bag, I encountered a well polished pair of military shoes, stuffed with a gun belt (but no gun), rolled military stockings, a soft campaign cap, and finally a fist-sized bundle of currencies which, when unrolled, contained not only German bills but also American silver certificates, British pounds, and Swiss notes. Even though I did not know exchange rates, it was obvious that this wad aggregated much more money than I had ever held at one time—enough to allow me to run far and fast.

I draped the jacket and pants over a chair back and could judge that they had been well chosen for someone of my size. The shoes were also appropriate, and I concluded, without knowing, that the insignia and ribbons were well selected and properly placed. One further check of the violated valise produced a manila envelope which contained three more unexpected surprises: temporary assignment orders for Corporal Dieter Meister to work at the Office of the Military Attaché of Germany in Prague; identity papers for the ersatz corporal (featuring a photo which I recognized as a miniature of the one which had once graced the Fischerstube billboard), and a first-class compartment ticket on the late Friday train from Berlin to Prague, leaving from the Lehrter Bahnhof about 24 hours from now.

I stared at the uniform for a long time. The nametag was sending a message to me, but it wasn't immediately clear to me why it conveyed feelings of profound sadness. I closed my eyes to consider the unsettling emotion and soon understood what it was.

When I was six or seven, a box containing my father's belongings had been delivered to our apartment at Dr. Hoch's Konservatorium, the musikakademie in Frankfurt am Main. On the lapel of a torn and soiled uniform a printed notation was pinned: Meister, Jurgen. My mother lifted the uniform to her cheek and cried softly for several minutes, then refolded it and replaced it in the delivery box, which I never saw again.

I know that my parents met there in the Konservatorium, where Father was a teacher of music and my mother, Eva Rosenberg, one of his students. My father, Jurgen, had won a piano competition in 1908, and apparently that merited his faculty appointment. Mother began her studies there about two years later, and their mutual attraction must have surfaced quickly, because I was born early in 1911. I was still very young when he went away to the Great War, and I filled that absence by keeping company with some of the older boys who were studying music there. Everyone said that I had natural talent for playing piano, and that seemed to facilitate my acceptance.

My mother always tended to spoil me by devoting as much of her time as possible to my instruction, and after my father's death we became even more closely attached to one another. With the help of the Konservatorium's managers, she received engagements to sing regularly at ceremonies and events all around Frankfurt, and I went everywhere with her. It was then that I first understood that familiar music often takes on greater meaning for people during wartime; my own experiences since then have confirmed that.

But, as you know, the Great War was not the only tragedy stalking Europe in 1918, and things got worse for me within a year after my father's uniform was returned to us. The doctor called it "heliotrope cyanosis" when he tended my mother's intense coughing at our small apartment, and she was immediately packed away to some isolated facility, soon to become one of the millions of victims claimed by the Great Influenza Epidemic of 1918/19. The Konservatorium staff burned all of the clothing and bedding from our apartment, and Dr. Sekles did the best he could for me, moving my few remaining belongings to a corner of the boarding students' dormitory. That was on my eighth birthday—the first of many I would be spending there as a stipendiat of the musikakademie. The generosity of many of its supporting donors combined to provide my education and living expenses there for a decade.

I'm not certain when I began turning to other males for the affection I had lost when my mother died, but I remember how comforting it was to curl up in the bed of an older boy and be assured of safety. There were abundant dangers outside the walls of the Akademie, but I had the generosity of the school plus the attentions of two or three talented students combining to shield me. In addition, my proficiency as a performer was advancing rapidly as a result of my total immersion with music and musicians. By the time I was 11 or 12, I was good enough to play at weddings, school performances, and private dinners. Just a short time after that, I was able to add taverns and even bathhouses to my venues. And with that, of course, there was the satisfaction of wages and tips lining my pockets.

I don't know when or whether I would have left those comfortable surroundings of my own volition, but the choice wasn't mine. Instead, the rising tide of Nazi intolerance resulted in an order by the Frankfurt City Council in 1932 that all Jews must leave Dr. Hoch's Konservatorium. My long-time patron, Dr. Sekles, and I were both among those dismissed by that order, and so I made my way to Berlin, where friends assured me there would be work for a piano man. Once there, I paused for a few days in a seedy bathhouse, where I met Miguel do Nacimiento, manager of the Fischerstube. He auditioned my musical skills and hired me to be the resident piano player in his tavern—and soon I was also sharing his flat.

There was no more time for indulging the memories a uniform and nametag had provoked. My immediate concern was avoiding capture or endangering a young woman who had become important to me rather unexpectedly. Once again, I was looking for an escape from unknown persons who would disrupt my life for the simple reason that somewhere in my lineage there was Jewish blood. Back in Frankfurt, I had been only collateral damage as the city fathers chose to wrest control of the Akademie from its prominent Jewish director, and I was swept out with the "undesirables." Now, however, I seemed to have earned my own significance by virtue of my closeness to the daughter of a prominent person. Thinking of Sofie, I reached into my pocket and drew out her handwritten note.

Then it struck me . . . "*debilitated as the result of a tainted Oyster.*" It was awkwardly constructed for such a precise writer, and the capital *O*? Oyster . . . Oster . . . Hans *Oster*! The newspaper headline. The Oster Conspiracy against the führer's life!! Sofie was telling me subtly that her father's position was in jeopardy as a result of his connection with the tainted Colonel Oster. And her father was *confined*—not meaning illness, but house arrest—at the lake. He was under house arrest at Lilkahaus until matters could be sorted out! Perhaps that was why Sofie had failed to arrive at the safe house in Rahnsdorf and why she now wanted me to accompany her to Prague.

I could easily understand that the general, who was also a loving father, did not want his half-Jewish daughter or her half-Jewish consort paraded in front of a tribunal of inquiry and offered as proof of his conspiratorial nature. As I thought through the random events of the past twenty-four hours, I discovered more fragments of a larger picture. It was one in which an apolitical young musician had accidentally blundered into jeopardy and might also pose a danger to others.

The train ticket was for an express departing the next evening. I still had time to consider whether to become Cpl. Meister and show up in uniform at the Lehrter Bahnhoff, with my papers and largesse, a few minutes before boarding time, after daylight had given way to the indistinct tones of evening. Or should I try to conceal myself in Frankfurt or Berlin, maintaining the lowest possible profile? I imagined that I had enough German currency to run and hide within Germany for at least three months. Wouldn't that be the prudent course? Always take the road that defers decisions until you know more about your available options. Right? If I were the only one who might be compromised by my decision today, I would clearly step away from familiar surroundings and hide. But someone who now meant a great deal to me might be left more vulnerable if I chose that course. I decided to weigh the alternatives further over kielbasa and sauerkraut; a full belly often improves one's ability to think.

CHAPTER THIRTEEN
Leaving Home – 1938

THE TRAIN RIDE
[From Dieter's Journal]

The desk clerk at Fremd Bathhouse was more than happy to share his room that evening, and I enjoyed the protective reassurance of another body near mine. I was careful not to make mental comparisons with either Miguel or Sofie, reasoning that this was nothing more than a favor exchanged for shelter. I slept well, even though I continued to weigh the proper course for the next day. More and more I understood that Sofie had gone to great lengths to facilitate my departure from Berlin, even including a generous dowry for the trip. By now she must know that I had not been apprehended in Rahnsdorf, and probably that I had wandered about the Humboldt campus for several hours, which could only mean that I was searching for her. The uniform and papers had to involve more than just Sofie; I was sure she did not have a closet full of military clothing or a drawer full of blank military order sheets. But a general or someone loyal on his staff could produce those things readily. I found myself hoping that the General and his daughter had conspired together to spirit the two young people to safety. It sounded worthy of a Russian romance novel, and I wanted it to be true. Perhaps, in the final analysis, that was the reason I chose the bold—and dangerous—course. I wanted Sofie's affection and her father's caring to be true things in a world that was quickly becoming treacherous and evil.

The uniform was a splendid fit. Before departing from Fremd Bathhouse, I donned it and examined myself carefully in the mirror, even returning several salutes to my image. I needed a close shave and a more military hair trim before becoming Corporal Meister. The nameless desk clerk was off duty until evening, and for a British five-pound note he was delighted to put my face and hair into condition worthy of a close parade inspection. He splashed my scraped skin with witch hazel and salted the insides of my shoes with talcum.

My old clothes and sparse belongings were stuffed through the Cesarean slice of the once-elegant valise, to be deposited furtively into the first deep trash bin along my route. I allowed half an hour to purchase a small duffel, more appropriate for a traveling corporal, and then I filled it with newly bought civilian clothing and the essentials a young soldier would need when off duty. It occurred to me that masquerading as a soldier could become very inconvenient at some point, in which case I should have at least one other complete "persona" in my duffel. At precisely 4:00 p.m., Cpl. Dieter Meister walked to the Blue Line kiosk to await the No. 9 bus, which would deposit him across New Order Square from the Lehrter Bahnhof. Every aspect of the anticipated adventure heightened my sense of excitement and danger, but above all, I found myself surging with the electricity of joining Sofie and setting out together.

The Bahnhof was a gigantic building with a very high glass roof, consisting of several parallel half-cylinders, joined together at metal seams. The structure seemed to amplify and project the sounds of locomotives as they entered or departed from the covered area. Steam escaped from piston housings in an extended *hissss!* and the air was pierced with the sharp, high-pitched whistles of departing trains. People moved briskly along the platforms separating iron rails, and very few really looked at the others contending for space. I wondered how many of these, as I, were assuming low profiles so as to pass the gate guards and professional watchers monitoring the narrowed points of passage. At the end of an autumnal day, there was a pink glow to the sky outside; it was homogenized as it streaked through the cloudy panes and filtered downward toward the tangle of rails. Walking deliberately and averting the direct glances of other pedestrians, I passed gates marked to destinations across Europe, then saw PRAGUE spelled in white letters at Gate 8. A train was already aside the platform, and through its windows and doors I could see the first passengers entering their compartments and putting bags into overhead storage spaces.

A platform guard looked my way and I had a sudden urge to turn and run, but instead smiled and produced my ticket, asking where the private compartments would be found. He motioned toward the rear of the train and turned his attention to a young couple struggling with a steamer trunk, apparently satisfied that a crisply dressed soldier needed no further assistance. A second guard nearer the rear of the train looked at my ticket carefully, then joked that I would be riding in style tonight, pointing to the next car, where most of the compartment doors were already closed. The entry door corresponding to the number on my ticket was open and the space inside completely vacant, but I lowered my duffel to the platform and remained outside the train, pretending to examine some part of my bogus papers in the better light there. Only fourteen minutes remained until the scheduled departure of the Prague Express. If I boarded now, there would be no turning back: once inside, I was committed to remain Cpl. Meister until I reached my destination.

One of the "arts" practiced in the Western World during the 1930s was that of looking casual and unflappable. It had been employed hundreds of times on motion picture screens by actors and actresses, and we all longed to be that coolly confident person who showed no outward hint of internal tension, even in the face of looming dangers. Usually our screen icons employed the prop of a cigarette to convey this sense of total control over one's immediate world. A long, thoughtful draw on the white tubes followed by a slow, drifting discharge of the smoke said, "I'm in my own world right now, thinking of things you might not even understand."

I had never taken up smoking, but, standing alongside the hissing cars of the Prague Express, I wished that I had done so. It would be so much easier to pretend disinterest while attempting to see everything going on around me on the platform. My own model for relaxed appearance had been the American pianist and composer Hoagy Carmichael, who resembled a pile of wrinkled clothing topped by half-closed eyelids and a crooked, wry smile. His songs often sounded that way, too, and I loved playing them to quieter audiences and wished that I could add Hoagy's nasal delivery to the laconic lyrics. I wondered how Sofie might interpret "Stardust" or "Georgia On My Mind" or "Lazy Bones." She would probably exude a delivery laced with humor and relaxed energy.

Six minutes until departure. Three military men engaged in intense conversation passed my car, followed by a businessman dressed elegantly. A dowager being wheeled by a porter approached from one direction and a young mother with two neatly dressed children from the other. I tried to whistle a Carmichael tune but found that my lips were too dry to muster a whistle, so instead, I tried to feel the imaginary chords and melody in my fingers as I looked up and down the platform again. If Sofie were coming, she would have to run now. All of the remaining passengers were moving at a deliberate pace, with flailing arms and tense glances at their timepieces. German trains ran on time, emulating the standard set in Italy by the Fascist Mussolini government.

A whistle blown by the platform conductor warned of two minutes remaining until departure. This would be when my movie idols would carefully press out their cigarette butts with the toe of a polished shoe and shift their attention to the next act of nonchalance. I folded my papers and slipped them into my tunic pocket and turned slowly toward the open door of my compartment, wondering what lay ahead for me. The dowager was seated on one of the two benches inside, arranging her small carrying case and looking up at me with incredibly beautiful eyes.

I thought that it might be a mistake to offer any sign of recognition until we were safely out of the station and our tickets and papers verified, so I put my feet up on the duffel and slid into a relaxed posture, a soldier catching up on his sleep. The "dowager" across from me took two books from her case and began reading one; the other slipped off the bench and onto the floor of the car, but she made no move to retrieve it. It finally occurred to me that I was to do so, and as I reached down to the book, I could see that a folded paper had been inserted inside. Now the slouching soldier in the first-class compartment had reading material to add to his casual appearance.

D—DO NOT RECOGNIZE ME UNTIL WE HAVE CROSSED BORDER!!!

You must think me daft to have sent you to Rahnsdorf, but I had to be certain you did not return to your room, where I fear you would have been apprehended and taken for questioning. Apparently a Gestapo informant at the Fischerstube reported that you regularly received notes from OVS, and that one note had to do with the führer and Berchtesgaden and money to be paid to you. In the current furor resulting from Col. Oster's aborted plot, there is even an effort to link OVS to that treachery and to scheming Jews. I tried to join you at the house, but could not. We can talk freely in Czechoslovakia. Don't keep this—it is NOT a keepsake for your heart pocket. Perhaps I am! How do you like me old and fat?

The great Deutsche Reichsbhan DRB 05-Class locomotive emblazoned with a red-and-black swastika moved the long train effortlessly from the Bahnhof, and we began the six-hour journey to Prague. We Germans were proud of our trains and locomotives; they were the best in the world, we had been told. A full display of Europe's finest trains was planned for the upcoming World's Fair to be held in New York, USA, in 1939, and we were assured that our superior technology in land transportation would be featured.

It took only a few minutes to escape the urban landscape as we gained speed smoothly. Dresden lay ninety minutes to our south, and an hour beyond that was Teplice near the border with the Czech provinces of Bohemia and Moravia, which were strongly German in their ethnicity. I assumed that we would encounter a checkpoint in the vicinity of Teplice, because the führer had already spoken publicly of the need to reunite the Sudetenland with our homeland, and tensions were high at such border crossings. I waited until the train was far from the last Berlin suburbs and whistling at grade crossings in open countryside, then I stood and made a stiff bow toward the absorbed dowager and walked slowly toward the lavatories and the between-cars observation platform.

Outside, I was alone in the cool, rushing air that washed over the small platform. The impact of wheels on rails tattooed the night with clickety patterns, and from ahead came the sharp warnings of the great engine's whistle as we sped past country roads and farm dwellings. Reaching into my pocket, I withdrew the penned note and tore small pieces from the main body one-by-one, allowing each to join the passing windstream until all had escaped my hand. Even an alert Gestapo snitch from the Fischerstube would have no hope of reassembling the provocative message which had recently passed between two masquerading travelers. This would have been another appropriate time and place for enjoying a cigarette, and I resolved to consider learning to smoke if my life continued to be punctuated with evasive travels.

The whole question of the Sudetenland seemed convoluted to me. The *Anschluss,* in the spring, had obliterated distinctions between Germany and Austria, which truly belonged together, and the same logic was offered with respect to bringing Germans living within Czechoslovakia into the thriving new Germany. With that accomplished, my country would be stronger and able to offer more opportunities to all German citizens. But somehow, our neighbors in Poland, France, and England seemed unconvinced that Germany had no other territorial ambitions, and they continued to hint at hostile actions against us. Lately, the Britisher Arthur Neville Chamberlain had visited several times with Herr Hitler to try to gain assurances that Germany would remain peaceful. Each time they met, we saw photos of smiling officials dining together and speaking rationally. They always spoke of productive and friendly meetings, and Germans everywhere welcomed the new respect our leadership had gained. Our führer was a master negotiator, and Germany had never been healthier.

I was uncomfortable with the realization that my pride as a German and my fear of the jeopardy imposed upon me by the German government were in sharp conflict. I didn't understand at all why my late mother's religion should make me a pariah and result in my running and hiding like a criminal. I had never ventured outside the law, and yet I was peering over my shoulder through imaginary clouds of cigarette smoke, trying to avoid the glance of law enforcement officers. Now, finally, I had become an arsonist and a fugitive pretending to be a soldier, traveling with bogus identification papers. Why? Because of a young Jewish woman who died two decades ago? It all seemed so illogical, especially in a country proud of its logical, scientific progress. I really needed answers so that I could start making intelligent choices. Somehow I sensed that one of those choices would unavoidably involve consequences to another young woman who had become so important in my life.

Stepping back into the compartment, I could see that Sofie had fallen asleep. She lay balanced in the corner of the opposite bench, with her legs curled beneath her and a shawl covering her upper body. An open book lay face down on the bench, and her luggage was stowed beneath. In the frumpy—and certainly padded—clothing and soft, grey wig, Sofie bore no resemblance to the young student I knew. Unable to speak with one another, I was deprived of even her warm voice. How illogical and frustrating to be alone with a special person, yet totally estranged because of some third-party policies regarding religion and politics. I wondered what it would take to get back to simpler times that could nurture our relationship. I closed my eyes and let my thoughts drift back to the pleasant evenings shared by the fire at Lilkahaus.

Miguel had smiled as we walked by the river. I liked it when he smiled, because there was a warmth which I imagined was meant just for me. I had first experienced the same feeling back at the Akademie when older boys approved of my music and chatted between themselves as to whose bed I would share that evening. I had favorites but never let it be known when I was disappointed at the outcome of their negotiation. With Miguel, however, I was exclusive, and that allowed me to speak more freely of the myriad thoughts and questions about our existence that crowded to the front of my mind when we were alone together.

His question had been, "Which are you, Dieter—a German or a Jew?" It surprised me, because I had no notion that the two were mutually exclusive.

"Miguel, I am both a German and a Jew. I was born into both. Nobody asked me which I wanted to be. I suppose that in my own mind I am more a German now, because I speak the language, study the history, and conduct myself as my fellow Germans do. I don't go to Temple or celebrate Jewish holidays because I no longer have a family organizing such things. But I am a Jew just as a black man from Afrika is a schwartzer. He may be an Ethiopian or a Rhodesian citizen, too—but he is a schwartzer. He can put on a Seville Row suit and an Eton cravat and spats and carry a walking stick, but then he is only a dressed-up schwartzer.

"I am proud of my country. It has recovered from terrible humiliation twenty years ago and is admired, even feared, across our continent. Our authors and musicians and engineers are celebrated everywhere. The world came to Berlin to attend the Olympics, and they left talking about the youth of Germany in superlatives. Our cities prosper and our neighbors seek our favor. I was born into this country; my father gave his life for it. I am a German and have no wish to be otherwise. But you see me as you would that well-dressed schwartzer, don't you? Because my mother was a Jew, you regard me only as a Jew acting like a German.

"No, Dieter," he raised his hand, deflecting my statement, "I see you as neither a German nor a Jew, but as a compassionate lover who understands my needs. Everyone is categorized by others according to the interface between them. I have no political or religious interface with you, so those facets are irrelevant. But our relationship is based upon an understanding which others can't appreciate as we do. If I ever have a need to be political, I will explore that subject with a political scientist. If I am seeking salvation, I will turn to a priest. When I am terribly hungry, I will find a good chef. But, at the end of the day, I need none of those very much. I need a sensitive musician who can be transported to another dimension in my company." And then there was his smile.

"ACHTUNG! WE WILL CROSS INTO SUDETEN, CZECHOSLOVAKIA, IN FIVE MINUTES. ALL PASSENGERS MUST PRESENT SUITABLE IDENTIFICATION TO BORDER CONTROL PERSONNEL, WHO WILL PASS THROUGH THE TRAIN. PLEASE HELP TO AVOID UNNECESSARY DELAY BY HAVING YOUR PAPERS READY FOR INSPECTION. ANYONE WHO IS UNABLE TO PRODUCE VALID PAPERS WILL BE ESCORTED FROM THE TRAIN SO THAT IT MAY PROCEED TO PRAGUE ON SCHEDULE. DANKE. HEIL HITLER!"

I was fully awake again and stepped into the corridor outside our compartment to put as much separation as possible between the bogus soldier and the phony dowager. Perhaps if they were viewed separately, their individual pretensions would be less obvious. As I closed the compartment door, I felt a hand on my shoulder, and I suddenly felt that urine was trickling down the inside of my thigh. "Cigarette, comrade?" asked a disembodied voice, and I turned to see a military uniform similar to my own.

"Ja!" I returned, instantly relieved of the wave of fear I had experienced moments before. At last it was time for me to become the patient, thoughtful smoker of so many motion pictures. How did they keep their hands from shaking? And how did they make the end of the cigarette pick up the flame offered by a lighter or Lucifer held nearby? I took the proffered cigarette and leaned toward the hand holding a flame, then I sucked air mightily through my first cigarette and felt my lungs explode in a convulsive cough, with spittle glancing off my sleeve and onto the lapel of the other's tunic. More coughing followed and I felt his hand slapping at my back rhythmically until I finally was able to swallow the remaining expulsions and look at my benefactor through tear-filled eyes. He was dissolved in laughter.

"Egyptian Royals," he said, holding up the cigarette package. "They are stronger than what you use, ja? Here, take the rest of this pack; I have many. Perhaps we can offer a smoke to the border guards so they will move quickly and not look into our bags. They love to steal things and claim they are contraband—bastards! Watch them try to feel up the old lady in there with you. They think it is funny to make them scream. Hide your money, too—they will relieve you of it and claim you are a smuggler. Hey, your cigarette has gone out. Want another light?"

"No—not now. I want to make sure my mother is OK. I'll see you after the border. Thanks for the smoke. Sorry about the spit on your tunic. It's dry already." We both laughed and I ducked back inside to remove the roll of currency from my bag and stuff it into the crotch of my underpants. I could see that Sofie was surreptitiously watching me and directing my attention toward the partially open compartment door with a flick of her eyes. I kicked it shut and said, "What?"

"Put two large RM notes in with your papers and hold them all in your hands. Don't reach into your pockets in the border patrol's sight. Turn out the compartment overhead light and get out of this compartment. I will deal with them. Go now!" The instructions did not invite a reply—this was a general's daughter taking charge, and I moved quickly to obey. In seconds

I was out in the corridor again with my papers in one hand and a package of Egyptian Royals in the other. The moisture on my thigh felt cool as it dried and I hoped that my uniform pants weren't wet through from the inside. Three men in uniform walked into sight at the end of the car and they knocked loudly at the first door. "Your papers, bitte!" It was time for me to be *ein unbedeutender Mensch*—an unimportant fellow, easy to skip over.

Ours was the fourth compartment on the corridor, and I was able to watch the border guards as they cleared each of the first three compartments with what seemed to be a cursory inspection. A brief glance at proffered documents and a peek inside the compartment seemed the norm. Soon they had arrived at #4, and the lead guard looked at me skeptically. "This is a first-class compartment, corporal. I am not used to seeing enlisted men treated so well. Are you someone special?"

"No, sir," I responded, "the ticket accompanied my orders, and I believe that my services were requested by our attaché in Prague. Many changes are happening there, I'm told." I extended the orders and identification, which he took summarily, glancing at the photo.

"It is hard to recognize you without a beard—when did you shave it?"

"When I received my new orders, sir. I was told that the attaché does not approve of facial hair. First impressions, you know, sir."

"Hmmm. What is in your hand? Cigarettes? Let me see them, please."

I handed the nearly full package of Egyptian Royals to the head guard, who immediately put them into his pocket. Then the two bills fell from my papers onto the floor of the train. He regarded them with a slight smile and turned to his nearby companions chuckling, "I seem to have dropped our beer money—please retrieve it for me and have a look at our special corporal's duffle inside the compartment."

They pushed through the door, leaving it ajar. I could see Sofie sitting quietly inside the dimly lighted compartment. She looked almost regal sitting on the bench; there was no suggestion of the disguised person beneath the frumpy façade. Both guards selected the military duffel from the rack and dumped its contents upon the floor. They kicked the contents about, in effect sorting them with their boots. It was a meager pile of clothing, reading materials, and toiletries. Nothing worth stealing.

They turned their attention to the dowager's expensive leather suitcase and pulled it down rudely for inspection. Almost as quickly, her cane flashed, slapping the floor immediately in front of the nearer guard. "Call your superior in here at once!" said the irate lady. "Perhaps when you read this letter you will mind your manners better and behave like civil servants should. I will need both your names and employee numbers—put them on this piece of paper and sign it." She placed a sheet of paper on the opposite bench and pointed to it. "Do it now!!" she demanded.

"Oh, you are important, Grandma?" one jested, and turned to the other with a lascivious grin. "Perhaps we should search your cavities, like in *Candide*—you are probably overdue for a good pat-down!" Both stepped menacingly toward the passenger, and I wondered when I would have to go to her aid, but my thought process was truncated by the sound of the cane contacting a shinbone, followed by a howl of pain. This was enough to bring the head guard bolting into the compartment, and with his arrival all movement seemed arrested, except for one guard rubbing his lower leg and wincing at the pressure.

"Let me see that letter, Grandma!" he ordered, extending his hand to enforce the demand. He lifted the page toward the light and read aloud: "The Bearer is traveling under my full protection. Please extend every courtesy due this office." The letter was signed by Reichsmarshall Hermann Göring, and it was embossed with the elaborate seal of his office. The head guard bowed condescendingly as he handed the letter back to the dowager. "Please excuse the behavior of my colleagues, madam. It has been a long day, and I fear that fatigue got the better of them. We will do everything possible to facilitate your trip from here to Prague."

"The names and ID numbers," Sofie repeated, "on that paper with the full signature of each. Make that *three* names, IDs, and signatures—yours, too. Quickly. You are delaying everyone on this train unnecessarily, and Reichsmarshall Göring will want to know why. Incidentally, I am not at all amused by the reference to *Candide*, but if you gentlemen are using Voltaire to justify violating women, then you should also remember Voltaire's best-known political quotation: *Dans ce pays-ci il est bon de tuer de temps en temps un amiral pour encourager les autres*, that is, 'In this country it is thought well to kill an admiral from time to time to encourage the others.' I'm sure that the principle would be equally effective applied to border *guards who rifle through belongings, steal money, and grope women."*

All three guards were visibly shaken and pale. My cigarettes and banknotes were placed on the bench, and they proceeded down the corridor briskly, not entering any other compartments. I looked with amusement and amazement at the disguised young woman who had just humbled three badge-heavy officials with her calm confidence. I turned to her and smiled, "You really have been studying assiduously at Humboldt, haven't you! That quotation was brilliant, *Frau* von Seigler, and your French is excellent, too. I am a fortunate man, indeed."

"You did your part well, too," she smiled, "but your smoking will require some practice before you can pass as an *homme du monde*. Now sit down and relax while I transform myself into someone more familiar, and I will fill in some parts of recent events which are probably confusing you. The most important thing is that we are both out of Berlin safely for now—and we are together, which means even more to me."

As she spoke, she locked the compartment door and drew the shade inside.

"I don't believe we will have any further interruptions between here and Prague," she observed. "The word will pass quickly among these midget functionaries that someone under the umbrella of Hermann Göring's protection is on board and has already taken three names. This will allow us to depart the train without interference—but if anyone is looking for the threatening passenger on arrival, it will be with an eye peeled for a salty septuagenarian. A fresh-faced student should slide by observers with impunity. However, you must depart among other soldiers if possible. Can you find your smoking companion and step down with him?"

Quickly, layers of lace and pounds of padding collected on the floor, and with each unbuttoning, more of the chrysalis was stripped away, until an elegant butterfly stretched her arms toward the ceiling of the compartment, then entwined her fingers over-head and looked at me with sultry, downcast eyes. *Aha! She is Theda Bara today*, I thought. I wanted more than anything to fold her into my arms and continue that way to Prague, but I knew that our safety would be directly related to the care with which we proceeded for the next hour. And so, I ran my fingers slowly through her hair until they rested upon her strong shoulders, and then I planted an affectionate kiss on each side of her neck and turned away.

"Please pull my bag from the rack and extract the cloth duffel from inside," Sofie requested. "Then pick up all of the disguise items from the floor and put them into the expensive bag and throw it from the platform between cars. The duffel is more appropriate for a student, and our observers will undoubtedly remember the senior lady's elegant leather bag and try to spot it on the platform." Once again, I was awed by the cool demeanor and unassailable logic of my . . . my what? *Mistress* and *lover* were demeaning terms, and there was no formal agreement to carry our relationship to a traditional level above that of "dear friend." So I was awed by my best female friend, the woman who aggregated everything I had imagined in a heterosexual partner.

"You are amazing, Sofie." I blurted. "Do you understand how totally admired you are? Do you understand my feelings? And, do you share any part of that feeling?"

"Please dispose of the bag—now, while we are slicing through lightly populated areas at top speed. With luck, no one will see the bag for weeks, and when it is discovered, some Czech peasant will treat it as a gift from God and will hide it in his closet like a treasure."

I took the bag, checked the empty corridor, and moved with all possible alacrity to the platform. We were, indeed, passing by cultivated fields, and with a quick movement I propelled Sofie's best luggage deep into a copse of trees near a small creek. It was out of sight in seconds, and I lighted an Egyptian Royal (with a very modest intake of breath) and stared out at the stars through the small puffs of white smoke I was learning to expel. Alone on the small platform, I smiled at the day's events and anticipated a night ahead with Sofie. Despite the overhanging fears of war and persecution, this was a nugget of sanity to be grasped and remembered.

Back in the compartment, Sofie was curled on one padded bench, examining a Humboldt textbook. She smiled as I entered, and asked, "Done?" I nodded in affirmation and sat back, awaiting some explanations for several recent challenges in my life.

"I'm certain you understand that suspicion has been directed toward Father ever since the Oster matter was exposed. Even though his career has been celebrated, the fact that Oster falls within the scope of Father's command immediately raised issues of proper supervision. A few officers directed inquiries toward Father—mainly to divert attention from themselves, I suspect.

"The Gestapo assigned to several specialists the task of compiling a full dossier on General von Seigler—not just his military history, which is exemplary—but the full range of his relationships and outside activities. Inevitably, inquiries were made in Krakow, and that disclosed his marriage and the birth of his daughter. His detractors were delighted to point to Lilka's Jewish roots, and they suggested that a high-ranking military officer once married to a Polish Jew and now supervising Hans Oster presented a potential danger to the führer. Father was relieved of his command temporarily and put under house detention until more facts could be ascertained.

"The insidious inquiry next moved to the general's daughter, who had been born and reared in Krakow, but, as an adult, matriculated in a leading German University. Many of my Humboldt friends were plucked from the campus, and somewhere in that sniffing exercise, the name "Fischerstube" drew attention. Both Father and I frequented the tavern, and a few questions of frightened students provided a connection to a Jew pianist from Frankfurt working there. A waitress, Greta, currying favor, reported that she had observed the passage of notes and money from a prominent general to an invisible piano man. She volunteered that you had mentioned to her an invitation to the führer's lair at Berchtesgaden and a large sum of money being paid to you. You can imagine that the Gestapo felt it had stumbled onto a hot trail.

"A logical interview was that with your homosexual roommate, who was thoroughly irked by our relationship, and he was happy to disclose your connection to the general's Jewish daughter, as well as your frequent visits to Wilhelmstrasse and Lilkahaus. The official 80 Wilhelmstrasse visitors' records disclosed that Dieter Meister was not only a visitor, but also that he had been embedded in the lavish evening accorded Charles and Anne Lindbergh. Even the Jewish-authored songs we chose made their way into the final report to Herr Himmler, and he issued orders to apprehend both of us quickly.

"Had you returned to your room, half a dozen goons would have roughed you up, and you would have been questioned at Gestapo Headquarters until you confessed to whatever conspiracy they chose. I thought I could join you in Rahnsdorf that night but soon realized that all of my movements were being observed closely, and that I might lead those goons directly to you if I strayed from the lake house.

"Your imaginative departure from the safe house was brilliant. It made my nipples hard to think of you slipping away in the fiery night, and I prayed that you would read my note with the same ingenious attitude and show up at the Bahnhof. But, you came very close to disaster at Humboldt. As soon as the Gestapo realized that you had slipped their ring around Rahnsdorf, they deployed stakeouts to the lake, the area around your flat, Wilhelmstrasse, the Fischerstube, and locations associated with me. You were identified on the campus by a very capable Gestapo operative, and I'm certain she believed you would take the bait and go to the address she provided. I don't know what sixth sense sent you elsewhere, but your complete disappearance finally convinced them that you are a professional, and a very good one. Are you?"

The loudspeaker interrupted before I could reply:

FIFTEEN MINUTES UNTIL HLAVNI NADRAZI STATION IN PRAGUE. PASSENGERS PLEASE GATHER YOUR BELONGINGS AND PREPARE TO LEAVE THE TRAIN IMMEDIATELY AFTER ARRIVAL. HAVE DOCUMENTS READY FOR PRESENTATION WHEN REQUESTED. DANKE. HEIL HITLER!

Sofie handed me a small card. "This is for your medical appointment at the end of the day. Try to be invisible until then—a bathhouse, a movie, or maybe a museum. It will take only a few minutes by cab from the Majestic Plaza Hotel on Wenceslas Square, to which anyone can direct you. Pay with RM and give only a few coins as gratuities—nothing out of character for a corporal."

I looked at the appointment card from the medical office of Dr. Juraslav Havlik, which noted that Dieter Meister was expected at 4:00 p.m. The office address was on Čiklova Street and the telephone number was printed at the bottom. "What ailment do I have?" I inquired of Sofie, "or is that where we can finally relax together and not have to speak in code?" I'm sure there was a hint of irritation in my voice. Sofie noted it, too, and smiled reassuringly.

"That's where Lilka is awaiting us. Dr. Havlik has been family for years. He has our full confidence, and we are very safe with him. Confirm your arrival by telephone an hour prior—say only that it is Dr. Havlik's 4 p.m. appointment. But *no name!* If the response is that Herr Meister should try to arrive on time, you are assured that there is no problem. Otherwise, return to the hotel and I will have you paged there.

"Now, go and find some soldiers and bury yourself among them as you leave the platform. No cigarette! If you cough loudly and spit . . . well, you know." She punctuated the instruction with a full, confident laugh, and I picked up my duffel and walked away in the direction of the next car. I thought that there appeared to be no limit to the surprises produced by the young woman I loved. That thought—or its completion—caught me totally by surprise, and my unexpected admission left me trembling as the train decelerated preparatory to its on-time arrival in Hlavni Nadrazi Station.

CHAPTER FOURTEEN

Prague – Autumn 1938

AN EDUCATION BEHIND THE GREEN DOOR
[From Dieter's Journal]

By design, I stepped into the path of the provider of my Egyptian Royals, and we greeted one another as old comrades. "Meister, where are you off to?" he queried, and I told him I had a physical exam requirement before reporting to my assignment. I intended to see a little of old Prague before the appointment time. He continued, "I'm told there is a great Czech whorehouse only five minutes' walk down Ruzova from here. Girls from Austria, Poland, and even France—and they *like* German soldiers! Not like the stuck-up cabaret types in Berlin, ja? You look like you have a schnitzel in your jodhpurs already -

"How about it? Want to come along? I have the address."

His observation reminded me that my small fortune was still concealed in my britches—although obviously not totally invisible—and I knew that there were hours to kill before I could seek the safety of Dr. Havlik's medical clinic. Perhaps the suggestion of a brothel was not so unacceptable as it first seemed.

"I'll walk along with you—I don't know your name—and see what this place looks like." His name, he told me, was Jurgen Deitz.

We were almost at the end of the arrivals platform, and no one had challenged us to present documents. At the taxi stand ahead, I watched as a familiar young woman entered one of the waiting vehicles and pulled away from the curb. Sofie had run the gauntlet of observers without setting off suspicion, and now she was melded into the traffic of the new day. I imagined platform watchers craning their heads to catch sight of a dowager with a deadly cane and an expensive traveling case. I wondered whether the matter would be forgotten or if her apparent disappearance would exacerbate the search. It might reach back to Berlin; no doubt the tale of a personal letter of safe passage from Hermann Göring could be explored and verified. Had any of the border guards been alert enough to note the name of the feisty old passenger?

My brow furrowed as these questions occupied my thoughts and Jurgen prattled on about the myriad pleasures awaiting us only a few hundred meters ahead on Ruzova. Before I could complete my review of alternatives, we were standing before a pine green door guarded by a gap-toothed female in her fifties who seemed delighted to see us. I concluded that morning traffic was considered a good omen for the day's business, and that the first train from Berlin was a frequent funnel for military customers.

Gap-tooth ushered us inside to a small sitting room warmed by a glowing coal fire. Several ladies more attractive and youthful than our greeter sipped coffee or tea from small cups and stole glances in our direction. Then they giggled over a remark I couldn't overhear, offered by a heavy-breasted member of the group. Jurgen walked to them and extended his hand to the tallest member of the klatch, who stood and winked provocatively at her companions as they withdrew together. That left me standing alone and very uncomfortable.

After a few uneasy minutes—and growing laughter from across the room—I had no choice but to engage them in some way. I walked toward the small, good-smelling knot of young women and held out both hands— one toward Fräulein Full-Front and the other to a tiny girl who looked no more than fifteen or sixteen. They all laughed approvingly, and my two smiling choices spirited me through a beaded curtain and down a long hall to the last door.

"How much for a good show?" I asked, sending them into a huddled discussion that produced a quick reply. "I'll double that if you can make it last a full hour," I offered, and they nodded enthusiastically while their loose-fitting gowns fell away.

I watched a virtual circus of touching, kissing, fondling, and licking unlike anything I had seen before. It reminded me that I knew very little about the female body and methods to excite and delight it. I wondered if Sofie knew all these things and if the female students at Humboldt regularly amused themselves in sessions like this one. I decided to move closer and realized that an erection plus my dowry of rolled currencies were combining to make it impossible to stand normally, so, without thinking, I unbuckled my belt and lowered my military trousers enough to create more space for everything. There was no ignoring my arousal, which quickly became the focus of the naked ladies. It was time to surrender.

The teen reached out and pulled me toward her. "Join us!" she invited, then added with obvious distaste as she focused upon my erection, "*Juder.*"

The larger woman put her finger to her lips to suggest they adopt a lower pitch, and, in Polish-tainted German, admonished her colleague. "All are welcome here, Ursula. Help our handsome soldier to relieve that impressive sausage of its stress while I finish with you." It was a race to the finish line which I had no desire to win but did, easily and noisily. We all collapsed into exhales of breath and laughter, and the Polska said, "That was only thirty minutes, soldier. What more can we do to earn our full hour's wage?"

"Get me a wet towel so that I may clean up, and then tell me what *really* makes you feel happy and complete when you are with a man. Are there body locations or techniques I should learn—for my girlfriend, at home? I would like her to believe that I am truly all she needs for her happiness, even after novelty yields to familiarity. So . . . ?"

"If we tell customers that, we will put ourselves out of business." said the little one. "But I must tell you that you are nicely equipped and very expertly circumcised. We see some ugly work in here, and it is always revolting to me to have to act pleased when I see those. What about you, Renate?"

"Ach! Everyone wants to bounce and fondle these melons, and men never learn that only the tiny ones—like yours, Ursula—really have a direct line to aroused feelings. So, I go on moaning like a foghorn, while feeling about as much as if it were my elbow getting the attention. Soldier, ask your lady what *she* likes, and don't be surprised if it is a close whisper in her ear or a finger dangled along her inner thigh rather than some tit-wrestle or jack-hammer. And, whatever she wants, give it twice as much time as you would think before you move on with *your* agenda."

"And my agenda should be what . . . ?"

"Your agenda should be to make her proud that it is you inside her. You must help her to validate her choice and know that she is not a fool giving herself to someone who could be as happy frequenting our green door. And let her see your eyes! Never divert them from her to a timepiece. She must believe that she is more important than the next event scheduled in your day—or night. She is not a flag-stop on the railroad of your life, soldier. And if she feels that way, you may become just another military tunic hung over her bedroom chair. Ursula and I can handle your urgency, but you will always know that our affection is feigned and purchased."

Ursula warmed to the discussion and decided to expound on the philosophy of engagement between the sexes. She offered that women everywhere in the enlightened '30s were longing for equal status, and so an easy road to happiness lay along the path that permitted either partner to be the initiator of intimacies. "You men think that only you have a timetable of need, which entitles you to interrupt us at any time. Give your girlfriend permission to do the same and she will always come back to you."

I thought to myself that Sofie had already claimed that privilege, and my instincts had been to validate her claim on me. Otherwise, I wouldn't be in Prague—or in trouble beyond the mere inconvenience of having one Jewish parent. Was I too pliant? Or had I already achieved the balance Ursula described? I wondered if I would ever return to the green door on Ruzova, or if the fact that I had enjoyed this visit compromised my relationship with Sofie.

My hour had passed, and I paid the double/double of my contract with a smile, then asked busty Renate if there was a quiet restaurant nearby. She gave me precise directions to one owned by her husband. I thanked her and started walking in the indicated direction. Then, when I was out of sight of the green door, I reversed my course and sought another place to dine. It wasn't guilt about patronizing the establishment of my whore's legal partner, but rather a belief that I should avoid their later exchanging observations regarding the new Jewish soldier in Prague.

The train journey, the cool morning, and my unanticipated "menage" had combined to make me ravenous, so I purchased a German-language newspaper and settled into a comfortable booth in a cozy restaurant overlooking the Vitava River and Vyšehrad Park. The menu cover informed interested customers that this area had been "the birthplace of Prague" hundreds of years earlier.

A few early luncheon patrons had already been seated; they appeared to be local businessmen, and most were greeted by name by the proprietor as they moved toward preferred tables. I attempted to listen to the conversations, but my knowledge of the language was not adequate to discern much, except I heard the name "Chamberlain" repeated often. My newspaper featured a report of resolved issues, which would diminish the chance of open hostilities. I wondered whether the overt hostility toward Jews had occupied any part of the time of the distinguished negotiators, or if only the integrity of national borders had been on their agenda. There were no questions and no answers regarding the displaced Polish Jews, only the expressed hope that France and England could broker a suitable compromise with the formidable new Germany. Strangely, it made me feel proud to be a German and I wished Miguel were with me so that I could tell him, "Miguel—today I am mostly a German!!"

The Majestic Plaza Hotel was easy walking distance from the restaurant where I had slowly consumed my luncheon. I first glanced inside the nearby Church of Saints Peter and Paul and then set out on foot toward Wenceslas Square. Prague's streets were lined with stately trees, now bared of their leaves, and there were fashionable shoppes and galleries everywhere, all suggesting affluence here in Czechoslovakia's principal city. By 2 p.m. I had arrived at the Majestic Plaza, and I entered through brass-handled glass doors into a well-appointed lounge replete with posh seating areas. As I had done in the restaurant, I sought a place where I would be inconspicuous but still within range of conversations in the vaulted room.

Here most of the residents were conversing in German, and their voices were loud, suggesting to me that they may have been drinking somewhat excessively during their meals. I was able to hear that they were attending a bankers' convention, and that their mission was to assess the country's business climate as Germany assumed a higher profile in Czechoslovakia. If the Sudeten issue were truly put to rest, new opportunities would abound—or so they proclaimed to one another.

For the first time I considered that Prague could become my default residence for a while if Berlin continued to be dangerous for me. As I mulled the possibility, I noticed a gorgeous Hamburg Steinway grand piano in the adjacent dining room. No one was playing, even though it was still the high luncheon hour. I pictured Sofie and me providing the most elite diners of Prague with a selection of popular American music, and the prospect brought a smile to my face. Why not? Hadn't we already been well received by Charles Lindbergh, Hermann Göring, and the cream of Wehrmacht officers and their wives? I could see the billboard on Reznika Street outside the Majestic: "Straight From Their Celebrated Appearance in Berlin: Two Sensational Young Jews!" I wondered whether Sofie would find that as amusing as I did.

At 3 p.m. I approached the concierge desk and inquired where the house telephones were banked. He pointed to a mahogany-paneled passageway across the lobby. A single hotel operator sat behind the bank and he offered to place my call and collected the local toll from me. Moments later, he directed me to Booth #6, and, when I lifted the receiver from its cradle, a male voice announced, "Clinic of Dr. Havlik—how may I help you?"

"This is . . . this is . . . the doctor's 4 p.m. appointment," I stumbled, nearly forgetting Sofie's instruction. "Should I proceed to your office?" What a stupid recovery, I thought. I must get better at this deception business to have a chance of avoiding apprehension.

"Herr Meister is expected at 4 p.m., and the doctor requests that he be on time for his appointment," came the response. I was satisfied with the answer and concluded the call with no more words passing between us. Glancing in the direction of the operator, I imagined that he unplugged a line from his switchboard at exactly that moment, and I wondered whether he had monitored my conversation. I continued to look toward him, but he did not turn his eyes in my direction, so I gathered my duffel and my newspaper and walked slowly back across the foyer toward the brass-handled doors.

A bellman summoned a waiting taxi from the queue near the hotel's entry, and he asked my destination—to relay it to the driver, I assumed.

Remembering my incompetence in making the telephone call, I decided not to respond to the bellman beyond placing a few coins into his extended hand. Hopefully his only impression would be "just another cheap German soldier, not worth remembering." Once inside, I opened the glass panel separating me from the driver and gave him an address written on a scrap of paper—not the exact address from Dr. Havlik's card, but one I assumed would be a short distance beyond his office.

CHAPTER FIFTEEN

Prague – Autumn 1938

THE HAVLIK CLINIC AND ITS OCCUPANTS
[From Dieter's Journal]

*T*he cab ride was, as Sofie had indicated, about five minutes from the Majestic Plaza along Čiklova. As we passed the correct address, I could look at the building and see whether there was anything unusual in the street nearby. Nothing drew my attention, so after another hundred meters or so I tapped on the divider glass and pointed to a corner where I wished to be deposited. There was no comment in return, only a nodded acknowledgment as the cab caressed the curbstone and slowed to a halt.

You are behaving like a fugitive! I admonished myself silently. Was I imagining that everyone in this city of one million inhabitants had been alerted to the possible presence of a piano man from Berlin? Apparently I was, but then the necessity for an encoded call before arriving at Dr. Havlik's—what was *that* all about? It was certainly becoming more complicated to be a Jew, I smiled. Better to be safe . . .

After the cab had turned the corner and disappeared from my sight, I wheeled around and retraced the short distance to the office address. It was a well-maintained building in a very attractive neighborhood, but I couldn't see any plaque or other marking that would identify it as a medical clinic, only the address numbers on the entry door. Dr. Havlik must have a very good practice and affluent patients who demanded privacy.

I mounted the three stairs leading to the entry and reached for the stylish brass turn-bell, which seemed to glisten from regular polishing. Twisting its key-handle, I could hear a clear bell sound on the other side of the thick door. It swung open immediately.

Sofie stood just inside, with her arms extended toward me. She had never seemed more beautiful! Her outstretched arms pulled me inside, then entwined around my shoulders as part of a full-body embrace, which I was happy to return in kind. As my eyes adjusted to the lower light level, I saw two other faces in the foyer. One was a woman whom I judged to be in her sixties, with short, henna-red hair inappropriate for her skin coloring. The other was a man in his late thirties or early forties, with tired-looking eyes set deep into a very pleasing and sensitive face.

So, I thought, I am finally about to meet Lilka Rudovska and Dr. Juraslav Havlik. Releasing the clinging Sofie, I presented myself to the others. "Guten tag, I am Dieter Meister, Sofie's close friend from Berlin. I have looked forward to meeting you."

"Please call me Lilka," the woman said in accent-free German. She smiled. "You already know my wonderful daughter, Sofie, and now I would like you to meet my son, the doctor, as we Jewish mothers apparently delight in saying. Juraslav and Sofie are half-siblings, he from my early twenties and she from my early forties. How do you like *that?*" she added with apparent pride and a full smile, which immediately made her look younger and less severe.

I was not prepared for this twist and probably stood open-mouthed for a moment. My immediate thought process was that the besieged General von Seigler had not only a Polish/Jewish presumed-dead wife, but also a half-Jewish daughter with a similarly flawed lover and now a half-Jewish Czech stepson. That was a lot of baggage for a prominent Wehrmacht officer in 1938, especially one being linked to an attempt upon the führer's life. And here were all of those "embarrassments" gathered under one roof in Prague. An uneasy sense of vulnerability was forming in my stomach.

That evening the four of us dined together in a tasteful formal dining room with the curtains drawn closed. Dr. Havlik had both a cook and a housekeeper, who doubled as servers during such meals. They were young Polish women who seemed very devoted to their employer and to his Polish mother. All of the conversation among them, including that which involved Sofie, was in Polish, so I caught only scraps, especially when the words were hurried or multiple speakers overlapped their remarks. From time to time, my dilemma became apparent, and one or another would provide a short explanation of the matter then under discussion. There was concern that Sofie's and my passage to Prague might have been observed. She seemed to discount the probability of that, noting that we had both departed from the station without incident.

Dr. Havlik asked me (in German) whether I agreed with Sofie, and I said that I believed I had blended in with other German soldiers on the platform and in the city. He asked how I had passed the day, and I told him about the park, the restaurant, and the hotel, but made no mention of my adventures in the brothel on Ruzova. Since we were just getting to know one another, I thought that such full disclosure might prejudice my opportunity to be accepted as a proper partner for Sofie. Besides, I had been careful to retrace my path after leaving, and to avoid mentioning my name to any of the ladies behind the green door. Only Jurgen had that knowledge, and he had other things on his mind once we were inside the establishment. I decided to tell the other diners of my caution in not giving the bellman my destination and directing the cab to a nearby address rather than that of the clinic. There was a nod of approval from Lilka, then Sofie said, "Some in Berlin think that Dieter is a professional because he has avoided them so expertly. I'm sure that any who thought that way before are thoroughly convinced now, because he has walked away from his job and his rented room leaving no trail at all. Only Father and his aide were aware of Dieter's disguise as a corporal, and I purchased his ticket to Prague myself and have not shared the information."

"What is the status of the Oster matter?" I asked. "Is your father still under suspicion? And who has the authority to clear him to return to his duties?" They were bold questions for the newest arrival at the household to be raising, and I wondered whether I had overstepped my bounds in doing so. Still, they appeared to be comfortable speaking with me present, and certainly each of us shared some element of common danger with the others. Even the two housegirls would be affected if our relationship to recent events in Berlin were detected. We were like some little cabal of plotters in a Bolshevik story. I recalled the voices of the local militia men in the house in Rahnsdorf describing the furtive nature of Jews and was suddenly secretly pleased that I had recently given additional evidence of that quality by eluding detection so cleverly. But to what purpose?

CHAPTER SIXTEEN

Prague – Autumn 1938

UNDERSTANDING THE OSTER CONSPIRACY

[From Dieter's Journal]

*S*ofie was the first to respond: "Lieutenant Colonel Hans Oster worked for the German Office of Military Intelligence. It is a Wehrmacht function, and thus Oster was indirectly within Father's scope of command. He was not a frequent visitor to our house on Wilhelmstrasse—which you know, Dieter—but he did like to relax with Father and his closest friends at Lilkahaus, and when he did so, he worried aloud about the führer's military ambitions. Oster was a career military officer and, like many of them, he had no desire to return to the horrors they had experienced at the end of the Great War.

"He conjectured that Germany was excusing many of the führer's eccentricities because his brash nature was quickly re-establishing our prominence in postwar Europe. We were a country in need of self-respect, and Hitler more than held his own in the company of the sissified Chamberlain, horny Frenchy Daladier and the buffoon, Mussolini, with his petulant posturing. Only Jews saw him as stepping over the line, and Jews were not accorded much respect by their fellow Germans. As a country, and on balance, loyal, good Germans thought that Hitler was moving us back toward prosperity and certainly to respectability.

"Oster was closer to the führer's developing policies than most Germans, and he concluded that Hitler was muscling himself into command of the military with a deliberate unannounced agenda to initiate a series of small 'conquests' involving our immediate neighbors—Austria,

Czechoslovakia and Poland—none quite big enough to bring the major powers into play, but each consolidating Germany's strength.

"He did the same thing with Germany's Jews, first forcing them to register for conscription, then making them add "Ruth" or "Israel" to their legal names for easier identification, then issuing new passports and other documents prominently marked with a red *J*. He finally prohibited Jews from holding teaching positions, practicing medicine, or owning some kinds of businesses . . . "

Lilka added, "Yes, Sofie, and he then ordered all the Polish Jews to leave Germany and return to Poland, but finagled Polish authorities into preventing them from crossing the border, leaving them in a limbo of misery, where nearly 17,000 disappeared . . . "

Sofie was still speaking. "In both venues, international and internal, it was like a water-drip execution, with no individual step sufficient to precipitate major protests, but a cumulative result that was entirely horrible. Meanwhile, he and Mussolini honed their war machines on the practice fields of Spain, with the willing assistance of Generalissimo Francisco Franco. You heard at our party, Dieter, how Hermann Göring and his aviators migrated there—to Spain—and perfected their aerial warfare techniques on the defenseless Spanish."

Dr. Havlik interrupted. "Sofie, my irate little sister, you are wandering from the subject of Oster. There is a pattern that must be understood to comprehend how a trusted Wehrmacht Colonel conceived and launched an assassination attempt. It developed like this: For each nation or group being gently assaulted by the führer, an epiphany of realization came at a different time. It was cleverly conceived and brilliantly implemented, with powerful propaganda always twisting the facts into glowing reports of another triumph by the German leadership. Everything was celebrated by huge, staged crowds waving flags and demonstrating a groundswell of rabid approval. Who would dare raise a negative voice in the face of such success?

"Hans Oster, as you said, Sofie, was a professional soldier. He watched the progression of the Nazi Party's power growth just as the rest of the military leaders did, and for a while he was unwilling to protest. However, in June, 1934, this all became more personal for him. You will remember that Hitler then massacred hundreds of SA storm troopers in what the press dubbed "The Night Of The Long Knives." Even general officers were not spared if they had shown the temerity to disagree with the führer and his party. Oster knew many of those murdered men, and he at last concluded that the whole Nazi regime was evil and corrupt—that it could not merely be "adjusted," or "re-tuned," but that it must be stopped.

"He believed that only by removing Hitler from power could the aggressive program be blunted, and he was able to get agreement from many of his professional military contemporaries on that point. But their agreement broke down when it came to how such a removal should be accomplished. Many thought that Hitler should be arrested and tried for his violations of our Constitution. Oster said that a public trial of Hitler would be the worst possible scenario. He said that Hitler alive would be like Napoleon or Rasputin, polarizing opinions and constantly resurfacing with ever-greater levels of violence in the German society. No, he wanted Hitler dead!

"He sensed that he couldn't sell the path of assassination to most of his fellow disenchanted officers. Some were opposed on moral grounds, and others were just afraid for themselves or their families if the plot were uncovered and avenged. So, he developed a 'plan within a plan,' like those intricate Chinese puzzles. The ostensible plan was to create a rogue commando attack on the Reich Chancellery, apparently attempting to put the Army in charge of government, allowing the country to revert to a proper Constitutional basis. The secret plan within that strategy was to have "random gunfire" break out against unidentified 'defenders' at the Chancellery, and for Hitler to be shot and killed 'accidentally' in the exchange.

"By September of this year, Oster had local military commanders in many areas of the country alerted to the possibility of such a military takeover of the Reich Chancellery, and he was convinced that they would react supportively in the aftermath, accepting Hitler's death as accidental when that became known. Only a few knew of the mission to eliminate Hitler. A handful of Oster's closest collaborators knew that the attack was to take place on September 28. It nearly happened, but someone got cold feet and leaked the plot to the führer's inner circle of advisors, and Oster was arrested immediately. So were many others, and the process of sorting out the co-conspirators from those not involved is now playing out, with Herr Himmler and Marschall Göring taking the lead."

Sofie again spoke. "You know that Göring and Father share a long friendship. Even though Father was confined temporarily to Lilkahaus, there was no serious question of his involvement in the Oster Conspiracy insofar as Göring was concerned. They met there and had a long discussion, which resulted in Göring's commitment to absolve Father publicly of any complicity. In the spirit of that day, Father disclosed my mixed parentage to Göring, and appealed to Hermann's own sentiments as a new father to obtain my safe passage from the country before Jew-haters could point me out and threaten to harm me. Göring did not want to know where I was going, so he provided a generic letter. He thinks I was headed somewhere to the west, possibly to England. Unfortunately, I had to use the letter on the train, something I did not want to do, and we are worried that it could direct dogged searchers to Prague.

"That is why it was important that you and I not communicate on the train or on the platform afterward. You were just another soldier in the crowd, and the feisty old lady with the letter of safe passage was not seen anywhere after the trip. Hopefully, with German military currently taking over parts of this country and Hungary and Poland grabbing some of its mineral resources, any temporary interest in two travelers from Berlin will evaporate quickly. Here in Dr. Havlik's residence and clinic, we can pause for a few days and consider our next options."

At last I thought that I understood the knotty problem of the Oster Conspiracy. The unanswered question in my mind was why a decisive leader like the führer had chosen to proceed so quietly after the conspiracy was uncovered. It seemed to me that he might have harbored doubts about the loyalties of many German leaders, and thus was unwilling to test those loyalties by giving the matter too much overt attention. Or perhaps there could be multiple plots to unseat him, and making the world privy to that fact would automatically result in the instability of his government. For whatever convoluted reason, Oster had disappeared from the newspapers. And—gloriously—General von Seigler was out from the shadows of doubt and able to concern himself with his daughter's wellbeing.

Once again I turned to my own involvement in something so complex and marveled at the fact that I was sitting in Prague with the conflicted members of an important general's secret family. Improbable as it seemed, I *was* in that room and now burdened with knowledge that could affect many people. Did General von Seigler even know that Lilka and Dr. Havlik were there with Sofie and me? I wanted to know more about the obviously intelligent Lilka and the Czech physician who was the half brother of my Sofie. Now there would be time for quiet conversations behind the drawn blinds, and I resolved to gather the facts that could complete my understanding of this Gordian knot. But, before I could begin, there was the exciting prospect of being alone with Sofie.

Juraslav (as he wished to be called) and I sipped after-dinner brandy while Sofie and Lilka chatted quietly and the Polish girls picked up the remnants of our dinner. I can't recall what we discussed, because my eyes returned to Sofie at every opportunity, and my thoughts raced back over the events of the past five months that had made her so paramount in my life. The mantel clock behind Juraslav moved at a glacial pace, and I knew that my responses were becoming muddled and incomplete. Finally, when it seemed I could wait no longer, I felt a soft hand on my shoulder and heard Sofie's voice observing that we were both sleep deprived and ready to retire for the night. *Hallelujah* echoed in my brain and nearly formed on my lips as well. I tossed down the last two fingers of my brandy, shook Juraslav's proffered hand, kissed Lilka on both cheeks, thanked the girls for all their attentions, and gathered myself to climb the stairs. Hallelujah!

"After you tossed my suitcase and wardrobe from the train, there was little left for me to wear in Prague," she began. "So, while you busied yourself waiting for your medical appointment, I went to a few of the shoppes near Vyšehrad Park. Unpack your duffel and put things into that wardrobe closet while I put on my new nightdress—but don't look until I tell you I'm ready, ja?"

I agreed, but on the condition that the process not be a long one. "You know that a man who owns one suit and a borrowed uniform doesn't qualify as an expert on *haute couture,*" I quipped. "Whatever you may wear tonight will be more flattering than the dowager's weeds you sported on the train ... and in any case, I will insist that it be removed in the briefest possible time." I wondered if she also saw the incongruity in my words—the homosexual eager to be with a naked woman. How totally bizarre it had become.

"Now!" she laughed, and I turned to see the tall, statuesque young woman with electric eyes caressed by a sheer, red silk sheath. Her shoulders were sculpted and bare; her nipples seemed ready to pierce outward through the fine fabric, and there was a decided dimple where the silk followed the indenture of her navel. This time my *hallelujah* found a voice, and I understood why I had risked so much, instead of pocketing my dowry and running away from Berlin to some safe haven. The most miraculous part of it all was that she found me attractive, and I resolved that I must give her total loyalty and honesty for as long as I had the privilege of her devotion.

So, Dieter, I thought, does that start with an honest exposure of your morning in a whorehouse on Ruzova? How much honesty and how much devotion are we pledging here? And what if the honesty belies the devotion and the whole thing trashes the happiness you are beginning to cherish? Just what are the rules of love? You have ridden a train to one of the world's most dangerous places to be with Sofie, and then enjoyed—well, mostly— an interlude with two local prostitutes before arriving at her door. Can anyone but you understand that it was all part of your loyalty and devotion? Do you even believe that yourself? Just as my thoughts and doubts were about to pound me into submission, they were interrupted . . .

"Come here. I need you, Dieter . . . "

CHAPTER SEVENTEEN
Prague – Autumn 1938

INSIGHTS INTO DR. JURASLAV HAVLIK

"Impetigo" was the one-word observation that passed from Dr. Juraslav Havlik to the young mother standing nervously outside his examination room. She registered no recognition of the word, and so he continued. "Impetigo is a common skin ailment, easily passed from one location on the body to another—also from one person to another, if there is frequent or prolonged contact. The skin is the body's largest organ, and it can be infected as any other organ.

"Your son has impetigo lesions in his nose as well as his under-arm areas. It usually appears first as an irritation, and then goes on to develop yellow scales or scabs. And, as you have seen, those can ooze liquid and become very ugly."

She now looked fearful, and a tear drifted down one flushed cheek, so he hastened to assure her that the disease had no long-term consequences. "It can be treated and cured rather easily through a regimen of careful cleaning and regular application of astringents to the affected areas. But you must make young Radek aware of *his* responsibility during the treatment. He must wash his hands frequently with soap and hot water, and he must *not* continue to touch the affected areas. He may *not* lift the scabs or let the fluid spread to other areas."

The coltish ten-year-old boy was silent, but his wide-eyed concentration on every word suggested that he was taking in at least as much as his confused mother. Dr. Havlik turned to face Radek and asked him, "Are there any *other* parts of your body where you have these same skin problems? You know, sometimes boys have their hands between their legs, and that's a warm, moist environment where impetigo can grow and spread easily. How about it, Radek? Should we make certain there's no more?"

The youngster had turned pink with embarrassment and then pale with fear at the suggestion he might have been exploring that forbidden area. Then he lowered his head and an adolescent-sounding sob escaped from his throat. His mother turned him to face her and asked aggressively, "Well, Radek, have you spread this disease to your pee-pee?" Before he could answer, Dr. Havlik began unbuttoning the lad's trousers and slipping his braces off his shoulders, allowing the rough corduroy pants to descend to his ankles. Then the doctor moved his hands skillfully around the boy's midsection and pulled his white cotton underdrawers downward, revealing an impetigo-free, full-standing erection, which caused the young mother to gasp audibly and the youngster to flush an even brighter shade of pink.

"Good for you, Radek!" the doctor smiled. "That's a real zinger!! Now, please leave it alone for a few days so that your impetigo doesn't travel south. Can you do that?"

"Yes, sir," came the quiet response, as Radek quickly hiked his drawers over the protruding tumescence, did his best to re-button his britches, and pulled the braces over his shoulders. Dr. Havlik turned away from the comical scene to avoid laughing as Radek hastened away to the waiting room. When he turned back, he was met with a solid slap across his face, delivered by the incensed mother.

"You are a perverted monster," she shouted. "You are not fit to be a physician!

"I would like to scratch your eyes out. I will go to the authorities and tell them to withdraw your license to practice. I hate you!!"

"Relax, ma'am—your son is entering his puberty, and there will be spontaneous erections brought on by dozens of stimuli over the next two or three years. Don't turn it into a catastrophe each time he stretches his britches a bit, or you will risk turning him into a misfit. He's a healthy young man and he must be allowed to be comfortable in that new status. And perhaps it is time to stop referring to it as his 'pee-pee.' It is a good, healthy penis, and you must stress the need to wash his hands if he decides to enjoy it."

He pulled a prescription pad toward him, scribbled some numbers and symbols, then added a signature which looked like a child's drawing of a flower. "Get this prescription filled. It is a powerful astringent you can blot on the lesions with cotton pads or gauze. Do that two or three times each day and the impetigo should subside by next week. If you see fresh areas of infection, soak them well. And get intimate enough with your son to allow you to talk about the undesirable consequences of spreading impetigo to his privates. It is very nasty when it gets established there, and much harder to cure than are areas exposed to air and sunlight. I'm sorry if this was unpleasant for you. I didn't enjoy it, either, but we should both move on without any hard feelings. Is that all right with you?"

"I'm so sorry, Dr, Havlik," she blurted through tears. "We are Jewish, as you perhaps know, and I am afraid every time Radek is in a situation where someone might notice that he has been circumcised. There is so much discrimination and outright hostility toward Jews these days. You can't understand it, I suppose, but I am wracked with fear of what may happen to us. Please forgive me for taking it out on you."

He placed a comforting hand on her shoulder while she regained her composure, then he looked downward and smiled. "Please understand that all of your communications with your family medical doctor are privileged and never to be revealed to anyone else. You may call me on any subject concerning your health, physical or mental, and I will give you the best advice I can muster. Now, go outside and hug your son— he's a good boy. And, by the way, I am also Jewish and am well aware of the burdens some people might want to place upon us. We must all look out for one another.

The young mother avoided his eyes for a moment, then lightly brushed his cheek with her lips and left the room without further conversation. Left alone in his examining room, Jura realized that he was very tired; he slumped into his padded chair and allowed his thoughts to drift back to another time and place.

CHAPTER EIGHTEEN
Poland – Early 1900s

JURASLAV'S EARLY MEMORIES

When, exactly, had Juraslav decided that he wished to be a physician? His memories went back to the age of five or six. Home then was in the industrial city of Łódź, in the middle of Poland. Nearly everyone he knew in Łódź seemed to be in the textile industry, and each day, long trains went toward the east, to Russia, loaded with cloth produced at the mills. His mother, Lilka, worked as a bookkeeper in the employ of the Scheibler Mill. Even though she was still in her twenties, she was well regarded by her employers and hence by everyone in the small community where they had an apartment.

Łódź, in Polish, meant "boat," but the Bzura River on which Scheibler Mill was situated was certainly not inviting for boaters. It was heavy with the waste of the industrial processes conducted along its banks, and Juraslav considered it to be disgusting. He heard that the city's name had been coined hundreds of years before industrialization— at a time when no less than eighteen rivers caressed the countryside—and when nearly every resident actually owned a boat and spent part of every day on the water. He visualized himself doing the same and promised himself that some day he would live by a beautiful river and could explore in a craft of his own.

It was only the two of them, mother and son, sharing the one bedroom—and cooking, eating, reading, and listening to a music box in the second room of their dwelling. Six days of each week, Juraslav walked to the SDKPiL Socialist Workers' Children's School a short distance from his house, where he was recognized as a very bright little boy who could speak confidently in Polish, Prussian-German, and a strange, third tongue which no one else understood. Some said it was a Gypsy dialect, learned from the tall man who visited the apartment most weekends, when Juraslav got to sleep by the music box, or gramophone, as some people were calling it.

The man carried a small black bag filled with the signature tools of a medical doctor, and on the pocket of his frock coat the name *Uniwersytet Medyczny W Łódź* was embroidered in gold thread. Lilka called the man "Tovar," and they spoke in the Gypsy tongue when they wanted to omit Juraslav from the conversation. He had recognized this early, and soon he understood nearly all of what they said, but he never let them know that. This allowed him to learn that Tovar was a medical professor at the Uniwersytet; that he enjoyed talking softly about the hidden parts of Lilka's body, and that he referred to Juraslav as his son whenever he mentioned him. Juraslav liked Tovar, and when he asked questions about the world around him (in Polish, of course) Tovar gave him long, understandable responses.

Tovar loved to play Gypsy guitar music on the gramophone; it was exciting music that galloped along at a breathtaking pace. Juraslav asked where it came from and learned that places called Hungary and Romania had many Gypsies, but that they had lately spread to Germany, Poland, Russia, and even Belgium. Tovar said that Gypsies did not, as most people, affiliate with the countries where they lived, but instead they carried with them loyalties to tribal leaders, who also moved across national boundaries. Juraslav asked Tovar whether he was a Gypsy himself, and for once he got only an enigmatic smile instead of a detailed response. And so, Juraslav decided that if he was Tovar's son, then he must be half a Gypsy—and half a Jew, like Lilka.

In 1905, after four years of recession and mounting political tensions, labor problems began to move westward from Russia into Poland. Józef Piłsudski, leader of the *Polska Partia Socjalistyczna,* the Polish Socialist Party, encouraged his supporters to work toward independence from Russian domination and closer affiliation with Germany. The Scheibler Mill interests sided naturally with Piłsudski, which seemed to exempt them from the riots and strikes plaguing many other employers in Łódź. Lilka was very valuable to her employers in this process of putting her fellow workers squarely in Piłsudski's corner, and, before long, accounts of the young woman's competence reached the Socialist Party headquarters in Krakow. There was an important role she could play at party headquarters, and there were rewards to be reaped if she would leave Łódź for Krakow.

Juraslav tuned his ear to the late-night conversation between Tovar and Lilka, soon understanding that it was about him. If Lilka went to Krakow, it must be alone. Juraslav would have to remain with Tovar in Łódź, moving to Tovar's small bolt-hole flat at the Uniwersytet and studying his lessons with the children of physicians rather than those of textile workers. Lilka's heart would be heavy without her son, and she would miss the warmth and intelligence of Tovar. Perhaps in time they could all be together again, but there could be no promise of that eventuality. And, what if Lilka refused the "promotion" being pushed at her? It was clear that she would lose her position in the Scheibler Mill, and there was even some question of Tovar's professorship, because the members of Karl Wilhelm Scheibler's family were major factors in the finances of the Uniwersytet. Was there really a choice? The answer was silence, followed a few minutes later by the rhythmic squeaking of the ancient bedsprings. That was the only part six-year-old Juraslav was not quite certain he understood.

During the following weeks, Lilka cried often and so miserably that an embarrassed Juraslav found himself wishing that the move could be completed, whatever the new arrangement—get on with it. Tovar spoke more often to him during this period, and even took him to the Uniwersytet to show him where he would soon take his classes and where the faculty children played games together. Juraslav liked the clean area by the Sokolowka River where the Uniwersytet spread itself among gnarled old trees and well-kept lawns. He asked to see where Tovar lived and where he worked, and was surprised that the small apartment had a beautiful view toward the river and was only two hundred meters from the laboratory building from which Tovar worked. He would be sleeping on an overstuffed sofa at the remote end of the L-shaped room where Tovar's bed was situated, and they both would use a communal bath and shower room at the end of their hallway. The residents of four other apartments along the passageway also shared the clean, tiled convenience.

Saying a final goodbye to his mother was emotional for both, but she promised that she would come to visit from Krakow and that he could spend Passover with her in the city on the Vistula, which was actually only 188 kilometers away. That prospect made the transition easier as they waved to one another in the Łódź railway terminal and Juraslav watched as the only caregiver he had known in his ten years moved slowly away from his view. When the final car of her train had retreated beyond the terminal building, he finally blew his nose free of the accumulated moisture and turned to his father with a smile. "Let's go home and watch the river!"

"I am in charge of the emergency pavilion tonight," the older man responded. "Would you like to pick up a book, some crayons, and a pad, and sit quietly in the receiving room? Sometimes it is empty and at others it is chaotic—that means very busy—and you must entertain yourself at the times when I am attending an emergency. Would you like that? When you get sleepy, I will have a nurse walk to the apartment with you and sit until you are asleep."

"Are you taking care of people who are hurt?"

"Sometimes I attend injuries. Other times I am dealing with people who are sick or have suffered an infarction—attack of the heart—or other inside organ. I never know what the problem will be, which makes the work exciting for me, but perhaps a bit gory for you at this time. Let's see if you can do it—there may be time for us to practice language, draw pictures together, or . . . "

"You may have to save lives!" the young Juraslav concluded with obvious excitement. "I should like to see that, Tovar!"

"Perhaps you should call me *Father* now. I think you know that you are my own son, don't you?"

"Yes. I never had a father before, and you were called Tovar, so I will have to get used to it. But yes, I really would like that. So, Father, let's go watch the river until it is time for you to save lives, and then we can walk together to the emergency clinic. Good?"

School was better at the Uniwersytet and the students were much smarter than the children of textile factory workers had been. Juraslav truly enjoyed the more interesting books he now received, and he prepared his lessons well. Tovar regularly sat with him by the window facing the river and checked upon the quality of Juraslav's work papers. He rarely found anything to criticize and thus found himself much pleased with his son's progress. They were rapidly developing a rapport that would have been more fitting for a pair of equally mature adult roommates. Juraslav took over the role of dinner cook for the apartment, which he added to his duties as cleaning boy. Tovar gave him a weekly budget for foodstuffs and invited him to the emergency room or operating theatre whenever Tovar was performing surgery.

Each two weeks, a letter written in German would arrive from Krakow. In them, Lilka described her duties as an analyst and policy aide on Piłsudski's staff, but she was cautious never to mention any of the German military people with whom she came into contact. She was equally careful to omit any commentary regarding the tense interrelationships among German, Polish, and Russian officials constantly crossing paths in Krakow. She saved her soaring adjectives for the quality of the music recitals and operatic performances she was attending as a part of her work, and she went to great lengths to obtain tickets for them whenever her son was able to be with her in Krakow. Those treasured visits happened three or four times each year, usually connected with a Jewish holiday, even though Juraslav now neglected all of the ceremonial attachments to his mother's religion.

When Lilka mentioned this omission, Juraslav gave her his reason: "I want to be a doctor like Tovar and save lives and fix infarctions and mend broken bones as he does, Mother. But, Tovar . . . Father . . . says it is very difficult to become a doctor if you are a Jew. The rules are different for Jews, and even when they do become doctors, some people won't be attended by them. Only other Jews. I don't want to miss the chance to be a doctor just because you are a Jew. Can you understand that, Mother?"

It was such a painful subject that Lilka decided not to risk breaking the spell of their days together. Instead she said, "Juraslav, I have heard that, too, and I don't know whether it is entirely true. So, let me think about it and talk to some of my friends here in Krakow, and when we get together next time I'll know enough to give you my advice. But, whatever that advice may be, this will ultimately be your decision and you should do whatever is necessary to make your fondest dreams become reality. I am pleased and proud that you are considering becoming a healer, and if that is your final choice, I shall do everything I can to help. Meanwhile, the most important thing you can do is excel in your studies and observe as much as you can at the Uniwersytet."

Juraslav knew instinctively from that day forward that eventually he would forsake Judaism if that were the price of becoming a part of the medical profession. His mother had left Łódź to pursue her professional life in the Piłsudski party headquarters, even though it had put distance between them, and he understood that choice and accepted the changed circumstances it produced in his life. Actually, his life away from the cramped apartment hard by the mill had proven to be much more palatable, and now it pointed the way toward his lifetime choice of profession. If Jews and Gypsies were not good candidates for medical universities, he would be in no hurry to disclose either of those building blocks from his past. He would instead present himself as a strong student with a commitment to the practice of medicine and an indifference to organized religions and politics.

CHAPTER NINETEEN
Poland – Early 1900s

THE KING OF THE GYPSIES / PHYSICIAN TO THE ROMANI

Tovar appeared to ration the information he shared with Juraslav, savoring each morsel until his son was ready to absorb it, and then launching into a new area with the rapt attention of the youngster. One evening as they finished dinner and looked out at the moving river, Tovar suddenly opened one of those doors.

"I wasn't born here, you know. My family was associated with a Romani leader named Gregory Kwiek, and he determined where his followers lived and when it was time for them to move on. We were from a place farther to the south, but Gregory saw the new industrialization of the 1890s as a chance to move into Poland, where *gadje* would welcome our industrious habits and innovative skills."

"Who are . . . gadje? . . . Tovar, I don't know that name . . . gadje."

"Ah, of course you don't. Well son, we were Romani, and anyone who was not Romani was gadje."

"And Romani? Who are Romani, Tovar?"

"Romani, my son, are many groupings of what gadje call Gypsies. We were Gypsies, and the leader of the group—which included the Havliks—was Gregory Kwiek. So, as I was saying when you interrupted, Gregory took us northward into present-day Poland to a town called Sanok, where Jews and Romani were appreciated. We brought with us richness not known in the new area—richness of music, literature, medicine, and human understanding.

"I was one of the best young musicians of our group—I could play the mandolin, the violin, and several kinds of guitars. You know the music I play on our gramophone? The kind you like, with all of the fast rhythms? Well, I played that music many nights around the campfires of our tribe. And then, when I was fifteen or sixteen, Gregory asked to see my hands. He said they were perfect—for a surgeon! He said that many in our entourage could play Gypsy music, but we needed more young men who could care for the needs of the family. "

"So . . . he told you that you had to be a doctor? He could do that? Just tell you? Is that how it was?"

"Well yes," Tovar responded, with just a hint of sadness. "Our society had to function as a unit, because we were frequently assailed by gadje. We had to be self-sufficient, and the elders often determined what skills needed augmenting and who could best fill those roles. If a young person had been selected to fill a role that was considered essential to our community, it was a great honor. I was proud to be singled out as a future healer of my people, and I immediately turned my attention to medicine. That began with apprenticing under the older medical specialists in our tribe, but there was a specific mission to learn about the newer medicines and techniques then being developed in Europe."

"Did you like it . . . medicine, I mean . . . did you grasp it with enthusiasm, as I do?"

"I did not have the option of liking or not liking, of doing or not doing. If I wished to stay within my community, I must do it. And so, when you must do something, Juraslav, do not trouble to ask yourself if you like it. Do not take the chance that your true answer might be negative. That could lead to a life of remorse. Enjoy what you must do and you will have a happier life. I liked medicine because it was the choice made for me. And, in truth, the elders were correct. I learned quickly and had the confidence of my tutors from the first. And, when the time came that my skills equaled theirs, they determined that I should leave the group temporarily and study in a formal university."

"This one here in Łódź, Tovar?"

"Yes—this very university. I was really quite young, but able to pass the entry exam easily and to skip many basic courses. It was the first time I had been outside the womb of my Romani community, and so frightening that I did nothing but eat, sleep, and study for a while. That made me a top student, and the faculty embraced me as a kind of prodigy. I wasn't, but I was better than any of my contemporaries. I was only twenty when I passed the dissertation and oral examination by the medical panel—that was in 1895. Suddenly I was a professional man in Łódź and uncertain if I wished to return to the Gregory Kwiek family in Sanok before seeing something of the world around me."

"So, did you tell yourself that you must enjoy that which you must do? Did you return at once to Gregory Kwiek with your new skills?"

"You are a quick learner, Juraslav! You are tossing my lesson back at me and asking if I followed the advice I'm doling out to you. How clever! But, you did not catch me in an inconsistency. Ha! I did the right thing and returned to Sanok and shared my augmented knowledge with my former tutors. I became the lead doctor to a collection of older practitioners and commenced a program aimed at improving the general health of our thriving little community. The gadje had not yet reacted negatively to our presence near the prosperous little town, and our Romani found work there and even formed local friendships. Our music was appreciated, and we were invited to perform in the city square and other public places. I picked up my violin again and took part in some of those recitals.

"It was at one of those that I was approached by a lovely young Polish woman carrying a violin. She asked if I would share the fingerings and bowings Gypsies use to deliver their dazzling, up-tempo passages. I was flattered and quick to respond, and before long I was spending time in the company of Lilka Rudovska. We shared both an interest in and a talent for music, and we agreed with one another that musical talent and linguistic ability are closely related. I taught Lilka the nuances of Gypsy music, and she gave me lessons in the difficult grammar of the formal German language. Then I helped her to understand the complex Romani tongue, and she added Yiddish to my language capability.

"Friday nights were our time together, and I would routinely close the clinic trailer at 5 p.m. and ride a saddle horse to the sturdy old home she shared with her Jewish family. Their food seemed bland to me—caravan peoples always add many strong condiments to fight the effects of spoilage, whereas established communities like Lilka's more often can enjoy fresh meat and produce from their own larders and gardens. They don't need the acidic sauces that burn Gypsies' tongues and clear their sinuses. However, both cultures consumed copious quantities of alcohol-based beverages with evening meals, and Lilka's family thought it amusing that I could keep pace with their Friday night libations.

"Eventually, I had to reciprocate and take my gadje lady friend to the large clearing I called home. At age twenty, your mother was very much in the fashion of women who caused Romani men to look long—she had a narrow waist and ample bosom, and her hair was a luxuriant amber-red. She could also play beautifully on her violin, which I thought would be a useful passport to my closed community. But all of those assets were ineffectual in gaining acceptance in the tribe of Gregory Kwiek, and the evening dragged along with frequent lapses in superficial conversations. I excused us from the table at the earliest possible opportunity, borrowed a dray, and drove Lilka back to her home in silence. Finally, she extended her hand to me and said that she understood that my people just did not welcome outsiders, even if they came in a spirit of friendship. I could only nod in agreement and drive slowly back to the closed community.

"During the following two years, our paths crossed occasionally, but there was never any meaningful conversation between us. I knew that Lilka had become active in the affairs of the community as well as the newly unionized workers in the town's textile mills. It was a terribly confused time, with many strikes and much violence, but she was able to keep the worst of this from affecting her employer's mills. This was unusual for a woman, but she was no ordinary female. Her talent for organization and her mastery of languages had made her a popular and effective leader, and genderless in the eyes of the townspeople.

"Then, one day, Gregory Kwiek himself sent for me. He acknowledged that I had been friendly with a gadje woman who now seemed to function effectively in the Sanok councils. He said that Lilka had delivered to him a request to meet with national Polish Socialist leadership to discuss the question of collecting tax revenues from Gypsy tribes within the nation. The inducement—which seemed to excite Gregory—was that Poland was prepared to revive the ancient title 'King of the Gypsies' and to bestow it upon Gregory. I knew that several countries had recognized Gypsy kings in return for their cooperation in controlling Gypsy activities, and I knew that Poland had once awarded that title, but the practice had lapsed a great many years earlier.

"Gregory asked if I could resume my acquaintanceship with Mlle.

Rudovska and see what would be required of him—and what benefits would accrue to him—if he were to be recognized formally as King of the Polish Gypsies. Once again, I was being singled out for a position in my community and, despite the fact that Gregory posed it as a question, it was truly an assignment. And, as you so easily grasped, my son, one should try to find enjoyment in what one must do anyhow. And so I accepted.

"Now I had permission to be with Lilka—not only on Friday evenings, but whenever it could advance my representation of the Romani people in Poland. I used the privilege liberally, and her next visit to our clearing was one filled with friendly gestures and flattery. Lilka was far too intelligent to miss the new significance, but she was also pleased to be back in my company and ignored the insincerity of my people. Before long, she asked if I would travel to Krakow with her to meet with Piłsudski officials there, and I accepted the invitation. So, my son, nearly three years after the young doctor and the Polish lady musician had first shared interests, they began planning their future together. How do you like that!

"My mission was a success. In 1898, Poland named Gregory Kwiek 'King of the Gypsies' with great fanfare and ceremony. He loved it! The new king pledged to provide the national treasury with a census of the Romani people within the borders of their country, and to assist the central government in assessing a head tax on those Gypsy inhabitants to defray the largely imaginary expenses of protecting and supporting them in Poland. Gregory and his core community received the promise of a liberal stipend to be paid progressively as the Gypsy census and tax were implemented. I was thanked by the new king, who also gave his blessing to our planned marriage. Before the end of that year, you were born in our house in Sanok."

"But, were you still a Gypsy once you married? Mother was a Jew and also a gadje. Did you go to live with your people, or did you cleave to hers, in town?"

"Good question! And one that vexed us at first. Selecting either alternative risked offending the other, so we set about finding a chair for me in Łódź at the university. We were able to do that, but powerful people wanted your mother to be located at the vast Scheibler textile mill, helping to keep those workers loyal to their German owners and to the

Piłsudski leadership, which leaned away from Russia. We had to live separately much of the time to give the impression that Lilka was firmly rooted in the workers' neighborhood, while I had to be a part of the medical faculty community, a few kilometers away. In many respects, it was like the old Friday night dates we had first enjoyed, but our devotion remained strong, and we shared our dedication to raising a fine citizen—you!"

"That's enough for now, Father. I have to put it in place in my mind, because I think that being a medical doctor may force me to make difficult choices, too. I need to think about the ways that might affect you, Mother, and others. Me, too."

Finally, the conflicting demands of politics, religion, business and medicine were becoming clearer to Juraslav, and he could appreciate the sacrifices his parents had made to create a loving home for him. He was proud of them and promised himself that he would face his own conflicts with the same resolve. He surmised correctly that the path would not be an easy or convenient one.

CHAPTER TWENTY
Poland – 1916

THE ROMANI DEPART FOR CZECHOSLOVAKIA

In 1916, when Juraslav was beginning his medical studies at the university in Łódź, Europe had become an even more treacherous place—especially so for Jews and Gypsies, and extremely so in Poland, which was being assaulted simultaneously by Germany and Russia. Lilka was devoted to her political work and well positioned in Krakow. She had a new baby and had long since eradicated all official records of her former ties to Tovar. Juraslav had been relegated to a private corner of her mind; she was extremely proud of him and satisfied that he had firm direction for his future. But she knew that he should not become identified with a partisan figure in the minefield of Poland.

Gregory Kwiek, King of the Gypsies, had prospered in his quasi-political role and had decreed he would eventually be succeeded in that suzerainty by his son, Michael. But, while he still held the mantle of Gypsy leadership, Gregory determined that his nomadic people should move with deliberate speed away from the frothing problems of Poland. He gathered the elders to solicit their concurrence, and he included Tovar in that discussion, because any such relocation would create medical issues as the tribe encountered diseases, accidents, and hostility. Once again, Tovar accepted the responsibility without question. He knew instinctively that he must give up his comfortable position at the university and join Gregory and his people on the long, perilous trek to the south.

The Gypsy king decreed that their destination should be a site near

Prague, where the Romani people were still welcomed and where their traditions could be maintained. They could move in small increments during the months after spring rains had abated and their caravans would not be bogged down in mud. Their relative prosperity, derived from the King's favored status, would permit the extended family to equip and larder themselves comfortably for the journey. Elders digested the proposition during long firelit meetings. They exchanged ideas about the eventual outcome of the Great War and concluded that, whoever prevailed, Poland would suffer in the aftermath. They agreed to sever their ties with the cities of Sanok and Łódź and began their preparations.

Tovar and Juraslav sat by the river's edge, where they often shared important conversations. The older man reviewed the discussions to which he had been privy, and he again invoked the standard of loyalty he held toward the people who had first carried him to this area and allowed him to become a well-regarded healer and teacher. Then he complimented his son upon his successes as a student and future physician and told him that it was time for them to be apart, each being true to his commitment.

Juraslav did not welcome the prospect of being alone but said that he understood the forces affecting each of them. He would continue at the university for so long as he could and would maintain regular correspondence with both his parents, fully aware that neither could be truly close to him in the fulminating climate of those times. Juraslav was mature beyond his chronological age of eighteen, but so were most of the young people who would survive the Great War and the influenza epidemic. Survivors would be the pragmatists who could assess the challenges of each day with imagination. Lilka and Tovar suspected that Juraslav had those qualities.

For the first time, Juraslav's buoyant approach to the study of medicine seemed bogged down with personal concerns, and he did not have a satisfactory explanation. More and more he strolled by the river and imagined it as the flow of his own life, trying to discover its source, its present stage, and its ultimate destination. His earliest memories remained those of the factory district of Łódź and his very simple life there. Throughout those years, his dependence upon Lilka had been the foundation upon which he built, and then she was gone and no woman had taken her place in his life.

He knew that Tovar and Lilka had parted amicably, but he sensed that Tovar, as had he, had experienced a void after Lilka's choice of Krakow and the Socialist Party removed her. And now, with Tovar departing, Juraslav had hoped he might resume closer contact with his mother, but another man—and now another child—had pre-empted that course. Finally, Juraslav admitted to himself that he resented his mother's choices. He was angry that she had easily bonded herself with a German military officer. And he was jealous of the new baby who was surely going to be heir to the attentions he had enjoyed exclusively as a youngster. Perhaps that was at the core of his inert feelings for women: he did not want to risk further disappointment or rejection, and so he avoided all but the most superficial contacts with the women of the university.

It quickly became a moot issue. Tovar's half of the apartment was rented by the university to one Adam Wodzinski, a young medical student from Posen. Adam inhabited a tall, graceful frame, distinguished by long, tapering fingers. That was fortunate, because he had a passion for the music of the great Polish composer Fryderyk Szopen—better known by his French name, Frédéric Chopin. He played the most demanding Chopin phrases effortlessly on the fine piano in the faculty lounge following each afternoon's lecture section. Juraslav knew from their first encounter that they were destined to share more than the rental payments.

Adam announced to Juraslav that his chosen field of medicine was that of surgery, and he regarded those afternoon pianistic sessions as a necessary training regimen for the strong and steady fingers he would need in the operating theater. Juraslav thought that the image of a young surgeon strengthening his hands on a diet of polonaises was classically romantic, and so he listened to each of Adam's informal performances with his eyes closed and his imagination in full flight. The disappointment of Tovar's departure was soon dissolved in his newly formed appreciation of the refined young man with whom he now shared living space. Once again, Juraslav was approaching his medical studies with elevated enthusiasm.

Adam knew nothing of politics, cared little for socializing, and was content to stroll by the river with his new friend, lecturing him on the merits of the "Waltz in D-flat major, Op. 64, No. 1," or reviewing the seamier aspects of Frédéric Chopin's ten-year liaison with a Frenchwoman named Aurore Dupin. Juraslav, in turn, was duly impressed that he now knew the proper name for the "Minute Waltz" and understood that the novelist George Sand was really a woman who had inspired the greatest Polish romantic composer—who most people assumed to be a Frenchman. While they were careful not to make a public display of their mutual affection, Juraslav and Adam were inseparable on the university campus, and most of their fellow students understood the nature of their bonding.

"We're sort of like Oscar Wilde and Lord Douglas, aren't we?" observed Juraslav one day as they ambled along the riverbank. Adam stopped still. It was obvious that he did not share the notion and indeed was offended by it.

"How can you say that?" he responded. "We are medical students, not aesthetes, and our attraction began with music and not buggering. I'm not in love with you, Juraslav—I like you because of your interests. We learn from one another, and we don't waste our time on frivolity, but we aren't a disgusting pair of perverts rolling around in whisky and cooking oil. Can't you see the difference? We are together because we were both rejected by women, yet each of us still needs the kind of quiet understanding that normally exists in good marriages. Don't ever compare us to those sick people—remember, Wilde went to jail and he died a recluse suffering from syphilis in a cheap hotel in Paris. You and I are going to cure ailing and damaged bodies so that the inhabitants can extend their lives and magnify their accomplishments."

Juraslav knew that Adam had struck a raw nerve when he spoke of the rejection he had never quite acknowledged. Lilka had chosen her politics over Tovar and him—then had connected as easily with a German and launched another life. He wondered whether Lilka's daughter would risk the same dismissal at some point and, if so, what consequence it might have in her choice of her most intimate companion. The little daughter's name was Sofie, wasn't it? Yes, it was

Sofie, and her father was a German military professional. Not much tenderness from that source, he thought. Little Sofie might be thrust into a hostile world and left to her own devices, much as Juraslav had been. Adam was right: theirs was an affiliation of convenience, but not one of blind passion. Just enough passion to get to sleep easier after a long day at the university. Just enough intimacy to create a sense of belonging, rather than one of isolation. He squeezed Adam's graceful hand and said, "You're right."

The next few years were indistinguishable one from the other in Juraslav's memory. His love for medicine was abetted by the formal studies and practical experience he received daily, and he knew that he was becoming a fine physician. At the same time, his love for music was more than satisfied through his contact with the prolific Adam, who encouraged Juraslav's skills and enriched his knowledge. The void which had been created by the departures of Lilka and Tovar was more than filled by Adam, who shared Juraslav's interests and also served as an adequate sexual partner in the privacy of their shared quarters. In a convoluted world, Juraslav recognized that he was blessed to be sheltered in the quiet safety of his professional studies, and he was careful to present himself to that small world with no hint of his underlying "imperfections." He knew that as a Jew, a Gypsy, and a homosexual, he aggregated some of the most reviled categories of the time and place he occupied, yet he was known only as a leading student with well-developed musical skills. It was a fine line to walk, but Juraslav had become adept at it.

From Lilka, he received periodic encouragement, but now it was limited to correspondence because he had no real desire to watch his mother fawn over her young daughter—especially so now that the German officer had become engaged in the Great War and the two females left behind had become interdependent. Tovar was quite different. He was too far away to visit, but he was engaged intimately in the healing processes which Juraslav loved, and their correspondence was peppered with the exploding knowledge of human injuries and diseases which typically expand during wartime.

Tovar had been rewarded for his loyalty to the Gypsy king during their demanding trek to Bohemia/Moravia. King Gregory had provided funding for Tovar to set up a private practice in Prague, where he had prospered. Their understanding was that Tovar would continue to consult with the Gypsy enclave on its major health concerns and would be available to treat any tribal elders who could not receive adequate care at their location. This role had included some interesting—and dangerous—services. Occasionally one of the younger Gypsy men was brought in with a gunshot wound, usually incurred during a theft in progress. There were also influenza victims and, of course, unwanted pregnancies among younger Gypsy women. The inconspicuous clinic in Prague was a valuable asset to King Gregory, and he made certain that Tovar was well compensated for his services.

In 1922, the fully accredited Juraslav was added to the staff at the university. Adam, too, had completed his training, and he informed Juraslav that it was time for him to rejoin his family in Posen and, perhaps, to seek a proper marriage, one suitable to the status which the Wodzinski family enjoyed in that city. Although Juraslav had always known that their shared affection would end once each was an accredited physician, hearing it in matter-of-fact terms from Adam was a harsh reminder of the earlier departures of Lilka and Tovar. Once again he saw himself as being relegated to the discard heap of someone else's life, and he wondered how many similar disappointments he was destined to experience.

CHAPTER TWENTY-ONE

Czechoslovakia – 1922 to 1938

DR. JURASLAV AND OTHERS AT THE HAVLIK CLINIC

The Gypsy king proved to be the solution to Juraslav's latest uncertainties. Gregory was growing older, and his son, Michael, had assumed some of his ministerial duties; Michael was already recognized as the heir apparent to the mythical crown of the tribe. An emissary from Michael Kweik came unannounced to Łódź and sought out the young physician after he had taught his final class at week's end. His message was brief but compelling.

"You are the son of Dr. Tovar Havlik, who has been both loyal and valuable to Gregory Kwiek for many years. He is revered in our councils. However, like Gregory, he is no longer vigorous enough to bear the full weight of his position, and we are anxious to create a smooth transition to the next generation. In Gregory's case, that will be a transfer to his son, Michael Kwiek, of the title he carries. In Tovar's role, we are hopeful that you can be persuaded to move to Prague and become the partner in Tovar's practice until he is ready to retire. Unfortunately, that may happen sooner than you have thought, because Tovar suffers from an illness that is diminishing him already. The elders believe that his life expectancy may be no more than another two years. Tovar has not shared this with you, but we feel that it is only fair to do so, if the knowledge would affect your decision. I expect that it will do so—no?"

Juraslav had asked for a few days to weigh the matter, but he knew instinctively that his years in the cloistered university were coming to an end, and that he must prepare himself to live outside Poland for the first time ever. He remembered Tovar's philosophy of learning to enjoy that which one must do anyway, and with that insight he considered how fortunate it might be to be reunited with his father and to have a private practice of medicine in a modern city. Even the prospect of mastering another language intrigued him, and on the third day of the emissary's visit, Juraslav committed to him that he would get his affairs in order and move to Prague at the conclusion of the current school term, only two months away. That seemed to please the Gypsy diplomat, who departed with a warm embrace, leaving behind a bank draft that was more than generous enough to cover all of the expenses he would incur in the process of relocating.

It seemed appropriate to pay one final visit to Lilka in Krakow, and he made that trip at his earliest opportunity. He found his mother quite familiar with the subject matter of his coming adventure; apparently she and Tovar communicated regularly despite the changed status of their relationship. He was also surprised at the instant affection he felt for Lilka's seven-year-old daughter, Sofie. She was enthusiastic to know him and eager to talk about music and medicine, his two mistresses of record. It was the most satisfying time he had spent in Lilka's company since his childhood in Łódź, and it helped him to understand better the currents of her life that had drawn her away from Tovar and from him. Long before the conclusion of his visit to Krakow, the enchanting eyes of his half sister had erased all vestiges of the green monster of jealousy that had haunted him for so long. He hoped that the young girl could become a part of his life in the years ahead.

The name of Dr. Juraslav Havlik was added to the stationery of the Havlik Clinic in Prague in the year 1922. He was approaching his twenty-fifth birthday, and for the first time in his adult life he was living outside the womb-like structure of the academic world to which Tovar had once taken him. It was a time when the world was awakening from an awful dream and rediscovering some of the subtleties of civilization. The Great War and the dark influenza epidemic were over, and Europe was embarking upon a new era of culture and prosperity. Juraslav noted quickly that many of the signs of change were more visible in his new environs than they had been in Łódź.

Gavrilo Princip, who had assassinated Austria's Archduke Franz Ferdinand and his wife, Duchess Sophie, had recently died in a deteriorating prison in Terezin, near Prague. While this was seen in hopeful editorials as heralding the end of an era of violence, with hope for a new era of civility, at the same time, not far away, an upstart political figure named Adolf Hitler was delivering impassioned speeches, proclaiming his strong Catholic faith, and excoriating Jews, Gypsies, and homosexuals as defilers of the German dream.

Near Prague, Michael Kweik had just been named the new king of the Gypsies, succeeding his aging but still vigorous father, Gregory, and the Havlik Clinic was burnishing its reputation in the sophisticated capital city of one million Czechs. Juraslav entered this charged atmosphere with solid credentials and a presumption of excellence, earned as a result of his father's work. Juraslav was determined to make his father proud, and during the ensuing two years he more than fulfilled that goal. In the bargain, he helped Tovar to exit the world content in the knowledge that his only son was a compassionate and effective healer. Tovar was only forty-nine when he died, but it seemed that he had lived for a century. His funeral was attended by at least four hundred Gypsies as well as some of Prague's leading medical professionals and a collection of disadvantaged souls who had been recipients of Tovar's *pro bono* generosity.

It was 1925 and Juraslav once again had no one to please other than himself. It was almost too much freedom. He recognized that his Jewish and Gypsy heritages both had the potential for imposing severe restrictions upon his life, but neither was a part of his primary identity now. Religious and political subjects were no part of the conversations he held with medical peers or with his patients. Instead, he cleaved to topics such as the development of new treatments and the extension of medicine's benefits to groups previously denied such care. In quieter moments, he wondered to himself whether those concerns were really a form of self-administered punishment—a salve for the guilt of having escaped the *Jew* and *Gypsy* labels he might have borne. No matter; he was happy being the celebrated young healer with many distinguished patients, and one who also dedicated time and energy unselfishly to care of the less fortunate.

This *persona* served as the cover he needed to explain his periodic visits to Gypsy encampments, military hospitals, and even houses of ill repute. He was admired at the leading medical association to which he belonged for his apparent willingness to forego compensation on those days when he departed from the Havlik Clinic and attended the baser classes. This reputation was worn with modesty by the humble physician, who let others create his legend of selflessness. It was pointed out in social circles that Juraslav Havlik was equally welcomed by musicians, political satraps, military doctors, brothel madams, and the incumbent king of the Gypsies. Only the fact that he had no apparent romantic attachment kept him from being regarded as the consummate medical figure of the Prague community. Perhaps there was just no time in his busy professional life for the frivolity of attachment—or perhaps some prior relationship back in Poland had left him with a heavy heart. Who could say?

Lilka and little Sofie came annually to Prague during the years immediately following Tovar's death. Juraslav sensed that it was a special treat for the youngster to get away from Poland for a week to enjoy the sights and sounds of sophisticated Prague. By the time Sofie was ten, there were already distinct indications that she would become a woman of many complexities and talents, and the two of them had conversations ranging from the purloined works of popular composers to the underlying political conflicts within Europe to the basic attractions of the sexes for one another. Lilka seemed amused and pleased that her two-generational offspring enjoyed one another's company, and she encouraged their exploration of the broad issues they chose. Occasionally she interrupted the dialogue with questions or comments, which rarely failed to amaze her son; she was an intriguing mystery, still thoroughly involved in the political issues of postwar Poland and apparently engaged in policy formation in the penumbra of influential leaders.

Then, as one of these yearly visits was being planned, Lilka had added an ingredient that troubled Juraslav. She asked whether she might invite and include Sofie's father, Wehrmacht Colonel Otto von Seigler, who would, of course, travel as a businessman under some suitable pretense. Juraslav had heard rumblings of German sentiment that all Romani men should be sterilized, and he knew that Gregory and Michael Kweik regularly met with their counselors to discuss strategies for avoiding the extinction of their Gypsy culture. There had been a proposal to take the extended family to India, and feelers had been put out to the new Italian leader, Benito Mussolini, regarding a possible Romani colony in East Africa. How would it appear to his patrons if they were to learn that a German field officer was a disguised guest under Juraslav's roof? Might he be branded as a traitor, in which case, could he disappear mysteriously and become another unsolved crime in Prague's police ledgers? He shared these concerns with his mother, who hastened to assure him that Otto's only reason for coming would be to engage in the family planning appropriate for Sofie's proper future.

Of course, Juraslav had yielded to his mother's persuasion; most people did. Nevertheless, as he greeted his houseguests on successive days, he was nervous and alert to any unusual persons on the periphery of his activities. However, no catastrophe had befallen them, and instead he soon found himself engaged in the warmth of a true family gathering. He even wondered whether Tovar might have fitted into the odd puzzle, and after a while shared that thought with the others. Sofie, now nearly thirteen years old, was at the center of their attentions and she participated eagerly in the process of charting her future. It seemed obvious that she had prospered in many ways in the strict environment of her Polish home, and all agreed that the productive equation should not be disturbed yet; however, it might be time for her to see modern Germany and understand the role her father was destined to play there.

Juraslav watched the interactions between Otto, a fit and militarily handsome 38-year old, and his mother, now a matronly 53, to see if there was any atavistic sexual attraction still in play between them. It was hard for him to imagine these dissimilar players in a romantic coupling, yet he understood that none of his patients could *ever* picture their parents behaving like that, which lay at the base of some warped rationalizations and bizarre behavior by children. Strangely, he had eventually absorbed the relationship between Tovar and Lilka and found himself enthusiastically approving of the squeaking old bedsprings in the cramped apartment on those nights when he slept near the gramophone. He knew that both of them would greet the new day with a smile, and that usually there would be some treat for him in payment for his removal to the farthest corner of the flat.

But—the young German soldier and the older Polish Jew from his office? What was the attraction there? Had it all been a part of Lilka's intelligence-gathering assignment? Or, had Otto been such a lazy hound dog that he couldn't be bothered to prowl the bars of Krakow for some tender Polish morsel? Had Otto even known of Juraslav's existence in Łódź when he began his liaison with Lilka, and how did the distinguished military officer regard him now? Juraslav could not resolve the puzzle easily, but he watched for a hand laid familiarly on a shoulder or a private glance conveying long-ago intimacy that might confirm that these two had been genuine in their affection, and that they now shared the same benevolent feelings toward his budding half-sister. He almost wanted to hear the quiet, tiptoed journey of one lover to the other's room late in the night to give cloture to his doubts. Regrettably, that never occurred. However, Sofie's parents seemed always to view their own planning with due consideration for the possible consequences to Sofie, and so Juraslav was convinced that both had been happy with the result of their unusual romance and that they would continue to negotiate the decisions of Sofie's future as friends.

Each ensuing year, a similar family gathering in Prague had been planned, although Otto was not always able to attend with the others. It had been ten years since they first assembled at the Havlik Clinic; now Sofie traveled south from her university in Berlin rather than accompanying her mother from Krakow. Juraslav marveled at the changes that had molded his half sister during that decade. She had become independent and resourceful but, miraculously, had retained the integrity and good humor of her earlier years. And she was stunning. Juraslav knew that most people lurched into a first impression, propelled mainly by an appreciation of pleasant appearance. Getting over that hurdle often allowed one to move to the next level, where the discovery of merit played out. Sofie must whiz to that mezzanine of evaluation, with nearly every new person she encountered being eager to learn more about the glowing young woman. *It is a gift!* he thought. *May she use it productively in this fast-moving world. She has inherited the best parts of each of her parents and has added her own charisma to the mixture.*

Music had early become a common ground shared by Juraslav and

Sofie during their times together, and they returned often to that common denominator. She listened intently to his guitar renditions of spirited Gypsy themes, and they acknowledged that many musical phrases from the nameless caravans had found new expression in the works of Bach and other celebrated composers. She observed that some of the plaintive Gypsy vocal laments were similar to the blues melodies being produced in America and copied in European cabarets. She was not shy about launching into a Bessie Smith vocal to illustrate her point, and Juraslav was quick to recognize that his little sister had a gift for interpretation and a very worthy voice with which to make her points.

With that background experience, Juraslav had no difficulty understanding Lilka's letter disclosing to him that Sofie had developed a personal attachment to a young German musician. He thought it was equally interesting that each had a Jewish parent, and it helped him to understand that this "secret," in the Germany of 1938, might have made the bond between them more profound. He had awaited Dieter's arrival with keen anticipation, interested and anxious to see the man to whom his complex younger sister had been drawn. Juraslav suspected—correctly so—that a young woman with Sofie's good looks, intelligence, and important connections had a wide circle of male admirers. Still, he did not know what to expect before Dieter materialized at the door of the Havlik Clinic.

He had judged the young man in military uniform to be only slightly older than Sofie, and he noted immediately that there was a gentleness and aesthetic quality about Dieter that belied his role as a fighting man. *Could he even be homosexual?* Juraslav had wondered to himself, but he dismissed the idea because of the obvious affection that flowed silently between the two young people. It was not what he had expected, yet he genuinely liked the young man, and he had learned quickly that Dieter was well read and tasteful. Undoubtedly Sofie had discovered many more positive facets of the young musician, and Juraslav had resolved from the outset to explore them.

The 1938 gathering of the family in Prague was also Lilka's first meeting with her daughter's lover, and Juraslav watched closely to catch some hint of her reaction to Dieter. But, of course, Lilka was the product of many years' training in the field of political intrigue, and she had long ago learned to mask her judgments and feelings behind a façade of pleasantness few could penetrate. He hoped silently that General von Seigler would be so occupied with his duties in Berlin that he would have to skip this year's clandestine family gathering. With one strong personality off the table, it might become easier to evaluate the three visitors who remained under his roof, and he knew that somehow it was important that he understand that human dynamic.

CHAPTER TWENTY-TWO
Prague – Late 1938

NAZI OCCUPATION // DJANGO PLAYS THE TROCADERO

Despite the agreeable intra-family conversations and reminiscences which filled their evenings together, Juraslav's guests became restive after two weeks of virtual confinement within the walls of the Havlik Clinic. One by one, they took short walks down Čiklova to nearby Vyšehrad Park. Lilka strolled to Wenceslas Square to purchase German newspapers, and Juraslav stood by the moving waters of the Vitava River, once again engaging in his favorite metaphor of life. All considered the same enigma: Were they being sought or even watched? Or had the family of General von Seigler been dismissed as unimportant in the process of resolving the unsuccessful Oster attempt upon the führer's life? Nothing they could learn suggested any danger to them, and collectively they longed for an opportunity to change the pace of their time together. Even Sofie and Dieter sensed that their togetherness could be enhanced if it could be projected beyond the comfortable room they shared.

Then it happened. Juraslav raised his glass at dinner one evening and said, "I have news!" They could tell that he was excited, when his normally downturned eyes caught fire and seemed to light all of his gentle face. He reached toward Dieter and Sofie and continued in awed tones, "Django is coming *here!*"

Neither of them understood. They glanced at one another for a sign of recognition, then looked back at Juraslav. "Django Reinhardt—the famous Gypsy guitarist. The greatest artiste in the world!" he offered by way of further explanation.

"You mean the French chap with The Hot Jazz Club?" asked Sofie, searching for a handle to Juraslav's unbridled enthusiasm.

"Yes. He's Belgian, but, yes—that's the one. He has wedded the jazz from the USA to our Gypsy rhythms and produced a whole new sound. His Quintette du Hot Club de France is all the rage in Paris, and they are on a tour of the Continent, which will bring them here to the Trocadero, on Reznika, for a few nights. We can all do with some entertainment and good music to clear our minds from the toxic events around us. So, my dear family, I have booked a table for dinner on Friday. Isn't that grand!!"

Sofie and Dieter knew better than to dampen Juraslav's upbeat moods, so both instinctively reacted with more élan than they really felt. "That will be splendid," Sofie blurted, and Dieter quickly added that he absolutely could not wait to hear Django and his aggregation. Lilka was laughing, and when the others asked why, she informed them that in the Romani language, *django* means, "I am waking up!" Juraslav remembered that Tovar had taught her the rudiments of his Gypsy language, and he could only imagine when it might have been necessary or appropriate for his mother to utter *django*. It was funny, he agreed.

Then Lilka asked if the group also featured a violin, her instrument of choice, and she received Juraslav's fulsome assurances that Stéphane Grappelli commanded "the best jazz violin in the world"—better than Eddie South, or even Stuff Smith. Both comparisons were lost on Lilka, but she feigned the same enthusiasm as the others. After all, just getting outside the clinic for an evening of good music—or *any* music—in the company of upbeat people would raise the spirits of the cloistered household. They were all overdue to "wake up." Even the Polish housegirls seemed to pick up the new mood, and Dieter thought he heard them humming as they went about their evening tasks.

When Friday came, all four dressed well and took a cab from the clinic to the Trocadero, where SRO signs had already been posted at the door. The milling crowd outside was upscale in appearance, and it was a cross-section of ages and nationalities, much as one would encounter at a large-city opera house. Dieter had decided not to wear his ersatz uniform, opting instead for his only suit and a tailored shirt he had borrowed from Juraslav. He was surprised at how well it fit him, and a glance at the mirror before leaving the Clinic assured him that he looked like a successful young Prague professional.

Juraslav was particularly dignified-looking—perfectly turned out in the style of a leading Prague physician. No doubt there would be fellow professionals and probably some of his patients at the Trocadero on a Friday night, and it was fitting that he appear cool and prosperous.

Lilka had touched up her gray roots with henna and, in a rare departure from her usual bland appearance, had applied rouge to her cheeks and color to her broad lips. Even more astounding, she had chosen an evening dress which gave due prominence to her ample bosom, making Dieter slightly uneasy. He realized that Sofie's mother was unintentionally reminding him of the full-figured Renate who dwelled behind the infamous green door on Ruzova. He decided that he much preferred Lilka's normal, unremarkable appearance, even if it made her look older than her sixty-three years.

However, all eyes that evening were justifiably on Sofie, who wore the simplest of straight-line gowns but still managed to look like a matinee idol as she flowed gracefully along the carpeted area under the Trocadero's marquee. Dieter laughed quietly to himself as he recalled the witch with the baneful cane assaulting a border guard on the train from Berlin. Could anyone ever imagine that this was the same person, minus some padding and a wig? Of course not. Even he had difficulty with that connection.

After Dieter expertly lit and enjoyed a cigarette among the growing circle of smokers outside the entrance, the quartet of family members proceeded inside to the well-positioned table reserved for "Dr. Juraslav Havlik & Party." A bottle of champagne, beaded with cold droplets of condensation, rested in a tall silver caddy beside their table, and four crystal flutes stood at attention near individual hors d'oeuvres plates. As they took their seats, Dieter glanced at the adjoining tables and realized that Sofie's entrance had galvanized several observers. How could he have failed to "see" her during those early nights at the Fischerstube? Was it because Miguel had totally muted his interest in women then? He wished he could air all of this with the three persons sitting at that table, but he was afraid that analyzing his emotions might break the spell of his relationship with Sofie, and he knew that he would rather swallow his doubts in silence than risk losing her. Perhaps *that* was the answer he was seeking.

No advance briefing could have prepared them adequately for the artistry of the Quintette du Hot Club de France, and at the end of each selection they joined everyone in the elegant room in prolonged applause, followed by shouted demands for more. Django and the others seemed happy with the favorable reception, and their intensity built with each successive offering, until the singular violinist Stéphane Grappelli finally seized the microphone and pleaded for an intermission to allow them to wet their whistles and stretch their legs. With that, the audience turned its attention to dining, and the metallic sounds of metal utensils on porcelain plates replaced the stirring Gypsy/jazz rhythms.

A few minutes later, a dark-haired older man with intense eyes approached Juraslav from the shadows, and his gnarled, powerful hands gripped each shoulder of the venerable physician. Juraslav looked up and, with a smile of recognition, rose and embraced the older man. Then, lowering his voice to a secretive tone, he said to the stranger, "Gregory, I should like you to meet my mother, Lilka Rudovska, my sister, Sofie, and Sofie's dear friend, Dieter Meister. Dear family, you now have the honor of knowing Gregory Kweik. I believe you will recognize his name."

Lilka extended her hand and smiled. "We have met before, Gregory. I am pleased to see you looking well after so many years. I am grateful for your assistance and also that of your son, Michael, to my Tovar as well as my Juraslav. You two have recognized and rewarded their loyalty to your family, as you once promised."

The former king of the Gypsies bared perfect, white teeth in a broad smile and said, "Mlle. Rudovska, if you have changed in a quarter century, it has been only for the better. Are you still the consummate violin virtuoso that our Tovar brought to Sanok when you were courting?" Without waiting for a response or even permitting one —as befits a true king—Gregory continued. "I would like to introduce all of you to Django and Stéphane. They are transiting Bohemia under the aegis of my son, Michael, and they enjoy the oversight, protection, and courtesy of all our Romani people in the region."

At the lightest clap of Gregory's hands, an assistant stepped forward and bent his ear to the old Gypsy's lips, then scurried off toward a small alcove on the far side of the large dining room. A few minutes passed, then the assistant returned, followed by the best guitarist and the finest violinist in the entire world. By now, Juraslav's guests needed no convincing that those superlatives had been truly earned, and the level of excitement they had feigned days before had been replaced by the real thing.

Musicians everywhere share a language the tin-eared world can never decipher, and the six people surrounding the Gypsy king soon entered that private domain together, commenting upon composers, performers, their instruments, and their art form. Dieter learned that Django's left hand had been severely burned in a fire years before, and as a result he could use only two fingers to create the array of intricate chords and solo performances of his art. That made him the more remarkable to the cognoscenti.

Stéphane and Sofie seemed drawn to one another, and he elaborated upon the history of his rare Stradivarius violin and his conversion from classical violinist to jazz icon. She told him of her vocal training and occasional public performances and the close link she felt to many of the great jazz singers in America and Europe. Would she consent to performing one number with the group during their last set of the evening? Did she know the work of the American composer, Cole Porter? The group had recently recorded his "Night and Day" as a jazz ballad, and Stéphane had arranged it so that the group's occasional vocalist, Jean Sablon, could perform it. Sofie, never shy about music, agreed that she would step before the microphone and deliver the plaintive lyric. She was already wondering how the whispered, deep style of Marlene Dietrich would fit with the melody and how it would be received by the many Germans in attendance. Stéphane was thoroughly amused by the prospect and said he felt confident they could pull it off without the benefit of even one rehearsal. Perhaps it would be even better that way, as spontaneous performances frequently were.

The Quintette du Hot Club de France continued to delight their international audience for another hour, playing several of their recording hits, including "Honeysuckle Rose," "Billets Doux," "Sweet Georgia Brown," and "The Lambeth Walk." Sofie had excused herself from the table, and Dieter suspected she had gone outside the room to practice some scales and warm up her best Marlene Dietrich voice. Then, with the end of the evening drawing near, the dapper Grappelli raised his hand to quiet the overly enthusiastic audience.

"We are going to give one of our 1938 waxings a different treatment tonight with the assistance of a young friend in the audience. Her name is Sofie Havlik, and she has consented to sing Cole Porter's wonderful ballad entitled "Night and Day" from his New York musical *The Gay Divorcee*. The song was first sung on the Broadway stage by the dancer Fred Astaire—who should never give up his dancing in favor of singing—but the composition has succeeded, notwithstanding that beginning." Laughter erupted; apparently the audience agreed with him. "Mr. Porter has said that Islamic calls to evening prayers, which he heard in Morocco, inspired the melody, but tonight, for the first time anywhere, you will hear it in the style of Marlene Dietrich in *The Blue Angel*. Let me add that our young friend has never worked with the Quintette before tonight, and we have not rehearsed this song together. Please welcome Sofie Havlik—a young woman of great courage." Light applause greeted the announcement.

Dieter might have been very nervous about Sofie's bold move except for the fact that he had previously been terrified that she was about to be introduced as Sofie von Seigler to a room peppered with German functionaries. When that didn't happen, he relaxed so completely that her appearance before a sophisticated audience did not faze him. However, Juraslav and Lilka were stone-faced as Sofie stepped to Stéphane's side and acknowledged his introduction. They had never heard her sing in public, as Dieter often had, and they could not have known the extent of her confidence or professionalism when she took on the identity of a vocal star.

Django set a slow and deliberate rhythm, softly quieting the audience. Then, Stéphane delivered a spare and compelling chorus, limiting himself to the rich lower register of his formidable Strad. Finally Sofie moved to center stage, with a lock of her hair dangled over one hooded eye in the style of Dietrich, and launched a butter-soft voice that Dieter had never heard before. Sofie at first caressed each note exactly as Porter had placed it on the music sheet, then she slowly added passion and more rough-edged tones to her delivery until she became Dietrich for her audience. Django had been prepared to cut the amateur off after 32 bars, but, instead, he rose from his chair and signaled her to explore wherever she wished in her treatment of the beautiful song. As the very best musicians can do, the Quintette bolstered each of her successive approaches to the great standard with imagination, finally allowing her to trail off to the dulcet tones with which she had begun.

Dr. Juraslav Havlik and his guests were exhausted, and only the impassive Lilka lacked a tear-track leading downward from the corner of an eye. The rest of the room exploded with appreciation, and even the Quintette set down their instruments to stand and applaud their new friend. Finally, the smiling Stéphane quieted the room. "I think we are as surprised and pleased as you all are," he quipped. "This kind of magic doesn't often happen without many hours of preparation, and I must tell you that we have all enjoyed a remarkable new talent here tonight. So, Sofie, please let me extend an open invitation during our stay here at the Trocadero. Please come by any evenings when you can do so, and let's see what other pages from our songbook you can decorate with your lovely presence." Loud applause and shouts of *encore!* greeted the musician's proposition.

When the audience seemed determined to hear at least one more song from Sofie, Django and Stéphane huddled with her briefly, and Dieter could see her shake her head affirmatively. Then she took the microphone from Stéphane and addressed the room in German:

"I am overwhelmed to have had the chance to perform with these five gentlemen. Just to listen to them would have been unforgettable, but to actually craft a song with their backing exceeds this girl's most unreasonable dreams. Now, it is getting late for all of us, but you have asked for one last song from me. I would like to dedicate it to my wonderful friend Dieter, who is an admirer of the chanteuse Josephine Baker. I will give you my interpretation of Miss Baker singing "Sleepy Time Gal." Thank you, Hot Club Quintette, for this opportunity, and thank you, Trocadero audience, for receiving me so graciously."

Stéphane and Django looked at one another with puzzlement in their eyes, and the Gypsy pondered, "This is an amateur? *Sacre bleu,* Grappelli—she is more suave than even *you!* Old Gregory has mined a nugget!" Stéphane nodded in quiet agreement, and they set the tempo for "Sleepy Time Gal," confident that the young singer would lead them all on a tour of Josephine Baker.

Dieter hoped that this time she would keep her clothing on—which, of course, she did—but somehow the versatile vocalist managed to convey all of Josephine's lusty message, much as she had once done in the great room at 80 Wilhelmstrasse. This time Dieter was able to enjoy the delivery with no overt worry about the possible untimely arrival of Lieutenant Klaus Kolb. He saw that Lilka's eyes had finally clouded over with a few unmanaged tears of pride, while Juraslav was looking directly at him, probably wondering how an insignificant musician like Dieter had qualified for the devotion of his sister. Finally, Dieter glanced at a table across the room where the king of the Gypsies sat transfixed. It had been an evening Dieter would never forget, and possibly the high point of his and Sofie's romance.

Once they were outside the Trocadero in the late-night stillness, the family group was also quiet, almost as if each was reviewing the splendid evening in hopes of discovering the magic that had propelled them. Dieter was the first to break the silence as he asked Sofie how she felt.

"Much as Cinderella at 11:50 p.m., I would imagine," she smiled. "Do you think I did justice to the opportunity they gave me, schotze?"

"You did! They weren't expecting anything more than a few laughs, and instead you became an important part of the evening's success. I'm certain that some people in that audience will be inquiring whether you'll appear again.

"Do you think I dare contact them to see if they were sincere? Or is it just out of the question to be appearing in public when hostile people are looking for us? Maybe we already crossed that line tonight. It isn't fair to have to pass up a career breakthrough because of some past history that has no bearing on my ability to sing and entertain. I hate that!"

Juraslav held up his hand to quiet her, then he smiled and became more deliberative, as he imagined a big brother should be under the circumstances. "Sofie, it is my experience that important decisions must not be rushed or made while emotions are so high. We should all enjoy this evening's events a bit longer and then, weighing all that's involved, try to find a way to grasp the apparent opportunity without endangering the close circle of your family and friends. What do you say?"

"Of course you are right. And I love you for understanding and caring," Sofie returned, adding a squeeze of his hand and placing a tender kiss on his cheek. "We'll take a fresh look at this tomorrow."

Strangely, Juraslav could not remember being the recipient of any similar show of affection from a female since the young mother of his impetigo patient had abruptly switched from animosity to appreciation. He wished silently that Lilka could escape from her rigid political mold and hug him like a mother, but that barrier had not been breached since their earliest days together.

"Mama, you were really skillful in your exchange with Gregory. He usually intimidates people with his glowering brow and dazzling smile. They send conflicting messages and people don't know which to believe, so they hesitate to engage with him. Perhaps that helped him to become king, no?"

"No!" the older woman responded. "He became king because he was willing to sell out his people's privacy to the gadje tax collector in exchange for a useless title and a small cut of the proceeds. It was not an honorable exchange, in my view, but certainly not unusual for an ambitious political leader. Very few of them die poor, Jura. Nonetheless, he *has* kept his promises to Tovar and to you, and for that I am grateful."

Dieter did not wish to fracture the ongoing joy of the evening, but he posed a question that had exactly that result. "What will become of our Gypsy population, Juraslav? Are the caravans going to be safe here, or will the new German-dominated government take the same attitude as it has back home?"

Juraslav seemed unusually dour, even for him, as he formulated his response. "Dieter, it is going to be dangerous anywhere the New German Order spreads itself. Nazi leadership has openly declared that Gypsies will have *no* standing within their new class structure. They will be pursued, tortured, neutered, and violated until they either depart voluntarily or perish. The Romani people are as surely on the chopping block as are Jews and homosexuals, and, in time, all of those people will be betrayed by persons close to them. I choose to remain here as a physician because I have taken an oath to heal and have made a promise to share the benefits of my education with my Gypsy cousins, much as my father, Tovar, did. But, with my ethnic profile, I should have departed for Africa or South America long ago."

Lilka opted to join the discussion. "We in Poland are trapped in a vise. The Germans, to our west, are treacherous, as you say, Jura. But, the Russians, to our east, are animals! They eat their own young and spit them into mass graves to rot in the first sunlight. Those two decadent cultures will meet and decide how to carve up the best of Poland, and then they will turn on one another ferociously. Animals! Mark my words. I have watched this simmering for years, and it is nearing a tragic boiling point. I have learned how to survive in the crosscurrents, but none of you should *ever* return to Poland, for there is a good chance you would die there."

Juraslav was again imagining his mother intimate with the young German officer, and he mentally added "survival" to the list of explanations he had compiled earlier. Perhaps sleeping with the enemy was one good way to remain a step ahead of the scythe, no matter which villain wielded it. If the strategy had served to protect Lilka and had also produced Sofie as a dividend, it may have earned Juraslav's grudging approval—at least a small measure of it.

As the jubilant party, now grown silent, neared the clinic, there was a stronger sense of family unity than before. Sofie snuggled closer to Dieter and Lilka held her son's hand between both of hers. "We must all be alert to events and persons around us," the older woman observed. "Trouble may come in many forms. I don't believe that the Oster matter will go away until an example is made, and, while we had no part in it, each of us is at risk when retaliation begins." Dieter wondered whether this observation reflected some specific danger which Lilka had perceived or if it was just the paranoiac reaction of someone who had spent too many years working in the ugly basements of political intrigue and betrayal. He would be alert, of course, but he must also do his best to create a useful existence for himself—possibly even including the incredible Sofie.

CHAPTER TWENTY-THREE
Prague – Late 1938

AN EXCITING PARTNERSHIP

Sofie and Dieter strolled slowly through central Prague and took in the many attractive vistas, stopping to examine the display windows of the more chic clothing stores. They both knew that their destination, the Majestic Plaza Hotel, might prove to be a source of opportunity they could celebrate but could just as easily disappoint them. Dieter hoped that it would be the former; he loved it when Sofie was happy and inclined to dance about in their shared room, humming songs and being her most tactile self. At those times, it was easiest to forget the growing uneasiness of German domination in the Czech capital city. Dieter thought he should try to cushion possible disappointment by acknowledging the unlikely possibility of Sofie's future appearances at the Trocadero. He smiled at her.

"You understand, don't you, that there could be reasons why the Quintette can't offer you the chance to sing with them again? There are contracts that limit the ability of performing groups to alter the makeup of their personnel or the way they organize their shows. Owners must have these clauses, or big names could shortchange them easily and ruin reputations. The performers move on, but the establishments—like the Trocadero—are fixed in a community, and they must hold to a standard or risk losing patrons."

"You don't think Stéphane and Django will let me sing again?" Sofie shot back. "Are you protecting me, Dieter? Am I a silly girl who imagined that she was appreciated by a room full of music lovers and a renowned jazz group? You must be honest with me."

"Sofie, this is beyond my experience. I am the product of a cloistered music school, and I have experience only at weddings, socials, and in a beer cellar. You are a true talent, but I don't know the rules—perhaps talent is only a part of the total equation. We shall learn together. Come—let's stop straying and get to the hotel and test the water. I am with you and I love you." The words had surprised him; they had seemed so natural as they escaped from his unconscious mind into his conversation. There it was. There it was!

Sofie's eyes twinkled their brightest. She squeezed his hand and said only, "So you do, Dieter. You love me."

They walked the rest of the way along Reznika in silence, finally mounting the steps to the array of polished brass marking the hotel's elegant entrance. Inside there was activity everywhere, with well-dressed people engaged in knots of conversation all across the lobby area. They paused only once to smooth hair and pick imaginary lint from their best clothing, then they presented themselves at the counter identified with a discreet brass pyramidal marker reading *MANAGER*. Behind the counter, a well-groomed man in an expensive suit did his best not to look at the young couple until it was obvious that they were not turning away. Then he looked at them over the top rim of his half glasses and said, "Is zere something I can do to assist you?"

Sofie detected the German accent and immediately responded in her most formal German. She said that she was friendly with Messrs. Reinhardt and Grappelli from Paris and wished to leave an envelope which would surely be delivered to them at the earliest possible time. She extended the envelope toward the man, and in the process focused her eyes on his, projecting much more confidence than she really felt. Dieter knew that Sofie was acting a part—he didn't recognize the character, but by now was familiar with the technique. Then it struck him: she was General Otto von Seigler, and there should be no questioning of her instruction. It had the desired result, as the man nodded obsequiously, diverting his eyes and saying simply, "Of course."

A moment later, his demeanor changed totally. A broad smile broke down the barriers in his expression, and again he said, "Of course!" Then he changed to familiar German, as if speaking to a close friend. "Of course!! You were the chanteuse who joined our guests at the Trocadero. I was there, Fräulein. The audience loved your Dietrich as well as your Josephine Baker. I hope that you are coming to say that you will sing with them again. I, for one, would enjoy hearing more of your renditions. It is a pity that you cannot perform here at the Majestic Plaza. I have been invaded by German businessmen, military officers, and politicians. They have taken our best rooms, they book our best tables, and they want us to be a copy of the best Berlin hotels. Alas, they also want to listen to German music during the cocktail hour, and we have not lived up to their expectation in that area. I need exactly the talent you displayed at the Troc."

Dieter again looked at the locked Steinway grand piano, which he had first noticed on his arrival in Prague. It was draped with a velvet cloak, and a stack of dinner menus had been deposited atop the closed cover. He remembered daydreaming about Sofie and him fashioning cocktail-hour ambience there, and he wondered whether that might really be a possibility. *The door is opened—step through!* He cleared his throat, but unlike Sofie, he had no commanding spirit to shape his words, so they spilled out as one might expect from a 27-year old piano player. "Sir, we *do* work together and have a repertoire which might fit your need. Would you ever consider an audition? We could provide background for the hotel guests at tea or during the cocktail hour, and you can assess the reaction. I can even tune your piano, if it needs attention."

"Dieter, you are getting ahead of yourself," Sofie interrupted. "My only purpose is to sing again with the Quintette while they are in the city. I haven't thought about applying for work. Perhaps another day we can address that." She turned her attention to the interested man behind the counter and thanked him for delivering her letter, deftly slipping a British pound note across the counter before retreating toward the brass entry doors. Once outside, she turned to face him and scolded, "You seem to forget that we are fugitives in this city. We can't just solicit for a job in a public place without exercising some caution. We need proper papers and we must determine in advance who we are—are we British, or Danish or what? How come you aren't in the German army? What language is our first? My God, Dieter—you would be uncloaked in the first week. I don't want you dragged back to Berlin to be introduced to the Oster Inquiry as the Jew who sleeps with General von Seigler's daughter. Let's tighten up, or we'll all be in trouble."

It was the first time Dieter had seen Sofie's coarse side, and even though he knew she was correct, he had been shocked by the directness in her voice. This was not the pliant young woman who shaped her body to fit next to his on the feather mattress of their lair at the clinic. No, this was the daughter of a general and of an intelligence agent, who knew instinctively the threats around her and who did not suffer fools to endanger her or those she loved. Certainly it was not a facet of Sofie that would nourish his newfound libido, he mused. They walked quietly back to the clinic, where Dieter excused himself and perused one of Lilka's German newspapers in a quiet corner of the sitting room. After an hour of that isolation, Juraslav approached him to inquire whether Dieter was feeling ill.

"No—just a bit tired, I think," was the half-hearted reply. Dieter looked up at the older man and saw that there was real concern in his expression, so he augmented the thought. "Sofie and I disagreed on something earlier. I was wrong, and I am contrite about it. She didn't hesitate to straighten me out on my error, but still it makes me unhappy that I disappointed her." Juraslav's arm went around Dieter's shoulder in a comforting gesture and he smiled in acknowledgment of the indecipherability of women's moods. It was the first time since his arrival at the clinic that Dieter felt close to the quiet doctor, and after a few minutes he realized that his anxiety had passed. Was there something that reminded him of Miguel's benevolent smiles? Perhaps.

A bellman from the Majestic Plaza Hotel delivered the small packet to the clinic. There were four tickets for each of the remaining evening performances at the Trocadero, and a dozen cheat sheets for chords and lyrics from the Quintette's songbook. Sofie could not restrain her euphoria, so she postured and glided about the dining room affecting dramatic poses, to everyone's amusement. Then she said excitedly to Dieter, "Schotze, we must find a piano and work through at least five or six of these. I don't want to scale out of my true range, and I want to think of the best style in which to portray each. Oh, gosh. I'm sooo excited I could split in two." It was a character out of some motion picture Dieter remembered dimly. He could not immediately name her, but in time it would come to him, he thought.

"There's a music store on Ruzova—beyond the Porte Verte," interjected Magda, one of the two Polish housegirls who had been observing Sofie's excited outbursts. "We used to go there to listen to records and try sheet music when things were slow." Dieter choked on the coffee he was drinking. Magda continued. "You didn't know that? Elsa and I were hostesses there for a year before Dr. Havlik bought our contracts and moved us out of that place. How old were we, Elsa—sixteen? We ran away from home in Gdansk to see Europe and when we were out of money, and hungry, the Porte Verte gave us a place to live as long as we were willing to mix with any drunk German soldier who wandered in. It was fun at first, but a few black eyes and bruised arms cured that. Dr. Havlik keeps all of the working ladies healthy and checks for syphilis and other things. He doesn't charge for his work, and he buys back the debts of Gypsy runaways and others who are too young to be there. He's an angel."

Dieter suddenly felt lightheaded as he realized that his first day's adventure in Prague was there on Ruzova and could easily have involved one of Juraslav's patients. The presence of the Polish housegirls had never been explained before, and now it made sense to him. If Sofie reacted to his indiscretion of talking to the hotel manager as he had, how might she have bristled at his visit to the neighborhood brothel? He had to say something, so he asked the Polish girls, "Is there a piano in a practice room at the music store? Could we try out some songs there?" They assured him many people did so, and the subject was closed. He wondered whether the girls ever got together with their former co-workers and if they ever talked about the soldiers who ambled into the place. Sofie was correct; he had to be considerably more cautious and circumspect or risk unacceptable consequences.

Sofie appeared with Django and the Quintette du Hot Club de France on half a dozen evenings before their tour moved on to Vienna, and with each appearance her professionalism seemed to attain new dimensions. The group quickly adapted to her style, and there was genuine amusement on stage at the young woman's versatility. Audiences applauded her enthusiastically, and the Trocadero even added a small banner below the Quintette's poster announcing, "This week only—song stylist *SOPHIA* will perform at the 10 p.m. show."

Dieter attended each of those late-evening performances, occupying a small table well removed from the stage so that his presence wouldn't distract Sofie. However, he was certain that once she grasped the microphone and closed her eyes, all possible diversions were dismissed, and the music owned her. She was scheduled to sing three songs during the late set, but prolonged applause and shouts of "encore!" yielded a fourth and sometimes even a fifth number before she stepped down. Each evening she carried a snifter of cognac onto the stage and placed it strategically near the guitar and violin cases. After each song she let a healthy gulp of the warm liquid slide over her throat, and it seemed to Dieter that the quality of her voice improved as the snifter's content diminished. So also, her body movements became more fluid and suggestive after a little cognac, and there was no doubt that her audiences and her fellow musicians also noted that and pressed her to reach further in her interpretations. Dieter knew he was jealous that so many people were suddenly sharing the mysteries of Sofie that had been exclusively his before the Quintette arrived in Prague.

When she did finally step from the stage to join him at the table, Sofie wanted to talk about each song and solicit Dieter's suggestions as to how she might improve her delivery. And then, there were the people. Gentlemen walked inconspicuously to the table and whispered words of appreciation for her performance. Dieter suspected that many of them wanted only to see the young songstress at arms' length, with the low lights of the room reflecting the slight moistness on her bare shoulders and her deep-cut dress revealing a little too much. They lingered beyond the time needed for their ostensible purpose, and most were led back to their tables by women who had been left sitting alone next to empty chairs. Dieter wondered whether they even noticed him sitting across from "Sophia." *Yes,* he thought, *I am jealous that she has so much talent, and I must expect that there will be many admirers if it continues to be displayed. How long will it be . . . ?*

Sofie interrupted his thoughts. "Did you recognize the manager from the Majestic Plaza, Dieter? He has been here twice, and tonight he sent his card with a note to Django, asking if I am going on to Vienna. I believe that he is interested in talking about—you know—singing during the pre-dinner time at the hotel. Would that be something we should consider? You were intrigued earlier, and I snapped at you. But, if it were done right, we could add interest to our time here. I am now 'Sophia, the song stylist,' and you are my accompanist. We can do German, French, and American songs—things people can't hear in most Prague nightclubs and restaurants. Shall we ask Lilka and Jura what they would advise? I know that I was the one who said we had to be smart about risks—but now I'm torn. Help me."

Dieter knew that the opinions of the others would be guarded, but that they might find it hard to resist Sofie's enthusiasm if she launched it in support of the idea. So, what was the alternative? Continue to hide within the clinic until . . . until what? If Mr. Chamberlain was correct and the political tensions of Europe had now been diminished, perhaps they could begin to be part of the exciting new order of 1938. Working at a luxury hotel in this lovely city certainly offered more excitement and opportunity than banging out songs in a beer cellar, and sharing the excitement with Sofie could lead . . . who knows where? He smiled back at Sofie and said, "If he offers us the chance to work together at the Majestic, I believe we should try to write a letter of agreement, setting out our weekly time commitment and the professional fee for our performances. We must have the option to approve any publicity the hotel posts, and we should open a bank account with a professional name and have drafts from the hotel deposited directly there. That way we can avoid most of the curiosity that could expose us."

"We could also change our appearance a bit, you know," she offered with obvious enthusiasm. I could lighten my hair and pile it high atop my head, and you could grow a moustache and part your hair down the middle like a Frenchie. I could even wear a wedding ring to suggest . . . " The thought had the wrong effect. "To make me appear older and more professional, you know. We wouldn't actually say anything, just let them reach their own conclusions. What do you think, Dieter?"

"I wonder if it would be useful to discuss this with Gregory Kweik. He seems to have contacts throughout the city, and there could be considerations beyond those we have identified. Besides, if we are out there in public at the Majestic, he may have Gypsy taxi drivers or cooks or bellmen or maids where we are working. I would feel much safer having someone listening if ever we must call for help. Besides, it was the Gypsy king who put you on stage in the first place, and he could no doubt foresee, even then, where it might lead—*n'est-ce pas?*"

"Oh—you are already a Frenchie!" she laughed, and the warmth of her reaction washed over him, convincing him that they could truly proceed with the idea of becoming a musical duet at the Majestic Palace. Still, he resolved to access the insight of the king of the Gypsies, someone forced long ago to consider the threats inherent in being different, and someone experienced at survival in a hostile world. He wondered to himself whether even the celebrated Django could have enjoyed his two weeks of celebrity in occupied Prague without the blessings of the king. It would provide valuable information and something of an insurance policy to consult Gregory, and Dieter resolved to ask for Juraslav's help in arranging such a conversation.

"We should go home now and end this nice evening with a proper flourish," the happy Sofie suggested. No, it was more than a suggestion— it was a promise of the superb chemistry that could flow between them and erase all doubts and troubles. It was why Dieter was in Prague and willing to take substantial risks to be a part of Sofie's expanding ambitions. It was why he no longer awoke in the night thinking of Miguel.

CHAPTER TWENTY-FOUR
Prague – Winter 1938/39

NOW APPEARING AT THE MAJESTIC PLAZA

"We must all learn how to continue our lives within the conditions forced upon us by circumstances beyond our control," pontificated the Gypsy king. "The blind man must still savor his favorite stew, and, in fact, the aroma and taste may become even more compelling because he is deprived of the privilege of viewing it in the pot. Do you think for a moment that Gypsies forfeit the pleasures of falling in love just because gadjes are intent upon driving them from their midst? Or, do you think that Jewish businessmen forget to count their profits when hostile eyes are fixed upon their places of business? You are young and talented musicians who are living in troubled times—that is certain—but do you believe for even a moment that abandoning your talent would diminish the threats you perceive? Hiding in plain sight can sometimes be even more useful than cringing in the shadows. Our oppressors shine their torches into the shadows when they are seeking us, and they know instinctively that the dirty work they do in the dark only serves to spread fear of them.

"You saw at the Trocadero that a musical group aggregating two Gypsies and three Frenchmen earned the applause of an audience which was packed with German military, diplomatic, and business people. In fact, they all paid a good price to eat food prepared by a Gypsy chef, washed down with wines grown by Frenchies while they listened to Gypsy guitars—and, of course, to a Polish Jew singer. How strange is that, I ask you? Well, the answer is that it is not rare at all. The strong winds that create angry waves on the surface seldom roil the ocean beds beneath. Even Nazis have families and take vacations and study the classics and seek out culture and entertainment and have doubts and fears about the fragility of our existence.

"Back in Berlin, you could be singled out, apprehended, and interrogated because you are a part of the puzzle of the Oster Conspiracy—oh, yes, I know all about that. You could even be instrumental in slipping a noose around the neck of General von Seigler because of your ethnic identities and the unfavorable light that may cast upon his motives. This is not a good time to return there. But you tell me that you have not been detected during your flight to Prague, and now you are immersed in a city of one million people who have come together from many cultures. You are part of a family group that owns and administers the business of a respected medical clinic, which has been in operation for many years. You are Sophia and Dieter Havlik, hiding in plain sight. What do you say?"

Dieter asked Michael if he knew of a source of credible identity documents to authenticate those two newly created citizens and in return for his inquiry got a broad, flashing smile which assured him that the Gypsy king knew the best forgers in all of Czechoslovakia. "Before we produce them, let's change your appearance slightly—are you to be cousins, siblings, or spouses?" he asked.

"I think we should be spouses," Sofie shot back. "We are affectionate sometimes without realizing it, and neither cousins nor siblings act that way. Besides, a marriage certificate plus a birth certificate would allow us both to be Catholics on paper, and that could take us out of danger if we are questioned. Do you agree, Dieter?"

Dieter knew he must agree or have a fulsome explanation for disagreeing, and so he merely nodded and, with that minimal gesture, became a "married man" after two decades of homosexuality. It amused him to consider it, but again he thought better of treating the serious subject with too much levity. "Would that make it more dangerous for Sofie?" he queried. "Because I would not want to deprive her of any protection she may enjoy because of her father's respected position." It was a thoughtful offer but one which was instantly shrugged away by the old Gypsy, who reminded them that one of the few institutions not being assaulted by the Nazi government was the institution of marriage—

particularly if blessed by the Holy Mother Church. He reminded them that it was all part of a disguise and not a real marriage, but with a sly wink he suggested that they make every effort to be convincing in their roles. Finally there was laughter in the group, and they raised their glasses to salute the occasion.

Juraslav and Lilka seemed convinced that the temporary solution would earn all of them additional time to monitor events and would divert attention from the young houseguests who otherwise had no logical explanation for their extended presence in Prague. They could be convincing as a young married couple, both of whom had chosen a career in music. Lilka would be returning to her duties in Poland soon, and the guise of a family reunion would swiftly lose credibility, but as an ostensible couple pursuing their careers in entertainment, Sofie—now "Sophia"—and Dieter would seem genuine. And, perhaps most comforting, with the oversight of the Gypsy king there would be help nearby and skilled eyes watching for signs of danger.

Joseph Goebbels stopped German periodicals, newspapers, newsreels, and radio from providing any further reports on the Oster Conspiracy. Colonel Oster was not detained any longer, and although there were several resignations from officers in high command positions, there were not yet any formal proceedings aimed at removing them from office. The führer complained about "cowardice" among his generals, saying that he should not have to "drive them to war," but his focus had clearly shifted to completing the domination of Czechoslovakia and making further inroads into Poland. Certainly these exploits should not have to share headline space with coverage of a cabal of officers intent upon eliminating their leader. He was to be glorified, and there should be no scintilla of evidence before the public that anyone of high station would question Hitler's value in the process of elevating Germany and true Germans. Career officers understood that this was a temporary calm in the storm—that, beneath the surface, Gestapo investigations would continue, and in time there would be retribution for disloyalty.

General Otto von Seigler was informed that the investigation into his possible complicity had established that there was none, therefore he was eligible to be returned to active duty in his former Wehrmacht capacity. Reichsmarschall Hermann Göring called personally to congratulate his friend Otto and to assure him that there had never been any doubt in his mind of this outcome. The conversation was a brief one, steeped in cordiality but ending with an afterthought. "Otto," queried the Reichsmarschall, "do you recall that I provided you with a note of safe passage when this whole thing was being blown out of proportion?"

The answer was affirmative, and Göring continued, "Well, do you know whether Sofie ever used that letter in her travels?"

"No, Hermann, I don't believe she has needed it, and naturally she would have contacted me if she had done so. It is probably in her possession still. Should it be returned—or destroyed—or what?"

"Unfortunately, such endorsements sometimes take on greater value than is intended, and so I try to make them date-specific and person-specific to avoid their misuse. I did not do that in this case. Not that Sofie would abuse my office intentionally . . . but if the letter were misplaced and fell into other hands . . . well, you understand. Perhaps you can mention the subject to her and even recover the letter and return it to my office. By the way, where is Sofie? I understand that she has discontinued her class schedule. I hope she's not ill, eh?"

"Oh, she is quite well, thank you. She wanted to take a little time off—an affair of the heart, you know—and thought that the late autumn would be the best time for that. I believe she is in the mountains with friends. I'll make a note to discuss this with her."

"Ah, good, my friend. Our children don't seem to remember things as we do, and an occasional gentle reminder helps them to be more dependable citizens. When you two do talk, please extend my fond wishes, and tell her that I still remember the lovely Gershwin ballad she performed for all of us when our American aviator friend came to town. She is a most charming young woman, and you are to be congratulated on her achieving that without a role-model mother hovering over her. An affair of the heart, you say . . . is she entering or leaving a relationship, Otto?"

"Alas, Hermann, she is her father's daughter, and there are too many 'enterings' and 'leavings' for me to stay current. I seem to recall that this time it is about a new relationship, and so—it would be an 'entering.' Were we ever so mobile with our affections?"

"Not unless the opportunity was there," the Reichsmarschall replied and concluded the interview with a roar of laughter that seemed, to Otto, to be too hearty for the words just spoken. A general's well-tuned instincts told him that the Oster Conspiracy was not buried so far below the surface as everyone now represented. More likely, the offended führer was merely lulling the conspirators into false security and waiting for an unguarded time to resume his efforts to punish them. Otto resolved to be very cautious and to warn his family to be likewise.

Each of the broad columns supporting the high ceiling of the Majestic Plaza's lobby had a glass-enclosed bulletin board where current events and attractions were communicated to guests and visitors. Late on a Sunday night, the hotel staff member who oversaw those announcements began placing a new poster on each bulletin board. The posters showed a headshot of an alluring young woman with her hair piled in random curls and her bare shoulders hinting of compelling femininity hidden just below the bottom border of the picture. The caption atop the photo announced:

Sophia

NIGHTLY

FROM SIX UNTIL EIGHT O'CLOCK

APPEARING IN OUR INTERNATIONAL LOUNGE

THE MAJESTIC PLAZA WILL FEATURE
CAPTIVATING VOCALIST

We Are Pleased That This Versatile
Singer Who Recently Delighted
Prague Audiences

Performing With The Famous

**DJANGO REINHARDT AND HIS
QUINTETTE DU HOT CLUB DE FRANCE**

Will Be Singing Exclusively For Guests
And Visitors Of The Majestic Plaza Hotel

*A special dinner menu will be
featured after each performance.*

Dieter examined several of the bulletin boards, as if the message might vary from one to the other, but he really wanted to process the content over and over until it sank in. They were really going to be able to test their offerings before the sophisticated patrons of a world-class hotel. They were going to be paid generously for the exclusive booking, even though the initial contract was for only three weeks. That should be time enough to determine whether they could work successfully as a team, whether they were good enough to attract guests into the International Lounge and cause them to tarry over an early evening drink before proceeding to dinner.

That had been the manager's concern: How could he capture more of the dinner crowd which assembled nightly in his lobby before proceeding to other Prague restaurants where they spent impressive sums on food and libations? If Sophia could seduce them into his cocktail arena, the maître d' might then approach patrons quietly with the invitation to consider remaining at the hotel for a special dining treat. The manager promised that, if there were more food and drink covers due to Sophia, her contract would be extended and the appearance fee renegotiated upward. A new star who could impact his revenues favorably would be well worth the investment, and he had already seen her magnetism at work in the Trocadero.

Juraslav had taken Sofie to an exclusive Reznika designer, known for haute couture among Prague's most glamorous women, and there she was fitted for half a dozen flattering dresses suitable for the early evening. It was his contribution to his half sister's new career, and Dieter agreed that the gowns were well worth their excessive cost. It was not only that they made Sofie look incredibly regal, but even more that they seemed to provide a boost to her confidence. When she slipped into each, there was a look of assurance in the product, and Dieter knew that the message would project into the room.

Next was the question of whether the patrons of the Majestic Plaza could be lured into changing their evening routines, adding a stop at the

International Lounge. The manager decided that Sofie's performance should begin with the tall doors opened and speakers in the main lobby subtly reproducing the sounds from inside the lounge. He mulled over the notion of not charging for attending patrons' first drink, but then concluded that such a gesture might cheapen what he hoped would be viewed as a very elegant performance. Instead, he proposed a champagne toast—on the house—for the re-opening of the once-popular International Lounge.

He placed a standing order for fresh flowers nightly on all of the room's fifty tables and brought in a lighting designer to highlight the performer's stage in a flattering hue. It even allowed the spotlight attendant to follow her as she moved through the room, in a style recently made popular in the cabarets of Paris and Berlin. Finally, he had the Steinway concert grand piano tuned and its surface buffed to an ebony luster so that it shone in the muted light. The room was attended by a dozen of his best waiters and four experienced bartenders, and it was ready to live up to its newly created claim of being "the place to be seen" in the early evenings of bustling Prague.

On their first night, Dieter sat at the piano in the empty room without touching the keyboard for nearly a minute. Then he began softly with a waltz from Chopin which allowed him to hear the refractory echoes from the walls and ceiling, all of which seemed to add to the richness of the fine instrument. The waiters stood at their stations quietly, listening to the beautiful melody as if it were being created only for them. A couple looked in and as quickly departed, then a second pair of guests stepped inside and stood listening to the classic piece. They were joined by two more friends who were more interested in chatting, and then the sound of bold laughter from one of the men changed the atmosphere. Dieter took it as his cue to switch the tempo, and the Chopin waltz morphed into a familiar German song, which elicited approval from the four, who decided to sing along.

The distinguished Dr. Havlik, in crisp evening wear, moved to a visible table, accompanied by four colleagues from the medical community. Then a barely recognizable Michael Kweik with a party of his most attractive caravan dwellers filled two of the tables nearest to the entry. In their wake, half a dozen curious dinner-goers ventured through the doors, where an attentive waiter directed them to a candlelit table and an ice bucket holding Möet & Chandon champagne, recently arrived from Épernay, France. It was on the house this evening, he assured them. The lure proved irresistible, and they settled in with the free bubbly to await the featured performer.

Within the next fifteen minutes, a combination of persuasive waiters, the hint of piano music drifting into the main lobby, and the active manager charming several of the hotel's well-dressed patrons aggregated a suitably sized audience, all enjoying their complimentary champagne—some already requesting a second bottle and receiving it with due deference. It was half an hour past the advertised opening time, and Sophia's entry could not be delayed further, so the manager strode confidently to the center of the International Lounge and tapped on the open microphone until he had everyone's attention. Then he began:

"Good evening, ladies and gentlemen, and welcome to the re-opening of the Majestic Plaza's International Lounge. I believe that you are about to enjoy a rare treat—rarer even than the Dom Pérignon you are sipping." Laughter rippled around the room. "As are many of you, I am a devotee of fine music and talented performers. Recently, I made it my business to attend an appearance here in Prague by the extraordinary jazz guitarist, Django Reinhardt, and his Quintette du Hot Club de France." Scattered applause around the room told him at least part of their audience would likely approve of what came next.. "I was not disappointed. But, for me, one of the highlights of that evening was a young singer who joined the group in four unrehearsed numbers and captivated a knowledgeable audience completely. That evening, I resolved that she should help us to re-open the Majestic Plaza's International Lounge, offering selections that are truly international. Please join me in welcoming *Sophia.*"

All of the lights in the room except the candles atop each table were extinguished, and then a pink-hued spotlight focused upon the tall, shapely 23-year old standing by the Steinway slightly above her audience with her eyes closed and her hands pressed against her hips. She wore a Grecian-style, full-length white gown, fastened over one shoulder with a gleaming silver brooch. The manager, now invisible in the shadows, silently approved the elegance of his performer's appearance, and he waited with all in the room until it was completely quiet.

The singer opened her eyes full, without any other body movement.

Dieter thought that he heard several restrained gasps from women in the room as they assayed the beauty that those eyes suddenly added to the young face, and then there was another silence which lasted for several seconds before the hands moved from Sofie's hips and clasped in front of her where the audience could see that she was holding a pen and a sheet of writing paper. She began with her softest lyrical speaking voice, as yet unaccompanied by Dieter; she was addressing the world-famous American actor, Clark Gable. She was speaking the words her character had written to the glamorous movie idol:

"Dear Mr. Gable, I am writing this to you, and I hope that you will read it so you know ... " Sofie proceeded to trace the poignant introduction which the young American, Judy Garland, had added to a favorite 1913 James Monaco standard the year before, changing the song's orientation and earning her rave reviews. It portrayed a youngster imagining herself to be in love with the mature picture star, pouring out her heart in a letter he would not be likely to see or read. Sofie's voice was reed-thin and vulnerable as she spoke the intro, and then Dieter's piano accompaniment began as the familiar melody line cut in and Sofie's speaking voice changed to a rich contralto.

"You made me love you—I didn't wanna do it, I didn't wanna do it . . . " As soon as the audience recognized the popular American offering, there was applause of appreciation for the manner in which Sofie had smuggled it into the room, and then they sat back to listen as she built a solid ballad rendition which thoroughly delighted them and made the manager more certain that his decision would be paying off. Already, the few remaining empty tables were being taken by patrons moving as silently as possible into the International Lounge to hear Sophia.

Dieter wished at times that he had been conducting an orchestra to truly support the imaginative and beautiful singer, but he was content that their first evening in the room was exceeding expectations and that the word would spread quickly that the lounge had a star. When they arrived at the Majestic Plaza for the second evening of their three-week contract, he noted that each of the framed announcement posters now wore a red banner across the bottom, reading *RESERVATIONS SUGGESTED*. He suspected that they would have to rotate the musical offerings and Sofie's gowns because some patrons would be returning and they would want to see the full range of Sofie's—Sophia's—art. It might require extra hours at the practice piano, but it would be enjoyable work because both of them thrived upon receiving a full measure of listener approval. He wondered what dangers this unexpected exposure might pose but decided to keep those thoughts to himself rather than risk denting Sofie's soaring confidence.

With each performance, the audience seemed more appreciative and the two young performers more satisfied with their decision to put their talent on display. It seemed to Dieter that there were more Germans than Czechs coming to the International Lounge, but he noted a scattering of British, French, and other nationalities, too. Each evening a few patrons sought them out to express delight or to encourage the addition of a particular song to the repertoire. Sofie was always gracious and usually able to converse in the same language as the visitor used. *After all, it is the International Lounge*, Dieter thought—*what could be more appropriate than a smorgasbord of songs and languages?* The manager noticed this versatility and encouraged them to engage the patrons whenever possible. Meanwhile, the number of hotel guests remaining under his roof for dinner spiked upward, and a new flow of early-evening visitors emerged. Perhaps it was time to pick up his option for an extended engagement.

Dieter was content that his role as accompanist was, as usual, anonymous, and that the focus of everyone's attention was Sophia. There were hundreds of capable piano jockeys in every major city, but she was demonstrating her uniqueness each day. He was even beginning to like her new image, with the piled hair and tall heels creating the impression of a towering person and the slightly scandalous gowns erasing all thoughts of the young university student she had recently been. He had also tinkered with his appearance, returning to the Freudian beard of his Fischerstube years and adding centrally parted hair and popular glasses. The identification papers magically supplied by King Michael and his sources carried photos of these altered countenances and established that they were Swiss subjects of German extraction. The manager seemed satisfied with these identities, and he also gave them Majestic Plaza employee cards listing their nationality as Swiss.

The second Saturday evening crowd was their best yet, with five additional tables squeezed into the room and a few tall chairs added beside the working bars. Sofie ended the first set with the current number-one tune in America, "Begin The Beguine," woven around a subtle Latin beat which allowed her to sway provocatively in a clinging black gown featuring a leg-revealing slit on one side. Dieter noted a boisterous table of German military men in the back of the room who voiced their approval a bit too loudly before they were expertly muted by one of the experienced waiters. When the intermission lights were raised so that waiters could fill additional drink orders and patrons could visit the conveniences, Dieter and Sofie moved to an out-of-the-way table where they could relax for ten minutes, accompanied by one of the Gypsy king's young lieutenants. Sofie's cognac was already at her place, and an ashtray was positioned where Dieter would sit. Song requests and some gratuities from enthusiastic patrons were delivered to the table by the maître d'hotel, and the two young performers sorted through them while enjoying their brief hiatus.

The voice came from behind him. "Dieter—is that you? Dieter Meister—Corporal Dieter Meister?" He turned toward the voice and saw that it was one of the military contingent from the rear of the room. Then the name flashed in his mind—it was Jurgen, the soldier who had supplied his first pack of Egyptian Royals on the train journey from Berlin. Dieter had wondered how he might react to recognition but had not rehearsed any plan for denying or dealing with it. Obviously Jurgen knew it was he; the question was merely to elicit a response, not to verify the fact, so Dieter decided to acknowledge his questioner in the calmest possible voice.

"Jurgen, my friend from the train—how nice of you to attend our soirée. How has your time in Prague been?"

"Hah, Dieter! Obviously it has not been so productive as yours. Your companions have advanced from an old witch on the express to a pair of whores on Ruzova to the toast of Prague nightlife at the Majestic Plaza. And have you also obtained a release from active duty at the Consulate to serve our country at the International Lounge? You must have a fascinating story to tell me, my friend. Perhaps I shall linger after your performance to share a drink and a story with you. Now, introduce me to this charming creature."

Dieter sensed that Jurgen had drunk too much and decided to move him from the table as quickly as possible, so he responded, "Jurgen, meet me outside the main lobby doors at eight-fifteen and we can exchange stories. For now, I would rather not interrupt Sophia's concentration—she is planning her second set, and the room is brimming with patrons. Here, let Draco help you back to your table." And with that, the powerful Gypsy inserted his body skillfully between the two and took Jurgen's arm as he turned him toward the table of military men. Dieter looked downward at his hands and could see that they were trembling. He wondered if he would be able to recover his composure before returning to the Steinway. A glance at Sofie revealed that she, too, was unnerved by the interruption, and he asked, "Are you alright to continue, love? Let's steal five extra minutes of intermission to compose ourselves."

Sofie stopped sipping her cognac and belted down the rest in a series of large gulps, then signaled the waiter to bring another. It disappeared as quickly, and Dieter could observe that she was breathing deeply, averting her eyes and tapping her fingers nervously on the tabletop. Their intermission had extended well beyond the planned fifteen minutes, and the room was making impatient sounds. "Let's go," she said. "I'll start with "Lili Marlene" for your military friends, and then we can go back to our prepared sequence." The pink spotlight picked up her movement midway back to the stage and, as it caressed her, Dieter could see an instantaneous return of the confident diva. Now if only he could do his part.

Somehow both became submerged in their second set performance, and Dieter felt that it was the best hour of entertainment they had provided since re-opening the International Lounge. Sofie—Sophia—took chances with her voice, extending its range and extrapolating phrases in French, German, and English. She also left the stage and passed through the audience, leaving the microphone and relying upon the strength of her voice plus the courtesy of her attentive audience to carry her lyrics throughout the room. She paused for nearly a minute in front of the now-silent military table and delivered a haunting rendition of the German favorite "In einer Nacht im Mai," which Marika Rokk had popularized that year, despite the Hitler regime's official disapproval of lighter music. The appreciative soldiers arose to applaud as she moved on. For her final offering of the evening, she once again moved effortlessly to the top of the Steinway and announced a tribute to the late George Gershwin "to every gentleman out there in our audience tonight—here's "The Man I Love."

At its conclusion, Sofie blew a kiss to each corner of the room and sprinted toward the safety of the small dressing room they shared, while the manager picked up the microphone to thank his guests for being there and express the hope that many of them would linger for dinner in the hotel. If they would present their International Lounge bills in the main dining room, they would enjoy a dinner credit for half of its sum. This appeared to set off an impressive movement toward the main dining room, and within five minutes the International Lounge was occupied only by busboys retrieving the empty cocktail glasses and assorted plates, napkins and tableware strewn through the room. Dieter closed and locked the Steinway, then proceeded toward the lobby doors and what awaited there.

CHAPTER TWENTY-FIVE
Prague – Winter 1938/39

THE CLOUD OF JURGEN DEITZ

Jurgen stood outside savoring a cigarette in the half shadows, and Dieter decided it might be a fitting start to their conversation to join Jurgen in a smoke. He had mastered the mannerisms of his favorite motion picture heroes, and there was none of the awkwardness of that first coughing, spitting, Egyptian Royal experience on the train. Jurgen was not inebriated, as he had thought, and he seemed to wear a much more mature look than he had projected in the lounge with his companions. Jurgen spoke first.

"Ah, Dieter—nothing these days is quite as it first appears, don't you agree? The young corporal riding in a first-class compartment should have alerted me, but alas, I was distracted by my amusement over the beginner trying to smoke and his ancient 'mother' sharing the compartment. Then I should have picked up on the incongruity of a German soldier not understanding brothel protocol, but I was too interested in my own enjoyment to notice. So, later, my curiosity led me to follow up with a visit to the Consulate, where they had never heard of Corporal Dieter Meister. Imagine that! And finally, my inquiries at the railroad office eventually precipitated a story about a passenger in your compartment traveling under the aegis of Reichsmarschall Hermann Göring.

"So tonight I am again surprised to find my pretend corporal appearing in Prague's finest hotel as accompanist to a talented performer. Moreover, he is closely protected by—how many?—by *several* professional goons in expensive suits. Is it a coincidence that the audience aggregates some of Germany's best-connected businessmen and their wives? Is it only by chance that he now wears a short beard, unnecessary spectacles, and a musician's hairstyle? Dieter—if this is your name—I believe that we may have more in common than our phony military tunics. I suspect that we are both in the employ of Herr Himmler as un-uniformed Gestapo specialists. Am I correct, my friend?"

"You know, Jurgen, I am not at liberty to talk about my work—just as you may not tell others about yours, eh? But I can assure you that any efforts to expose me would meet with great disapproval. Those 'goons' you observed are not always so identifiable, and I cannot vouch for them as either prudent or gentle in their protective measures. My assignment is specialized, and anything or anyone preventing me from carrying it out may necessarily be removed from my path. I hope that you won't risk that, because it would not even be my decision. Naturally, I will pass the substance of this conversation to my superior and will recommend that we proceed as if nothing occurred. Is that fair?" He took a deep drag on his cigarette before crushing it out with a rotating movement of his polished shoe, as if to make a point to his interrogator.

Jurgen winced slightly, then extended his hand. "Let's both walk away as if this conversation did not happen. Be very careful—Prague is awash in intrigue. I know that you have professionals covering your movements, but shifting loyalties and panicked reactions can still produce extreme danger for anyone working in the shadows. We will undoubtedly meet again. Until then, I wish you good luck, Dieter. Heil Hitler!"

"Heil Hitler," Dieter shot back as he motioned to Draco, barely visible nearby, to summon a cab to the doorway. He wondered if the agitated Sofie was also nearby or if her departure from the hotel had been as swift as her flight from the International Lounge half an hour earlier. He watched as Jurgen made his way back into the hotel lobby and wondered whether any of King Michael's people would track his movements. Then he reflected upon the possibility that he was now regarded—at least by one German—as a part of the feared Gestapo network which was spreading itself into Czechoslovakia. He would rather have remained totally innocuous and invisible, but at least the suggestion of a Gestapo connection offered temporary protection. Next would be the unwelcome confrontation with Sofie.

"Let's start with the two whores," Sofie said, before Dieter could even extend a greeting. "Why does that Jurgen fellow from the train talk about two whores? Have I totally missed something since we came to Prague? Tell me about my fiancé and two whores before I read it in the newspaper or learn about it in some other embarrassing way, Dieter. Tell me!"

"I should have told you earlier, Sofie. It was innocent, or better—unintentional —but I just didn't want to share it because . . . "

"Come, Dieter—tell me an innocent way in which you have become known for your association with two whores, or any whores at all. I am intensely curious."

"It was when I left the train and tried to become inconspicuous by walking among other soldiers. Remember that? I fell into step with Jurgen, who had offered a cigarette on the train, and we proceeded down the platform chatting as I watched you get safely into a taxi. Out into the city streets, we walked together, continuing our conversation, until we were on Ruzova—that's very near the Bahnhof—and we arrived at a green door, which is a brothel. The very place where Jura sometimes attends the women's health needs and where our Elsa and Magda were rescued. There was a woman seated at the door who motioned us inside, and I did not want to make myself conspicuous by turning away. He—Jurgen—soon selected a lady, eh, whore—and I was alone with several more who were looking at me. I could not run away, and I did not want to take one to a room, so I thought that taking *two* would give me another option. I asked them to give me a show—you know, a she/she show—I could watch without fucking. I was thinking about us. Do you understand?"

"And the two whores did a show for you? You watched them and did nothing?"

"I started that way, but, well—it excited me. It was new to me and I got aroused watching and they saw that and—well—they started doing to me what they had done to each other and I just . . . I just . . . "

"You forgot all about me and fucked two whores just to appear like a normal German soldier? How self-sacrificing, Dieter!"

"No—I didn't. I was—I was finished before that became an issue, and I don't think I would have done that, but the decision wasn't necessary, and we talked for the next thirty minutes about women. I wanted to learn more about—well, about the things that you want and men don't do. Does that make sense, Sofie? I have been in homosexual relationships since childhood, and now as an adult I find that I love a woman but don't know enough to make me confident."

"And, what of this Jurgen? He seems to have remembered much about you, considering it was only a casual meeting of two soldiers."

"He is Gestapo, Sofie. He is Gestapo and he thinks I am, too. He noted the incongruity of my compartment on the train in an area where corporals aren't usually riding. And he saw that—I don't know—that I was a stranger to brothels. So then he asked for me at the Consulate and learned I wasn't on their roster. And he poked about the railroad office until he uncovered some strange report about Reichsmarschall Göring protecting a traveler that day. And finally, he recognized me at the Majestic Plaza and saw that I was guarded by what he called 'goons,' and his conclusion was that I'm a Gestapo agent, here to monitor some of the Germans who are taking over Prague's economy."

"I don't like having Gestapo interested in your identity. They are all about gathering information and betraying people. He will want to find out who your boss is and what your assignment is, and before long there will be frustration because those answers don't exist. I believe that Jurgen is a potential danger to all of us, Dieter. How much of this do you think he has shared with others? I wish I could speak with my father, because he would know how to deal with it, but I'm not even sure whether he is being watched by Gestapo. The Oster Conspiracy won't just dissolve—it will be pursued at some level and those involved will be weeded out—even if it disappears from the newspapers completely. Herr Goebbels is able to turn on the press when it suits his purpose and to muzzle them when he wants to kill a story. That may be the most ingenious weapon of our führer—controlling the attention span of citizens and convincing them that the leader is wiser and more benevolent than is truly the case. How I hate this whole Nazi mess!"

"At least, have we put aside the question of the two whores? It would kill me to lose you because of something so stupid as hiding that from you or going there in the first place. Do you understand?"

For the first time in hours she smiled slightly, and then, biting her lower lip, she said, "Dieter, I think I must offer you a few 'shows' to speed your engine, and you should explore a few of the techniques your professional teachers demonstrated. You may have to telephone the Rahnsdorf fire fighters again to cool us down! Pour me a cognac—I may need to abandon some inhibitions just to leave the lights on. Loosen your belt and watch Sally Rand right in your own bedroom!" He poured two cognacs and bolted the door. At least the most immediate problem he feared had apparently been resolved.

The Gypsy king plus Draco and another large man whom Dieter recognized as a waiter from the International Lounge sat across from Jura, Sofie, and Dieter in a small restaurant patronized by middle-class Czech families. The conversation had been convened at Juraslav's suggestion after he had heard the report of Jurgen's unexpected appearance at the lounge. Once the facts of the conversation had been repeated so that all were dealing with the same considerations, King Michael said, "We know this Jurgen—he was part of an advance guard which came here even before Hitler sold his specious argument to the British and French. Now he is under the Prague Gestapo chief, Gunther, and he is overseen by the German political chief for Czechoslovakia—a rotter named Reinhard Heydrich. The Germans and Poles both knew that our government might fall easily, and they busied themselves with identifying the resources they would seize when the opportunity arose. Jurgen is an accountant who would like to become a master spy. He is ambitious and is a disgusting sycophant, currying favor with his superiors and constantly reminding them of his supposed brilliance. Advising them of a secret Gestapo agent in the area about whom they knew nothing would be a coup for Jurgen."

"So, you think he has already told them he has recognized Dieter—a mystery Gestapo agent?" Sofie interjected.

"Absolutely not!" responded the king of the Gypsies. "He needs many more answers to present a well-documented disclosure. If he reveals fragments, they will steal the matter away from him and he'll derive no advantage at all from the incomplete intelligence. Jurgen will continue to poke and dig until he can piece together a bomb. Then he will try to convince them that he should assume a key role in the ongoing investigation. He wants to be considerably more than a Gestapo accountant with no decision-making authority. At the Port Verte, he boasts to the girls that he is a spymaster, and he shows them his official Gestapo identification and a silver pistol he is licensed to carry. The girls call it his dick!"

Juraslav spoke for the first time. "There are several ladies at that establishment who share information with those of us who feared a Nazi takeover. Germans from the army, the financial community, and the political leadership frequent the Port Verte, and their tongues seem to loosen with their other inhibitions. Our Romani community has been able to ensure its safety more effectively by knowing in advance of plans to arrest people from our caravans or to seize assets that belong to us. I don't know how to put this delicately with my little sister here, but an appealing woman can often obtain more information from a lonely man than even torture could produce. We are forced to use resources like that all too often."

Michael resumed his control of the conversation. "I believe that it would be in everyone's best interest if Jurgen could be assigned to someplace very far away from Prague at the earliest possible time. If you are all in agreement, Jurgen can be packed and ready to leave within 48 hours. He will probably leave without even saying goodbye to any of you."

"And his bank account may show a recent large deposit which is withdrawn on the day he departs," added the large waiter from the International Lounge.

Dieter's eyes were wide as he digested the suggestion. He had no doubt that, with Jurgen gone, a potential threat to Sofie, her father, her brother, her mother, and to Dieter himself would be neutralized. He remembered the day when he had first thought his lover Miguel might intentionally endanger Sofie and him—long before their relationship had coalesced to its present intensity—and he knew that even then he had briefly imagined himself eradicating Miguel. If he did not oppose the current idea, he knew he would be complicit in Jurgen's disappearance. And, of course, "disappearance" was only a way to avoid saying "murder."

"Explain the money thing," Dieter offered. "I want to understand— are you buying Jurgen, or . . . "

"Sometimes when people disappear," Draco began, "there is a brief inquiry to try and ascertain a motive. Authorities and others look for infidelity, dishonesty, terminal disease, mortal enemies, or other logical reasons for an unexpected departure. It would be possible to set up a 'straw man' to supply a satisfactory explanation and avoid more probing. Someone else could open a large bank account in his name—about which the mark knows nothing—and the account could be closed by the same someone on the mark's departure date. A few papers left behind might create the strong suggestion that our late friend took some kind of payoff and ran. It costs nothing but is effective because it seems logical to the superficial inquiry."

"You would not be considering this if it were not for my error, would you?" asked Dieter.

"Probably not," replied the Gypsy king. "We are not inclined to do injury to anyone unless and until that person threatens us and forces our hand. Jurgen is a pest, and in his Gestapo accounting work, he is a part of the German plan to seize the assets of others, including those of the Romani people. But, that avarice is not unique to Jurgen and it would not abate without him. However, in your case, Jurgen embodies the threat. Without him, there is no threat, so his departure really could change matters. Do you see the difference?"

"I do now," said Dieter, "and I don't think I could be the one to turn thumbs down on Jurgen. I must record myself as opposing the solution we have discussed, but I must thank all of you with my entire heart for the willingness you have shown to step up to this threat against us. You are more courageous than I am."

After another successful evening at the lounge, Dieter and Sofie strolled together along the walkway beside the slow-moving Vitava River. They were quiet until they were totally alone on the cobblestones, and then Sofie asked softly, "He was there again tonight, wasn't he?" Dieter merely nodded in agreement, and so she continued. "He isn't going to let go of this. We are going to search for his face in the crowd wherever we go, and inevitably we are going to lead him inadvertently to the people who are most dear and special to us. When we mail letters, they might be retrieved and read; when we call on the telephone, we will have to consider that someone may be listening—and when we do anything different from our routine, we will wonder whether it is being monitored and recorded." Again he nodded silently.

"I'm not willing to do that, Dieter," she asserted. "I am finally building the career I dreamed about, and I am living with an artist and man whom I adore. I understand that it violates my life-long ethical commitments to even contemplate eliminating an irritant like this one, but it is equally abhorrent to me to consider throwing away the elements of my happiness and to endanger my loved ones because an ambitious accountant believes he can make me some kind of chattel in his career-advancement scheme. Can you understand?"

"Of course I can," he returned. "This leech threatens my happiness at least as much as he does yours, and I would applaud a random lightning bolt frying him like pork rind in a hot fire. But I wonder if approving that result when it is *not* a random accident would then make it easier for me to crush other people for other reasons until I became a really evil person. I'm already an arsonist, an adulterer, and an arch-criminal, and that is only the *A*s, my Sofie. Seriously, what would you think of me if I said that I approved Jurgen's mysterious disappearance, knowing that my approval had put it into motion? Would you wake up in the night and think that you were sleeping next to a murderer?"

"Perhaps there is another path," Sofie mused. "What if I could explain this conundrum to my father and suggest that a transfer of our friend could remove the threat? What if some Wehrmacht office in a city far from here needed a good accountant with intelligence-gathering experience, and Jurgen's record came to their attention? It could be a good career step upward, so he might actually put aside this unfortunate 'hobby' of investigating you and set other goals for himself. Would you feel as guilty if a random lightning bolt struck someone in that city later on?"

"I would not want to know about it—ever. But, if Jurgen's career took another direction, it would lighten our lives considerably and allow us to do some more enjoyable things—such as advancing our musical careers and our personal relationship. Do you think your father would involve himself in such a ruse? And would Jurgen ever be alert enough to detect a connection between his pursuit of answers to my identity and sudden orders taking him away from Prague? Could moving him away actually move him closer to recognizing the core issue? Gestapo operatives think abstractly, always seeking real explanations for illogical situations. Thus far, he has noted the incongruities in my identity, but he has moved to an incorrect conclusion. However, when that conclusion can't be confirmed, he will most likely back away and continue to seek other explanations until he arrives at one that does fit. I would not want that to happen."

Sofie thought about all he had said. She loved the integrity as well as the intelligence of the man standing next to her. She wished there were an obvious "right" answer, but every course seemed to have a potential flaw. After a long pause, she said, "Dieter, this isn't going to be resolved unless I can speak with my father, and I am not certain I can do that in a letter or if I should risk a telephone call. What would you think if I traveled to Berlin after our commitment at the Majestic Plaza is completed—a short vacation, ostensibly to shop for dresses and consult my music teacher on new material?

"I could slip away to Lilkahaus and get father's best thinking and also learn the current status of Oster. Besides, it has been quite a while since I have seen him, and, after you, he is the most important man in my life. It would only require four or five days away from Prague. What do you say?"

Now it was Dieter pausing to mull over the idea and not quite ready to embrace it. His daily routine with Sofie in Prague, despite the limitations of fugitive life, was basically happy and fulfilling. They turned to one another for so many things, from sexual fulfillment to professional growth to the simple pleasures of conversation and discovery. Sending her away, even for a few days, might risk all of the things that had become so important to him. Once again, the seeming injustice of his accidental religious affiliation creating a hazard to so many important objects of his affection came into focus, causing him to blurt out, "Why must being part Jewish affect our every decision when we don't even practice the religion? Why does the return of Germany to world prominence have to carry such an exorbitant price tag for some of its citizens? Why must I be sending you away in order to continue having you with me? Yes, of course, Sofie—you must go to Berlin and we must find a way to take Jurgen from here. And, in time, we will encounter another obstacle, and another, and yet another. Beyond mountains there are—well, more mountains, as the legend tells us."

"Then let's become the very best mountain climbers we can be and stop the self-pity, Dieter. I am a soldier's child and more than ready to fight for my happiness. You must make the same commitment." It was said quietly, but Dieter knew that it was at the core of Sofie's approach to life and he must conform or watch their relationship dissolve.

CHAPTER TWENTY-SIX

Winter 1938/39

SOFIE SEEKS HELP

The manager was distressed that his top-drawing act would be leaving the Majestic Plaza, and he quickly moved to ascertain whether more money would change that. Dieter assured him that family matters required Sophia to travel away from Prague, and that the manager did not have to worry about her suddenly materializing in another cabaret, competing with the International Lounge. After a short discussion, he did obtain the manager's verbal commitment that a new contract at a higher appearance fee could be negotiated after her return. Dieter also hinted at the possibility of a late-night appearance in a room suitable to Sophia's style—something featuring her on the weekends, where she could introduce new material and hone her skills. If that were to be the price for filling dining-room tables and pouring hundreds of drinks each evening, the manager would surely consider it.

Dieter was pleased to tell Sofie about his productive conversation. Planning something together for after her trip seemed to assure him that this would be only a temporary separation. Still, he had nightly qualms about letting her leave, and often found himself clinging to her in his sleep as a small child might hold a prized security blanket. There was almost no reference being made to the purpose of the trip, and it was all open-ended as to how she would communicate and when she would return. Juraslav purchased Sofie's train ticket, which showed her to be Sophia Havlik, a citizen of Neuchâtel, Switzerland, traveling to Berlin with a Swiss passport.

When the fateful day arrived, Sofie carried only one small bag, and she summoned a taxi at the Majestic Plaza to transport her alone to the Hlavni Nadrazi railroad station, rather than having some driver note that he had been summoned to the Havlik Clinic to carry a departing traveler. It was just one more of the string of inconveniences her fugitive lifestyle had thrust upon her, and she resented all of them. Because several thousand people had by now attended her performances, Sofie also abandoned the appearance she had crafted for Sophia, and she left Prague with a simple bun collecting her hair; low-heeled shoes muting her height, and student clothing from another life helping her to be unremarkable. She cast her eyes about carefully, half expecting the ubiquitous Jurgen to be in the hotel lobby, but gratefully she saw no familiar faces at all, and she was certain that her departure had gone unnoticed.

She would not attempt to call General von Seigler's private number until she was safely off the train and swallowed by Berlin. Perhaps a call from a small restaurant or an apothecary's shop near the Bahnhof, she thought. The two had long ago rehearsed a "distress language" for such occasions; if either wanted to let the other know that it was undesirable or unsafe to continue at that time, the code was a reference to "grandmother's birthday." It had never happened, but she had thought it through many times. As a young student, it was fun to have a secret "get lost language" with her father, but now she hoped it would never be uttered. There was one additional piece to their code: if the cautionary words about grandmother were injected by either into their conversation, they agreed to try to meet on the following day near a favorite bust of Goethe in the large library, Zentral und Landesbibliothek. The time of their meeting would be two hours earlier than whatever time they mentioned in conversation.

As Sofie's train started north from Prague, Dieter was seated on a bench staring at the bare branches in Vyšehrad Park, near the church of Saints Peter and Paul. He heard a plaintive train whistle in the distance and wondered whether that was Sofie's train and whether he should have been on it, too. He walked slowly into the unfamiliar church and stood for several minutes, thinking of how to request some kind of divine intervention to protect the young woman leaving on that train—and also to bring her back to him safely. He watched as others lighted small votive candles, and then he did the same thing, mumbling the words of his improvised prayer over his offering. The little ceremony made him feel better as he walked back along Čiklova toward the clinic. It was less than three months since he first came to Prague in his corporal's uniform. It seemed like years; so much had changed. And now, the fugitive half-Jew had prayed in a Christian church! What more incongruities would follow as he sought a normal life in abnormal times?

General Otto von Seigler had celebrated his forty-ninth birthday alone at Lilkahaus, watching a cold sunset over the lake and opening a bottle of Martel cognac to toast his survival amid the wreckage of several military careers that followed the aborted Oster Conspiracy. There had been multiple interviews with Gestapo investigators, and all of them had eventually asked about his years in Poland and his short marriage to a Jew there. Had he engaged in the political intrigue for which Lilka Rudovska was known? Did they remain in contact after their marriage was dissolved? Was their daughter Jewish? Where was she now? He assured them that the marriage had been an idealistic attempt to legitimize an innocent child, who long ago embraced Catholicism and was currently pursuing musical studies, visiting several European centers. He had sent money to his ex-wife during the Great War, to assure his daughter's wellbeing, and that daughter, his only child, had come to Germany to study and to live with him as soon as he could provide her with an appropriate home. Sofie von Seigler had not returned to Poland, and she identified herself enthusiastically as a German.

Otto knew that his examiners varied their questions and returned to the same theme frequently in an effort to catch him in some contradiction, but he was much too canny to be tripped up in a narrative he had rehearsed for years. And so, gradually, the frequency of their visits dwindled, and instead he began receiving episodal assignments from Wehrmacht Headquarters. There was a major deployment of equipment and manpower underway, and General von Seigler was credited with being one of the country's best conceptual military planners. His assignment involved preparedness for several possible scenarios, beginning with a rapid assimilation of parts of Czechoslovakia and forays into Poland. Control of borders with the Low Countries must be maintained— and might involve rapid movements to their heartland— while remaining alert to the possibility of resistance from French or British forces on the continent. The Master Plan called for "neutralizing" Russia while this intrigue played out; the führer told his military advisors that he could negotiate a treaty of mutual accommodation between the two major forces.

There had been no mail or telephone calls from Sofie in Prague, and General von Seigler had made no overt effort to contact the Havlik Clinic, where he knew she had gone. He wondered about the young man for whom he had supplied orders and uniform items. Loyal staff members whispered to him that the Gestapo professionals had been thoroughly frustrated in their attempts to establish Dieter's movements after the mysterious fire in Rahnsdorf. Their conclusion was that he was a professional—but a professional *what*?

Was he reporting to someone high in the Gestapo on his observation of commissioned officers? Was he someone's low-profile bodyguard? Did he have a direct line to Berchtesgaden, as one informant had reported? They knew only that, on multiple occasions, he had managed to "de-materialize" while being watched by professionals, who normally could not be thrown off the scent of a target. Otto was amused, because he had spent enough time in the company of the young man to conclude that he was nothing more or less than an apolitical musician with a huge crush on his daughter. Sometimes frustration was the mother of legend, and Dieter's pursuers had placed him on a pedestal in an effort to excuse their own failures. He hoped that Dieter had used his good fortune to blend into some distant landscape where he would remain out of sight for many more months. Eventually, other developments would entirely obscure the Oster Conspiracy, and the Gestapo resources still assigned to the matter would be refocused onto other priorities. "Buy time!" he thought. "Buy time, and do your job efficiently."

CHAPTER TWENTY-SEVEN
Winter – 1938/39

TWO LITTLE GIRLS FROM GDANSK
[From Dieter's Journal]

After you had departed for Berlin, Sofie, I sometimes sat alone in our room at the clinic and enjoyed a cigarette late in the evening. Many of the things I associated with you—intimate reminders, like your combs and brushes and favorite bar of perfumed soap—were still in their usual places. They made it easy for me to imagine that you, too, were still nearby and might push the door open and walk in at any minute. So, when there was a quiet tap at the door late one evening, I was confused momentarily by the soft voice asking, "Dieter—are you awake?"

It was Elsa, one of the two Polish housegirls we had gotten to know at the clinic. But then again, it wasn't Elsa—something about her voice and the intrusion were out of character, and that added to my confusion. I was afraid that something awful might have happened and she had been sent to inform me, so I stood and faced her, fearing the worst. She said simply, "Dieter, I need you to put on a warm sweater and join me in the kitchen. I've made a pot of coffee and I must talk to you about some things without interruption."

Minutes later, Elsa and I were seated across from one another at the kitchen table with cups of hot coffee and a plate of small cakes between us.

"How would you describe Magda and me?" she asked. The question was totally unrelated to my expectations at that moment and I didn't respond, so she asked a second time. Apparently she thought it was important, or that it would lead to something more pertinent, so I collected *myself and responded.*

"Well, if someone asked, I guess I'd say you are two little girls from Gdansk who have been befriended by Dr. Havlik and now assist him at his clinic. I wouldn't go into events in your lives prior to that, although I have some idea of them, as you know. Why is this important, Elsa?"

"What you have described is exactly what we are trying to convey to the world, Dieter. But suddenly this clinic and all of us here have become endangered, and it is now necessary for us to take you into our confidence and reveal an identity that you will not recognize so easily. Maggie and I are career operatives in Poland's SWW. We work for Europe's finest intelligence service, and our low profile as housegirls enables us to escape notice."

"Help me to understand that," was all I could respond.

"As you know, Poland and Gdansk have forever been surrounded by hostility, Dieter. Our country, Poland, is a perpetual buffer between aggressive Russians and Germans. Our city, Gdansk, was carved away from Germany by the League of Nations as an independent city-state after the Great War. But its citizens continue to have conflicted loyalties, and Germany's leaders regularly threaten to annex the area again. Maggie and I grew up as fiercely patriotic Polish youngsters, resolved that our culture would prevail despite the military superiority of neighboring bullies. We met when we were university students attending patriotic rallies and meetings, and before long we were together inquiring about career opportunities."

"In Gdansk you spoke both German and Polish, correct?"

"Yes—plus adequate Russian and English. We were fit and we had been very good students. From the outset, our SWW interviewer was encouraging, and, as we learned more about the compensation plus the opportunity to move about Europe, our enthusiasm grew. Within weeks, we were rewarded with an invitation to become provisional trainees, and we entered an intensive program to provide us with the investigative skills we would need, plus survival skills for dangerous times—like the present.

"After training, we were assigned to a handler—Sofie's mother, Lilka Rudovska. Her office had already anticipated the encroachment of Germany into Czechoslovakia, and she had the beginnings of an outpost here, with Dr. Havlik actively assisting Gypsy immigrants. We remain a part of Lilka's intelligence group, which has been very useful to Poland. You know the rest."

I was amazed by this account, and of course I wanted to know whether you had known any of these details when you arranged for us to slip out of Germany. Certainly, if you knew, your father must have known, too—and he had facilitated our disappearance. He had placed your wellbeing above all else. In every part of this intrigue, there are wonderfully selfless people, and I continue to ache with guilt for the consequences of my carelessness. Elsa had helped me to understand our situation better, and with that understanding I knew that my own involvement was about to become even more challenging.

CHAPTER TWENTY-EIGHT

Berlin – Winter 1938/39

A VISIT HOME

Sofie had seated herself in the second-class coach of the local train to Berlin. Her seat companion was an older gentleman—perhaps a farmer—who smelled of garlic and dried sweat, but who nevertheless was intent upon charming the young woman with very large eyes. He offered her a slice of blutwurst, which was skewered on the point of his cracked hunting knife. It was undoubtedly homemade and proved to be quite tasty when she sampled it. By accepting the wurst, she immediately became eligible for a long draught from his bottle of homemade wine, which was wrapped in an old newspaper. It tasted like paint remover—or at least as she imagined paint remover might taste. The second swallow was a bit better and, with a crust of his black bread smeared with sweet butter, the third swallow elicited a positive reaction from Sofie. *"Der Mensch ist was er isst,"* she said, smiling at her gap-toothed admirer. *A real man is what he eats.* His reaction was a hand laid gently on her arm.

"Danke," he smiled back at her. "You are in the springtime of your life—des Lebens Mai—and I am going home to die soon, yet we can share a pleasant moment and a light meal on a train away from our individual problems. That is good in these bad times. I hope your trip produces great happiness, Fraulein."

"And I hope yours yields long life," she rejoined. They both closed their eyes and thought of other places and other people. Sofie remembered her last, anxious train ride away from Berlin and contrasted it with the relaxed feeling she felt today as she went back toward her father's protection. She wondered if she would ever develop that level of reliance and comfort in Dieter's care. Or might she always be the backbone in a relationship with him? She decided that it should be the subject of their father/daughter talk over dinner at Lilkahaus.

After the old man left the train at Teplice, Sofie was alone in the small compartment. She was relaxed from the country wine and happily contemplating her recent success as a cabaret singer in a major room. She had kept a copy of the lobby poster announcing her appearance in the International Lounge in order to show it to her proud father. It was wonderful confirmation of her ability, and she hoped she could return to Prague and resume singing as quickly as the best solution for "the Jurgen problem" could be agreed upon. As she mentally reviewed the options in hand as well as the possibility of a solution involving her father, she was interrupted by the loudspeaker:

ACHTUNG! WE WILL BE CROSSING INTO GERMANY IN FIVE MINUTES. PASSENGERS PLEASE HAVE IDENTIFICATION PAPERS READY FOR INSPECTION SO THE TRAIN WILL NOT BE DELAYED. HEIL HITLER.

How good it felt to be traveling in her own clothing, rather than the uncomfortable disguise of her last trip! How much less anxiety she felt not having to worry about a companion and the need to be consistent in their responses. And how much she looked forward to being back in her own country soon. As the train slowed to a halt, she opened the compartment's door and turned up the ceiling light. She stretched her arms and legs and awaited the border guards.

"Guten aben, Fraulein—your passport or papers, please." He was young and quite good-looking in his uniform. He smiled pleasantly and extended his hand to receive the requested documents, and Sofie immediately proffered her ticket and Swiss passport.

"And your purpose in visiting Germany would be?" Again it was a pleasant question, so she replied quickly that she would be visiting friends in the country and getting some musical coaching. She said that her profession was as a musician—a singer, in fact—and she unfolded the Majestic Plaza poster and held it out proudly. He looked at it and nodded in approval.

"And we are a citizen of Neuchâtel Canton in Switzerland, correct?"

"Ja!" she confirmed "Neuchâtel—*haus und hof*, all that I have comes from there."

"Perhaps not your perfect German? If I recall correctly, Neuchâtel Canton is one of the French-speaking parts of your country, but you are very much at home in the German language. How does that happen?"

"I told you—I am a singer. And I showed you that I am featured in an International Lounge. I must not only *sing* in five or six languages, but to do my job correctly, I must also *converse* in each of them with our many wealthy patrons. Would you prefer that I speak to you in French to verify that I am from Neuchâtel?" It was said with a broad smile, but there was a challenge in the response.

"Ah, what a fine suggestion!" he laughed. "Tell me—the old codger who shared your compartment and let you drink his wine—remember? I would say he was about seventy years old. How old is that in Neuchâtel?"

"That would be *septante*," she replied without hesitation. "Obviously, you know that we Swiss do not express the numbers 70, 80, and 90 as do our French cousins who use the vigesimal counting system. So, tell me, if I had responded, *soixante-dix*, as a Frenchwoman would have done, would you have plucked me from your train and sent me to a dungeon?"

"You are too funny, Sophia Havlik from Neuchâtel! I wish you much success in your singing career. Perhaps I shall save up my shekels and catch your act in Prague after your return. Heil Hitler."

With that, he moved on, and Sofie pulled a flask containing cognac from her bag and let the warm elixir slide down her throat and soothe her roiled nerves. She hoped that this did not portend a journey too full of challenges. She might not always be able to con the curious or deflect probers. But wouldn't Dieter—and even Lilka—have been pleased with her resourcefulness as well as her mastery of French? Even though she had acted contrary to the lesson of one of her own favorite French adages, *fou qui setait passé pour sage*—literally, *a fool who holds her tongue may pass for a wise person*—she told herself, *it would be wiser to remain less verbal in the future, dear Sofie!*

The Gestapo "guards" who had sat near the entrance to Lilkahaus for a fortnight had not returned recently, and telephonic contacts from Wehrmacht Headquarters had increased both in number and in the level of responsibility implicit in each successive assignment. There had even been social invitations once again, but of those he had accepted only a summons from the spirited Emmy Göring to an informal "stag roast" at Carinhall, to be attended by a few close hunting friends of Hermann Göring. At that event, there had been no mention of Oster or of any of those absent officers whose names had earlier been linked with Lieutenant Colonel Hans Oster. It was almost as if nothing unusual had happened on September twenty-eighth.

General Otto von Seigler had spent a quarter century within the German military and had held positions of authority throughout the Nazi years. He knew never to trust still waters—in fact, to be more alert than ever when the smiles became too broad or the handshakes too warm. He felt like a barefoot woodsman tiptoeing through a field of baited beartraps, and he hoped that his more cautious approach to social contacts did not signal the apprehension he was feeling. When someone did note that he no longer socialized as much, Otto was quick to point out that his hostess/daughter had been absent, and that it was she who had the knack for organizing such things. Once, he had even added that some friends had insisted upon introducing him to a single woman, and that it had made him uncomfortable. Actually, the proffered "candidate" had manifested some very fetching qualities, but he had declined the obvious opportunity because he thought he might be compromised in the process.

Those were the thoughts on the periphery of his consciousness as he sat reading a military dispatch on the Czech situation. It was quiet and lovely at Lilkahaus—and then his private telephone interrupted the silence with a noise like a fire bell in a church. He lifted the receiver and in his most stentorian voice announced, "General von Seigler."

"Poppy—guess who!" said the happy female. "I hope I'm not taking you from anything too wonderful, but I wanted to hear your voice. How *are* you??"

"Ah, well—a little sad tonight because it is your grandmother's birthday, you know, and I still miss her. I was reading her favorite verse from Goethe, remember it? *Gebraucht der Zeit! Sie geht so schnell von hinnen*—use each hour, for they glide away swiftly. I really should look up the rest of the quotation, because it has to do with being more efficient and putting things in good order, and that helps to slow time's passage, or so Goethe thought. And what of you? I hear good things about your music. Does it go well?"

"Poppy, I'm very happy with the chance I've had to perform with fine musicians in front of demanding patrons. But perhaps I should call tomorrow when you are free. What would be a good time?"

"Let's say about 3 p.m. Auf Wiedersehen. We'll talk soon."

Otto did not trust the recent hiatus in house surveillance to insure that telephone lines were not tapped, and the mention of grandmother's birthday would have sent a pointed message to Sofie in their dusty code language to break off the call quickly and not disclose anything. He hoped that the Goethe quotation and the mention of an hour on the following day would serve to reunite them in a quiet corner of the large library at 1 p.m. Suddenly he was elated at the thought of sitting, if just for minutes, with his only child.

Sofie had no trouble decoding her father's intended message, and she set out to find a small *pension* where she could pass the night in obscurity like any of the hundreds of other young people visiting the capital. She would try to find one near the *Zentral und landesbibliothek* and would walk to that big library at noon when diners filled the streets. Once inside, she could locate herself at a reading table within sight of the Goethe bust, which was to be their meeting spot. How could she introduce the subject of Jurgen, if their time together was very limited or they were being observed? She decided to commit the matter to a brief written piece, which could be concealed inside a book. She wrote:

> *A military accountant named Jurgen Deitz who is a non-com about 27 years old attached to G office in the city where we once celebrated reunions, has fixated on my friend and has temporarily concluded that they are doing similar work. Jurgen endangers several people by pursuing the matter. If Jurgen were reassigned to other location all concerned would be happier.*

When she had finished, she reread the note and concluded that it conveyed nothing beyond the necessary facts. No addressee, no signatory, no names, no locations. It also made no mention of some people's suggestion that Jurgen simply disappear, but she hoped that Otto would understand that her travel to present the problem connoted its seriousness. He had always stressed the desirability of disclosing as little as possible in writing, and this appeared to meet his criteria. Sofie folded the note neatly and placed it inside a pocket edition of Goethe's *Faust,* which she reckoned would provide a touch of irony to tickle her fond father's fancy.

At noon on the following day, Sofie strode through the main library doors and climbed to the third level, where she knew that the bust of Goethe resided in an out-of-the-way alcove, in a section reserved for the German classics. She had acquired a notepad, a newspaper, her copy of *Faust,* and some pamphlets describing the library itself. Then she found an empty reading table about twenty meters from the classic marble bust of the heavy-browed writer, and she seated herself where she could observe Herr Goethe and his pedestal without appearing to do so. There was not much to see; few browsers came to the third level, most preferring to pick through periodicals and current books by Nazi luminaries on the main floor or to eat the tasty snacks and drink the strong Arabic coffees offered in the readers' cafeteria.

At 12:45 she suddenly saw the uniform—the well-tailored tunic of a general officer, with no medals or ribbons of accomplishment other than the polished designators of rank displayed neatly on stiff epaulets. He was ascending the far stairway slowly and deliberately, wearing a crisply curved officer's headgear with a shining black bill. Just below the bill, dark tanker glasses hid much of his face, but the size and movements were familiar, and she waited as he moved laterally to the statue, with his back in her direction. Sofie thought to herself how magnetic and how commanding he looked. He projected authority and confidence as he moved to where Goethe stood, and then he continued beyond toward the next alcove. She was relieved that there was no one moving in his wake, or for that matter anywhere near where he had ascended to the level.

"Captain Kolb will make a striking general some day, don't you think?" asked the deep and welcome voice. The speaker was standing directly behind her, and when she turned, he was wearing a modest business suit with the coat collar turned up, as many German men did on cooler days.

"Poppy, I love you!" she blurted unexpectedly, happy that the sound of her voice did not carry beyond the immediate area they occupied. "How did you? Who was—? Oh, you're so amazing—I never saw or heard you, and all of what I was doing was intended to see you first and make certain you were alone. Can we talk here?"

"We may talk until that young officer ascends again, which will be my signal that others may be coming here. Then, I'll slip away and he'll remove his epaulets, cap and glasses and chat with you about joining him for lunch. Do so if you can. Klaus has always been devoted to both of us."

"And what is this business of having a double, or whatever he is?"

"Many general officers now have adjutants who can wear their uniforms and be mistaken for them at a reasonable distance. You might think that the major purpose of this was to deflect danger, but I'm told that it was started by married officers with mistresses. The führer is serious about his Catholic faith and takes a dim view of philandering by his top people, and we are all living in an atmosphere of betrayal. Klaus rides in open cars at public ceremonies and stands on reviewing stands when I haven't the necessary patience. Unfortunately, I haven't got a mistress or a jealous wife, so Klaus has yet to realize his full potential."

"Poppy, you are too, too funny, and I do love you deeply. But I need to ask a favor that may be difficult to accomplish. I wrote a cryptic note, which is inside this copy of *Faust*. Why not sit and read it while I go to the restroom, and destroy it after. If we still have a few moments, I'll add some detail." She scampered off toward the central stairway, and the "businessman" stood near a tall window thumbing his way through the pocket copy of Goethe's classic and reading her description of "the Jurgen problem." After a short time, he watched her return with a feeling of enormous pride: she walked with long, graceful strides, and all of her movements bespoke rich maturity. His daughter! His beloved child!—now an incredible young woman.

They stood in the shadows and spoke in muted tones. He told her that his sources had told him about her success with Django and then her solo appearance at the Majestic Plaza. She gave him the poster from the hotel's lobby, and watched as he read it, moist-eyed. He told her that the

Oster matter was disturbingly silent but probably still in the hands of determined investigators. He was not certain whether he was really cleared, and their communications must continue to be guarded. She told him about her difficult trip into Czechoslovakia, and he laughed out loud at her resourcefulness.

Finally, Otto turned to the matter of a proud father's concern. What about Dieter? Was he a good partner? Did he understand her needs, and did he protect her against the dangers she must face? Otto expressed his deep fears about the direction German National Socialism was taking under the maniacal leadership of the führer and his sadistic henchmen. He worried that the artistic Dieter might not sense the extent of the danger because of his preoccupation with music and with Sofie. They agreed that Dieter had demonstrated uncanny self-preservation resources in Rahnsdorf, at Humboldt University, on the trip to Prague, and within that perfidious city. Then Sofie got to the matter of Jurgen, and Dieter's poorly considered decision to patronize two prostitutes and to let Jurgen learn too much about him. Now that they knew Jurgen was Gestapo, he had to be steered away from his interest in Dieter. Once he understood the truth about Dieter, everyone connected with Dieter would be exposed and endangered.

"I will inquire and see what I can learn about this Jurgen. If I can do so, I will spirit him away to some other location and make certain that he is very busy there. But, if that can't be done—quickly—do not hesitate to go to 'the Romani alternative,' notwithstanding Dieter's sensitivities. Do you understand?" Otto wanted to add, but did not, that the other alternative to protect Sofie, the Havlik household, and himself might be the disappearance of Dieter. Jurgen and his Prague superiors could not easily pursue a missing Jew. He hoped it would not come to that, but it must remain under consideration.

As the black-billed military hat reappeared ascending the main stairway, Otto gave Sofie an envelope filled with Swiss banknotes and a scrap of paper with an international telephone number. "That number will put you into direct contact with Klaus without involving me. You can trust him to get messages to me, and you can rely on anything he tells you about my situation. Let's plan to meet again shortly after the new year—perhaps in Neuchâtel, eh? Your new hometown. Oh yes, I know." He planted a kiss on her cheek and moved down the rear staircase with impressive athleticism.

Sofie looked across the dining table at Captain Klaus Kolb and wondered if she had ever really noticed him before. Certainly his voice, in normal conversation, had surprised her today. She could recall having heard two- or three-word responses in the past, all delivered with traditional military crispness. Now, as he formed whole sentences with normal inflection, it was entirely different. There was also an occasional smile to soften the stern military countenance, and it surprised her because there was a hint of shyness plus some genuine humor in the relaxed face. Her father had suggested the conversation, and Sofie wondered what he had hoped the benefit would be.

"Fräulein Sofie, I have known you since you first arrived from Krakow, and I am aware that you have always been the paramount person in General von Seigler's life. You should know that, and you should also know that he has always performed his duties with honor. I do not know of another officer so imbued with honesty and justice. However, we are living in treacherous times, and there are others who are less honorable. They are unscrupulous in advancing themselves—they will destroy the reputation of anyone in order to serve their own ambitions. As much as your father may question the wisdom of our national leadership, he would not be a party to murdering those leaders. Instead, he would step away from his career. But, before this Oster matter is put to rest, you may yet see public claims that General von Seigler was complicit or at least inattentive in allowing it to proceed. He wishes you to know always that such claims are untrue. His legacy to you is one of integrity and honor, and that should be your heritage to the next generation."

Sofie was still unclear as to why this conversation was necessary. Her father always had a purpose when he arranged meetings or prepared messages. He also addressed delicate matters directly—himself. He did not assign unpleasant things to associates, which was one reason for the very high esteem in which he was held by fellow officers. Clearly Klaus was dedicated to her father, and he was privy to many of the most personal elements of Otto von Seigler's life. "Thank you, Klaus. Even though I know those things, it is good to have them reconfirmed by others who are close to the situation daily. But, what exactly do you see ahead for all of us? Where is Germany headed in 1939?"

"Fräulein Sofie, no one here knows those things exactly. There is certainly a master plan in a few minds—most likely those minds that meet at Berchestgaden and stare over mountaintops while Wagner plays in the background—but those encompassing viewpoints are not shared at the working level. What we *do* know is that mobilization is proceeding along the border with Poland and that the inaction of England and France has allowed a bloodless coup within the German areas of Austria and Czechoslovakia. The ease with which this has proceeded is emboldening the architects of Germany's future, and I expect them to take what comes easily and see where resistance is finally encountered.

"The insidious part is the way in which they keep most citizens united loyally behind them. They have set up 'target blame groups' within our community and are using traditional animosities to attribute all of our troubles to those groups. You know the stereotypes: our finances are manipulated by mysterious Jew families; our personal assets are stolen in plain daylight by bold Gypsies; our youth are corrupted by immoral homosexuals in raunchy clubs; our culture is assaulted by suggestive music from abroad; and, of course, our traditional national enemies sought to humiliate and emasculate us in the aftermath of the Great War. Anyone who belongs to or sides with any of those groups is the enemy of the State and deserves to be punished. Anyone who supports the State is to be rewarded. No wonder that hundreds of thousands are willing to turn out and wave swastika banners just as an 'insurance policy.' It is mindless—and for the moment it has seemed to raise the profile of Germany and the lifestyle of most Germans."

With that, he moved to the substance of the meeting, drawing closer to her to avoid the possibility of being overheard by other diners. "Your father has entrusted me with certain of his assets to liquidate. He has instructed me to use the net proceeds from the sale of those assets to set up a joint numbered banking account with you in Switzerland. When that is completed, you will be able to access the funds deposited there without reference to him. He intends to add to the corpus of the account from time to time, but only when it can be accomplished without creating suspicion. Although I will be your co-signatory, I will not withdraw funds. However, he requests that you recognize an annual management stipend to me, equivalent to 2 percent of the average balance in the account during the preceding twelve months. Do you understand so far?"

"I understand what you have said but not the motivation behind all of this. What exactly is happening, Klaus? Is he in great danger?"

"No one knows, Fräulein Sofie. It would not be reasonable for Oster to be completely ignored, and in the course of time the führer will find a way to single out those who were complicit—and when he does so, there will be an object lesson for others. Your father does not know whether he is absolved from blame or whether he is being given sufficient rope to hang himself. If there is a reversal, there would be no time to set up such an emergency fund. So he prefers to do so now and have your 'insurance policy' in place. You are a fortunate daughter; it is a comfortable amount."

"Please tell him that I shall use it prudently, and that I will always respond to his needs from that source if needed. And yes, Klaus, I will send a draft to you each December recognizing the two percent stipend. But, perhaps you should give me an address or account number for those payments. It would not do for me to be searching for you and calling attention . . . you understand. Can you suggest something?"

"Fräulein Sofie, I have purchased a small vacation home in Almeria, Spain. The mailing address is on file with your new Swiss banker. You need only request that the amount be forwarded to the caretaker at that address, with no reference to me. It will be taken care of. But before any of this may take place, you must first visit the bank and execute the signature cards. You will then be given a coded access, which only you will know. After that, your requests may be transmitted by mail or cable, using your encoded identity. Your father hopes that this facility will help you to realize your dreams, no matter what course the problems of Europe and Germany may take. You already have a contact for me through which I can deliver messages to him. Hopefully all of this will pass, but until it is definitively over, you must both proceed with great caution."

"Thank you, Klaus, for your loyalty and integrity toward both of us. We shall not forget—you know that, don't you?"

"Yes, ma'am," he smiled. He left a small card on the table with the address of the Bank Julius Baer in Zurich and the name of its assistant manager. "*Sparen bringt Haben.*" Sofie recognized it as the German adaption of an old English observation: a penny saved is a penny earned. She wondered who had saved the pennies that would now be hers.

CHAPTER TWENTY-NINE

Prague – Winter 1938/39

PERSISTENCE OF THE GESTAPO

Jurgen Deitz, wearing a recently purchased business suit, strode to the main desk of the Majestic Plaza hotel and tapped lightly on the silver bell. When no one responded, he rang more impatiently until a head appeared from the door behind the reception counter.

"May I help you?" was the greeting. It was after 10 p.m. and most guests had been checked in hours earlier. The lobby was quiet, with only the sounds of a few late diners filtering through the closed doors of the main dining room. "Sir—may I be of some service? Are you a registered guest?"

"I am a frequent patron with a question. Are you the night manager?" It had just the hint of impatience or irritation, so the protruding head was followed by a body, and soon the two men faced one another at short range across the leather-inlaid reception desk. "I asked if you are the night manager of this establishment. Are you?"

"I am an assistant manager, sir. How may I serve you? Do you need a room? Unfortunately, we are fully booked, but I can recommend—"

"I am disappointed in the Majestic Plaza and seeking an explanation. Three weeks ago you were attracting the best Prague night crowd. Your International Room—or whatever it is called—"

"That would be The International Lounge, sir."

"—that room. It featured a chanteuse who delivered enjoyable contemporary songs, accompanied by a German pianist. Dieter something. So what do you do? You build a reputation with locals as well as your transient guests, and then you drop the whole thing? Why? This place is dead again!"

"I'm very sorry, sir, that you are disappointed. I fully agree that it was a delightful act, and it helped build our dinner crowd, too. We even added later performances in view of the popularity of Sophia—that was her name—but she did not renew her contract at the conclusion of three weeks. I believe that she went home to Switzerland for some family matter. Our manager may be able to tell you when they are to resume. I know that he has expressed an interest in signing them to a longer contract. That's all I know, sir."

"Switzerland, you say. I thought he was German. Dieter Meister—that was it. Dieter Meister. Does that refresh your memory?"

"I didn't know my memory was being tested, but I don't believe that the name was Meister. I think it was Havlich or something like that, and I'm relatively sure they were Swiss. Come back during daytime business hours and the manager will be here. He had to record their passports and he would have signed their paychecks. Is there anything else this evening?"

"Nein. Guten abend. Heil Hitler!" A loose flip of the wrist and he was gone. The assistant manager watched his departure, scribbled a note to his superior, and slipped it into the box marked *Manager*. Something about the rude fellow said Gestapo; perhaps it was the over-shined military shoes peeking from beneath an ordinary business suit. They were everywhere these days, looking for Jews and Gypsies—poor bastards. He wondered why anyone would be checking on a piano jockey and a sexy singer. They seemed like really nice people. Come to think of it—did Switzerland ever produce any jazz singers or contemporary musicians? All he could remember were accordions and yodeling. He retrieved the note and wrote the name *Havlik*. That was it. He had taken a reservation from a Dr. Havlik when the act first opened, and he was related to the performers. He wondered whether this bit of information could fetch a small monetary consideration. Perhaps he should forget about leaving the note and just keep his eyes open for the unpleasant Gestapo person. No doubt he'd be back soon.

Gestapo Lieutenant Colonel Edward Gunther was impatient about nearly everything in his life. Because of Gunther's obvious intelligence and instinctive nose for illogical situations, he had been an early recruit of the canny Heinrich Himmler. Those little inconsistencies that most officers were too busy to notice seemed to register quickly with Gunther, and he pursued investigations with the mind of a criminal rather than that of a lawyer, which he was. This novel approach had led to several early successes in the period immediately following the Reichstadt fire.

Himmler, the powerful leader of Hitler's shadow police, kept Gunther close by as the Gestapo machinery was assembled, frequently seeking his advice. But with all of his natural abilities, Gunther was still an annoying human being, never accepting the premises or arguments of others and always swift to embarrass them when he discovered a flaw. This troublesome tendency was exercised indiscriminately, and Gunther's superiors as well as his minions were frequent victims. They all dreaded it when Gunther interrupted a group discussion with his usual entry wedge, which began, "Contrary to the opinion of my distinguished colleague, Herr Zo-und-Zo, we would be remiss if we were to overlook the following . . . " The sword would be set firmly between the shoulder blades of whoever was being skewered that day, and everyone within Himmler's inner circle was fair game.

Once the führer had outmaneuvered British Prime Minister Chamberlain at Munich and won a "free pass" to annex parts of Czechoslovakia without fear of reprisal, Himmler saw the opportunity to create an assignment for Lieutenant Colonel Gunther which would be both useful and a relief for the strained internal relationships at Gestapo headquarters. Gunther would be a perfect choice to organize and lead the new Gestapo unit operating out of Prague. He could audit the many German interests that were pouring into that country and assuming control over many of its productive resources. There was real concern that profits might be concealed or even spirited outside the country by opportunistic bankers and entrepreneurs.

There was also the matter of the Jews and Gypsies who had already vanished into Czechoslovakia from points in Poland and Germany. They were a threat to the Master Plan for Europe, and it was necessary to obtain much better information about them—and then to dismantle their leadership. Gunther had the devious mind necessary to weed out those intrigues and to effect a most efficient housecleaning of the subversive elements. Himmler even imagined using the "Gunther Experiment" as a possible pattern for similar controls within Germany. It could be for intelligence what the Spanish Civil War had been for military machinery: a sort of proving ground without the high level of consequences attached to failure. Gunther's model could be fine-tuned for application to any populace that later came under Germany's dominance.

But—and Himmler hated to admit it, even to himself—it would be a relief to move the irritating Lieutenant Colonel Gunther several hundred kilometers away from Berlin, where his annoying forays would have to be in the form of secret dispatches, rather than the dreaded "contrary to the opinion of my distinguished colleague . . . " onslaughts. Dispatches could be read, analyzed, and defended before they rained down on unprepared fellow officers. Himmler's Gestapo could still enjoy the benefits of Gunther's brilliance without having to mediate the disputes he kindled with his abrasive personality. It seemed like a workable solution, and Himmler silently congratulated himself upon its implementation. And so, Gunther was transferred to the command of Reinhard Heydrich, the Stellvertretender Reichsprotektor with primary responsibility over all of the newly annexed areas of Bohemia and Moravia within Czechoslovakia.

Gunther had, of course, requested and gotten a team of well-schooled professionals to form the core of his satellite operation. He first needed language experts who could work comfortably with the many dialects spoken within Czechoslovakia. It was an "assembled" political entity, but not one with uniformity of traditions, beliefs, or languages. That had, of course, been the nucleus of the führer's debate with Chamberlain—the presence of so many ethnic Germans within certain Czech provinces and the fervent desire of those people to be united with the language and customs of their heritage. If they continued to be denied that natural affinity, surely there would be bloody rebellion, but if they could be reunited with the expanding and grand Germany, peace would prevail and Germany would have no more territorial ambitions unrequited. That was a promise! "Peace in our time" could be sold to an anxious world, and the führer's ambitions could proceed unhindered.

Gunther got the team of language experts easily, many of them already local residents of the country being assimilated. He next requested the muscle and brains, contingencies needed by any good secret service organization. It was in the "brains" category that Jurgen Deitz was delivered to Prague. Jurgen could examine a bank statement or a balance sheet with lightning speed, and his attention was drawn magnetically to the "soft" areas, where transactions were hidden and profits could be tucked away from the tax collector. Jurgen disliked Jews because he had been outmaneuvered by some Jewish businessmen early in his accounting career, causing him intense embarrassment. He viewed a Gestapo position as a platform from which he could gain a measure of revenge against such people and when the opportunity arose, he grasped it.

Much as Gunther had been, Jurgen Deitz was disliked by his co-workers in Germany because of his ambitions. Jurgen liked the swaggering power of the Gestapo, and he longed from his first day in the organization to be more than an accounting specialist. Similarly, as Gunther had done, Jurgen regularly pointed out the shortcomings of associates in an attempt to raise his own profile. And so, these two exiles had come separately to Prague for similar reasons and were now integrated into the Gestapo's relentless effort to intimidate and control ordinary citizens within their territory.

The assistant manager had just relieved the day staff at the main desk of the Majestic Plaza when he saw the unpleasant fellow sitting in a lounge chair across the lobby. He was reading the current edition of *der Spiege*— or at least pretending to do so—as he monitored the movement of a trade delegation that was chattering as they walked toward the main dining room. The same military footwear belied his business suit—actually a different suit from the one he had worn the night he pounded upon the night bell. How nice that the Gestapo was developing a sense of sartorial style, he thought. Next they will probably become sommeliers and start ordering something other than the bad Rhine wines, which always gave their identity away at good restaurants.

When the lobby had cleared, the assistant manager strolled toward the seated figure, who was now busy appraising a shapely escort dangled on the arm of a local businessman leaving by the front doors. "Good evening, sir. Didn't we speak recently?" the assistant manager offered.

Jurgen looked up and smiled condescendingly at the hotel employee wearing a nametag on his blue suit. "When might that have been? Did you make a reservation for me? I don't believe I recall."

The assistant manager knew that Herr Gestapo recognized him, and he immediately resented the unnecessary attempt to belittle him before according that recognition. So he decided to parry the unkind thrust with his own professional arrogance. "Ah, perhaps I am mistaken. I thought you were the toothpaste salesman from Dusseldorf who needed to borrow a house tie to enter the dining room. I'm sorry, sir." He turned and started back toward the desk and could hear footsteps trailing him as he did so. Herr Gestapo would like to speak with him now that the formalities had been played out. Because that had been necessary, the price of his information would now be doubled, he resolved.

"I asked you about the singer and her piano accompanist," Jurgen confirmed. "You said that they were Swiss and had gone home. Do you recall that exchange? It was only a few nights ago."

"Yes, sir, I do recall. I believe that I could retrieve information on each of them from our confidential records, but, of course, doing so would violate my work contract, and this is a very rewarding position for me. I cannot imagine endangering my job only to satisfy the idle curiosity of a patron who is not even a hotel guest. Do you understand my concern?"

"Of course. Of course. But if I were to pay for a room, might we explore further the question of entertainment attractions being offered to guests of the hotel? After all, there are many establishments from which one may choose, and such choices hinge upon the overall profile of each hotel under consideration. For example, the Czech businessman, Herr Skvarla, who just left the lobby. Where did he meet the charming creature who accompanied him out the door? Does the Majestic have an ability to provide introductions for the lonely? Perhaps that lies within the province of the night manager?"

"Assistant manager!" came the quick retort. "If one were to book a room for, say, two weeks, there would be an easier rapport between staff and guest. Certainly there could be more specificity about future and past entertainment features. Here are our room rates—for our finest rooms, you understand. If you would like me to do so, I could hold your advance payment and let you know when a two-weeks' accommodation is available. I will need a name and telephone contact."

Jurgen smiled. The assistant manager was no fool and very good at the shakedown, but such a contact at this central location might prove to be valuable for more than just solving the riddle of Dieter Meister. Two weeks' advance room rent probably equated to a month's salary for the assistant manager. Jurgen decided to risk it and peeled off several crisp banknotes, sliding them across the counter. Then he scribbled *Jurgen Deitz* and a telephone number onto a piece of hotel stationery. "I'll expect to hear from you within the next two or three days—do you understand?" It was a threat, and the assistant manager realized that this was one thrust not to be parried.

His secretary knocked respectfully on Lt. Col. Gunther's open door to get his attention. When he looked her way, she informed him that Accounting Specialist Jurgen Deitz was requesting to speak directly with him on "a matter of importance."

"Deitz? Accounting?" blurted the annoyed Colonel. "Tell him to prepare a one-page summary and I will decide whether the subject matter is of sufficient importance to merit a conversation."

"Sir," she said quietly, "he knows that is our procedure but believes that the matter should not be committed to writing. He seems adamant. Do you still want me to tell him to prepare a written summary?"

"Himmel! Tell him he has five minutes—and it had better be important, or his liberty time will be cancelled for the next two months. If he wants to risk that, show him in and then close my door."

There was another, harder, knock on the doorframe, and Jurgen Deitz stepped just inside, then ripped a straight-armed "Heil!" toward his superior, who reflexed a limp imitation of the salute and motioned that the door be closed and the intruder be seated.

"Thank you, Colonel. I would surely not presume to bother you with anything trivial, but I believe I have uncovered something substantial which is deserving of your attention as Gestapo commander in this region."

"Continue. Five minutes. Spare me the unnecessary crap and get to the point."

"Yes, sir. On my way to this assignment from Berlin, I met a man on the train who was wearing a corporal's uniform but was seated in a first-class compartment. Unusual, but explainable. He claimed to be attached to the Consular Office here in Prague. We chatted and smoked together and then walked to the Porte Verte, a brothel on Ruzova. It was totally foreign to him. Again, unusual but explainable.

"My professional curiosity was sufficiently alerted that I visited the Consular Office on my own time to speak further with him, but no one there knew his name and no one of that description had been added to the staff recently. Very unusual and not easily explainable. A few weeks later, I encountered him working as a piano accompanist to a woman singer at the Majestic Plaza International Lounge. His appearance was altered, but I was certain it was the same person and began observing him. Then I engaged him in conversation.

"He was very circumspect but gave me the impression that he was somehow engaged in the same work as you and I, and that it would be unwise to uncover his activity. I noted that there were goons protecting him in the shadows—one even escorted me away from him in a rough manner. Again, totally unusual and now requiring an explanation. So, I checked our pay roster for the name I had seen earlier on his identification badge—Corporal Dieter Meister—and found no one of that name and no new addition to our payroll around the time of his arrival.

"I continued to attend performances at the International Lounge but did not contact him further. I just watched him to see what his mission might be. There were many trade delegates and other prominent people at the hotel, and he might have been in contact with any of them. Several sent notes to his table, and several walked there to exchange words with the man and with the singer he accompanied, but I could not get close enough to learn anything, and the goons always retrieved any scraps of paper and facilitated his departures so that I could not follow him."

"You have gone well beyond your assignment as an accountant, Deitz," interrupted the attentive Colonel. "I hope you haven't fucked up anything in a way which will reflect badly upon my office. Herr Himmler is not a forgiving man."

"Let me finish, sir; there is more. Both the singer and Meister were soon gone from the hotel even though they were a popular attraction, and so I compensated the assistant manager to learn more about them. He said they were a Swiss couple from Neuchâtel, Switzerland named Havlik, and that they, or more precisely 'she,' had returned to her home to attend to family matters. He expected them to return and resume their work shortly. Sir, I have checked and there are no Havliks or Meisters in the tax rolls of Neuchâtel. Again, very unusual and truly suspicious, because it confirms that they presented false documentation to their employer here."

The Colonel pointed his pen menacingly and said, "Am I to understand that you are bothering me because a piano player and a singer are using false documents and have disappeared? Do you understand that people all over Europe are obtaining false documents these days and many of them are moving about secretly? That does not make them spies; usually it makes them exiles and, in time, normal police work takes care of them."

"Sir, please hear me out for one more minute, because there is a final piece to the puzzle. I asked at the railroad records office about the passenger Dieter Meister on the day we both traveled here from Berlin, and there was something unusual that day. A passenger in that compartment was traveling under the aegis of Reichsmarschall Hermann Göring. So, I then asked our Berlin Headquarters whether they knew of a Dieter Meister connected with Göring's office—and the name *did* mean something to them!

"How so?"

"Sir, he—Meister—had been watched and trailed by skilled Gestapo personnel, but he seemed capable of evading them. They concluded that he had been superbly trained. They also uncovered interviews alleging monetary amounts paid to him by someone in Berchtesgaden while he was once again working as a piano player!"

"And why was he being followed, Deitz? Do you know that?"

"I know only that it had to do with an investigation being conducted by Reichsmarschall Göring's office. When I attempted to learn more, I was refused categorically. Why would Reichsmarschall Göring protect someone and also pursue and monitor him? Why would an operative with those skills be entertaining at a hotel in Prague? This is why I wanted to speak with you. I am not certain whether we are dealing with a highly placed fellow intelligence operative or with a clever intruder. In either case, it would be important to know, don't you agree?"

"Is there anything more?"

"Perhaps. The assistant manager recalls sending a hotel messenger with a package from a hotel guest to the Havlik Clinic, a private medical facility on Čiklova near Vyšehrad Park. He also confirmed that a Dr. Juraslav Havlik made reservations and attended performances at the International Lounge—that is, performances by the two Havliks from Neuchâtel. The name Havlik is not uncommon in this country, but the coincidence should be explored further—in my opinion, that is, sir."

"I will look into this, Deitz. You may *not* pursue it further unless I so direct. Stick with your accounting. Understood?"

Jurgen understood that he had, indeed, uncovered material of importance and that Lt. Col. Gunther would now preempt all of his work and present it as his own. There would be no sharing of credit if it were due, but there would be condemnation of his *ultra vires* probe if the matter of Dieter Meister proved embarrassing. He would have to consider the risks of taking this matter to someone higher and incurring the wrath of Lt. Col. Gunther. How badly did he want to advance his own career?

CHAPTER THIRTY
Zurich - Winter 1938/39

THE SPOILS OF WAR

Bank Julius Baer's principal offices were located at Bahnhofstrasse 36, near the heart of Zurich's financial district. There was no commercial marquee to distinguish the bank's entrance; instead, the classic marble façade was marked only with discreet brass letters located to the right of a very solid-looking, dark wooden entry door. There was no exterior posting of the days or hours of normal business at the bank. Regular clients already knew those facts and, of course, the most distinguished depositors could call upon their personal bankers at *any* time and obtain access to their assets upon very short notice.

Sofie had been informed that she could request to meet with Assistant Director Heinz Bartel whenever it suited her, but she had decided against any such display of privilege or eccentricity and instead presented herself unannounced at the reception desk at 3 p.m. on a Friday, a time when she supposed that most banking for the week would have been concluded.

She was seated immediately in a small, private meeting room which had no windows and, upon her request, the receptionist had produced a fresh cup of aromatic coffee accompanied by a small offering of sweet biscuits, each wrapped in foil, bearing the bank's distinctive logo. Then, for ten minutes, Sofie was alone with her thoughts as she once again questioned the wisdom of this unaccompanied excursion to a new and somewhat strange city.

Her reflections were interrupted by the quiet entry of a bespectacled, bald man in his fifties who extended a soft hand and said "You are Sophia Havlik? How do you do? I am Assistant Director Heinz Bartel, and I will be your account manager. What language do you prefer for our conversation, Miss Havlik?"

"English would be my choice, if that is agreeable to you, Herr Bartel. It seems to be the growing standard in commerce and banking these days, and many of the newest financial concepts are best expressed in their language of origination, don't you agree?"

"How astute of you as a young woman to have noted that trend," was the patronizing response from Heinz Bartel. "May I assume that you have a financial background, Miss Havlik?"

"Please do not make any assumptions about me, Herr Bartel," came the crisp reply. "This will be an impersonal banking relationship. I am the bank's creditor and I will expect excellent service and strict confidentiality, for which I will be charged your usual account maintenance and transaction fees."

"Of course. Bank Julius Baer has earned its reputation serving private clients who value anonymity. May I point out that we are available to our preferred depositors every day of the year, and that your assets can be accessed on very short notice—usually our responses are set in motion within 24 hours of your properly submitted requests. I will provide you with your contact paths for wire, telephone, registered mail, express delivery, and even proxy instructions. You will be identified only by a code number and a series of responses to three questions. Obviously you will want to guard them carefully, because someone else presenting the same number and responses would be able to access your assets. Of course, you may always contact me at the bank should you need assistance in any phase of the relationship, but even I will not implement an instruction without the proper code and responses. Do you wish to provide us with a point of contact where we may send pertinent messages to you?"

"Not at this time." Sofie responded. "I will include response instructions in each of my communications to you. Because I move among several locations, those contact paths will not carry over from one request to the next. There is, however, one annual transfer of funds at each year's end to a single payee in an amount equal to 2 percent of the average daily balance in the account during the preceding year. I understand that the transferee and routing have previously been supplied to you. Is that correct?"

"Yes, we are aware of that, Madame. You will have to execute a separate instruction, which I have prepared, to cover those annual third-party distributions. I have been directed to forward a copy of your executed instruction to the intended recipient when you and I have completed the necessary paperwork. Is that agreed?"

"Of course," she responded. "But please make a second carbon copy for me. And, when the annual distributions are made, I will require a confirmation that shows the calculation of the amount and confirms that it has been duly sent to the recipient. Now, may we get on with the basic documents required for me to assume possession of the account? What will be my opening balance?"

Assistant Director Heinz Bartel extended his manicured hand, which conveyed a slip of white paper containing a sum denominated in Swiss Francs. Sofie looked at it and immediately fought to control her facial expression, as she felt a wave of anxiety spreading through her body. The paper reflected a balance of nearly two million Swiss francs, easily enough to provide a lifetime of comfort. She hoped that the diminutive banker had not noted her astonishment, but when she glanced up at him she saw a condescending smile that said that he understood that her benefactor had exceeded all reasonable expectations.

Less than an hour after she had entered Bank Julius Baer, someone newly wealthy named Sophia Havlik departed, offering a firm handshake and a cordial nod to Assistant Director Bartel. With their work completed, he had offered to provide a bank driver to return her to her hotel, but she had declined politely and, with formalities concluded, she walked toward the electric streetcar stop on Bahnhofstrasse, where she took the first trolley in the direction of the international train depot. Her traveling valise had been stored there in a public locker, and she had resolved at the onset of the day's adventure that she would retrieve it and depart from Zurich as swiftly as she could, leaving the least possible evidence of her visit for any curious eyes to review.

With the small bag in hand, Sofie traced a desultory path through the Bahnhof's corridors, trying to ascertain whether anyone was following her. Then she turned abruptly into a ladies' restroom and waited just inside the door to see if anyone entered closely behind her. When that did not happen, she occupied a closed stall and changed from her chic business suit into an inexpensive-looking dress topped with a warm country shawl. She then removed the dark wig she had worn to the bank and added a pair of unflattering reading glasses to complete her transformation.

A totally unremarkable Sofie emerged from the convenience together with two other women who had entered a few moments before, and she made her way quickly to the track that had been posted for the evening train to Berlin. She knew it would be departing soon, and she was relatively certain that no one save the employees of Bank Julius Baer had known of her brief visit to Zurich. The long day had been stressful for Sofie, and she wished earnestly that she could settle back with a snifter of cognac in the dining car and relax for a while. However, nothing would be more out-of-character for the plain woman occupying a second-class compartment to Berlin that evening, and she did not want to attract any attention to herself. How strange, she thought, that on the day she had acquired a fortune she was making every effort to appear ordinary.

CHAPTER THIRTY-ONE

Prague - Winter 1938/39

DIGGING DEEPER

The adjutant knocked on Gestapo Lieutenant Colonel Gunther's door. "Sir, there is a call coming to your personal line from our headquarters office in Berlin. They have requested that you be available to speak in about ten minutes from now. May I give them that assurance?"

"Of course you may. Do you know the subject matter?" responded the wary officer.

"No, sir, but the call is from Herr Himmler's office, and it may be he calling you. That is his usual procedure for assuring that he has the availability of the precise person with whom he wishes to speak. It was specific that the call will be for Colonel Gunther and no one else."

The annoyed and somewhat nervous Colonel arranged and re-arranged several items on his desktop. He laid out a notepad and several sharpened pencils, then poured a glass of water from his carafe while attempting to anticipate the reason for a personal summons from headquarters. When the telephone rang, he plucked it from its cradle and announced crisply, "Heil Hitler! Prague Headquarters. Lieutenant Colonel Edward Gunther here. Guten morgen."

The familiar voice on the other end was clear and calm. "Edward. Good to hear your voice. It has been too long, my friend. We must discuss two matters this morning. First, I must ask if you know an accounting specialist in your command named Jurgen Deitz. Do you?"

After a brief hesitation, Gunther said, "Yes, sir. I recognize the name and believe I can put a face with it. He joined us three or four months ago and has been assigned to auditing several commercial accounts."

"Precisely, Edward. Is there any reason why he should be communicating directly with this headquarters, out of normal channels?"

"Not that I know of, sir."

"And, Edward, would you not normally know if such direct contacts had been authorized?"

"Of course, sir. We maintain very disciplined staff procedures, and my personal authorization would be required to circumvent our usual protocol."

"Interesting, Edward. Because Specialist Deitz has apparently been in contact with an investigative unit here, attempting to gain information regarding a fugitive person. Would that be related to the auditing tasks he has been assigned?"

"No—er, no, sir. I understand your point, sir. Can you identify the fugitive person? That is, are you at liberty to tell me the name of the person about whom Deitz is inquiring?"

"Edward, I am at liberty to do as I choose in this organization, but I know of no reason to disclose the information to you at this time. Do you?"

"Sir, this is my only knowledge of the matter, but I am in firm control of my Czechoslovak unit, and I would be gratified to be included in any matter concerning someone under my command here."

"Yes. Commendable, Edward. Commendable. But, perhaps it won't be an issue, because we have received a request to release Deitz for assignment to a Wehrmacht command in the East, on the Polish border, where we have seen some increased activity of late. Would you object to our granting that favor?"

"Sir, Deitz has been here a relatively short time. I have little personal familiarity with the quality of his work, but I find it unusual for a request to be made to our headquarters for an ordinary accounting specialist— unless, of course, he has some unique knowledge, as of a particular industry, or region, or even language. Is that behind this request, sir?"

"It would be my conclusion that Deitz probably possesses some unique knowledge not necessarily a component of his military specialty which is of interest to someone highly placed. I suggest that you stand down from the matter and we shall resolve it here. It has been good speaking to you, Edward. Heil Hitler." *Click.*

Lieutenant Colonel Edward Gunther swept all of the items atop his desk onto the floor with a single, angry motion and a loud profanity.

Jurgen Deitz remained methodical and painstaking in his dogged efforts to learn more about the enigmatic Dieter Meister, and as he reviewed their personal contacts mentally he noted there was an important omission from his inquiries – the two ladies with whom Dieter had passed time at the Porte Verte on his first morning in Prague. Dieter's awkwardness and inexperience had been the subject of humorous commentary among the regulars for a short period, but then it seemed to be forgotten amid business as usual.

He sought out the youthful Ursula one quiet evening and engaged her in conversation; she had very precise recollections of Corporal Meister, who had demanded little, but tipped generously. She confirmed that the man was probably Jewish, and in answer to Jurgen's inquiry about subsequent visits to the Porte Verte, Ursula said that to the best of her knowledge Dieter had never returned. However, she had recognized him on one of her visits to the music store on Ruzova, where he was accompanied by a tall, attractive woman who appeared to share his interest in music.

Jurgen suspected that the female companion was the singer known as Sophia—but was she also the mysterious traveler on the train from Berlin who had brandished a letter of safe passage from Reichsmarschall Goering? Why would two musicians go to such elaborate lengths to hide their identities? And if they were not merely musicians, what else could they possibly be?

Even before he departed from the Porte Verte that night, the inquisitive Gestapo accountant had added a page of notations to his ledger, and he left feeling confident that he was getting closer to some explosive revelations with career implications for him.

Juraslav and Dieter dined together, as they frequently did after Sofie's departure for Berlin. They had chosen The Balalaika, a small restaurant near Wenceslas Square, where Romani specialties were the featured dishes and Gypsy musicians frequently performed. It was more a treat for Juraslav than for Dieter, although he, too, was developing a taste for the highly seasoned food and racing rhythms. They were sipping after-dinner drinks and enjoying a haunting mandolin solo when Magda and Elsa entered the restaurant and joined them at their corner table.

The two young Polish women bore little resemblance to the housegirls Dieter had encountered when he first arrived at the Havlik Clinic. Tonight, they wore stylish dresses and were professionally coifed. Their faces had been enhanced with eye makeup and other well-applied cosmetics. The general impression was of two professional men meeting two attractive lady friends for dinner. Dieter thought to himself that the SWW had done an excellent job of training these two informants—or were they spies?—so that they could be practically invisible while gathering information in a foreign city.

Juraslav ordered two more of the Romani cordials, and the four friends raised their glasses together in a mock salute. Finally, after some meaningless chatter about food and weather, Juraslav leaned farther forward and, with a questioning tilt of his head, said simply, "Well?" Elsa responded first.

"He has been a busy fellow. He has quizzed the assistant manager of the Majestic Plaza and has bribed him to learn the nationality and status of Dieter and Sofie."

Magda interrupted angrily. "That pompous little bastard! He's getting rich from behind that counter! We pay him to use us as escorts for visiting German businessmen. The Gestapo bribes him for confidential information on hotel employees and guests. The Gypsies kick back a part of their pay as bellmen, drivers, or waiters. There's more integrity in a whorehouse, Jura!"

Juraslav chuckled and shrugged his shoulders. "You're correct, but let's accept it and try to stay on the subject of Jurgen Deitz. Is there more?"

Elsa resumed, "I have been told that he requested an interview with Colonel Gunther, the Gestapo chief here, but my informant did not know the subject matter of their conversation, only that it was of brief duration and that Jurgen seemed disturbed afterward. That same source was able to tell me that he—Jurgen—has placed several telephone calls to

Gestapo offices in Berlin, which is a new pattern for him."

Magda had composed herself after her angry outburst and proceeded with relative calm. "I followed him to Hlavni Nadrazi, to the office of the station master there. He remained for nearly an hour. I conclude that he was seeking information on the passengers from Berlin the day he came to Prague. Actually, those records are poorly maintained, if at all, and I doubt they could be helpful to him. He would learn much more from the border guards' logs."

"Why don't you suggest that to him?" shot Elsa. "The poor fellow must be awash in frustration." She laughed at her own humor, but the others remained thoughtful, trying to imagine how much Jurgen had learned.

Dieter sat silently, feeling contrite about all of the intrigue and concern that had been precipitated as a result of his foray behind the green door with Jurgen. He felt constrained to contribute something to the conversation. "We should learn something soon from Sofie's trip to Berlin, shouldn't we? Her father will tell her if a transfer can be arranged, and that could obviate all of this mess I've created."

"Sofie will contact us with new information when she can do so safely and when there is something concrete happening, but that could require several more days," offered Juraslav. "We agreed that she would send a bogus medical update, telling us that our patient is being transferred to another hospital, or, alternatively, that the patient's condition remains unchanged and critical, if no re-assignment is being processed. You understand that if her father is still being investigated in connection with the Oster matter, he may hesitate to draw attention to himself by initiating such a request. Then we might have to consider other ways to dispose of Jurgen."

"There is a final item on our friend which could be important," Elsa continued. "Earlier this evening, he presented himself as a patron at the Porte Verte and purchased an hour with Ursula—the small girl you know, Dieter. Jurgen has a regular girl at the house, and he has never before shown the slightest interest in Ushie. But tonight, he seemed intent upon cultivating a relationship with her, and he asked about the soldier who had accompanied him there one morning. That would be you, Dieter.

"Our friend Renate—the big-busted one—learned as much as she could from Ursula, and then she called me immediately. Renate believes that Ursula told Jurgen that Dieter is a Jew and that he has a girlfriend with whom he shares an interest in music. By itself, that's pretty innocuous, but added to the profile Jurgen is compiling, it might offer useful confirmation."

Juraslav looked serious. "With every day and each added morsel of information, this Jurgen becomes more potentially dangerous to all of us and to the cause we all serve. We must set a reasonable time limit on our forbearance and make certain that Jurgen is not permitted to continue his probing beyond the critical point. I favor any solution that promises to remove him from Prague by the end of next week. We need to consider two or three alternative action paths that can accomplish that."

A quick glance around the table brought confirmation from everyone—this time even including the reluctant Dieter, who thought to himself that abetting a murder might possibly be amended to the catalog of his transgressions. All, of course, emanated from the one flaw in his genetic composition—it was maddening!

CHAPTER THIRTY-TWO

Berlin - Winter 1938/39

CLARIFICATION

Sofie stepped from the train in Berlin precisely on schedule at 8:45 p.m. and walked a few blocks to a café where she did not believe there was any likelihood of encountering friends. The place was slightly musty-smelling and the interior was dark. A sign in the window advertised the presence of a public telephone inside. Sofie looked around and saw nothing threatening, so she ordered a draught beer and picked two small sausages from the free lunch offering for patrons. It was easy to see that the older counterman sympathized with his impoverished but attractive patron, and she wished she could erase his lines of compassion by telling him that she had two million Swiss francs ready to lighten her burdens. Hah!

A second draught and a third sausage later, she entered the public telephone enclosure and dialed the number she had scribbled—in reverse order—inside the back cover of her Swiss passport.

"Kolb!" was the one-word greeting, followed by silence. When she was sure there would be nothing more from the recipient, Sofie was nearly as economical with her response, "Humboldt music student here," she blurted.

Klaus Kolb relaxed at the sound of the familiar voice, and Sofie imagined his face showing some of the empathy and shyness that had surprised her during their lunch at the library. "Miss Sofie, are we at liberty to speak? Where are you?"

"Near the Bahnhof in a small pub. I just returned from making arrangements for my friend in Almeria, and all went well. I was wondering whether your senior associate might be available to dine with me tonight?"

"I'm certain he would welcome that opportunity, but I will need a little time to contact him and arrange it. Perhaps he will want me to retrieve you. Can you remain where you are and call me again in thirty minutes?

"Yes. If I have another draught, I don't believe I'll be hurried. Please try to reach him, Klaus, and I'll call you in thirty minutes."

Sofie fiddled with her beer stein, not really wanting to consume a third ration of beer before embarking upon a serious conversation with her father. She glanced frequently at the wall clock, wishing that she could accelerate it, but instead it seemed that she was having the opposite effect, and she knew that she was tweaking the curiosity of the bartender by doing absolutely nothing. Finally, as the twenty-fifth minute inched by, she slid from the elevated bar chair, intending to return to the telephone, but as she did so, another patron slipped into the public booth ahead of her.

"Doesn't that make you furious?" a familiar voice intoned. How had he gotten here? Her eyes conveyed the question, and General Otto von Seigler continued, "We have perfected a good caller-identification process for our personal telephone lines in order to avoid some callers and to facilitate personal chats with others. The system operator was able to locate your call as coming from this quadrant, and it was relatively easy to pinpoint your exact location once we had that."

"Oh, Poppy, you are so clever! Why can't I be around you more often? I always learn something new and fascinating when we are together. Can we go somewhere for a quiet dinner? I promise not to be too inquisitive about your work —or to smoke cigarettes—but there are some things I need to discuss with you, and I have missed you." She took his strong hand between hers and squeezed hard to emphasize the point.

"Klaus has our car at the curb and I have called ahead to Lilkahaus, where we can enjoy some nicely aged venison and schnitzel with a bottle of Bordeaux—I know you'll like that! The monitors have been withdrawn from around my city residence, and I'm integrated into central military planning again, but still I am not fully comfortable dining in a public restaurant until all questions related to the Oster attempt are settled."

Once they arrived at Lilkahaus, the two dined happily together for the first time in many months, each filling in details of recent events. Sofie spoke of her single-name popularity as Sophia in Prague after her success with Django and his illustrious Quintette. She praised Juraslav and his Gypsy connections for their acts of kindness as well as the protective curtain they appeared to extend, and she made many references to the rapid transformation of Prague itself into a quasi-German metropolis. She expressed the hope that she might return soon to Prague and to her dear friend, Dieter—but not while that posed any risk to others.

Otto acquainted his daughter with the enigmatic twists and turns of the Oster inquiry. He had concluded that his value to the German armed forces had never been in question, but that detractors had cited his early marriage to a Polish Jew as some evidence that his loyalty might be compromised. Flush with the success achieved in the Sudetenland, he expected additional bold initiatives elsewhere along Germany's borders, and his own experience in Poland together with countless military honors appeared to have lifted him above any further entanglement with the Oster plotters.

"I finally felt comfortable with the suggestion you made about transferring Jurgen Deitz away from Prague, and I believe that the process has been initiated," he began. "His personnel records establish that he was born and spent his early years in the town of Forst, which is walking distance from the border with Poland. Most residents of Forst have working knowledge of the Polish language, and they integrate well with their neighbors to the East. I did not personally submit a request for transfer, but a Major Fritz Heller, who oversees budgets at our Wehrmacht control center near Forst, was encouraged to add a 'local lad' to his staff, and Deitz's service record was the only one of those supplied to Heller which fell within the parameters of the job description. If Heller's request is granted, your intrusive Gestapo friend should be plucked from Prague within a few days. Do you still believe that his removal will stop the probing into Dieter's identity?"

"I cannot guarantee it, Poppy. He may already have shared his concerns with others, but he is an ambitious man, and our friends in Prague believe that he wants to earn the full credit for exposing Dieter. If that is accurate, he would need more complete information than what he has collected thus far. We believe that accounts for his intense observation of Dieter and me. He is still trying to complete the picture. And, remember, his early conclusion was that Dieter is also a Gestapo operative. If that were the case, and Jurgen Deitz's meddling caused the failure of someone's pet project, he would probably be cashiered out of the Gestapo and sent to an undesirable infantry hovel. Sorry, Poppy, no disrespect to the Wehrmacht, but—well—there's more glamour in Gestapo work."

Later, Sofie reluctantly opened another avenue of discussion that was important to her—the sizeable fortune deposited at Bank Julius Baer in Zurich. She knew that her father had compiled a distinguished military career and that he had very few personal indulgences to waste his income, but still it seemed unlikely that he could accumulate so much from his salary alone. Although Otto had not been comfortable discussing some aspects of his life with his daughter, he understood that the quality of their ongoing relationship as independent adults would likely be shaped by the willingness of each to share such details. And so he cautiously began.

"The period from 1932 until now has been very rewarding to many of those at the helm of the Nazi—that is, National Socialist—movement. As you understand, the political philosophy of our leadership revolves around the acknowledged ability of enlightened central government to promote new ideas that can create a stronger Germany and share the rewards of that prosperity among the greatest number of Germany's legitimate citizens. To accomplish this, government must be in a position to decide when a productive national asset is not being well managed and able to expropriate that asset and redirect its development.

"For example, our leadership determined that Germany's financial community had long been corrupted by secretive Jewish banking families, who profited unduly through their lending practices—even to the point of gaining control over some of their own corporate customers. Central government was able to impose new regulations that avoided those abuses, and government-chosen managements have been substituted for many of the former abusers. You saw that initially in Austria, where banking was badly corrupted. It has now been cleansed and absorbed into our own system, and the crafty Jews who were profiting from banking there are no longer to be found."

Sofie had heard the explanation many times previously, because the German Minister of Propaganda, Herr Goebbels, never passed up an opportunity to identify the malefactors or to herald their removal from authority. He had pointed with pride to each new government initiative and each additional layer of central control, always burnishing the images of key leadership personnel and, of course, the führer. Clearly, the nation's international profile had been enhanced in the process as dynamic new personalities had replaced tired, old icons. However, nothing in this explanation moved from the general to the specific: she was still uninformed about the two million Swiss francs and was not going to be satisfied with a simple Nazi economics lesson.

"Poppy, are you telling me that after removing selfish troublemakers from positions of power, it has been appropriate to reward the team members who have implemented the transition? Doesn't that just substitute one oppressive group for another? I have heard rumors that our friend Reichsmarschall Göring has amassed a fortune of art and artifacts, all seized from those very malefactors. Also, it is said that many high-ranking officers have demanded bribes from fleeing Jewish businessmen to assure their safe passage abroad. Are there hundreds of secret accounts in Swiss and English banks, all fed with the blood money extracted from Jews who are running for their lives?"

For the first time that evening, General Otto von Seigler banished the benign smile from his countenance and resumed the personality of a Wehrmacht field officer. "It would be dangerous to point out that contradiction during these times of change, Sofie. There is an adage that reminds us that the ends justify the means, and Germany is now in the process of shedding many tired ideas and personalities in favor of a system that can assure equitable sharing of our nation's wealth. In that transition, supporters may fare better than detractors for a time, but history will be the judge of the overall benefits of our embrace of National Socialism."

Sofie sensed that she would continue to hear only tired platitudes if she was unwilling to press her question about the money, so she squared her shoulders and returned to the slippery subject. "Then, Poppy, how have *you personally* been rewarded for your role in effecting the changes?" It was an aggressive question, out of character for the loving and respectful young woman, but she was determined.

"Many senior military officers have been offered opportunities to invest in new government-financed entities. I have availed myself of those opportunities, and my confidence has been rewarded generously. The same has been true for cooperating industrialists, bankers, merchants, and government leaders. And, Sofie, please consider how the combined efforts of those supporters have raised our country's profile throughout the world! The new Germany is admired and accorded great respect, and I have seen no criticism of our internal policies from any credible source. Have you?"

"Poppy, I am a graduate student studying music and the performing arts. I am primarily interested in refining my talent and crafting a pleasant existence doing what I love—performing for appreciative audiences. I will be happy within any political structure that permits me to do that peacefully. But here I am, darting among the shadows and behaving like some Mata Hari because my mother is a Polish Jew and my male companion had a mother named Eva Rosenberg, who died twenty years ago. We didn't corrupt the banking system of Germany and we don't threaten the national priorities of road-building or geographic expansion. How many *other* Jews, Gypsies, homosexuals, Communists, and foreigners are being forced into panic, as we are, by a government which proceeds like a road grader, flattening everything to its liking?

"I want the ability to be just a little different, so long as I am honest, hard-working, and law-abiding. I don't want a tone-deaf government minister telling me what music I must perform or what ancestors my companion must have. Am I unreasonable?"

Her father put his hands on Sofie's shoulders and looked squarely into her magnificent eyes. "Sofie, as you grow older you will see that many good policies can appear flawed when individual cases are examined. We try to evaluate success by the broad results, not the exceptions. If, let's say, the government decreed that all German school children under the age of 12 be given daily rations of whole milk to build strong bones, and one child choked to death while drinking milk, would that make the program a bad one? Of course not! We are asked to be patient until the overall results may be assayed. So—how do you see Germany today compared to ten years ago? Better, eh?"

"I'm not sure, Poppy. I wish I could divorce my view of the new

Germany from the misery it is causing me personally. And, as you said, I may still be too young and inexperienced to separate the two. But, another thing: Suppose the führer makes all good decisions and enacts really excellent laws and carries Germany to world prominence as a benevolent dictator, yes? What happens when all of that unbridled, centralized power passes on to another person—a successor who is totally malevolent? Would we not then have a pliant nation in evil hands? By concentrating so much power and acceding to the cult of the individual, don't we make our society more vulnerable?"

"You have incorporated too many assumptions into one proposition, Sofie. *Any* form of government can be corrupted, but in a strong, healthy country there are appropriate counterweights. Other institutions, such as the military, stand ready to prevent the abuse of power."

"Poppy, do you mean reactions like the Oster Conspiracy?" Sofie could see instantly that it had been the wrong direction to take her argument, as her father slouched deep into his chair and waved a hand, as if in surrender. "I'm sorry, Poppy, but wasn't that an attempt by patriotic military professionals to unseat a central power which they deemed to be running amok? I know that you were *not* one of the plotters, but . . . "

The discussion was already over, and both father and daughter sought to regain common ground for a topic of conversation with which to end their dinner. Otto spoke first. "When will you return to Prague?" he queried. "And to Dieter," he added, as a quick afterthought. "Are you planning to resume your public singing there, at the Majestic Plaza Hotel? If so, I must find some pretext which will allow me to visit Prague for a day or two, just to sit anonymously in your audience and celebrate my good fortune."

"Poppy, nothing would make me happier than to sing for you in that beautiful setting, but I have decided I should not risk a return to Prague until Jurgen Deitz has departed and I'm no longer haunted by his eyes staring at me from the dark corners of the lounge. So, I am considering making a brief trip to France, where I might have the opportunity to work for a few sessions with Django and Stéphane. I learned so much from them about timing and interaction between performers in just a week while they were in Prague. Since then, I have developed my own sense of audience management, so I believe they would allow me three or four numbers each evening, and I am rich enough that I can do it without being paid! I can travel to Paris as Sophia Havlik from Neuchâtel and not attract any attention at the border."

She continued, "Dieter and Juraslav get along well, and I can communicate with them through messages to the clinic often enough to know when it appears safe to return and resume performing there. Hopefully it will be only a brief separation. What do you think?"

Otto responded, "I agree that you and Dieter should not resurface together immediately after Jurgen departs for his next assignment. If he has mentioned you to associates, the two events could be connected and some other eyes might be fixed upon you from the dark recesses. Yes— take a sabbatical in France with your mentors and call me at the private telephone number I gave you—each two or three weeks—even if only to confirm your safety and to learn the status of matters in Prague and here ... and, I would urge you to be cautious about your newly acquired assets. You are a twenty-four-year-old musician, Sofie, and that sounds like a description of struggling finances to most people. No need to subsist on day-old bread crusts, but don't book a suite at The Crillon, either."

Sofie brightened. "Poppy, I can't move as silently as you, but I have developed a stealthy side, and I will stay in character."

On the following morning, Klaus Kolb drove Sofie to the early train to Paris, and soon a young Swiss musician was staring out her compartment window at Berlin, wondering when she would next see it— or Lilkahaus, or the father she so adored. An inner sense alerted her to the possibility that unexpected events could conspire to delay all such happy reunions.

CHAPTER THIRTY-THREE

Prague - February 1939

HUNTING THE HUNTER

L t. Colonel Edward Gunther skillfully manipulated a coin so that it "walked" across the back of his fingers, turning over one half revolution between each crease. Not many people could perform the trick, but then, not many had the patience to cultivate that degree of control. The Gestapo commander for Prague prided himself on disciplined thinking that sorted through seemingly irrelevant details and weighed probabilities until everything fitted together nicely.

He had by now obsessed over Jurgen Deitz for several days, but the puzzle only grew more challenging as he did so. Deitz was intelligent and he was ambitious, too. Deitz had thought that the young German soldier with whom he had traveled on a train from Berlin to Prague was bogus— why? Because he was in a first-class compartment which he shared with an old lady, to whom he referred in one remark as "his mother." However, after their arrival, the two had not remained together. Instead, the soldier had walked down Ruzova with Deitz to a brothel. And the old woman—had anyone even seen her again? Because she had produced a courtesy letter from a powerful national leader, there were officials at the Prague station alerted to her arrival. Apparently none had identified her among the arriving passengers. Curious, no?

The soldier had said that he was to work in the consular offices, but that appeared to have been a fabrication. Then later, Deitz had encountered the same young man—who had by then altered his appearance—working in an excellent hotel frequented by visiting

Germans, with whom he interacted. At the hotel, the man was piano accompanist to a young female singer.

Deitz had concluded that the man was an agent of *some* German intelligence agency, which was why he initially brought the matter to his superior's attention, obviously hoping to advance his career by doing so. When that produced no results for him and he was ordered to drop the matter, Deitz had persisted, attempting to circumvent normal lines of authority to learn what he could from other Gestapo sources in Germany. There he had learned that a "Dieter Meister" had been sought but had frustrated efforts through a series of skillful escapes. And finally, Deitz had gleaned from the assistant manager of the Majestic Plaza that the piano player was named Dieter Havlik, a resident of Neuchâtel, Switzerland.—which was another fabrication. Yes, Deitz had been right to be suspicious, but what rational explanation could be assigned to all of the deceptions he had uncovered?

The coin slipped sideways from Colonel Gunther's ring finger and rolled a few feet away from his desk. As he retrieved it, his secretary announced that his 4 p.m. appointment—Accounting Specialist Jurgen Deitz—had arrived and was waiting. "Then show him in!" commanded the senior officer.

"Deitz! Good to see you—Heil Hitler! Here, take a chair here by my desk, young man." After establishing that they were now on much more cordial terms, he continued. "Do you recall our earlier meeting, when you shared your concerns about a 'Dieter Meister' and you described certain incongruities which you had observed?"

"Of course, sir."

"At the conclusion of that interview, I directed you to cease your investigation—but apparently you ignored that order. Correct?"

"Unfortunately, correct, sir."

"And you are, of course, aware that contradicting a direct order from your superior can result in disciplinary actions, yet you persisted—and with what result?"

"Sir—my apologies. The ongoing search for rational explanations did continue, but *never* at the expense of my assigned duties. I am a naturally curious observer of all my surroundings, and the inconsistencies in Dieter Meister begged for clarification. If I had encountered anything more, I would have shared it immediately with this office and risked the consequences you describe."

"Deitz, who is Wehrmacht Major Fritz Heller? And why has he requested *your* transfer from this command to his staff in Forst?"

There was no immediate response from Jurgen Deitz, and it seemed apparent that neither Major Heller nor his personnel request meant anything to Jurgen. Finally, he looked directly at his superior and smiled conspiratorially. "Sir that confirms it! My probe has made someone uncomfortable, and the requested transfer is an attempt to shield Meister—or whatever his name is—from any further scrutiny. Whoever initiated that request had access to my personnel records and knew that I am from Forst, which lies hard by our border with Poland, you know. He wants the reassignment to appear credible and logical—an accountant from that town with intimate knowledge of the area and of the Polish language. Don't you see?"

Colonel Gunther walked the coin across the backs of his fingers again and his brow furrowed. It was the kind of analysis he had often made himself during his ascent to command authority, and it seemed to fit nicely into the mystery of Dieter Meister. On its last rotation, the coin again dropped to the floor and rolled to the chair where Jurgen Deitz sat anxiously awaiting some acknowledgment that he may have provoked the transfer request through his probe. Deitz retrieved the coin and walked it across his own hand quite expertly, then smiled and handed it back to his superior. "The smaller coins are even more difficult, yes Colonel?" he smiled, with the faintest hint of sarcasm.

"I am going to approve your transfer to Forst, but will convey my regrets that it may not be accomplished until you can complete an important audit upon which you are working for me. That work is estimated to consume about three weeks of your time—not an unreasonable condition for an area commander to impose in a response to a field major, eh? After all, the Third Reich is supposed to last for a thousand years, and twenty-one days in the life of an accountant should not put that grand plan into serious jeopardy.

"One final thing, Deitz. I am not in the habit of condoning disobedience, and you have willfully disobeyed me. Now, I am telling you: peel this banana and keep the process one hundred percent within *my* parameters. There will be *no* tangents and *no* leaks. No bragging in brothels about your new mission for the Gestapo commander and no unauthorized calls to Germany. If I suspect for a minute that you are working at cross purposes to me, you will return to Forst *in a box*! Do you understand?"

"Sir. I will clear every step in advance with you, sir—and I will request a personal meeting anytime there are new details to share. Thank you for your confidence. I will not abuse it, sir."

Colonel Gunther knew that the image of an undraped casket being unloaded at the Forst railroad depot had produced the desired effect, and he was confident that the obviously bright Deitz would make every effort to complete the inquiry successfully. "There is one more thing, Deitz. If you are regularly at my door, that will draw attention, so please just deliver a daily one-page summary to my secretary in a sealed envelope, and if you encounter a true emergency, call me at this number, which only I answer. Good luck with your work. Heil Hitler!"

Jurgen returned the salute but remained at his commander's desk for one more moment. "Sir, have I your permission to take the local train as far as the Teplice Border Station to speak with the immigration guards there? Three of them interacted with Meister and the old woman, and perhaps there is a thread to be retrieved there."

"Permission granted. Heil Hitler!"

The first days following Sofie's return to Berlin had given Dieter a needed break from the tensions of performing in public, plus those added by a Gestapo agent seemingly picking away at the fabric of Dieter's identity. However, by the second week of her absence, time—devoid of energy—became progressively more discouraging. During the hours when the clinic received its patients, Dieter sat in his room and read the periodicals which Magda and Elsa carried back from whatever they were doing in the city.

Most evenings, the four inhabitants dined quietly together. Even though "the girls" prepared those meals, they sat as equals at the table, and there was a sharing of newly gathered information regarding the quickening pace of Germany's aggressive actions toward its neighbors.

"Poland's situation is nearly impossible," observed a concerned Elsa. "The country's leadership is divided, and the army is ill-equipped to resist the panzer units camped near our borders. Added to that, we have the reality that it may be far more acceptable to be occupied by Germans—who are at least Christians—than by the godless Soviet animals. If that is to be our choice, of course."

Juraslav added his concern that France and England had encouraged further German adventures by meekly condoning the absorption of Austria and large parts of Czechoslovakia, all in the name of satisfying Herr Hitler's desire to repatriate Germans in those countries, and, of course, to avoid another Great War with all of the remembered horrors of that conflict only a generation ago.

The Low Countries, Scandinavia, and the Baltic Nations all sent sycophants to Berlin, seeking assurances that they were not slated for "liberation" by the Third Reich. Everyone was told exactly what he wished to hear, but Juraslav was certain that those assurances had no value and that Germany would be free to continue its outrageous behavior. All of this produced an aura of gloom around the small coterie of expatriates sitting together nightly and awaiting some outside word as to how they should proceed before their options began to close.

Three weeks after her departure from Prague, Sofie sent a telegraphic message addressed to the clinic:

> STATUS UPDATE / PATIENT #412-1938: THIS PATIENT NOW SCHEDULED FOR SPECIALIZED TREATMENT IN GERMANY AND WILL BE TRANSFERRED AS SOON AS RECENT PROCEDURE HAS HEALED STOP ESTIMATED TIME BEFORE TRANSFER IS 21 DAYS AS REQUESTED BY ATTENDING PRAGUE PHYSICIAN STOP NO COMPLICATIONS REPORTED BUT NORMAL CAUTION RECOMMENDED STOP J BAKER RESIDENT BERLIN FULL STOP

Juraslav passed the message to his dining companions with obvious disappointment. "Three more weeks exceeds the tolerance we had agreed upon. We must consider whether our vulnerability can stand up to that period of possible exposure."

Magda responded immediately. "Obviously, it will depend upon how Deitz spends those three weeks. If he is confined to his normal accounting work plus the business of packing and turning over his files while preparing to depart, that could be benign and acceptable, but if he continues on the same mission of uncovering Dieter and Sofie, three weeks more would be intolerable.

"So, I believe that our effort should be to observe as closely as possible what Deitz is doing with his remaining Prague time. His movements and contacts will provide the answer. Elsa and I should share primary surveillance, and we should incorporate the help of Renate at the Porte Verte and Romani employees at the Majestic Plaza. There's also a secretary within the Gestapo office who watches him as closely as possible. We'll know soon enough if Deitz still presents a threat. If so, we are obligated to neutralize the threat. Do you all agree?"

There were nods of approval from around the table, and they began assigning daily responsibilities on a shared calendar. Elsa would be the first to establish and maintain visual contact, and she would communicate to the clinic by telephone if she needed support. Juraslav would contact the Romani leadership and also pay a personal medical visit to the Porte Verte to alert Renate. Dieter must remain hidden in the clinic but available to coordinate telephone messages from the others.

Dieter sensed ominous forebodings that the extended time and close monitoring of Jurgen would necessarily result in some tragedy. He thought that somehow it was an inappropriate consequence for one who had merely offered to share his cigarettes with a fellow traveler on a train. It seemed a bit like his own innocent entanglement in so many intrigues, and the entire complicated mess now made him weary. He wished that he and Sofie could be working some small room far, far away from Europe's problems. Could that ever be recaptured?

CHAPTER THIRTY-FOUR
Paris - February 1939

OLD FRIENDS / NEW HORIZONS

Sophia Havlik from Neuchâtel, Switzerland, arrived at the Gar del Este in Paris, where she took the underground to Montparnasse Station—near to the Jazz Emporium, a large café popular with music enthusiasts from across Europe. Despite the tensions gripping the Continent, Paris seemed vibrant, and the Emporium was obviously preparing itself for another capacity evening. Several billboards posted in the windows and others freestanding on the sidewalk announced that Django Reinhardt and Stéphane Grappelli were in residence, and that a substantial cover charge and minimum would be in effect for all performances. It all seemed so wonderfully normal. Perhaps that was one of the greatest gifts of good music—shutting out the ugliness of the real world for a brief, surreal period of total immersion.

Sofie put those ruminations aside and applied her charm to a doorman, convincing him to allow her to enter the closed café where she could hear the Quintette rehearsing for its evening performance. She did not immediately interrupt but rather hovered near a bartender who was arranging the tools of his trade and who only nodded in her direction as he continued turning the labels of familiar bottles toward the rail where jazz aficionados would begin to gather in another hour.

The Quintette stopped frequently to make jot reminders on their charts, each to remind them of some special treatment that one or another would employ to embellish the popular standards their audience would be demanding. The ballad they were rehearsing was Johnny

Green's beautiful "Body And Soul," and from the direction of the bar they heard a female voice ask, "Wouldn't that be perfect for a vocal by some sultry girl singer?" All five musicians halted their playing and looked toward the source of interruption. Stéphane was the first to recognize the speaker.

"Mon Dieu . . . is that the toast of the Prague Trocadero right here in our little Emporium?" His broad smile assured Sofie that she was welcome, and the others quickly recognized her and joined in extending a warm greeting.

"I'm looking for the opportunity to continue my musical education and came to Paris—to my best teachers—to inquire whether I might apprentice for a week or two. After you moved on from Prague, our random Trocadero partnership helped me land a three-week gig at the Majestic Plaza, and I'm told that it was well received. However, I've also learned that solo performers learn mainly from themselves, and that can be a slow and even painful process. Please—I hope I'm not being bold— but would you consider letting me perform a few numbers with you while I'm here? If we can actually rehearse them, I believe they could be better than at the Trocadero.

"I need to purchase new stage dresses here in Paris, and I'll select something which your patrons will notice—and I'm not asking to be paid anything but the experience. So, gentlemen, what do you think?" She did her very best to let her eyes ask the question in a most appealing way and then waited for the answer she hoped to hear.

Django lit a cigarette thoughtfully and smoothed his Adolf Monjou– style, pencil-thin moustache. Then he looked directly at the young woman. "Sofie—*this* is our home city, and jazz people come from across Europe to listen to us here. We regularly introduce our best material at the Jazz Emporium, and we even cut many of our recordings right in this room with live audiences. I hope you can understand that trying to add an amateur vocalist would totally upset that balance—so it would be quite impossible to consider your request. Right, gentlemen?"

Then he suddenly laughed and clapped his hands together like a playful little boy. "Hah! You really believed me, *ma chère*! Of *course* we will cut you a slice of our evening—beginning tonight. We all had a circus in Prague watching your improvisations, and our audiences there called you back—how many times? Two, three encores each night, no?

Let's play "Body And Soul" from the top and modulate to a D-flat chorus for Sophia. Then you can run over to that boutique in the Montparnasse Plaza and pick out your first Paris frock. I'm sure you can find something just right for "Body And Soul," eh? Just the right amount of 'body' for the Emporium crowd!"

Sofie squeezed her eyes together, interrupting the escape of a wayward tear, then she threw her arms around Django's shoulders and planted a full kiss on his forehead. "Thank you! Thank you all. The Trocadero was incredible for me, but Paris with the Quintette exceeds my most ambitious dreams. I promise you I'll give your audience the best "Body And Soul" they've ever heard. So: What should we plan for the first encore?"

There was warm laughter from all of her companions, and she allowed herself to enjoy the moment with abandon. There would be time enough later to remember that she could not disengage totally from Europe's frightening circumstances or from several endangered people whom she loved dearly. But that sobering reminder was not permitted to mute her explosive happiness, and she moved forward to the rehearsal stage determined to attack the evening performance with all of the energy and competence she could muster. This could be the defining evening of her career, and Sofie vowed that it would be her signature performance.

CHAPTER THIRTY-FIVE

Prague – February 1939

SWW AT WORK

Elsa sipped from a demitasse cup loaded with strong Arabic coffee and took tiny bites from a slice of sugared kuken, which left traces of white powder around the edges of her full lips. She had been seated at the sidewalk café across the boulevard from Prague Gestapo headquarters for nearly an hour, and she could feel her toes complaining with the cold. The Romani counterman inside the café had been alerted that there would be a telephone call for "the Polish lady seated under his awning," but no call had come, and the lady appeared determined to make the meager fare last all morning if necessary.

The double ring, common to Prague telephones, caught him precisely as he began a fresh brewing cycle for the expected second wave of boulevardiers. He dropped the receiver in annoyance, then retrieved it, issuing a soft Gypsy curse at no one in particular and spitting out the name of the café to the caller.

"Let me speak to the lady seated outside your door—wearing a raincoat and with a pink satchel from the Bata Department Store on the chair by her side." Obviously, the caller could see the café from some nearby vantage point; the Romani counterman wondered what intrigue he was abetting. He proceeded to the window and knocked upon the glass to attract the raincoat-clad patron. She was at his side with remarkable quickness and took the telephone from its resting place.

"Yes. Thank you. How soon? Wearing what? Carrying a document case, you say. Thank you." She disconnected and immediately dialed a number from memory. "Maggie, we are doing a hand-off at Hlavni Nadrazi in just a few minutes. We will both take the local to Teplice and we can decide how to proceed once there. It is a nothing town except for the border-crossing activity, so we need cover. Ask Jura if he has any Romani women friends with babies near Teplice. If so, have her meet the train with a baby and show it to us like old friends on the platform—that always seems innocuous to men. Even Gestapo animals tend to dismiss women emoting over babies as being a zero factor.

"There may be a lunch counter at the station or nearby from which we can monitor our target. He has booked return passage from Teplice, leaving about ninety minutes after his arrival there. If you can, bring a change of clothes so that one of us can be on the return train without—well, you know the procedure, Maggie."

"Congratulations, Elsa. You were right about his getting more from the border guards—he seems to have worked that out, too. Damn! That could be the spark to blow this whole thing. I must hurry—see you at Hlavni. Bye."

Jurgen Deitz was charged with excitement that morning, He was now working directly with the top Gestapo officer in his area on a matter which he knew instinctively could have profound career implications for both of them. And, following the current assignment, he was headed back to Germany—to an installation near Forst, where his few close relatives still lived.

Jurgen had thought often about the described "courtesy letter" from Luftmarschal Göring, which had been intended to assist someone on the train—probably Dieter Meister, or perhaps the old lady sharing his compartment. If that letter contained a name it would—or could—provide an important clue to Dieter Meister's real identity and mission. Perhaps it would even explain the enigma of a Jew wearing a Wehrmacht uniform. He silently congratulated himself upon this superb bit of reasoning, which again proved—to Jurgen, at least—that he was a natural in the intelligence-gathering profession. All of his euphoria prevented him from noticing the young woman who fell into step a few meters behind him as he departed from his office to walk the short distance to

Hlavni Nadrazi Station. That omission in turn caused him to miss the coincidence that the same young woman was later sitting with a friend in the waiting area for his departure.

When they arrived at Teplice, Magda and Elsa stepped quickly from the train and bolted toward a young woman pushing a baby tram, who waved at them like an old friend. The three of them exchanged meaningless baby superlatives as they watched Jurgen amble by and request directions from the stationmaster, who pointed to some low, swastika-emblazoned buildings. They were the barracks and office of the official border guards, charged with inspecting the contents and passengers aboard trains passing from Germany into Czechoslovakia. As he walked away, the three women opened a picnic basket at a public table and began sharing morsels of grilled goat meat and a bottle of local red wine.

Forty-five minutes later, the young mother wheeled her carriage away from their picnic, and Magda and Elsa visited the public toilet, where they made changes in their clothing and hair, somewhat altering their appearances. Then they sat separately in the station house with a few others who were awaiting the southbound local train. They were relieved to see Jurgen walking back to the platform shortly before the train's scheduled arrival time, seemingly engrossed in adding to the contents of the document case which both had noted earlier. When the train ground to a stop, they were careful to enter the same car as Jurgen, but from its opposite end. Once inside, Elsa produced a deck of playing cards, and the two unremarkable-looking women gave the impression of being totally absorbed in some kind of card game, rarely glancing in the direction of the Gestapo operative who was hurriedly scribbling notes only three rows away from them.

Fifteen minutes into their return trip, Herr Deitz left his seat carrying the document case, but leaving his coat and newspaper in the overhead baggage rack. He walked purposefully in the direction of the dining car, which had been pointed out by their conductor. "Three cars to the rear, mein Herr." Neither Elsa nor Magda attempted to follow but set their cards aside and watched as their assignment disappeared through the swaying cars. Elsa suggested that one of them walk to the dining car if Deitz had not returned within the next fifteen minutes, and both checked their timepieces to be certain they did not wait too long to check on him.

When it was time, Magda slipped into the aisle and took a few steps toward the dining car. Then the train braked suddenly, causing her to lose her balance for a moment, and soon it was grinding noisily to a full stop in open countryside. She started again toward her intended destination, but two train crewmembers sprinted through the car in apparent confusion and told everyone to remain seated. Elsa grasped the sleeve of the conductor's uniform and asked if the train had suffered a mechanical problem, to which the conductor responded distraughtly, "No, Fräulein, but apparently one of our passengers has fallen from the train. I believe he was walking from car to car and lost his footing as we passed through Litoměřice—a small town two or three kilometers back. Now we must wait for the police.

"Actually, I believe that the poor fellow was seated in *this* car and had gone to the dining car for something to eat. My guess is that we will not be detained for long; this is a single-track run, and we will be holding up other trains before long. Besides, he is probably dead, and we can't help him by waiting, ja?" Elsa was horrified that their quarry may have died suddenly while both of them sat only a short distance away.

When the conductor had walked on, Magda leaned toward her companion and whispered in a frightened voice, "Elsa, this is not good. We can assume that Deitz didn't fall or jump, but rather that he had help dying. That surely means someone else was watching him today, and even though Jurgen didn't see us, we may have been noticed. We cannot stay on the train all the way to Prague—what is the next scheduled stop where we can drop from sight?"

"That would be Lidice," was the quick response. "I agree; we should step quickly away from the train just as it departs from Lidice station and try to find a bus into Prague. And before we return to the clinic, we must call to be certain it is safe to do so. Dieter is there, but I hate to tell him on the telephone that Jurgen has died. You know how he feels about that, and he may even assume that it was we who—you know."

"I wonder about that document case he was carrying. Do you think it was lying with his body, or—"

"Don't be naive. That case was probably the reason he was done in and it is going to be part of another probe into Dieter's and Sofie's identities. The Gestapo will put all of this together soon, and we have a decision to make. Jurgen is no longer a 'stop point' for protecting all of us. We waited too long, Maggie. We let personal consideration for Dieter dictate our course. And we both know that is unprofessional. You and I have to get back to thinking and performing like SWW *professionals*."

"Then we must get through to Lilka and tell her that the clinic is exposed and everyone should leave."

"And where do we go? Things are bad at home, too. Germany gets bolder every day, and unless France and England announce that they will defend Poland, Hitler will cross the border and grab what he wants. I'm not loyal enough to work in some whorehouse in occupied Poland, being abused by German soldiers while I grub for scraps of information. I don't know about you, but I'm ready to go to England or America and be ordinary. How do we do that, Maggie? How do we?" She blew her nose and gazed out the window at nothing in particular. Then she nearly growled her concluding thought. "If we had slit that fucker's throat and dumped him in the river two weeks ago, this whole operation could have continued indefinitely!"

CHAPTER THIRTY-SIX

Prague – February 1939

TOO MUCH KNOWLEDGE

Lt. Col. Edward Gunther watched the progress of the gold coin across the backs of his fingers. A thought teased his conscious mind: I can do this flawlessly with my *right* hand, but I have never even attempted it with my left. A common error. Work only in one's comfort zone; don't venture where there may be less familiarity. How many lessons can be learned in unfamiliar territory? How many clues go undetected because of our reluctance to "leave home" and innovate?

It wasn't an organized thought, but Edward Gunther imagined that there could be an indictment of his work within the truism as he sorted through it and watched the coin's progress. What if his reliance upon Jurgen Deitz and Deitz's singular obsession with the mysterious soldier on the train had distracted him from an even more obscure trail—that of the feisty old lady in the same compartment? Could she be the important person and the soldier only peripheral? How could a skilled researcher like Gunther learn more about an old lady who rode from Berlin to Prague on a train four months earlier?

His ruminations were interrupted by a knock on the office door. "Sir? I must have a word with you," intoned his usually phlegmatic adjutant. "One of the members of our staff has suffered a fatal accident today. He fell from a moving train an hour north of here, and apparently died instantly."

"Name?" inquired the colonel.

"Jurgen Deitz," was the quick response. "He was scheduled for reassignment and apparently completing some work prior to leaving Prague. Sad, no?"

"Yes," said the impassive Gestapo chief. "We must notify his family as well as the unit to which he was being transferred. Will you please draft two letters for my signature? Include the standard commendations for excellent service and an additional month's pay to the decedent's survivors. Let's get those out at once. Is there a police report on the death?"

"Not yet, sir. But I understand that he was seen speaking with a man in the dining car and that they left together, walking in the opposite direction from the car where Deitz had been seated."

"And his belongings?" asked the officer. "Were they recovered?"

"His outer coat and a newspaper were in the overhead rack where he had been sitting, and he had his identification papers, some photos, and quite a sum of cash in his billfold. They were on his body, sir."

"Anything else? Reading materials? Notes?"

"Apparently not, sir," answered the adjutant.

"Then that will be all for now," said the Colonel, effectively dismissing the younger officer. Once he was alone, Lt. Col. Edward Gunther slid a document case from under his desk and continued analyzing its contents. There were two notepads filled with handwritten, dated notations. Each was in a kind of personal shorthand Col. Gunther was able to decipher easily. Entries were dated, and the earliest were about 60 days before the last, which bore today's date and said:

> *Treplice. BGds rotated 2 wks. Crnt pers say rcds sho incident @ train on arr date. RM Göring safe psg letter in possession of fem psgr in comptmt bkd w illegbl name – possible 'Sigwitz or Seglitz." BGd desisted. Oldr FM Psgr not IDd deptg train Prague. Appearnc altered? flu possbl connct Göring / Seglitz*

"Possible change of appearance," Gunther muttered to himself. It intrigued him and apparently had also drawn the attention of the unfortunate Jurgen Deitz. In the margin, Deitz had added two notes to himself:

Could old Frau Seglitz (?) be yng Sophia Havlik? Both were companions of Dieter Meister. Why wd. either be important to H. G.?

Col. Gunther thought it ironic that his young accountant had been so adept at probing the mystery but had also been so clumsy that he necessitated his own elimination. One with more training and experience would have known better than to go out of channels in a matter of concern to persons of standing. Gunther expected that the death of Deitz would now reveal the authority who had wanted to summon Deitz from Prague to Forst. He doubted that the request was Heller's but more likely someone Heller would accommodate. He would be expected to contact Heller, and, if he were skillful, could obtain the information without appearing to be probing.

The larger question was what use Gunther should make of the information once he possessed it. He would be able to "bank" it together with a catalogue of personal secrets he had hoarded for future use. Blackmail was a potent tool for any rising Gestapo officer, and Edward Gunther had already accumulated and stored many treasures that were never intended for public disclosure. He wondered whether Deitz should have been allowed to pursue his prey a little longer before meeting with a tragic accident, but, no—Deitz was a talker, and the true value of the information would be its exclusivity.

He placed a small gold coin on the back of his left hand and painstakingly guided it over three fingers before it escaped his control and fell to the floor. With a little more work, he would be able to master the movement.

Sofie—Sophia—the Sensational Swiss Songstress, discovered recently in Prague, made a successful musical debut at the Jazz Emporium in Montparnasse. Even though Paris was extremely edgy, awaiting Herr Hitler's next bizarre moves, the City of Light continued to be a mecca for sophisticates who were still interested in superior food, outrageous American music, and beautiful people. Sophia's performing dress radiated *haute couture* to her international audience, and her cognac-softened voice, embracing the lyric of "Body and Soul," elevated the status of love above mundane concerns about a new European conflict, at least for a while. Django and Stéphane exchanged delighted expressions of approval, and the audience made no secret of its elation over finding a new treasure at the Emporium that evening.

At the conclusion of the session, Django asked, "How long will you be with us in Paris?" to which Sofie shrugged a non-response, saying that her plans were unsettled. At least ... perhaps ... a week or two, following which she would return to Neuchâtel. There was tacit agreement that the new musical partnership should remain intact for whatever time Sofie stayed in Paris. In a remote recess of her mind, Sofie realized that she was nourishing the quiet hope that she might continue in France for much longer than she had originally thought possible. Circumstances had conspired to advance her musical career beyond anything she had imagined a short time ago, and while she was here, she vowed to enjoy that bounty. There was talk of "peace in our time" among British and French leaders and, if that really resulted, she could visualize her rapid ascent on the Paris musical scene.

It was the one part of the troubled world around her where she had a degree of control. By concentrating all of her energy on each song she rehearsed and each audience she faced, Sofie believed she might gain recognition as an important new face on the musical scene. If that scene were truly blessed with peace and prosperity, she would have covered several giant steps by maximizing her exposure with the wonderful men of the Quintette. And then? Could she still bring Dieter back into her life if she didn't return immediately to Prague and to him? A quiet smile softened her face as she walked out of the Emporium, passing through Montparnasse and back to the cramped room in the small hotel which would be home for now.

At the Havlik Clinic, Dieter and Juraslav reexamined together the two morsels of outside information that had filtered through to them during the last twenty-four hours. The first, from Sofie, told them that she was going to France for a brief visit to fill the buffer interval between the reassignment and departure of Jurgen Deitz and her own reappearance in Prague. She hinted that she would like to have Dieter inquire about when they might again work the lounge at the Majestic Plaza, so that her return could be explained easily by the resumption of her career there.

The second, from Janusz Kwiek, now recognized as king of the Gypsies, succeeding his father, Michael, reported that the Litoměřice police had acted swiftly to declare the death of "the German tourist, Jurgen Deitz" an unfortunate accident, "possibly the result of excessive alcohol consumption prior to boarding the train." The investigation had been closed officially and the mutilated remains of the visitor returned to his next of kin in Forst, Germany.

"We know from Magda and Elsa that Jurgen appeared to have been traveling alone on the train and that he seemed normal and alert when he left their railroad car, walking in the direction of the dining car with his document bag." Dieter intoned mechanically, as if creating a detective's checklist. He continued, "and Janusz has assured us that none of his people were complicit in anything which would have resulted in Jurgen's accident. Only the young Gypsy mother who greeted Elsa and Magda at the Treplice Station actually observed him."

Juraslav interrupted, "Let's assume that we can also omit General von Seigler and his affiliates from consideration, since there was already a transfer order in process and he would never want to draw attention to the individual—Deitz—for fear his involvement would be uncovered. Don't you agree?"

"Mmmmm, yes. So could it be that the most likely causal connection would be to Deitz's own Gestapo organization, which could cause the local police investigation to take the swift and abbreviated course it did, and could get the body out of the area immediately? That's frightening—the idea that his own associates eliminated Jurgen. Are we being logical, or have we overlooked something obvious, Jura?"

"Well, if Deitz had actually pulled together enough facts to link Sofie and Dieter to the general, and if it could be demonstrated that Göring helped the two of them to slip out of Berlin before they could be incorporated into the Oster thing, that could be a bombshell. If he had all of that in his document case, can you imagine that the case and Deitz might be high priority for a Gestapo thrust? That's the kind of dirt they thrive on—the things which make big names subject to blackmail, Dieter!"

"All right, I can see that. Now, here's one more consideration in support of the idea that the Gestapo did it. Jurgen was in a public place—a train, right? And someone lured him from the dining car in the opposite direction from the seat he had occupied earlier and pushed him to his death. But there was no commotion, as there might have been if an unknown person started muscling him out of the dining car. He just stood up and walked away normally, as if he were accompanying someone he *knew*! Doesn't that suggest that he encountered an associate—or superior—and walked willingly from his comfortable seat in the dining car?"

Juraslav's brow furrowed in thought, then he continued in a much lower, almost conspiratorial, tone. "Dieter, here is the danger I see. A Gestapo agent acquires all of the information Deitz has compiled and realizes that he has most of the pieces of an embarrassing relationship that has been covered up. There is still one huge flaw: just as everyone else has done, he has failed to locate the fugitives! The mysterious Dieter Meister, who disappears at will, has done so again, and Herr Gestapo has only a story but no culprits. So, wouldn't Herr Gestapo try to be patient and nab them before making his case in Berlin? I think so, Dieter—I really think so."

"Then we must not fall into the trap. We can't just resume singing in the Majestic Plaza if grabbing us is the last step in assembling this leverage. I feel as if I have already betrayed so many people by my blundering here, and I would be mortified if Sofie came back to Prague only to be seized by some Gestapo thug and used to ruin her father's career. I'm miserable, Jura. Simply miserable."

The older man embraced him gently and tried to protect him from his self-criticism, but he knew that Dieter had endangered everyone in the clinic and so could only join him in lamenting. As their embrace lingered, both realized how close they had become, and each sensed the beginning of a new interdependence in this hostile place. Dieter finally released Juraslav's hand and, with an air of finality, said, "We must get word to Sofie that she cannot come here or return to Berlin—she will have to remain in Paris until all of this intrigue has been put to rest. However long . . . " But the words trailed off and gave way to a shrug of resignation.

CHAPTER THIRTY-SEVEN
March – 1939

OLD ALLIES ADDRESS NEW ISSUES

The telephone reception from Warsaw to Berlin seemed unusually clear. Lilka Rudovska reflected upon the fact; usually "others" would be listening, and that resulted in crackling noises and gaps in the connection. After being connected with the regional operator, Lilka had given her the private number for *Lilkahaus,* and a few moments later she heard the resonant voice of her long-ago lover and husband. As always, he seemed to project confidence and authority, and for a moment she imagined them together in her small flat years ago, totally comfortable and delightfully intimate. As she had done many times before, Lilka wondered briefly what their lives might have been without the stigma that had attached to her nationality and religious affiliation. Could they have remained together and raised their daughter? Or would the political alliances of Europe have torn them apart, as happened earlier with Tovar?

"This is Otto von Seigler," the voice repeated. "Who is calling?"

"My name is Lilka Rudovska and I am inquiring about a beautiful young woman who combines our best properties," Lilka answered playfully. For a brief moment, twenty-three years seemed to melt away, leaving two proud parents exchanging pleasantries. From Juraslav, Lilka had heard all about Sofie's appearance at the Majestic Plaza, but Magda and Elsa had later recounted the abrupt end of that engagement, as a rogue Gestapo functionary entered their lives and threatened to uncover their identities.

"I have arranged for that Deitz fellow to be reassigned to the Polish border," Otto interrupted. "Once he has departed from Prague, Sofie can return and be reasonably certain that no one is peeking into her windows. We believe that his intense surveillance was a personal mission—not part of any official Gestapo probe of Sofie and her friend."

"Then you are not aware that the fellow is dead?" Lilka questioned. "My girls in Prague reported that he was crushed under a train near a town named Litoměřice, not far from the old German border, yesterday afternoon. They were observing his trip to Teplice, where he apparently questioned the border guards, still trying to identify the two travelers with whom he had entered the country."

"Had Deitz learned anything important?" the concerned Otto asked, hoping that the Gestapo soldier had not been murdered because he had already identified Sofie.

"We don't know that, but he had been carrying a document case which probably contained the results of his investigation since he began his probe—that would be many weeks ago. The case and its contents are in other hands now; someone wanted the information and did not want our young antagonist, Deitz, to be in possession of it. Apparently Deitz's death was as important as the document case to some interested party."

"Could the Gypsies have done this?" Otto asked hopefully.

"Apparently not. They have been following Deitz's movements— you know, they are *everywhere* in Czechoslovakia—but they deny any complicity in his death. Jura believes them, and he has concluded that this was another example of intra-Gestapo treachery. Do you know the Gestapo commander in Prague—Lt. Col. Edward Gunther?"

"No, not personally, but his reputation is one filled with much personal ambition and few scruples. He was posted out to Prague because many of his fellow officers in Berlin found him personally offensive. I believe we must assume that Gunther now has whatever facts and scenarios the young accountant was able to piece together, and Gunther's higher position will allow him to ferret out the remaining parts to the puzzle."

"And would that put you in jeopardy, Ottobert?" the concerned Lilka questioned, using a term of endearment long forgotten.

"Probably not, my love." He unconsciously rejoined. "My only vulnerability is in the matter of Oster. Hermann's office controls that investigation and Hermann already knows everything about you and

Sofie. He is fond of Sofie and was helpful in spiriting her away from Berlin, although he doesn't know where she has gone. Hermann's wife, Emmy, has intervened with him on behalf of several Jewish people, and she, too, likes Sofie. No, I believe I can avoid danger here. I am an integral part of the staff again and they need my knowledge . . . ”

“ . . . of Poland,” she completed his thought. “Your leader can't be content to digest only Bohemia and Moravia; he must latch onto Danzig and subjugate many of *my* people before he is satisfied. The little bastard!”

“Now, Lilka. Most of the residents of Danzig are ethnic Germans—and remember, it is a ‘Free City,” not an integral part of Poland. That was all settled at Versailles, when we were humbled by every nation on the map of Europe. Please forgive us if we now flex a little muscle and revive our national self-esteem. Hopefully our leadership will be balanced in satisfying a few territorial needs and will be content to consolidate a few fragments of true Germans who have been chipped away from their Fatherland and now desire to return.

“Let's get back to Sofie,” he continued. “She carries a Swiss passport and she has departed from Prague and gone west to work on her voice training. I have seen to it that she is financially independent, and she has proven to be capable of protecting herself on her own. Her friend Dieter is still with Juraslav, but the Gestapo in Prague poses a problem for him, and I believe that it is time for him to leave there and seek a safer location. He is not so circumspect as Sofie and may even present a danger for her if he is with her, so I will suggest to them that they give some time and distance to one another.”

“So, you are saying they should not be together for awhile?” Lilka confirmed.

“That is my preference,” Otto responded. “Dieter unwittingly created considerable—how can I say—considerable curiosity here in Berlin by slipping away with apparent ease. Not just once, but several times! As a result, he has aggregated much more importance than he deserves. Several professionals have been quick to attribute qualities to him that he doesn't possess. Lilka, he is nothing more than a musician with no political agenda. He was—or perhaps is—a sensitive homosexual. Our daughter reached some other part of him and they formed a mutually dependent team, as young people often do. Sofie is not a primary target for any agency, but Dieter has created such consternation and frustration that he is regarded as a sort of 'mystery agent.' He, of course, will be apprehended, because his luck will evaporate in time. I don't want Sofie to be in his company when that happens, because it is possible that no one can then extricate her from the situation. You understand that, no?"

"Of course," Lilka responded, pleased that Sofie's primary caretaker was still actively looking out for her. "If she contacts me, I shall stress the need for extreme caution until we are sure that these dangers have passed."

Otto and Lilka had both enjoyed the rare conversation. Each realized that loneliness heightened the need for old friends, and, even though their liaison had taken place decades ago, some vestige of those shared times brought comfort now. He completed the call with, "Take good care of yourself, old girl. These are uncertain times." She reciprocated the sentiment, understanding that they might soon be on opposite sides of a confrontation of nations that would forever separate them. After Lilka rang off, Otto listened for the telltale sound of any other listener closing the line, but heard none. He wished there had been words available to him to tell her how much she had added to his life, and he vowed to have them at the ready if they got another chance to speak before the inevitable conflict began.

CHAPTER THIRTY-EIGHT

Prague – later in 1939

THE COMPLEXITIES OF AN INSIGNIFICANT CASUALTY

"Ach—so, Edward—your young accountant—the one who went out of channels, eh?—is no longer with us, you say? Any insights regarding his untimely passing? I imagine you are also shocked by this turn of events, ja? And just when he was being reassigned to a post near his home, I understand. A pity, Edward—a real pity!"

Lt. Col. Edward Gunther listened to his superior's voice over the telephone and thought he detected some of the infamous Himmler sarcasm being aimed his way. He knew that he must exercise extreme caution and select his words carefully to avoid falling into some trap of inconsistency. No doubt the conversation was being evaluated by others and recorded for future action, if any seemed indicated.

"Heinrich, I had spoken with him only a few days ago, and we discussed his forthcoming redeployment to Forst. He was committed to completing some assignment here before his travel date, but appeared quite happy to be returning to the area nearer his family. Nothing—I repeat, *nothing*—in his manner or attitude suggested suicide to me. The Litoměřice police looked into the circumstances of his death immediately, and their conclusion favored the explanation of accidental death with alcohol a possible contributing factor. I will forward a copy of their final report of the accident so that you may have it in your files."

"And do your files reflect any other incidence of excessive drinking by Deitz?" asked the Gestapo leader. "Surely a committed imbiber doesn't wait for a train ride to get himself inebriated. It is much cheaper and easier to do in a friendly neighborhood bar. How about it, Edward? Any history?"

"There were occasional reports of what was termed 'anti-social behavior' in one of our best-known Prague brothels, but Deitz was young and in a foreign city. What is more normal than an occasional drink and a romp with the ladies—to change the pace, you know? Nothing in his evaluations suggests that he ever underperformed his duties as a result of drinking, or for any reason. On the contrary, he is described as being well-organized and given to detail."

"So, then, Edward. Did he leave behind a *handbuch* describing the work he was doing when he fell from a moving train in Litoměřice? Do you know what he was so committed to completing before leaving your command? His inquiries to Berlin were all about a mysterious Dieter Meister—apparently a resourceful chap who moves easily in the shadows, giving some of our best operatives headaches. Could he have been following Meister? Or could Meister even have done him in?"

"That is an excellent question, sir. One which I will be pursuing. But, no—there was no handbuch listed among his belongings recovered from the train, and none reported as being on or near his body. I have ordered that his effects be removed from the room he occupied and from his office at this HQ. They will be inventoried and retained in our lockup. You shall have a full report. I will also look into this Meister—he is not in your command, I assume?"

There was no response, a condition Edward Gunther disliked, because he could visualize the canny Himmler sitting with his fingertips pressed together, reading some invisible script on the ceiling of his vast office. What inconsistency was the Gestapo chief sorting through? Tiny droplets of perspiration formed on Gunther's forehead as he awaited something further from the telephone earpiece. Finally it came.

"Edward—no word of this to anyone but me. Do you understand? It may be nothing, but there are too many unexplained inner workings for my simple mind to grasp at one sitting. I know that I can count on you to be ... prudent. Yes, prudent, Edward. Heil Hitler!" *Click* and *click* again as the director's handset and then the recorder disconnected. Lt. Col. Gunther dabbed at his brow with a handkerchief and resumed his examination of the document case that rested beside his desk. He made a mental note to insert a dental appointment into his desk calendar on the date and at the approximate time of Deitz's accident. Dr. Jandl, his dentist, would gladly make a parallel entry in his records when informed that the tax audit of his books had found everything to be in good order. The power to tax was, indeed, the most effective form of leverage, and it could buy many favors when strategically withheld.

Lt. Col. Gunther departed early from his office that evening, with the document case he had recently acquired hidden beneath his bulky uniform raincoat, which he had draped casually over his arm in distinctly non-military fashion. "Perhaps I can make it home before the sprinkles come," he smiled at his reliable secretary. She glanced toward the window but prudently desisted from noting that the skies appeared clear and the weather relatively mild.

"Shall I forward callers to your apartment line?" she asked, although she suspected that the uncharacteristic early departure signaled his desire for privacy.

"Only calls from Berlin," he responded. "I have some personal business to attend, and most things remaining on today's calendar can wait until morning. Guten abend."

"Heil Hitler," was her tepid response, to which he retorted only a simple, "Yes." She rarely saw Col. Gunther so absorbed, and she wondered whether the unexpected death of young Specialist Deitz had been upsetting for him. She noted that he had reviewed Deitz's personnel file earlier in the day and wondered whether that was what had been concealed so inartfully beneath his raincoat. *Don't go there!* she reminded herself. Sudden deaths could be hidden traps—especially so in this center of intrigue. *No—don't go there!*

Lt. Col. Gunther had been examining Deitz's notebook retrospectively, beginning with the most recent entry and gradually tracing Deitz's movements and observations backward in time toward the recorded beginnings of his curiosity about Corporal Dieter Meister. He had paused and reread notes made following an interlude with a prostitute named Ursula:

Jew/perhaps homosexual/musician/attractive, tall female companion with some romantic connection and some musical connection/needed a location to remain out of sight in Prague before some appointment later in the day/customer of the music store on Ruzova/definitely not military/adequate finances to allow generous extra tip.

Not much about the mystery woman in that set of notes, he reflected. She was tall, attractive, and musical. Probably it was she who sang with this Dieter Meister at the Majestic Plaza, and probably it was she riding in the compartment with him on the train from Berlin. But who was the disguised woman traveling from Berlin who preferred not to be recognized and who might even have merited a letter of safe conduct from the second-highest official in the Third Reich? A mistress, perhaps? But certainly not of the newly married Göring. Most improbable. What then? Some friend of Göring had wanted to ensure safe passage of a woman and had obtained a favor in the form of the letter. And while that letter had been displayed to the border guards, it had never left the woman's possession, but it had gotten the intended reaction from the guards. Deitz concluded that the woman had changed in appearance before departing the train, and neither she nor her distinctive luggage had been noted by alerted platform watchers.

If she was truly that crafty, she had undoubtedly disposed of her traveling clothes, disguise, and luggage before arriving at Hlavni Nadrazi Station that morning, and the person who walked past observers on the platform bore no resemblance to the old witch they were instructed to follow. In fact, if she was "a tall and attractive young woman," the fools probably did enjoy looking at her and had to be reminded of their assignment.

Gunther wondered whether publishing a generous reward notice for an "expensive suitcase and clothing dropped accidentally from the train near such-and-such a location on such-and-such date" could possibly inspire some local person to come forth and claim the money. There were not many population centers between the border and Prague, and a notice in the newspaper of each town might produce something. He put the thought aside for the moment, promising himself to revisit it later.

A more interesting thread for now was Deitz's notation that the assistant manager at the Majestic Palace had eventually identified the musicians as Sophia and Dieter Havlik of Neuchâtel, Switzerland. He had offered the additional information that Dr. Juraslav Havlik of Prague had attended the Havliks' early performances together with other city residents. Col. Gunther would request a report on Dr. Havlik from his staff in the morning, to see whether his attendance at the performance had been motivated by normal curiosity about a performer with the same surname or some closer connection to the musicians. Perhaps one of his people could also visit the good doctor's office as a patient and make useful observations before there was an obvious Gestapo interest manifested.

Colonel Gunther had no doubts about his ability to unmask Dieter and Sophia Havlik, but he had considerable uncertainty regarding the path he should take once armed with that information. He knew that the path was leading higher into the pyramid of Nazidom, and at each level the penalty for a misstep would be more frightening. Himmler already disliked him, and if someone in Himmler's peer group declared that Gunther was an annoying pest, he could be crushed like an insect. Wasn't that exactly what had befallen the unfortunate Deitz?

CHAPTER THIRTY-NINE

Prague – March 1939

TWO LITTLE GIRLS FROM GDANSK AT WORK

Magda worked over the encoded dispatch from Lilka, making penciled notes on a small pad as she finished each sentence. When she had finished she sat for several minutes before calling to her associate. "Elsa . . . Elsa . . . come in here. We have something to discuss."

Elsa had just bathed and washed her hair, which she was drying with a large towel. She was faithful to the daily strength-training routine prescribed by her SWW superiors and had been doing her morning bends and presses for nearly an hour before immersing herself in the warm water. Magda admired the sharp definition in Elsa's unclothed arms and legs. Even though she appeared to be a small woman, Elsa was capable of inflicting serious injury to any unsuspecting opponent, and Magda had witnessed occasions when the explosive Elsa had repelled unwanted advances with a fury that left large welts and even broken bones in her wake.

But now Elsa was comfortable and smiling as she walked naked through the room of her best friend. "Good morning! *Kochasz mnie?* Ha-ha—good one! Nobody loves me because I'm a whore. What have you been reading?" she asked. "Is that Lilka's response to our last communication? Does she understand the fragile nature of our continued presence here? Did we make ourselves clear?"

"She says that a shadow government will be set up in Paris or London soon, because the assessment is that Hitler will move on Poland before winter, and when he does, we must have a command post which is outside the zone of immediate danger—in case no one comes to help us repel him, you know. We—you and I—can elect to be attached to that headquarters and collect intelligence within the friendly host country."

"You mean we are offered the chance to be whores in France or England? Do you think the pigs in those countries would be any better than the trash we must bed here? Could our country possibly use our minds instead of our bodies for a change? Are you as angry as I am with this, Maggie? It is demeaning, and it is not what we were trained to do. Damn them!"

"I think it would be different, Elsa. I think they are talking about our being attached to the shadow office in some capacity—enabled to meet gentlemen from the diplomatic or intelligence services of our host country and to socialize with them. It's not the same as sitting on a couch in a brothel waiting for a horny soldier to make his selection. Really, it is much less demeaning, and we could set our own schedules, you know."

"Maggie, I am disgusted with myself. This is not what my parents expected their only daughter to be. I can't accept the idea that the only way we can help our cause is . . . you know . . . seducing people; getting them drunk and stealing their secrets when they're disarmed. It's not honorable. How can they ask us to do it? Don't you hate it?"

"Really? Probably not . . . hate. No, I don't hate it because I feel that my femininity is enabling in a way. It gives me power to extract information that some harsh form of interrogation couldn't ever pry loose. And, that's kind of ironic to me—do you understand? And the sex is just an exercise—like the stuff you do to stay fit. I consider it a routine, where I have four or five steps to complete and I check them off one by one until I'm having a drink or a cigarette with some fellow who has a stupid smile and a limp dick, and who wants to tell me how important he is, so he tells me things which are the secrets of his office. Every so often, I even enjoy the sex myself, although usually I only run my checklist and wait for the afterglow."

"You're better at it than I am, Maggie. All I feel is anger, and I have to fight off my inclination to blacken their stupid eyes or break their trespassing paws. I actually bit one major—nearly took a chunk out of him—and had to tell him he was so good that it drove me mad. He wanted to hear that, so he laughed and didn't report me or anything. I'm really afraid that some day I might . . . "

"Forget it. What can we say to Lilka? Shouldn't we let them move us away from Prague and get us to a safe city? There will be time after that to decide whether to refuse any more of the whoring. They can't force that on us; they can only ask. And you know we can say *no*. If we just refuse any more, the worst that could happen is that we'd be dumped from the service and left to our own devices in a safer place."

"No. No, they wouldn't let us just walk away. We know too much. We think that the Germans are the only bad people because they threaten our homeland, but, believe me, our secret service is just as heartless, and making us safe and happy is no part of their mission. The SWW owns us, and we will probably continue to render service on our backs. Sorry I vented on you, but it feels better just to say something. Let's tell Lilka we can be ready to leave here on twenty-four hours' notice and ask her how we are to travel to our next assignment."

Lieutenant Colonel Edward Gunther carried his outer coat over his left arm. Unlike the evening before, it was not being used to conceal any folders or papers, and it freed his right arm to offer the Nazi salute to uniformed guards at the door to Gestapo Headquarters/Prague. He seemed to be in unusually good spirits as he pranced past staff members in the outer office, pausing to extend greetings here and there along the route to his inner sanctum. At the tall oak door that protected him from the office noise, his secretary motioned with her head and in a barely audible voice said, "The report you commissioned is in a red folder atop your reading desk, sir. Shall I hold calls until you have a chance to read it?"

Colonel Gunther smiled his agreement with the suggestion and asked for his favorite cup of dark Afrikan coffee. Then he draped his outer coat over a side chair and took his reading glasses from their case. His most comfortable chair was already positioned by the light atop his reading desk, and a sealed red folder lay immediately beneath the green-shaded lamp. Inside was a single sheet which contained the report he had ordered, and Col. Gunther wondered if it would answer any of the vexing questions surrounding the late Jurgen Deitz and his quarries, the elusive Dieter Meister and his mysterious companion, Sophia.

JURASLAV HAVLIK, MEDICAL DOCTOR

RESIDENCE: HAVLIK CLINIC / ČIKLOVA STREET / PRAGUE (SINCE 1922)

DOB: March 1, 1898. Łódź, Poland

FATHER: Dr. Tovar Havlik. Trained at Łódź Medical Sch.Poland. Polish citizen attached to Gypsy community near Sanok, Poland, which later migrated to Czechoslovakia. Dr. Tovar Havlik founded the Havlik Clinic and his practice was apparently successful. His son, Juraslav, became his partner in the Clinic in 1922 and became its sole proprietor after Tovar Havlik's death.

MOTHER: Lilka Havlik (née Rudovska). Polish. Jew. Public employee and union organizer. Reported as deceased during Great War but possibly alive in Poland. If so, Lilka Rudovska may be married to hotelier Liv Zimmerman from Krakow. A woman identified as Lilka R Zimmerman is said to direct several SWW intelligence agents in this area.

OTHER FAMILY: Never married. No children. Half sister Sophia Havlik, Swiss.citizen b. 1915 Krakow. Possibly appeared Prague November 1938 as singer in Majestic Plaza Hotel with Swiss piano accompanist Dieter Havlik.// Multi-lingual. Currently believed to be in Paris France as music student and performer. Dieter Havlik may be pseudonym for German citizen Dieter Meister who has been sought by Berlin Gestapo Unit #43 for some time. Dieter Havlik (Meister) was pianist in Fischerstube tavern (Berlin) frequented by Gen. Otto von Seigler and his staff . General von Seigler was implicated in Oster Conspiracy but vindicated by investigation conducted under aegis of RM Hermann Göring.

Gen. von Seigler has one daughter, Sofie—born Krakow 1915. Mother listed as deceased, 1918.

MEDICAL TRAINING: Graduated w/ highest honors 1921 from Uniwersytet Medyczny W Łódź Poland

MEDICAL SPECIALTIES: Public health. Immunizations. Inspections of licensed public facilities/employees. Gastro-internal medicine. Minor surgery. Consultant to three Czech medical faculties. Dr. Havlik has been published in several medical journals. His articles are all related to public health considerations.

PROFESSIONAL ASSOCIATIONS: First Faculty of Medicine, Charles University, Katernska 32 Prague / Visiting Specialist Bulovka University

Hospital / Advisor to Ceska Farmaceuticka Spolecnost- Prague

POLICE RECORD: No record of any infractions found. Dr. Havlik has not traveled outside the country within the past five years.

GENERAL OBSERVATIONS: Dr. Havlik enjoys good standing in the medical community and the Prague community at large. His practice appears to be financially sound. He does considerable *pro bono publico* work in Gypsy encampments and licensed brothels. We could find no indication of marriage or personal romantic attachments, which raises the question of possible homosexual classification. He is reputed to be a trained musician. He speaks several languages, including Gypsy dialects. Household help consists of two nondescript female employees observed to be age 30 or less.

Col. Gunther was stunned by what he saw. "A rats' nest of spies!" he muttered to himself. "Fucking Deitz saw something and I choked him off. A master Jew spy sitting in Poland with a small army of whores across Europe, picking up secrets from businessmen and soldiers in brothels. Right here under my nose a doctor who is the son of the Jew provocateur—and he earns his sterling reputation by caring for the bait. They probably take their days off at the clinic—or use it as their communications center. And, on top of that, a Wehrmacht General has a daughter by the same Jew spy, and when he comes under suspicion in a plot to kill the führer, he gets RM Göring to help him smuggle his Jew daughter into *my* city with a bodyguard the Gestapo can't seem to catch. So what do I do? I blot out the only Gestapo agent smart enough to sniff some of this out. *Scheisse*, Edward! You have absolutely shit the bed!"

A jar of pencils ricocheted off the great oak door, followed by a drinking carafe and an inkwell. Outside, his secretary recognized the sounds and did not hasten to respond to Gunther's shouted summons. She wondered how his cheerful mood had evaporated in only thirty minutes and realized that the confidential report she had typed probably precipitated the tirade. After she could delay no longer without risking her own safety, she opened the door a crack and saw the Chief of Gestapo Operations/Prague rolling a gold coin across the back of his left hand and giggling like a drunk. "May I do something for you, Colonel?" she offered timidly. There was no response, so she repeated the words more audibly. Finally, after a second repetition there was recognition.

"Please have those new special agents of Reichsprotektor Heydrich's—Donner and Gnoff—come to this office at once—with sidearms and outer coats. I will be sending them on a short mission immediately; they are supposed to be among the best-trained men assigned to this region and this may require all of their skills."

"Yes, sir." she responded, and quietly closed the door behind her.

Elsa and Magda each filled small, undistinguished traveling suitcases with essentials and their preferred clothing. The balance would be donated to the Gypsy camp outside Prague, which had been alerted to send a small truck to the clinic after nightfall. In exchange, they would have gold and silver coins which could be secreted on their persons, plus safe carriage to the Hungarian capital of Budapest, 600 kilometers to the southeast. After confirmation of Lilka's decision to utilize their services in England, the preparation for their departure had been achieved with professional efficiency, and by dawn it would be impossible to find any remainders of their long residence with Juraslav. To their own "donations," they added all of Sofie's clothing and shoes—the items which Dieter had enjoyed visiting in the closet of the room they had shared. Dieter watched the process with quiet resignation, reminding himself that at one time he had regarded these young women as unimportant servants and peasant girls. How amazing, he thought, that they could pass so lightly through the perception of another person. The SWW had selected and trained them wisely to remain invisible.

Their activity was interrupted by urgent knocking at the rear door to the clinic, and when Elsa responded to the summons, Dieter could see a middle-aged woman, dressed in the typical highly tailored garb of a business professional, who partially covered her face with a high neck scarf. He could not recognize her features, nor could he hear the hurried conversation between the woman and Elsa, but within moments the caller was gone and the chatter inside the clinic had ceased abruptly. Outside on the street, he watched as the woman entered a waiting taxi. His only clue to the exchange was his recognition of the vehicle and its driver; it was one of the ubiquitous Gypsies who had guided Sofie and him to and from the Majestic Plaza during their brief career there.

Elsa called for the other three to join her and listen carefully. "We are alerted that two Gestapo "standers" are being dispatched here to find out who are the occupants of this building and to take Dieter to their commander if they find him. Apparently they are very capable men recently arrived from Berlin, and we are warned that they will force their way in if necessary." Dieter was amused, even in the stressful atmosphere of the room, that Elsa had referred to the Gestapo men with the derogatory term *stander*, usually reserved for an erect penis. He thought to himself that it probably reflected a whole catalogue of unpleasant contacts necessitated by the work which Magda and Elsa selflessly performed for their government.

"Dieter, why are you smiling?" she demanded. "This is not one bit funny and we are all in danger. Pay attention so that we can have some chance of getting through the next couple of hours without suffering another tragedy. You get a warm coat and hat and your heaviest shoes and walk toward Vyšehrad Park immediately. Take some money with you, but if you get hungry don't go into a restaurant. See if you can find a street vendor and keep moving. Do you remember the telephone number of the clinic? Good! Call back at 7:15 p.m. and don't say anything. Just listen, hang up and do as we tell you. Now go!!

"Juraslav, put on your medical coveralls and all of the doctor junk—stethoscope, eye-reflector, anything you can think of which looks as if you are examining a patient. I'm going to be the patient—I need one of those white wrap-arounds—and I'll be sitting on the examination table with my back exposed to you, between you and the door to the examination room." She began disrobing with deliberate speed, stuffing each item of clothing into a canvas bag like those they had been filling for the Gypsies.

"Maggie, you are the nurse receptionist. Answer the door and try to persuade them that you may not interrupt a medical examination in progress because of ethical considerations, but let them convince you otherwise. Dr. Havlik and I will look surprised, then indignant after the door opens, and we'll have to extemporize after that. Use the time remaining until they arrive to move as much of the clothing in bags as possible to the back entrance, where our friends will be picking it up tonight. Do we all know what we are doing, now? Dieter—why don't you have those shoes on yet? Those *Schutzstaffel* must not find you here or we will all spend tonight in some lockup. *Schnell*, Dieter!"

He realized that Elsa was the heavy hand in their little group of exiles, and that she was very good at her profession. By now she was quite naked but unembarrassed and slipping the white examination gown around her surprisingly toned body, while Magda trailed three of the canvas bags out of sight and Juraslav converted himself into the prototypical examining physician, complete with a clipboard and documents which looked like a patient's medical records. Some rubbing alcohol had been smeared on Elsa's bare skin so that the room even smelled like a working medical office. Dieter congratulated himself upon finding his shoes, gloves, coat, hat, and money, and he slipped out the rear door, moving quickly toward the sidewalk where he could blend in with other pedestrians walking toward the park and the Church of Saints Peter and Paul. A glance at his watch showed that it was a few minutes past 4 p.m. He wondered what the next three hours would bring.

The two fit-looking men were in their mid-thirties. Each wore an expensive brown suit and gleaming shoes. If one looked closely, one could see that their hands were heavily veined and calloused, even though the fingernails were professionally manicured. If anything contradicted the intended appearance of businessmen, it was probably the precise, short haircuts, which almost shouted "military," despite their efforts at civilian disguise.

Lt. Colonel Edward Gunther allowed himself a few moments to absorb the outward appearance of the highly rated and decorated specialists, who had recently been added to his command by Reichsprotektor Reinhard Heydrich, as they stood before his desk. Then he motioned them into the visitors' chairs directly in front of him—the ones where the light shining from behind him gave Col. Gunther a decided advantage in eye-to-eye confrontations.

"Heydrich tells me that Donner and Gnoff are equivalent to a squad of street police—that they can interrogate with great persuasive effect and inspire total candor. I am impressed, because the Reichsprotektor is very spare in allocating praise. I have a special assignment for you. It is one which has frustrated many of your colleagues, and it could prove to be a dangerous quest, although I'm assured that you are not strangers to such challenges. Before I outline the chore, I must have your assurance that all that transpires and everything you may learn in the process will be shared totally and exclusively with me. No written reports and no contact with other Gestapo offices from this point forward. Is that understood and agreed? Good! If that confidence is broken—or even cracked a little—by either of you, I assure you that *both* your careers will be destroyed. So, as you can see, I am making it important for each of you to monitor and encourage the performance of the other as well as to accomplish your assignment."

Col. Gunther leaned forward and looked directly into the faces of the two men, aided by the strong light entering the room from behind him. When he was certain that his point had been stressed adequately, he recounted the desultory path of Dieter Meister from a tavern in Berlin to the circle of luminaries assembled at #80 Wilhelmstrasse to a safe house in Rahnsdorf to Humboldt University to Prague. He stressed that Meister appeared to have elaborate cover, ranging from his appearances as a musician to military and diplomatic status to his alias as a Swiss subject. He added that the mysterious figure seemed to have friends in high places, including perhaps RM Göring and General von Seigler in Berlin, and that the late Jurgen Deitz, God rest his soul, had reported a circle of "goons" who had provided Meister with shadowy protection. No doubt they had caused Deitz to be crushed under a train just because he inquired about Meister!

Most important for Col. Gunther was the fact that Meister *not* be harmed but instead delivered to him with as little fuss as possible. There was still the possibility that the man was someone's special agent, and even the name of the führer himself had come up in the course of earlier investigations.

"And so, here is the name and address of a clinic in the city where they know about Meister and where he may even be living as Dieter Havlik. Go there today and get inside. Interrogate the residents. If you find Meister, bring him to me, and do whatever you must to keep the occupants of the building from alarming others. If he is not there but there is evidence that indicates he has had a presence there, immediately set up around-the-clock surveillance that is as low-profile as possible until

I tell you otherwise. Contact me immediately when you have Meister—but in all events, get back to me in twenty-four hours with a progress report. Any questions? No? Then, good luck. Heil Hitler!"

Magda did not see a car arrive at the curb, but she heard footfalls on the clinic's porch, followed by the ringing of the brass doorbell. She did not immediately open the door in response to the sound, but instead stole a furtive glance at the two men standing outside through a side window. She saw only those two and concluded that they had come alone. With that assurance, she inquired through the door, "May I help you?"

"Public Health Authority! We have the new Patient Information Forms which medical facilities are required to complete, and we would like a few minutes with Dr. Havlik. Now!"

Magda knew that the German National Socialist government was intent upon gaining greater control over medical services, and these two Gestapo visitors had ingeniously validated their visit under the cover of that power grab. She resolved to play out the ruse, as instructed, so she opened the entry door slightly and said, "I am Dr. Havlik's nurse assistant. Perhaps I can provide the information that is called for. Unfortunately, the doctor is with a patient and cannot be interrupted."

Borg Donner pivoted the door to a full open position with one hand, nearly lifting Magda from her feet in the process. He and Horst Gnoff were inside immediately, closing and locking the entry door behind them. "Fräulein, where will we find Dr. Havlik? Please do not make us impatient—this is a matter of importance."

"I'm sure it is important to you, sir, but the medical profession's first obligation is to its patients, and it is an inflexible rule that the patient's privacy must be respected. You will have to wait with me in this reception area until Dr. Havlik finishes his examination of Frau . . . that is, of his patient, and comes out through that door." She nodded her head toward a particular door in case the Gestapo lads were not bright enough to choose the correct one. "Please let me see the forms and perhaps we can make more efficient use of your time that way."

"Sit at your desk and keep your hands folded in plain sight, Fräulein," was the next command from Donner. "Horst—keep our nurse assistant compliant while I look in on the doctor. If she moves from that spot, shoot her." At least the pleasantries were now concluded.

Donner took three quick strides and opened the door that had been indicated. It led into a large examining room with several glass-front cases of instruments and medications on one wall, a cluttered desk and chairs opposite the cases, and a pure white examination table under an overhead canopy light in the middle of the room. Behind the table was a tall, slim medical doctor, holding his stethoscope against the upper back of a blonde female patient, who was facing toward the Gestapo agent. When the door burst open, the patient had grasped the medical gown that had fallen from her shoulders during the examination, and she now clasped it to the front of her body to conceal her bare breasts from the intruder.

"Please be at ease," Donner smiled, in a tone and with a look which conveyed exactly the opposite message. "You are Dr. Juraslav Havlik, ja? And you, madam—who is the good doctor examining today? Would you be one of the legion of ladies sent out from Poland to spy on the diplomats and military men of other nations? Are you surprised that I know about such a mission? Well, today you do not have the cover of some sex palace to shield you. In fact, you have precious little between you and the world, eh? Please raise your hands and let go of the gown. Let's have a look at those puppies with cold noses you are covering."

Juraslav uttered a weak protest, but Elsa said, "It's all right, doctor. I have nothing to hide from your visitor." She allowed the gown to yield to gravity and it dropped below her breasts and gathered in folds on her lap. She averted Donner's prying eyes and noticed that the second man had also shifted his attention from Magda to her bare torso, so she extended her hands outward to the sides with palms upward as if to complete a burlesque presentation. Then she grasped the gown and again covered herself.

Donner barked, "I did not say you could re-cover yourself," and he yanked the gown totally away from her body and cupped her breasts in his hands like two ripe pears, flashing a lascivious grin at his fellow agent. "We should have been doctors, Horst—this is good work!"

Donner saw the back of the small woman's right hand raised as if to slap his face, but he made no effort to move because he was certain that only her hand would be hurt if she struck him. He did not see the scalpel cupped in her fingers and did not anticipate the speed or precision of the backhanded delivery, which sliced through the center of his right eye and nicked the bridge of his nose. Her return thrust was even swifter, with the scalpel entering the left side of his neck below the jaw line and severing the common carotid artery, splashing rich, red blood randomly across Elsa's white shoulders.

Horst Gnoff reacted instantly to the unexpected attack, drawing his Walther P38 pistol and raising it, preparing to fire at his badly wounded partner's assailant, but before he could perfect his aim or get off a shot, a single bullet from a VIS Polish Eagle pressed directly against the back of his neck shattered two vertebrae and severed his spinal cord, causing him to crumple like an unsupported puppet. Magda quickly returned the weapon to her apron pocket and stepped over the two dying Gestapo agents to embrace her trembling friend. "It's over—no more *schrecklichkeit* from these two. Breathe deeply, dear. You had no other choice. Now we must hasten to erase all evidence of this."

Lt. Col. Edward Gunther was restless. Even the precise passage of a coin over the back of his fingers failed to divert him, and so he walked to various locations within his well-appointed office—straightening a picture, rubbing a fingerprint from a glass surface, picking dead petals from the flower arrangement his secretary had provided. It had been nearly twenty-four hours since he dispatched Donner and Gnoff to visit the Havlik Clinic and possibly to apprehend the elusive Dieter Meister. If the mission had been successful, Gunther would soon possess a bargaining tool for future leverage with Himmler, Göring, and von Seigler—three of the most powerful men in his government. Even if they had failed to capture Meister, Col. Gunther was confident that the clinic would provide valuable information about the phantom agent and the itinerant daughter of General von Seigler. Only ninety minutes more, he thought. He had been specific with the specialists: call after twenty-four hours with a status report.

The rude bell of his telephone ended his desultory walking and thinking, and Col. Gunther was on the instrument with animal swiftness. "Gunther here! What can you tell me?"

The voice on the other end was unfamiliar. "Colonel. Colonel

Gunther? Colonel—I have unbelievable—I have unbelievably unpleasant
. . . you will not be able to . . . Colonel Gunther, the new agents Gnoff
and Donner were apparently run over by a train last night, and a local
policeman came upon their bodies—badly . . . very badly . . . mangled,
sir. It was in the same town as that where Jurgen Deitz fell under a train.
It is like a curse, sir. Sir? Are you there, Colonel?" Only a whispered
profanity punctuated the air before a click signaled that the Chief of
Gestapo Operations / Prague had terminated the call at his end.

Could it be possible that this Meister is *that* good at his trade?
Gunther decided to send a full investigative team to the Havlik Clinic at
once to seal it off and to examine every scrap of information there. But
. . . somehow he knew already that the location would be totally
sanitized, with only the automobile of his special agents to confirm that
they had, indeed, visited. Already he was mentally conjuring a fabrication
for his report to Headquarters—how he had nearly captured Meister
until . . . until what? How could he distinguish his failed efforts from
those of the others who had been humbled? The deaths of three Gestapo
agents were now going to appear on his Prague record, and none could be
justified.

Then the figurative "other shoe" dropped. "Wait," Gunther said to
no one in particular. "If the bodies were taken to Litoměřice and
deposited by the tracks there, it was a message to me. It says that
Meister—or whoever did this—is aware that I dispatched Jurgen Deitz. It
threatens me with disclosure for that death in addition to whatever blame
may attach to the loss of two specialists. It is my career—my career! This
scoundrel has me by the balls." The palm of Gunther's hand was
pounded against his forehead several times in self-deprecation as the
usually confident officer mumbled *Dummkopf!* with each blow.

He walked to his window and stared at the street below, where still
another tweak to his pride conspired to ridicule him. In the reserved
parking space marked *Chief of Gestapo Operations* resided a black car,
which he recognized as one used by special agents like the unfortunate
Donner and Gnoff. "The impudence!" he spat. He was approaching total
frustration, but he realized that he was also developing a grudging level of
respect for his phantom quarry.

CHAPTER FORTY
Czechoslovakia – Summer 1939

SEEKING A WAY OUT / HELP FROM THE GYPSIES

After depositing the two lifeless bodies near the railroad bed outside Litoměřice, Draco had driven their official car to the center of Prague and parked it beside Gestapo headquarters. The first reserved space in the lot was unoccupied at night and no one observed his hurried departure in a waiting van. By morning, the decrepit van and its six occupants would be far away, and chances were that the parked staff car would go unnoticed for several additional hours. The clinic had been cleaned and emptied of all its contents, including boxes of medications that would soon be transferred to Gypsy caravans in the dense wooded areas to the northeast of Prague.

Jura, Dieter, and the two young Polish SWW women rode in cramped silence through the night, taking turns helping their driver to circumvent the checkpoints that could be anticipated outside populated areas. Draco knew the geography, as did their Gypsy driver, and so they navigated flawlessly and undetected for nearly 90 kilometers until they turned off the highway onto a two-rutted lane more appropriate for horse-drawn transport. Soon, that also diminished into a barely flattened pathway beneath ancient trees. Four armed men challenged them, then waved the van onward into a clearing, where Dieter could make out a grouping of covered caravans and some armed men huddled around well-managed fires.

"This is where we must leave you," said the Gypsy driver, and Draco helped the four new refugees from their uncomfortable positions in the van, laughing as each rediscovered folded legs and stretched tired arms toward the blackness above. "You ladies will move with the caravans, which are soon headed southward toward the border with Hungary. Get some dirt under your fingernails and put olive oil on your skin and in your hair—you look too Polish right now."

"Dr. Havlik, we have several people here with intestinal problems and a few young men showing signs of the clap. We will need your help to get them all ready for the journey during the next few days, while we complete our other preparations. And Dieter, we have an abandoned German army truck hidden in a barn near here, which you can learn to operate, I think. If so, we have saved your corporal's uniform from the closet at the clinic, and you may be able to leave this area without endangering our Romani travelers. I don't believe you could pass as one of us, and the price on your head is too high to risk. I'm sorry."

Juraslav put his hand on Dieter's arm reassuringly and said, "You will be my assistant for so long as the medical work may require, and then we will depart together. Don't worry! We are safe for a few days, but he is correct—we cannot endanger these people who have no part in the current conflict. Agreed?" Dieter nodded without comment, but his thoughts brought an unexpected smile as he reflected: *Now I must be totally corrupted. I can be viewed as a cheating homosexual Gypsy Jew arsonist who is accessory to the murder of three German officers. No wonder they don't welcome me as their houseguest!*

Lt. Col. Edward Gunther was in the foulest mood his staff could remember. His irritation extended to the most trivial of things, and no one was spared a portion of his vitriol. It was whispered that he had been outwitted and humiliated by a nest of Polish spies and that his arrogance had contributed to the gruesome deaths of three of his own Gestapo agents. The discarded vehicle parked in his designated space plus the unexplained but understood departure of his Czech secretary added to the humiliation collecting around the Prague Gestapo chieftain. He understood that worse might lie ahead if all those details ever reached the attention of Heinrich Himmler, and he resolved to do what he could to prevent that.

Col. Gunther wondered whether Meister's eventual capture (and he was certain it would happen in time) should even be disclosed to superiors because of the danger, to him, of having them revisit this whole sorry episode. And of course there was the possibility that his prey, when captured, could provide additional details of even more ineptitude within the Prague office and could link him to the unfortunate Jurgen Deitz. By now, Col. Gunther had dismissed any vestiges of the earlier notion that this Dieter Meister person might be an agent of the German Reich. No, Meister's value lay in his potential to embarrass important people in Berlin, and that should also be his value to Col. Gunther.

"When I get you, I shall keep you in my arsenal," Gunther mumbled to the phantom he imagined in the parking space below his office window. "You may yet be my ladder to higher office rather than my dénouement from this one!"

When dawn broke over the clearing, Dieter could judge better the size of the Romani encampment. He estimated that there were at least two hundred men, women, and children soon to launch their trip to Hungary in a score of covered caravans. Apparently they would be protected by at least a dozen mounted outriders carrying arms. All of those he observed appeared to have some role in the coming transition, and they moved about efficiently making their preparations, suggesting to Dieter that they had done this many times before and would likely be successful in moving farther from the threats of the Third Reich.

A steaming breakfast porridge was delivered to Jura and him by a young Romani woman, who asked that they be ready to receive their first patients later in the day. She also delivered a change of clothing donated by men from the tribe, and both shed their Prague clothes happily and donned the new ones, which were loose and comfortable even though noticeably used. Dieter examined himself in a mirror fragment that was tied to a tent pole, and he congratulated his reflected image for having retained the full beard of Majestic Plaza vintage. With the application of a little olive oil, even he might be able to pass for Romani!

Their young male patients began to file in one by one, and each reluctantly agreed to the request that they drop their britches before the gadje strangers. Before long all were relieved to learn from Dr. Havlik that they had contracted something called "impetigo" rather than the dreaded syphilis, which they knew had diminished so many European monarchs and patriarchs. Jura gave each a small bottle of astringent and a wad of cotton, then told them to go first to the nearby stream and wash their lesions thoroughly with strong laundry soap and later to clean away any crusts, scabs, or fluids with the pungent liquid in the bottles.

"Keep your hands—and everyone else's hands—away from those areas until they are normal for two weeks." Juraslav commanded. This brought peals of laughter from the boys, who elbowed and pushed one another at the suggestion. "I'm *not* jesting," Jura interrupted. "You will get more and more of this unless you let it heal properly. Two weeks! Hear me?" For the rest of the day he patrolled the ablutions taking place along the stream and observed as each boy carried out his instructions with the cotton and astringent. Finally he told them to put on clean pants, if they owned any, and to wash the ones they had been wearing and dry them inside-out in the sunshine. He seemed satisfied that this part of the tribe's medical problem had been addressed properly and resolved to continue with the diarrhea sufferers on the following morning.

The diarrhea victims were, surprisingly, all women. After considering this coincidence, Jura inquired whether the women of the tribe had a different diet from the males. One shyly stepped forward and in a soft voice said, "Our men like us to eat lots of the crustaceans which we can gather along the river bank. They say," she giggled, "that it makes us better lovers when we eat those." All of the women shook their heads in agreement. Dieter asked if that could be true, and Jura smiled conspiratorially and whispered to him.

"Poor things; with diarrhea, they probably have to tense their abdominal muscles to avoid soiling the bed during intercourse, and no doubt they race urgently to conclude for the same reason. But, I'm certain that it *seems* more intense to their partners." He told the assembled ladies to stop eating the crustaceans and added that he was giving them some medical powder to dust very lightly over the meat, poultry, and fish they were preparing each day. He added that it would disappear quickly from sight, but would help cure the problem. "It is called potassium nitrate," he said. His patients took four large bottles of the white powder, promising that they would use it as instructed.

The medical consulting was a welcome diversion from the concerns of recent days and the headlong dash away from Prague, but when night fell on the fourth day of their visit with the Romani people, Jura and Dieter sat by one of the fires and agreed that they must address the important and intimidating issues of planning a reasonably safe exit from Czechoslovakia.

Jura asked, "Could you see through the truck windows as we drove to this spot? Did you notice that we travelled parallel to a river—the Ohře—for many kilometers?"

"I saw glimpses of water, but it seemed that we turned off frequently and then returned to the river road. Correct?"

"Yes. Draco's family owns a refuse collection business, and their trucks serve small communities along the route we travelled, so he knows how to weave around trouble spots. The Ohře comes out of the mountains to the west of here and moves swiftly to the area around Litoměřice, where it joins the Elbe and goes on to the North Sea. Draco's truck picks up all manner of garbage and waste, then they dump it into the Ohře, where the current moves it along."

"Ah, but eating crustaceans pulled from the banks could make someone ill!" Dieter observed. "And that's what you believe happened to the Romani ladies. But what of the powder you left with them?"

"Potassium nitrate is a preservative sometimes called Chile saltpeter; it is used to extend the useful life of meat and fish." Jura responded. "It is also reputed to diminish males' libido. The army says it works, but I really don't know. In any event, it should improve the quality of their perishables and—who knows?—if the men of the caravan become less demanding, perhaps they will view their women as being more so."

Once again, Dieter found amusement in the day's events even amid the stress and uncertainty of his own situation. "You are too funny, Jura." he laughed. "How could I survive without you?"

CHAPTER FORTY-ONE
Czechoslovakia – Summer 1939

FIRST CONTACT WITH THERESIENSTADT

Jura asked whether Dieter had noticed a vast, dark assemblage of old stone and brick buildings flanking the Ohře, which he said they had passed along their escape route from Prague. But Dieter responded that he had not. "It was dark, and I was trapped under the girls on the floor of the van," he chuckled.

"It is an old fortification from the late 1700s, built by the Austrian emperor," Jura explained. "It had no real value as protection for the region—which was his intent—but there was space for a jail and for billeting of troops and even for housing the poorest. The emperor named it for his mother, Maria Theresa, so it was called 'Theresien.' The Archduke's assassin was kept there for years, but nobody had a real use for the place because people got sick if they lived there too long. Some combination of dampness and mold and foul air, I imagine.

"However, our newest conquerors, from Berlin, have concluded that it would be a fine place to house any undesirables they encounter here. They have renamed it Theresienstadt and added that it is a friendly village being delivered over to the Jews and others, where they may realize a protected life among their peers. They intend it to be a music and arts showplace which can disabuse the world of its notion that Nazis are cruel to certain groups."

"Will they really do that?" Dieter asked. "They seem adept at promising but deficient at delivering. I don't believe I'd have any interest in becoming a resident there. Let's work at getting out of here safely, Jura."

CHAPTER FORTY-TWO

Prague – Late Summer 1939

THE GESTAPO NET TIGHTENS

"Ah, Major Heller. Good of you to return my call," oozed Gestapo Colonel Edward Gunther, who knew how to charm even without much practice. "Do you recall Accounting Specialist Jurgen Deitz, who was to be transferred to your command from mine? But who celebrated his good fortune a bit too vigorously and fell to his death from a train? I believe it was you who requested him, and I am wondering whether you knew Deitz or his family personally. As matters heat up with Poland, I will be assisting in establishing the Gestapo operations there, and when I visit Forst I would feel it incumbent upon me to pay his family a courtesy visit."

"How thoughtful of you, Colonel," responded Fritz Heller, already sensing an ulterior purpose and wishing to avoid any unnecessary involvement with the unpopular and ill-reputed Gunther. He continued, "No, unfortunately I did not know them or him. I was ordered to add an accounting specialist with Polish language proficiency, and his was the only available folder which met the full criteria." *That* should close the matter, he thought to himself.

But Colonel Gunther was not to be dismissed so easily. "Do you recall where the order originated?" he countered. "Perhaps I could go to that source for more . . ."

"Ah, Colonel, we have gotten massive numbers of transfer orders to build this attack force. I could only guess that the Deitz matter came from Wehrmacht HQ. Er—for some reason, it jogs my memory that an aide to one of the general officers probably contacted me."

"General von Seigler, perhaps?"

"I really couldn't say. Of course, that would be possible because Otto has been heavily involved in matters concerning Poland, you know. But I really don't recall that detail."

It had been a model of nimble verbal footwork, but after applying his "Gestapo filter" to the attitude as well as the words of Major Heller, Gunther concluded that General von Seigler had indeed initiated the request and had done so in a way which he hoped would obscure his involvement. Deitz had been hard onto the trail of Sofie von Seigler and Dieter Meister, whose disguised flight from Berlin to Prague was intended to protect the General from possible embarrassment during the Oster investigation. Von Seigler had wanted Deitz moved away from their new location in Prague. Moreover, Reichsmarschall Göring had abetted their escape from Berlin with a safe-conduct letter. Gunther knew that he must find one or both of the fugitives before open warfare with Poland erupted and usurped everyone's full attention. Border crossings from Czechoslovakia and train stations around the country should be alerted to the fugitives' names and descriptions. Gunther would not be denied his quarry again!

CHAPTER FORTY-THREE

Czechoslovakia - Near The Polish Border Late August 1939

FUGITIVES

Neither Jura nor Dieter had ever driven a motor vehicle, let alone explored the mysteries of the engine and gears that propel them. So, for three frustrating days they fumbled with the old heap they had pushed out from its hiding place in the barn. Of course, they understood the purpose of the crank dangling from the front of the engine housing, and they took turns coaxing coughs of life from within the mysterious tangle. Once or twice it threatened to turn over, but as often it snapped backward, delivering painful impacts to the forearms of its tormentors.

A young farm girl, whom they judged to be about eight or nine years old, came by each day to watch their labor with amusement, and, in exchange for their coins, she produced bread, wurst, and a nondescript, fermented beverage. On the fourth day, she dragged a large military container filled with fuel to the barn and pointed for them to pour it through a port concealed under the crinkled fender. They followed her instruction. "Now it go!" she smiled.

The three of them pushed the beast to the top of a long incline, deciding to allow it to descend with gravity's help while one of them stomped on the gear pedals, hoping to engage them by accident. They had identified a magneto switch and the small toggle to place it in the *On* position, which they correctly assumed would be a condition necessary to achieving ignition of the fuel.

Dieter drew the short straw of the driver, and he positioned himself for the descent after he and Jura agreed that he should jump for his safety if necessary. Half a minute of bouncing downhill and an explosion of black smoke left the vehicle shaking violently at the bottom, where its engine achieved an ongoing hiccupping status, with little puffs of smoke emanating from a pipe beneath the chassis. Jura and the girl caught up to Dieter where gravity had left him, and she indicated which pedal to depress while ramming the massive gear lever into its forward position. Finally, she pointed toward a two-rutted track leading away from the gully and said, "You go Opava that way." It was the name of a town to the east near the Polish border, which Jura recognized.

Dieter took Jura's hand firmly in his and smiled, "We should have purchased a horse from the Romani." Both laughed and waved to their young friend, then putted away on what would be their final day of freedom together.

Jura had convinced Dieter that their best opportunity lay to the east, across the Polish border. "We can travel eastward until we intersect the Oder River, and then if we go southward along its course, we should encounter several small towns—like Opava—where it may be possible to cross the river and enter Poland. Once there, it will be easier to contact Lilka or others in Krakow who can help us."

Dieter had believed that, with his Swiss passport, he would fare better going westward in the general direction of Switzerland, and from that neutral country begin an effort to reunite with Sofie. However, Jura had drawn a simple map in the sand showing him that too much of German-controlled Czechoslovakia and Austria lay between them and the nearest point in Switzerland. No, going east would be much shorter, and the possible availability of help from friends would be much greater if they could get to Poland. And so, on September 1, 1939, they began chugging and quivering along a stream in the general direction of a town called Opava, with no knowledge that it was the same day on which German forces commenced their onslaught against Poland.

CHAPTER FORTY-FOUR

Paris – September 1, 1939

ON THE LEEWARD SIDE OF THE STORM

Sofie was on a shopping trip alone in Paris when she placed the call to a telephone number she had memorized while on her visit to Zurich. It took a discouragingly long time before the connection was completed, but when she heard the condescending voice of Herr Bartel, she was relieved, notwithstanding her dislike for the banker. After identifying herself and providing all of the encoded enabling numbers, she instructed Herr Bartel to open a second, conventional account with 20,000 SWF from her existing dowry. The new account would be a joint account with a Swiss citizen named Dieter Havlik, from which Herr Havlik could at any time withdraw all or part of the corpus or credited interest without the need for her co-signature. Herr Havlik's encoded password would be "80 Wilhelmstrasse." His instructions were to be honored at any office of Bank Julius Baer.

The entire transaction consumed less than 15 minutes, but Sofie was confident that Herr Bartel would execute her instructions perfectly.

With that accomplished, Sofie called the private telephone of Klaus Kolb and informed her father's faithful aide that she had created a modest provision for her piano-tuner friend at Bank Julius Baer but was sure that Kolb's annual stipend would not be materially diminished by that assignation. If he were able to get the information to Dieter, his account name was the one on his Swiss passport, and his password was the address where they had first met. Kolb thanked her for her honesty, then added that Sofie's trust had been augmented recently, thus his annual 2 percent stipend would actually be greater than he had anticipated.

"How much more is in my account, Klaus?" she asked with trepidation. He responded that he believed it might have doubled since her visit to Zurich, which caused her to choke with disbelief. Did this mean that still more Jewish family belongings and treasures had been confiscated and more Nazi pockets lined with the loot? She knew without asking that that was the case. She hung up with a brief goodbye to Klaus and sought out a sidewalk café where she could purchase a snifter of cognac.

Sofie became thoroughly inebriated that evening and had no recollection of her return to her hotel room. When she finally awoke, it was midmorning, and she ordered up a full breakfast to her room in an attempt to settle her roiled nerves and complaining stomach. An hour after finishing, she dressed and walked to a Paris office of Bank Julius Baer, where she established her identity and requested confirmation of her current balances.

A very respectful bank officer returned shortly and presented her with a ledger card showing that her principal account had an available balance of SWF 4.2 million, and a joint account (combining her name and that of another person) contained an available balance of SWF 20,000. Getting drunk hadn't changed anything; she was still very rich and very disturbed by the genesis of her wealth.

CHAPTER FORTY-FIVE

Near The Polish Border – September 1, 1939

THE WHEELS COME OFF

The revived clunker and its two disheveled passengers moved along back roads, always making corrections for east, as its passengers determined, at a thundering velocity just above 10 kilometers per hour. There was no way to estimate how far the fuel would carry them, and they had little confidence that they could restart the balky machine if its engine ceased to turn over. However, the primitive nature of their truck and their shabby clothing seemed to provide them with immunity from interest. Instead, they encountered amused waves from people along the way, and they returned those greetings with good humor.

Then, to their dismay, two military motorbikes with sidecars loomed in the distance to their rear and overtook the dilapidated lorry with breathtaking, dust-belching velocity. Dieter steered to the right side of the roadway, preparing to be interrogated, with little hope that their contrived explanations would gain acceptance. "This is probably the end of our odyssey, dear Jura," he lamented, and Juraslav squeezed his extended hand in a gesture of resignation. It had been a wonderful, shared adventure, he offered.

The speeding cyclists narrowly missed the quivering truck as they sped by, showering pebbles and dust over the two sorry-looking travelers. One soldier shouted an insult and raised his finger as they passed, and Jura returned a proper "Heil Hitler" from the passenger side of the wooden driving bench. "We are such sorry-appearing *merde* that no one is interested in us!" he shouted at Dieter over the growling noises of the engine and the creaking and cracking of the chassis. "We are invisible, Dieter!"

The summer day was long, and at 6 p.m. there was still abundant light remaining for driving. It was actually easier to identify "east" as the sun dipped toward the western horizon behind them. They passed a road sign that proclaimed that the Village of Opava lay 5 kilometers ahead, and, gloriously, the entrepreneur who had erected the sign had added that he offered "Petrol For Sale" at his establishment.

"Keep your fingers crossed that our limousine has another 30 minutes of fuel," Dieter smiled. "If so, we can fill it *and* our bellies in Opava, and find a comfortable haystack for the night."

Lt. Col. Edward Gunther dreaded each ring of his private telephone these days. Those calls rarely signaled good news, and at the moment he expected more fallout from the recent failures under his command. However, during business hours, the distinctive bell of the red instrument could not be ignored. "Colonel Gunther!" he barked into the mouthpiece. "Please state your business."

"Sir, we believe that two persons of interest to you are being detained at a border crossing near Opava."

"Would that be a man and a woman?" his voice erupted hopefully. He did not want to give any names because the caller had not yet identified himself.

"Sir, it is a Czech medical doctor and a Swiss gentleman, who share the same surname of . . . "

"NO NAMES!" Gunther bellowed. "Where were they proceeding?"

"Into Poland," was the quick reply. "We had received our daily alert bulletin covering several prospective travelers, and these two made no effort to present false documents. I am reasonably certain they are individuals your office desires to detain and question."

"I'd like to raise their heads on pikes," Gunther mumbled inaudibly, but for his caller, he intoned, "Please do not harm them unless they make a serious effort to flee. And make certain they do not dispose of anything in their possession. What alerted their captors?"

"We heard news today that our Wehrmacht units have crossed into Poland, and we did not want any men of military age to try to join the

Polish defense forces. Several have been detained here today, Colonel. Are these two volunteers or military people? They look more like road hobos or Gypsies, and their vehicle is little more than junk. What should we do next, Colonel?"

"My adjutant will pick up this call and take down your driving instructions. We will proceed as quickly as possible to your location and take charge of these prisoners, if they are who I believe them to be. Good work. Heil Hitler!" Gunther called for his adjutant and then began gathering a few essentials for the two- or three-hour drive he anticipated. He had not been to Opava previously but now looked forward to his first visit with keenest anticipation.

"Did we do something wrong, Jura?" a confused Dieter questioned. "We just drove to the crossing point as others were doing. It appeared to me that people moved in both directions—workers and shoppers—and that the border guards were indifferent."

"Dieter, we were new faces to them, so they requested identification. I heard them repeat *Havlik* and then we were ushered into this holding room. Someone alerted them and they will now go to that someone with their finding."

"Jura, I'm afraid we will be outed, and that cannot be a good thing for either of us. Should we try to escape before they know more? If we can reach the riverbank, we could swim to Poland. What do you think? The river isn't broad here and they are busy with other things. Let's just stroll away and try it!"

"I'm not so young or strong as you, Dieter. But I'll divert them with questions or feigned illness if you want to try it. With just a few minutes' head start, I believe you could disappear in the crowd along their main street, and then you could find a secluded spot from which to enter the river. Then Poles on the other bank may come to you with assistance."

"No. We'll stay together. It has gotten us this far and I prefer to take my chances as part of a team. If you don't think you could jog and swim to safety, then we will wait here—together. Just as you did when the Gypsies said they would turn me loose, and you said I would not be alone. We are a good team, Jura."

"Guten abend. I am Lt. Col. Edward Gunther," he began. "You gentlemen have been detained because you are suspected of being participants in a Polish espionage activity headquartered in Prague. That activity has precipitated the deaths of three German officers, and your involvement could cost you your freedom or even your lives. Do you understand? Good! I am in a position to make things less onerous for you, but my generosity will be directly proportional to the assistance and information you provide to me. So, gentlemen: Who are you, and why were you attempting to cross this border today?"

Dieter and Juraslav looked at one another to see which should respond and how they should define themselves.

Colonel Gunther spoke again. "I can place one of you in another room and interrogate each of you separately before you concoct some fabrication together. Would you prefer that? If I'm forced to do so, we will just shoot the less cooperative one and concentrate our generosity on the good collaborator. So—what will it be?"

Juraslav spoke. "I am a medical doctor, as you can easily confirm in Prague. I have served the city's citizens and visitors since 1922, and my father did likewise for a long time prior to that. I have *never* inquired into the occupations of my patients; whether saints or spies, I have tried to treat their illnesses ethically. It is possible that some who have been my patients were antisocial, but that would be true of any physician's work. After all, we are Christians, don't you understand? And Christian charity must extend to all!"

Colonel Gunther turned toward Dieter. "And you? Are you Nurse Nightingale to this conscientious healer? Hmmmm?"

"I am the doctor's cousin from Switzerland, as you can see from my passport. Alas, I am not trained in medicine, but instead in music. I was employed recently at the Majestic Plaza Hotel in Prague, and during that time, I stayed with my cousin. I was there when criminals struck his clinic. We ran for our lives when shots were fired there."

"Very good!" smiled Colonel Gunther. "But why did you not flee to the nearest police station instead of running all the way to the Polish border? Was that because *you* were firing the shots? Come quickly—a logical explanation for *that*, Herr Doctor."

"Of course," began Juraslav. "I was examining the wife of a Prague police officer when two men burst in to rob the clinic. She was injured, and the policeman, who was in our waiting room, responded to her screams. He and the intruders shot one another. We were all told to flee as fast and as far as we could. We have no side in this matter. As a physician, I am sworn to do no harm. I would not fire shots at others, Colonel."

"You are both very original," Colonel Gunther again smiled. "While I check further on your accounts of the murders at your clinic, I shall keep you as my guests at a quaint village north from Prague. It is called Theresienstadt—do you know it? No? Well, you shall. And when we next speak, perhaps you will have an explanation for how two corpses took the train to Litoměřice and jumped off there. Also, I will need the name of your female patient, doctor."

"Herr Colonel, you *know* that patient/physician confidentiality prevents me from disclosing that. You know that I have taken a sworn vow not to break that confidentiality. Sworn on our Holy Bible, Colonel! I would feel like some perfidious Jew if I broke that pact merely to gain personal favor."

"Ah—so you would, Doctor. But, your cousin has made no such sworn promise. Perhaps he will come up with a name for me, and then I would need no further cooperation from you. So both of you please enjoy Theresienstadt until we have our next conversation. And please extend my best wishes to Fräulein von Seigler if you find her there."

When the Gestapo commander had finished the brief interrogation, he departed in his staff car, leaving the two captives with guards who locked them into the rear compartment of a military vehicle and drove them back to a holding area not far from that old stone fortress by the river. There they were stripped and hosed down, then given simple white prison-issue pants and tops. There were no laces in their shoes or drawstrings in their pants, and the shoes were not designated for right and left feet—just slip-ons with leather soles.

Each had a bedroll, and their cramped, shared room had a bucket for toilet use, which was to be emptied once daily into a large pipe leading from the exercise yard to the river. There was a common shower for the entire barracks, which had multiple cells like the one to which they were consigned. Strong lye soap bars were lying on the floor of the shower room, but there was no sign of towels, brushes, toilet tissue, or eating utensils. Jura thought that the cellblock smelled like an open sewer, and he was sure that any superficial skin cut could become massively infected if exposed to the place.

"So—what happens now?" Dieter asked. "Are we just abandoned here, or will we receive some kind of instruction and routine?"

"They will keep us guessing and try to make us anxious to speak about our connection to Sofie and her parents. That's my view," responded the older prisoner. "It could be weeks before that happens, and in the interim we must try to imagine a way to pass the time and a way to leave this cesspool."

Lilka Rudovska's desk was heaped with dispatches from the front, none of them good news. German Panzers were swift and deadly, and they would force Poland's capitulation in only weeks. There was no hope held out for British or French intervention, and the USSR had executed a non-aggression pact with Hitler in which each country had agreed to stand away from the other's territorial moves. "In time they will clash," Lilka said to no one in particular, "but for now, Germany can gobble up our territory with impunity."

A secretary interrupted Lilka's thoughts as she entered with yet another printed sheet. "I believe you should read this," she said with an audible sigh of resignation, and she turned away quickly after placing the single page atop the growing pile.

BUDAPEST / 1 SEPTEMBER / FOR LILKA/ ADGAM AND ASLE OUTSIDE STOP ARUJ AND RETEID STILL INSIDE STOP PROCEEDING TO NEUTRAL PORT STOP WILL REQUEST TRANSPORTATION FROM THERE STOP ASLE

FULL STOP

So, her Prague agents had departed Czechoslovakia successfully, but her son and her daughter's friend might no longer be free. She wondered whether the whole matter of the clinic and its connections to Otto von Seigler would be exposed now—or would Jura and Dieter be perceived as just two more suspicious men picked up in a routine sweep? In any case, she must try to alert Otto, and she resolved to see whether his secure telephone remained a useful conduit.

The conversation had none of the personal warmth of their previous chat; it was fast and factual. Havlik Clinic was no longer in business. Dr. Havlik and a young man might be detained. The rest of the household had resettled farther to the south. In return for those tidbits, Lilka was requested to have anyone who might chance to encounter Dieter let him know that he had inherited a little money and have him contact Otto's aide for details. This time there *were* two distinct *clicks* after Lilka rang off, but Otto judged that the brief conversation had been sterile as respects disclosing any information that could put people into jeopardy.

Neither had mentioned Sofie either by name or by identifiable reference, although both were concerned that she might be vulnerable in the aftermath of the clinic's unmasking. Sofie had always before had a protector nearby, but now she was outside the umbrella of those caretakers, and the world was becoming more hostile with each new day. Both knew instinctively that when the Wehrmacht's campaign in Poland was concluded successfully, the Low Countries and France could expect German incursions, too. If Sofie remained in France, she might be endangered by the spreading conflict.

Lilka had read that the celebrated Quintette du Hot Club de France was initiating a tour of the British Isles, and she resolved to attend a scheduled performance in London's West End and to steal a little time with Sofie if she were traveling with the group. She wanted to do so without disclosing their relationship to observers; the SWW was resented by many, and if Sofie were continuing with her public performances, she should not be identifiable as the daughter of a Polish spy, or, for that matter, as the daughter of a Wehrmacht general. "Sophia Havlik from Neuchâtel, Switzerland" was a wonderfully neutral identity for one who wanted only to entertain, and Lilka vowed not to damage that façade.

CHAPTER FORTY-SIX
London - 1940

THE QUINTETTE'S FINAL TOUR

Lilka was surprised at how pricey The West End bistro was for aficionados of the Quintette. There was an admission price, a stiff music cover charge, and a three-drink minimum. And—for any who might become peckish during the evening—the price of a slice of roasted beef atop a longbread was about what dinner at Simpson's On The Strand would cost. Yet, when she was ushered to a distant corner table, she could see that the bistro would be overflowing with the Quintette's enthusiasts well before their performance was slated to begin.

The billboard announcing their appearance pictured a suave Django and his brother, Joseph, holding guitars, and the dapper Stéphane cradling his Stradivarius. Behind them were Pierre "Buro" Ferrat (also a Gypsy) and Roger Chaput. There was no mention of a vocalist, but on the chalkboard near the entrance, someone had noted that "Sophia" would be joining them that evening—along with a choice of Shepherds' Pie or lamb chops for adventurous diners. Lilka was hungry but ordered only a glass of Bordeaux wine, since she knew that she would be consuming three of them.

When the musicians finally entered the room, three hundred pairs of hands applauded for what seemed like a minute, and the Quintette waved back at their fans with engaging smiles. Then there was the usual tuning of instruments and shuffling of music sheets until finally Stéphane raised his hand and quieted the room.

"Dear friends: We are pleased to be back on this side of the Channel and flattered that so many of you have come to The West End to spend a little time with us. We're going to open with a number you'll all know, and dancing in the aisles *will* be permitted to "The Lambeth Walk"! With that, the joyous sounds of the Quintette burst over the audience, and a visitor from afar would have believed there was not a worry in the world that night.

Finally, Lilka spotted Sofie seated with a heavy-set but darkly attractive woman at a bad table, one from which the occupants could not see the performers on stage. Sofie had a cognac glass cupped protectively between her hands, and she was dressed in her favorite deep red color, in a frock that was distinctly French and provocative. Lilka thought that Sofie looked older and thinner, but of course she was now past her twenty-fifth birthday, and she probably dieted to stay comfortable in her chic French dresses. The two women were in deep conversation, and Lilka concluded there was absolutely no chance that her daughter would detect her presence in the audience.

After an hour of their familiar offerings, the Quintette announced a 15-minute break. When they returned to the small stage, it was Django who spoke. His English was much more accented than Stéphane's, but he had practiced a short routine of information about the group and their itinerary on the current tour. He ended by saying, "I would like to introduce two very special ladies who are seated around the corner in the cheap seats." He waited for the laughter to die down, then continued. "For those who can see them, please welcome my companion, Naguine"—again he waited politely for their applause to slow—"and a talented young lady who favors us with her renditions of the signature songs of some of the world's best-known vocalists. Here—from Switzerland—is our own Sophia!"

Lilka watched her daughter move confidently through the tables toward the stage and saw the appreciative stares of 150 English gentlemen as they appraised the tall young woman in the skimpy red French dress. She heard one quip, "Who cares if she can sing—just so she walks around the room a few more times!" inciting some bawdy laughter from the room. But she definitely *could* sing, and within minutes the room was captivated by her stylings, which ended with her salute to the late George Gershwin and her soft delivery of "The Man I Love."

After quieting calls of *encore!* Stéphane promised that Sophia would return later, and Sofie retreated to the semi-concealed table and a newly filled snifter. It was time for Lilka to approach her.

When Sofie recognized the woman who was approaching her table, she flashed a delighted smile and bounded to her feet, arms extended to initiate an appropriate familial embrace. Lilka responded with a discouraging frown and softly cautioned her daughter that there might be people in the room who knew Lilka's SWW position—and that she would rather not have them know that Sofie, or Sophia, was her daughter. With that formality completed, Sofie's dining companion, Naguine, graciously relinquished her seat at the small table to Lilka, and mother and daughter savored their first eye-to-eye conversation in nearly two years.

Sofie had to be told that Dieter and Juraslav had been apprehended by the Gestapo and interned in Theresienstadt, but Lilka approached that subject gently, first recounting the fact that the young 'housegirls' had departed Prague safely, and the men might have to perform as professional musicians in "the village that Hitler gave to the Jews." The fact that they were prisoners was not specifically explained, and Lilka wondered whether Sofie truly understood the nature of the Nazi occupation of the Sudetenland.

Sofie told her mother that she believed France would successfully avoid German domination, since Hitler was consolidating his gains in Czechoslovakia, Poland, and the Low Countries and did not need an elevated conflict with France and England. If that were the case, then she, Sofie, would be well established in the French music community soon and ready to help Dieter when he was released from that place Lilka had described. It was a naïve viewpoint, but with only a few minutes together, Lilka chose not to contradict or correct her daughter.

"Where is your home now?" she asked, and Sofie told her that Django and Naguine had a cozy weekend cottage in Salbris, in the center of France, which Sofie occupied alone, since they preferred the swifter life of Paris. She continued that she had sufficient resources from her father to travel and to book hotel rooms as needed. When her current tour with the Quintette in Britain concluded, she had plans to vacation on the French Riviera during the late summer when the holiday crowds had departed. After that, she would try to book musical appearances for the autumn and winter seasons.

Lilka was amazed at how Sofie apparently regarded her profession as providing immunity from the world calamity around her. It reminded Lilka of the account she had heard earlier of Dieter's mother, who thought that the Great War and the influenza epidemic were for others and that her own marriage and singing career would surely resume. Was Sofie's attraction to Dieter somehow the product of that myopia? She wondered and worried for her daughter.

CHAPTER FORTY-SEVEN

Theresienstadt – Winter 1939/40

SETTLING IN
[From Dieter's Journal]

After three weeks, during which we saw no one but our silent guard, who dumped nondescript mush on our tin plates and purple fluid into the communal drinking jug, we finally had the first official contact with our warden. He was waiting for us in an open room we hadn't seen previously, and his questions concerned only our musical abilities.

My sole performing instrument was the piano; I could still sight-read musical scores, even though I had worked for years improvising songs in a bar. Juraslav offered that he could coax music from anything with strings, but he had not been formally schooled in music so couldn't read music from a score. Those answers seemed to satisfy the man, who departed without further questions. Another two weeks dragged by before the next contact. During that time we spoke in low, guarded voices and tried to assess as much of our new surroundings as the limited views through our barred cell window and quick glances from the walled exercise yard would permit.

I told Jura, "I can hear others speaking at times, and hear fragments of instrumental music which is *not* from a gramophone. Remember, we were told that Theresienstadt houses musical and artistic people."

"That may be true," Jura returned, "but we appear to have no talents of interest to them. I was expecting to be asked about my medical specialties, but perhaps physicians aren't needed in the perfection of the Third Reich. Only strutting administrators required, eh?"

Eight weeks after our arrival (if the day scratches on our whitewashed cell wall were correct) I was led out of the cellblock and to a building that appeared to be an auditorium. It was about 300 meters from the cellblock. I was amazed that the auditorium contained an abused-looking Petrof piano that was missing one leg. It sat on a raised stage, amid scores of individual music racks and scattered portable chairs. It was a scene that suggested a sizeable orchestra might have assembled there recently.

"Please sit and limber your fingers for a while. Herr Schächter will come here shortly to evaluate your abilities."

"Do you mean the Czech pianist, Rafael Schächter?" I asked, with more than a hint of amazement that the celebrated leader of the Vienna Philharmonic Orchestra might possibly be auditioning inmates at Theresienstadt. There was no response to my question—clearly this was not a conversation. I was simply chattel in Theresienstadt—one whose value hadn't been evaluated officially. So I did as ordered and played scraps of music on the Petrof, alone in that large room. It was a surprisingly good piano, although I knew that with small pliers or a child's skate key I could bring up some slightly flat notes and improve the timbre. Perhaps Director Schächter—if that was really to be my evaluator—could be persuaded to let me tune the instrument. It would help break the boredom of Theresienstadt to have such a responsibility.

When I finally "auditioned" for Director Schächter, I played both classical and popular selections from memory to his satisfaction. "You will do as a supplemental member of our performing group—that may save your life," was his brief, chilling comment. Director Schächter then gave me a small stack of music sheets to study before the next rehearsal, and I requested a pen, ink, and a pencil—ostensibly to add notations to the sheets. I had already conceived of keeping a journal for you—or perhaps for me—to combat the monotony I could foresee. I would later hoard as much paper and as many pens as possible to fill the endless void.

Director Schächter also handed me two clean, pressed shirts and a pair of crisp cotton trousers—with a belt! "These are for public performances. Take good care of them!" he cautioned. I certainly didn't have the temerity to ask how one did that while crammed into a two-person bolthole with no bureau or closet, but I resolved to find a way. For now they would remain folded under my bedroll during the daytime, and they would never be near the purple stuff we were given to drink, or the shared fecal bucket.

Finally, I respectfully posed the question of how the Petrof was tuned, and by whom. I said that my tuning experience included some of the finest instruments in Berlin, but I stopped short of offering an account of the unlikely adventures on Wilhelmstrasse with a Wehrmacht general, the Oberbefehlshaber of the Luftwaffe, the world's most famous aviator, and a half-naked girl. Apparently the unadorned story was sufficient to get Director Schächter's attention, and I became the official tuner of the Petrof, with plenary permission to visit the auditorium for two hours each week in order to attend to my tuning assignment. It coaxed my first smile since entering this awful place.

CHAPTER FORTY-EIGHT

Forst, Germany – Winter 1939/40

MILITARY HONORS

Lt. Col. Edward Gunther had been well received in Forst on his initial visit, as he evaluated his temporary assignment as consultant to the structuring of a Gestapo presence within the newly conquered areas of Poland. He reflected that he would not have been so highly regarded and this important task would not have been entrusted to him if his recent Prague embarrassments had been reviewed critically in Berlin. He welcomed the opportunity to resuscitate his flagging image and resolved to present an energetic profile while in Forst.

Perhaps it would be a nice touch to contact the family of the unfortunate Jurgen Deitz and convey the personal condolences of Deitz's last commanding officer. After all, even though military families were inured to the possibility of combat casualties, a clerical officer in a peaceful, occupied city was not expected to meet a violent death. It was an easy matter to extract the address of Deitz's parents from the deceased agent's personnel folder, and Col. Gunther learned that the family owned a farm only a few kilometers from Forst.

He drove himself to the well-kept family homestead just four kilometers outside the city limits and parked off the road near the principal building, a Low Country–style residence. Col. Gunther stepped up onto the porch and knocked sharply on the solid wooden door, using a mounted knocker that was carved and painted to look like a woodpecker. It amused the Gestapo chieftain to observe the simplicity of rural people, and he anticipated that they would be duly impressed by someone wearing an officer's dress uniform adorned with four rows of multi-colored decorations and campaign ribbons.

A man who appeared to be in his mid-fifties opened the door and sized up his unannounced visitor, then asked if Col. Gunther was an officer from his son's Prague posting. The unexpected question surprised Col. Gunther and shook his composure enough to require a swift retort. "I was Jurgen's commanding officer, but how would you perceive that, sir?" was his hastened response. "You must encounter German military personnel often in and around Forst—there are hundreds billeted here— why ask *me* about a connection to your late son?"

"Because that is the only reason an unaccompanied Colonel would visit my house," was the man's response. "I have awaited the time when such a visitor would drive onto my property and attempt to explain why my only son drank too much and fell from a train. I don't believe that account, Colonel, and I am very curious to know why and by whom it was fabricated."

"Your son was a Gestapo operative, and we deal in many intrigues," Colonel Gunther extemporized. "You might be correct in your skepticism. I cannot add anything to the official findings except my deepest regrets."

"But you are Lt. Colonel Edward Gunther, and Jurgen was performing one final mission for *you* before he shipped back to his new posting in Forst. Isn't that true?"

Colonel Gunther knew it would be futile to deny what the man had already deduced correctly. *Perhaps that is where young Deitz had acquired his talent for logical deduction*, he thought. So he decided to put the best possible face on his response. "Jurgen was tracking a rogue agent as his last Prague assignment, and that may have contributed to his death," he explained.

"But, Colonel—who delivered that fatal stroke?" asked the older man. "Who was uncomfortable with Jurgen's activity? Was he ever threatened with harm if he persisted in his pursuit? Was he ever given the prophetic warning that he might return to his home in a pine box if he continued his investigation? No—don't lie to me, Colonel! Jurgen communicated regularly about his accomplishments and his suspicions. He was so very determined to be an excellent professional, and he worried that his efforts might be expropriated and he might be eliminated. Did that happen, Colonel Gunther? Now you may speak, knowing that it is *not* to a fool!"

Lt. Col. Edward Gunther drew his Mauser Schnellfeuer pistol and pointed it directly at the man. "You are a stupid and insulting peasant! An officer of the Third Reich need not tolerate such offensive insults!" he shouted.

A single shot shattered the tranquility of the early evening, but it was too far away from any populated area to reach any ears except those of the three persons in the farmhouse: Colonel Gunther; Jurgen Deitz's father; and Jurgen's mother, who now stood over the colonel's fallen corpse, cradling a still-smoking P. Bauer & Son hunting rifle in her trembling hands.

"Come, Mother—we must get this villain and his car away from here. We can take him over the Aultbridge and leave him in the Polish woods. Germany will need to report at least a few casualties from this brief skirmish with Poland, and Edward Gunther can be decorated as one of Hitler's heroes."

Lt. Col. Edward Gunther's decomposing remains were discovered two weeks later. He was identified only by his uniform, because marauding carnivores had picked his exposed parts clean of skin and some opportunistic Polish farmer had relieved the corpse of its valuables and official identification. No one reported the neat hole behind his ear, and he was officially decorated as a casualty of the glorious Polish campaign of September 1939.

Of course, the death was not acknowledged at Theresienstadt, thus Dieter and Juraslav were left to their imaginations as to why there was never a follow-up interview with their captor. No one seemed to know or care that they were prisoners, except those charged with assembling musical groups. And so they began three years of solitary confinement together, with only music, one another's company, and Dieter's journal to cushion the sadness, suffering, and sheer boredom of Theresienstadt.

The conquest of France became Hitler's paramount objective in May 1940, and, once again, his opponents' resistance dissolved quickly. Various new French "leaders" emerged and sought to form a government for occupied France, and multiple sites vied to become the seat of such puppet rule. Paris capitulated to a formal "prance-through" by the führer and his impressive, goose-stepping legions, but if there was any damage to the City of Light, it was superficial, and the entertainment community resurfaced quickly to serve the new patrons sitting at their tables.

Sophia's popularity was growing, especially when she delivered favorite ballads in perfect German, with the spotlight caressing increasingly exposed areas of her perfect skin. She wished that Stéphane could return from his exile in England to lend new vitality to the group, but otherwise it appeared that she bobbed along on the crest of history's new wave without incurring much personal hardship.

But, that was the superficial appearance. Beneath the façade of the increasingly polished performer, she thought often of Dieter and wished she could curl up by a fire with him again. She wondered where her father was deployed and whether anyone was occupying her beloved Lilkahaus. She knew that her mother was toiling with Poland's exiled leaders in London, but there was no way to join her there. She hoped that Jura and Dieter were still together and could keep one another's spirits from flagging. Sofie was lonely and depressed, and she drank too much cognac, too often, and . . . *no, don't go there*, she thought. *What you do to keep your emotions in check is a temporary expedient. All of this isolation will be over one day and then we can return to our normal lives.*

CHAPTER FORTY-NINE
London – Spring 1940

REUNION AND RECAPITULATION

Lilka had not seen Elsa and Magda personally since her final visit to Prague. They had maintained regular shortwave communications for many months after that, but they ceased exchanging even those messages following the sudden need to close the clinic in Prague and the decision to move the two younger women back to the provisional headquarters of Stuzba Wywiadu Wojskowego outside London. Lilka was now sixty-five years old, yet her energy and dedication to Poland were unabated. Consequently, she was disappointed when she first heard that the two younger women had apparently lost their taste for fieldwork and were expressing doubt that Poland's future could ever be revived. It was proving difficult to inspire enthusiasm amongst many of her countrymen, following the lightning-fast passage of Germany's mechanized divisions through the Polish countryside in September 1939. Many of them now correctly anticipated similarly swift capitulations of the Low Countries, Scandinavia, and France, leaving only England in the West to oppose Hitler's forces.

The three women came together following Magda and Elsa's well-managed retreat from Prague through Budapest. Gypsies camped near Uzhgorod, Czechoslovakia, had guided them to Hungary—stealthily, via backroads, at night—and had hidden them in caravans during the daylight hours. Unfortunately, Gypsies had by then become increasingly subject to attacks by Czech police, who sought favor with their German overlords by coming down hard on the itinerants. Two work camps for apprehended Gypsies had been established within Czechoslovakia—one in Lety and one in Hodonín— and the young Gypsy king, Janusz Kweik, was advising his followers to leave their caravans and blend into local communities, or else to abandon Czechoslovakia altogether.

The compatriots met in a small hotel that offered luncheon specials to office managers in the region around Eaton Place. The composition of such luncheon gatherings had changed rather swiftly from something traditionally resembling exclusive men's clubs to an array of mixed tables with increasing numbers of women in the room. Britain's men had gone to war, and women had replaced them behind many of the area's desks. By now, there was nothing unusual about three women sitting together and ordering the businessmen's special at the Dundee House. Each had a pint of stout in front of her, and after brief greetings, they joined their glasses in a quiet toast to their beleaguered country. Lilka spoke first.

"I can't tell you adequately how indebted we are for your work on behalf of our common cause. And I can't begin to express my personal happiness that you were able to slip away from Prague after that ugly attack on the clinic. I understand that the official Gestapo report of the incident sounds like an ambush by a division of armed assailants who dispatched two of their finest. I only wish that Dr. Havlik and young Dieter could have escaped Czechoslovakia with you—but I understand that the caravan's leaders determined that would have endangered all of their people. Is that essentially correct, Elsa?"

"It is," the attentive younger woman responded. "The caravan was preparing to move away from Nazi-occupied provinces of northern Czechoslovakia. There were rumors that all Gypsy men in the area were going to be sterilized—or just murdered—and the elders were unanimous that it was time to depart. Dr. Havlik and Dieter might have been identified at any search point, and everyone would have been slaughtered when it was discovered that they were being concealed by the Romani."

"We last saw them fiddling with a broken old truck, and if it could be operated, they planned to drive to some crossing point and then look for help in Poland. None of us knew that Poland was about to fall, and that it offered no hope of sanctuary. We didn't know anything of the Polish invasion until the Hungarians began boasting of their new opportunity to seize some Polish assets."

"So what did you do from Budapest to here?" Lilka queried.

"The usual," Magda sighed. "We traded favors for train rides, truck rides, and boat rides until we reached Portugal, and then we were able to contact you and get booked on a military flight to London. Branka housed us in Lisbon and got us some decent food and clothing until there were vacant seats on the airplane coming to Stansted. It was our first time riding an airplane, Lilka. Have you flown? It is remarkable!" It was also the first time they had all smiled during their luncheon get-together.

Lilka inquired about the remaining Gypsy "assets" within the Prague region, and Elsa responded with sadness that those who had not been imprisoned had either fled or died under the Nazis' heel. "Of course, there are a few exceptions. Some of the Gypsy network there was made up of native Czechs—not the immigrants from Poland, Germany, and Austria, but locals whose ancestors had settled much earlier. For those, it was possible to stay in the region and to continue directing their family interests, hiding their Gypsy ties deep below the surface of their lives. Most now attend Roman Catholic Church services, and all abandoned traditional Gypsy clothing and music. The few who accomplished this transition remain as committed as ever to the eventual defeat of the Nazis, and they must be regarded as a valuable asset in future planning."

"Good! And what about yourselves?" Lilka inquired. "What plans are you making for your future—during and after this war? It *will* end at some time, you know—and we *will* reestablish our Polish culture when sanity returns to Europe."

Elsa took a long swallow from her pint, then deliberately set it aside and rubbed her hands together, indicating a shift in the conversation. She chose her words carefully. "Lilka, each of us has turned the question over and over since killing those two Gestapo standers in Prague and running for our lives through the European countryside. None of this is easy, you know, and we have become as devoted as sisters during the past nearly five years. But after endless discussions, we realize that we are going in different directions from this point forward.

"Maggie has family in America—in Chicago, America—and they have invited her to come and sample the life there. She has a tourist visa from the American Consulate near here, which will allow her to remain for up to a year, with the financial guaranty of her family members there. If it proves to be the opportunity she is seeking, she can apply to become a citizen, as have the members of her family there. She can put sufficient distance between herself and the events of the past five years to emerge as a fresh, new person in a fresh, new ambience. I applaud that choice, and I know that you will agree."

"And you, Elsa?" Lilka continued, without acknowledging the obvious request for tacit approval of Magda's direction. "What do you envision for yourself?"

"Maggie and I are different from one another. I cannot imagine myself assuming a new lifestyle that will allow me to eradicate the past from my memory or from my attitudes. When I think of being married or having children, I cannot believe that the things I have done won't impact those relationships horribly. There has been violence in my nature and an ugliness in my behavior which are like Lady Macbeth's bloody hands. I cannot wash myself clean of those realities."

"And so?" Lilka raised her brows with a penetrating inquisitiveness.

"And so, I must continue to be what I have become. I am one who exploits her charms to steal from others. I am an actress and a whore. I deal in deception, theft, and illicit sex. I speak half a dozen European languages, and I know the back streets of many key cities behind the new German lines. You could not possibly train someone to do what I can accomplish easily. So I wish to return to the Continent, sufficiently funded to operate in the areas where valuable information can be extracted and communicated back. You know that I will be a loyal—and ruthless, if necessary—asset for as long as I can preserve myself. Is that what you wanted to hear, Lilka?"

"Yes, it is. And Maggie, I am totally in accord with your choice. I will do everything possible to facilitate it. But I do not want to burden you with any further knowledge of Elsa's next assignment, so we should end this discussion now and just enjoy a lovely luncheon shared among three devoted friends. Long live Free Poland!"

CHAPTER FIFTY
Theresienstadt - Czechoslovakia – 1941

COPING WITH BOREDOM
[From Dieter's Journal]

M y individual "day scratches" now cover a large part of the best-illuminated wall of our cramped cell. Three empty beverage cases and a straight-backed wooden chair with one arm missing have been formed into a working area, and several nails are driven into the thick columns that support the brick walls; they serve as clothing hooks. However, by far the greatest luxury in our room is the single electric light bulb which hangs above our improvised desk, allowing Jura and me to read, write, and study musical scores—and scribble this journal—after sundown darkens our limited world.

Each of us now owns a larger cache of clothing, which reflects the fact that many musicians who have come to Theresienstadt subsequently become ill and eventually are transferred to a place in Poland named Auschwitz. When they depart from this old fortress, they do so without luggage, and usually they donate the clothing left behind to friends before it can be confiscated by the guards. I acquired a warm outer coat, which has become my prized possession, used to cover both of us on cold evenings in our unheated cubicle. It belonged to "Old Jacob," a Czech Jew who was one of the first musicians to be interned in Theresienstadt. When Old Jacob's coughing became uncontrollable, he was herded with several others into a waiting railroad car, which was then appended to a longer train destined to the East. I caught a last fleeting glance of the emaciated old man peering out through the slotted side of his railroad car, and that memory has convinced me I must find a way to get out of here before our captors decide it is time for me to depart as Old Jacob did.

Jura and I have been allowed to venture outside the barracks walls more frequently now. Music practice sessions, the weekly tuning of instruments, and a few concert performances account for much of that outside time, but we have also been assigned to clean the Theresienstadt officers' dining hall after evening meals. Often there are sticky scraps of food clinging to the plates we scrape, or even short draughts of malt in the cups left behind. The cleanup is loathsome on Friday nights, because religious restrictions require that fish be served to the mainly Roman Catholic officers, and the discarded fish bones, entrails, and heads became disgusting six or seven hours after the meat has been stripped off for cooking. We prisoner/cleaners are required to render it all spotless and odorless within three hours after the officers depart. We must have the putrid garbage cans and their contents sealed and rolled to the gate leading outside the prison wall, where they are retrieved about dawn on Saturdays.

Fridays are also "beer and song" nights for the soldiers and guards, and I have become their accompanist. As a result, on Fridays, I'm often outside our cell from the end of the dinner hour until after midnight—first cleaning the garbage, and later playing an old upright, which reminds me of my former unappreciated freedom back in the Fischerstube. Of course, when my thoughts drift back to Berlin, there is always that image of my Sofie stepping up from a table to deliver a captivating vocal to her appreciatve friends. What wonderful nights they were, and how swiftly they passed into memory! And now—now I carry those private thoughts delicately back to a damp cell and slip under the warmth of Old Jacob's discarded coat, shared with Sofie's dying half brother. A half-Jew and a half-Gypsy pooling our body heat in a molding pile of brick and stone—and we are among the luckiest residents of Theresienstadt!

Lately Jura has become noticeably less animated and robust. His coughing has increased, and a few droplets of blood speckle his bedroll. For the first time within my memory, Jura isn't attending to the medical needs of others—he has been forbidden to do so, and his own health issues are neglected as well. However, he continues to urge me to perform regular exercises, and makes certain I get the best scraps from the plates we wash. I'm much leaner than when we arrived, but surely as fit as circumstances *permit, and I owe that to Jura's care. And so we pass what seem like endless days, most of which are indistinguishable one from another—except for that increasing army of lines scratched into our wall. There are now over four hundred of them.*

CHAPTER FIFTY-ONE
Lisbon, Portugal – 1941

THE GENERAL'S VACATION

With the Polish Campaign completed successfully and most of France and the Low Countries under effective German occupation, General Otto von Seigler hoped that his führer would give the tired German armies sufficient time to rest and repair. Some officers younger than he were petitioning for an immediate preemptive invasion of Britain. During 1940, the Luftwaffe had attempted to force England's capitulation by launching air strikes at the British capital, but the overall result had been disappointing. Nearly twenty-five hundred Luftwaffe planes plus their skilled aircrews had been destroyed in that air war, and the English appeared to be more resolute than ever.

British forces on the Continent had been trounced in battle but had escaped successfully through a retreat across the Channel from Dunkirk, and any attempt now to invade their homeland would surely encounter much more effective resistance than that which had characterized the short battle for France. In addition, there was the possibility that the USA would come to Britain's rescue, posing a much stronger defense against Germany.

Otto and other conservative members of the inner circle of military advisors could no longer muzzle the aggression of less circumspect officers, and Otto was becoming concerned that the nation's resources would be overextended and vulnerable if conflict with either the USSR or the USA were precipitated by a German assault on Britain. He could sense that his conservative viewpoint was losing traction in success-emboldened Berlin, and he needed time to review the Wehrmacht options—as well as his own.

General von Seigler was overdue for two weeks of mandatory military leave, and he decided to spend that time in Portugal, which was somehow "away" from the war's fury. He had only one personal friend there, a man who had failed miserably after inheriting one of Germany's best-known industries. The man's name was Hugo Stinnes, Jr. and his company had been familiar to Germans a generation earlier as Hugo Stinnes Schiffahrts GmbH, a major shipping line with worldwide operations. His father had been profiled on the cover of America's *TIME* magazine in March 1923, where he was called "The New Emperor of Germany."

But, after his father's early death, mismanagement—probably that of his son—had resulted in an unprecedented collapse of the company, and Hugo Jr. had departed from Germany in disgrace to seek anonymity in neutral Portugal. There he enjoyed the protection of the dictator Antonio de Oliveira Salazar, who was in many respects a carbon copy of his Spanish neighbor, Francisco Franco. Both wisely sat on the sidelines during the current war.

Hugo Jr. and Otto had been schoolmates as youngsters, before one entered the military service and the other bankrupted his family's shipping business. They had maintained irregular correspondence over the years, and Otto now had a reason to chat with his disillusioned and disgraced friend in Portugal. As they dined together in a waterfront café, the two old friends covered years of personal history, then turned to the contemporary European conflict.

Despite Portugal's official neutrality, Oliveira Salazar was now being forced to supply Germany with scarce tungsten necessary to its military machine. To "balance" that favor, he had continued to allow transatlantic visitors destined for England to transit the Azores and Lisbon. The pioneering US airline Pan American regularly landed its impressive Clippers at those Portuguese facilities. Recently, one of those flights had carried Wendell Willkie, an American financier and political figure, to England to negotiate terms of a "Lend-Lease" arrangement that would supply warships to the British on a basis that did not impact Britain's dwindling financial reserves. Portugal was maintaining its delicate equilibrium, and Otto was truly interested in learning from Hugo Jr.

how the country had evolved that survival technique.

Late in the evening, Otto decided to get to his discreet personal inquiry. "Hugo," he asked, "Do you still have ships going west across the Atlantic from here—ships flying a neutral flag which the U-boats will respect?"

"Well, my friend, it is no longer like the old days, but I do have a small fleet of tramps plying to and from ports in South America. And thus far, the undersea fellows have not sent torpedoes into any of our hulls. Between us, there are hundreds of Jews fleeing each month through Lisbon, and we manage to accommodate some of them, even though our tramps have few passenger staterooms or amenities. They are eager to pay for passage, using just about anything they own as currency. It is all very sad, Otto."

"And if I had someone who wanted to sail with you to South America—without creating an official record of the journey—how would I arrange that? And how would I compensate you?"

Stinnes wrote a telephone number and a telegraph address on the reverse side of his calling card, then replied. "Please let me know what I may do, my dear friend. I am not a Nazi, but I am always a German and I am always here for my friends. Don't worry," he continued, laughing, "I will pick your pocket clean when I hear from you, but for tonight, please allow me to pick up our dinner check."

When he returned to his hotel, Otto observed the handsome bartender watching him closely, and he wondered why he was getting the attention. He thought that he might have seen the man before, but that couldn't be possible. It had been many years since Otto's last visit to Lisbon. Now, wearing civilian leisure clothing, Otto could be a tourist from any of a number of European countries. No, he was being paranoid, he concluded. Each of them probably looked like someone else from the other's past.

The balance of his vacation time was spent in sunshine—and in the company of a delightful young Polish refugee whom the concierge had suggested as a dinner companion. The two strangers chatted in Polish and in German, reminding Otto nostalgically of another Polish woman twenty-five years earlier in Krakow. When Otto raised his wine glass in a toast "to Lilka," his companion only smiled and said, "No—I am Branka."

About the time when Otto returned to his post in Germany, Lilka Rudovska received a telephone call from her SWW associate, Branka, in Lisbon. She listened to details of recent sailings and the estimated numbers of persons from both sides of the current conflict who were fleeing from war-torn Europe through the neutral port of Lisbon.

Then Branka mentioned that she had spent several days—and nights—in the pleasant company of a German businessman who was on vacation leave in Portugal, using an assumed identity. She said that the gentleman appeared to know a great deal about the German military leadership and its pursuit of objectives in Poland, and that he had unusually good command of the Polish language.

The man had expressed concern that Germany might unwittingly overextend its armed forces and try to vie with the Soviets for control of the Balkan countries. He had stated his own preference for extending peace feelers to Britain before matters between those countries deteriorated even further and a major conflict exploded—one which could bring the United States into the war on the side of the English. He believed that, at present, many Americans still favored neutrality from the European war, and he had stated that in Middle America there were sizeable concentrations of citizens who identified with Germany and wished to avoid conflict with the most powerful European nation.

When Lilka asked the name of the "businessman," she was not totally surprised that the response was "Otto." With a few more discreet inquiries she was able to assemble facts establishing that Wehrmacht General Otto von Seigler had traveled alone to Lisbon and spent fourteen days there, during which time he had consulted with the expatriate Hugo Stinnes, Jr. Lilka's report did not include any conjecture regarding her own curiosity about the purpose of that meeting. Was it to explore Sofie's possible departure? Or for Otto himself? Or did it concern third persons unknown to Lilka? Otto would be embarrassed to learn that he had shared the company of one of Lilka's SWW professionals, but if Lilka contacted him to learn more, that fact would be obvious to him. She decided to weigh the matter carefully before placing a call to his personal telephone.

How curious it was in wartime, she thought. One conflict long ago had brought her into contact with a young German officer, with whom she had produced a talented daughter. Twenty-five years later, she and that officer found themselves on opposite sides in a monumental struggle, but their personal trust remained intact, as did their devotion to their daughter. And now, with her country defeated and occupied by his, she suddenly had a thread of vulnerability reaching into his life through an operative who actually reminded her of the young woman she had once been. Wasn't there a Wagnerian opera based upon that theme? Lilka produced a rare smile as she thought of Otto bedding her shapely proxy and allowing his tongue to run on too long as he reflected upon matters which could not be discussed in the official meetings which he attended. Her little P-3 network remained among the most effective intelligence-gathering organizations yet devised.

CHAPTER FIFTY-TWO
Theresienstadt, Czechoslovakia – Spring 1942

AN OLD FRIEND
[From Dieter's Journal]

*T*his is day #940 on our wall, and I believe that it is Saturday, March 28. Yesterday was a Friday, and a stressful day for me. Of course, all Fridays are unpleasant because of the ritual fish dinner and its smelly aftermath. I find it nearly impossible to eat any of the Friday scraps, because I can already smell the rotting bones and guts dumped into the garbage cans in the kitchen, and somehow even my strong stomach says *no, thank you* to ingesting any part of those stinking river creatures. It may be because I am reminded of Jura's attentions to the diarrhea-stricken Gypsy wives, and his explanation regarding the refuse being dumped into the river.

One more thing puzzles me about the Friday ritual. I know that Holy Mother Church has decreed that good Catholics not partake of meat on Fridays, but Miguel once told me that the rule officially exempted people of Spanish origin. When I asked why that would be true, he said, "Economics, dummkopf! Because the Spanish-speaking countries produce meat as one of their only saleable commodities, they would be deprived of 15% of those revenues if one day of meat consumption per week were proscribed by the Church, and that might affect parishioners' loyalties and especially their tithing into the collection box."

I have heard grumbling among some of the officers and guards here who say that soldiers on duty should also be exempt because they need all of their strength—to kick old Jews onto the trains, I suppose. The whole thing is too weighty for an imprisoned piano tuner to resolve right now, and I will leave it to the führer and Pope Pius XII to ponder when they have spare moments. I don't look for that to happen soon, because both appear to have major concerns elsewhere. I'm told that their only remaining communal topic is the "problem of the Jews," and after 940 days in this rock pile I am convinced that few Jews, Gypsies, or homosexuals will be left in Europe at the conclusion of this war, whichever side wins it.

But, despite my tirade at Fridays, I am suddenly thankful to Fridays and my extra duties disposing of the remnants of the Friday dinners. On those evenings, the kitchen produces enough putrid waste to fill four metal garbage barrels. Jura and I must seal them at the top and firmly affix the cover of each. Then we transport them on a low dolly across the central yard of Theresienstadt to the main entry gate leading to the river road. Guards open the gate for us, and while they watch we wheel the barrels outside and place them by the roadside, atop a poured concrete dock from which they can be retrieved by refuse collectors. Very early on Saturday mornings, the barrels are carted away, and empty barrels are left in their place on the dock. Jura and I wheel those empty barrels back to the officers' kitchen on Saturdays, and the cycle repeats.

On March 27, we carried the full barrels to the gate as always. But on March 28, when we stepped outside the gate to retrieve the empty replacement barrels, the fly- covered full ones from Friday night were still there. As we awaited instructions to deal with the problem, a disgusting-looking truck bounced toward us on the river road, surrounded by a small cloud of flies, insects, and road dust. The driver shouted an apology—his truck had blown a tire, and he was delayed on his rounds. The driver was our old friend, Draco!

We are not permitted to exchange any word of conversation with outsiders, and under the surveillance of the gate guards our only communication with Draco was with eye signals and subtle head movements. But Jura and I agree that Draco recognized us immediately and that he will communicate in some way. We are guessing that there will be a "feeler" inside the returned barrels next Saturday, and we will be asked to respond in the following Friday's garbage.

I have not been so happy in months! I cannot wait for the next container of smelly fish parts so that I can initiate communications—with someone!

CHAPTER FIFTY-THREE

Salbris, France – Spring 1942

BECOMING RESTLESS

Sofie was surprised that her call was answered on only the fourth ring; she had expected longer delays in calling from France to Germany, but a familiar voice responded with one word: "Kolb." It was followed by dead silence, so she decided that she should proceed with caution.

"I am calling to inquire about our mutual friend, the Übermensch," she laughed. "He has not called or contacted me in some time. Can you give me any news of him?"

"Ah, Fräulein—alas, he has been away from Berlin for weeks, and the demands upon him are very heavy. You would be pleased with his appearance—very robust and energetic—but our extended lines to the east have created logistical nightmares, and there are few with his knowledge of such problems. I know that he would welcome news of you, and if you feel comfortable relaying through me, I will certainly deliver your message."

"Klaus—you have been supremely loyal for as long as I can remember, and naturally I trust you. I would like him to know that my musical performances still go well, although there are fewer people in the audiences—in fact, they are principally German military groups relaxing from their duties. No English or Americans can visit Paris, and the French stay behind their shutters and wait for something they can't articulate. Please ask if he knows anything about my former accompanist; there are none here as good as he was. I have to know if he is well and if I can anticipate working with him again."

"And if there is any word of him, how may we reach you? Is there a military unit in your location to which a dispatch envelope can be sent?"

Sofie assured her father's aide that there was a small local military headquarters at L'Hotel de Valaudran in Salbris, and that a communication sent there and addressed to Kapitan Dietrich Schultz-Kohn (marked for delivery to "Django") would find its way to the little guest house which she occupied. Then she paused to reflect upon her next thought. Why not? "Klaus, he has not seen me perform in public, and I'm privileged to be working with some of the best musicians in all of Europe. Do you think he could be persuaded to take a weekend in Paris and give us a listen? Nothing—nothing—would make me happier, Klaus. I have truly learned a lot since those first songs at the house on Wilhelmstrasse, and I would love to show off for him. Really. What do you think?"

"I think I should make him aware of your wish. Since Paris fell to our army, a great many senior officers have scheduled little 'training missions' to the Moulin Rouge or have undertaken other Parisian refresher courses. Who knows—he might even require that an aide accompany him for the weekend. I cannot promise that he'll consider it, but will do my best to place the option directly under his nose until it gets his attention. Are you there all weekends?"

"Lately, yes. We drive up to Paris on Friday mornings and return to Salbris on Sunday afternoons. That way we can do three or even four shows, and the money is good for all of us. If it were not for the war, it would be a really agreeable time for me, but of course, reality sets in again after the final encore. I'm terribly lonely, Klaus. Please do your best to convince him, hmmm?" When she hung up the phone, Sofie realized that she was crying uncontrollably. She wondered whether she should have remained in England at the conclusion of the Quintette's last tour, or if she should have stayed in Prague with Dieter and Jura and taken her chances with them. But, of course that was not the answer. Sofie poured a snifter of cognac and stared out at her little garden through the amber liquid. She had never missed Dieter more than right now, but there was a real possibility that she would never see him again.

CHAPTER FIFTY-FOUR

Theresienstadt, Czechoslovakia – Summer 1942

VERDI'S REQUIEM
[From Dieter's Journal]

Jura and I heard the news with total disbelief. A delegation of distinguished persons under the auspices of the International Red Cross would be coming to Theresienstadt to make an independent determination of conditions here. It was a bold step by the Nazis to defuse the notion that their detainment camps were places of incredible hardship and suffering. Instead of closing the fortress to visitors, they announced they would be opening the gates and holding a "day of culture." Jura said, "They can't get away with it, Dieter—these are skilled observers and they will see past fresh paint and new haircuts—they will count the inhabitants and calculate that they must literally live atop one another. They will test the water supply and know that typhoid courses through these corroded old pipes. They will smell the raw mold in the corners and even more the fecal matter tossed into the ditches leading to the river. No, Dieter—this will backfire and expose the inhumanity of this place!"

Jura had done his best to organize work details to clean up the typhoid sources, and in that one area he had actually gotten a small measure of help from the camp commanders, but not enough to stem the tide of typhoid-related deaths which seemed to flow like a river in this place. But, the message went out: the encampment was to receive its most thorough cleaning and face-lifting since its original dedication in 1790. Excess inhabitants would be moved temporarily to other locations, and Theresienstadt's best musicians and artists would be put on display as never *before.*

I had not understood the phenomenon of beaten-down prisoners suddenly pitching in together to hide their collective misery. Perhaps it was fear that if we failed this important test, things would be even more intolerable in the aftermath. Or, quite possibly, if we produced basic improvements, they would be ours to keep. Or maybe just the camaraderie of a common cause took over. In any event, key parts of our prison were transformed into something eminently presentable. And, as the "day of culture" approached, our population was pared down drastically to contradict any possible accusation of overcrowding. The sickest and least attractive residents were loaded onto those midnight trains bound for the East; we knew they would return empty with no account of the passengers who had left us.

Each of the Theresienstadt performing musical groups rehearsed for extra hours, and every shopkeeper, schoolteacher, or artisan was given the assignment of making his particular activity appear as a model of good management. Naturally, the transformation was concentrated into small facets of our overall environment, but we were instructed—on pain of death—that only those authorized samples of Theresienstadt would be available to the inspectors. Shamefully, our distinguished visitors allowed themselves to be herded through the staged exhibits, and none of them demanded to look behind the locked doors or shuttered windows of the real encampment.

The final gilding of this figurative lily was supplied by one of our most distinguished inmates, the renowned Czech conductor and choral director, Rafael Schächter, who led his inmate choir magnificently through Giuseppe Verdi's complex and massive Requiem. Although we realized that we had all contributed to defrauding the international team of visitors, I must confess that we secretly swelled with pride that evening. How ironic! Maestro Schächter was to repeat the stunning recital at least a dozen more times before he was shipped off to Auschwitz Birkenau for "special treatment" by our captors.

For me, the summer of 1942 held even greater significance above and beyond our fleecing of the International Red Cross and its distinguished evaluators. By now I had perfected my weekly interchange of short communications through "garbage-pail mail." As Jura and I had anticipated, Draco had scribbled a short note and adhered it with chewing gum under the lid of the clean cans we retrieved on Saturday, April 4, 1942. It was our first word from the outside in 947 days! Draco told us that Lt. Col. Gunther had been killed more than two years earlier, while working behind the lines in Poland. That explained our total abandonment within these walls. With both Jurgen Deitz and Col. Gunther deceased, I wondered whether anyone remained who cared about Sofie's and my pertinence to the Oster matter.

Subsequent weeks brought more unexpected revelations from Draco. Because Col. Gunther had initially decided not to report the capture of Dieter Meister to his superiors, the "phantom Meister" had remained an unsolved mystery for the Gestapo. The deaths of four of Meister's earlier Gestapo pursuers (Deitz, Gnoff, Donner, and Col. Gunther, himself) tended to authenticate the rumor that Meister was an extremely dangerous professional. Quite recently, a bold attack along the roadway between Prague and Dresden—resulting in the death of Reichsprotektor Reinhard Heydrich, Hitler's top political official in the former Czechoslovakia—had been attributed by some to the mysterious Herr Meister. The successful attack was cited by many nervous Gestapo agents as evidence that Meister was continuing to operate within the provinces around Prague.

Under those circumstances, it was no wonder that two musicians named Havlik being detained at Theresienstadt were totally ignored.

Draco also confirmed our worst fears about the trains that departed regularly from our fortress, headed to the east. They were carrying thousands to their certain deaths each month, and if we were to avoid that same fate, it would have to be by finding a way to escape from Theresienstadt. Draco let us know that the few remaining members of the former Czech Gypsy community were now blended into the local citizenry, but he assured us that we had resourceful friends outside the walls.

I had to find a way for two men to leave the fortress alive, one of them increasingly ill and unable to undertake heroic moves. And, once outside, we needed a solid plan to get to a neutral country before we could be hunted down and killed as a deterrent to others with similar aspirations. That night, Jura and I began a systematic evaluation of possible escape scenarios, and from then onward we would take turns, one proposing an escape route, the other acting as devil's advocate, trying to foil the plotter. It was an improvised parlor game which we at first called "Disappearing from Theresienstadt," and later simply, "Escape." The nightly contest became key to maintaining our spirits and our sanity. Eventually it was also to yield an effective exit strategy.

CHAPTER FIFTY-FIVE

London – Summer 1942

FRAGMENTS OF THE NETWORK

As she promised to do, the resourceful Elsa had occasionally smuggled personal letters to Lilka through the diminished SWW network. In the summer of 1942, Elsa wrote that she was once again stationed in Prague. The letter actually came through Branka in Lisbon, which brought an amused smile to Lilka's well-creased face as she wondered whether the handsome General von Seigler had ever realized that his vacation "conquest" had been one of her SWW associates. Perhaps at the right time that could be her *touché!* to complete a trans-Channel conversation with Otto. But there were more pertinent bits of information in the recent letter. Elsa had already commenced sending encoded dispatches to the diminished SWW in London regarding German encampments in Bosnia. Each relayed a wealth of information, and Lilka assured herself that at some future time all of this spadework would be useful in the reformation of Europe.

The determined "Little Girl From Gdansk" was now working as a cocktail waitress in the restaurant of big-bosomed Renata's husband, currently a favored watering hole for younger Germans in the city. She had reestablished her contacts with the ladies of the Porte Verte but vowed not to be one of them. Her occasional dalliances were very private arrangements in the city's best hotels, and they were limited to those that could yield important data as well as generous contributions to her personal retirement fund. Somehow the revised arrangement appeared to make it more palatable for Elsa—a fact that gladdened Lilka somewhat, although she questioned how much longer Elsa would be able to project youthful vitality. Probably all of that physical training bought a little extra time, but she hoped Elsa would step away from it before some young swain called her an old whore and broke her heart forever.

Elsa had recently contacted Draco at his family's business, and the stoic Gypsy giant had confirmed that recently he had seen both Juraslav and Dieter on his garbage rounds near Theresienstadt. They had developed a weekly secret exchange of brief communications which contained enough information to confirm that both were surviving the rigors and deprivations of the facility until now, but that their tenure at Theresienstadt had already exceeded the normal life expectancy of inmates there, leading to the inevitable conclusion that they must seek a way out. Draco had made them aware that their pursuer and captor, Col. Gunther, had died without identifying his "catch" to Gestapo superiors, so they were known at the camp merely as two homosexual musicians. "Homosexual?" Lilka reacted. She understood that on the German scale of hatred, homosexuals were not quite so despised as Jews or Gypsies, and that—plus their respective talents—might account for the fact that they had survived for so long.

The letter concluded that, if Lilka wished to communicate something to Juraslav Havlik or to Dieter, the most effective routing would be back to Branka in Lisbon with instructions to move it along to Elsa at the restaurant in Prague. She also asked Lilka to send any news she might receive about Magda. Obviously there was a great feeling of loss after they went their separate ways, and she still regarded Magda as her dearest friend in the world. Lilka resolved to inquire whether Magda had reached "Chicago, America," and rejoined her family members there. How different their lives must be, she thought. But now America was becoming more involved in war around the globe, and all of its citizens and residents would become engaged in some aspect of that national effort.

Lilka also must get word to Sofie in Salbris that Dieter and Jura were surviving behind Theresienstadt's cold, ancient walls, and that it might be possible to transmit short communications to them through "the old network" of SWW and Gypsies.

CHAPTER FIFTY-SIX
Theresienstadt – Late Summer 1942

THE 20TH REUNION OF UNIWERSYTET MEDYCZNY W LEDOZI CLASS OF 1922

Juraslav listened from the corridor leading into the performing auditorium. He had not heard such a commanding delivery of Chopin's "Waltz in D-flat Major" in many years—in fact, not since those late afternoons in the faculty lounge at the Uniwersytet. His ears had not deceived him; when he turned the corner and looked toward the raised Petrof he could make out the tall form of Adam Wodzinski, with his trademark high wrists and long, supple fingers whizzing through the piece.

"Wodzinski! You? Here? Adam, Adam—I can't believe it! How long? How long has it been?" Jura grasped the familiar hands with his own trembling ones. "My God, Adam—tell me everything. I can't—am I dead? Tell me I'm not."

"Jura—dear Jura! I think we may both be dead! There, hold my hands for a minute so we can be sure. Hah! This is my third day here, and I was beginning to think that no happiness could ever penetrate this place, and then I see you and hear your voice again. This is incredible! How long have you been here, my friend?"

"Longer than three days—more like three years. Every day is a line on the wall of my cell, and I'm running out of space for more. I'm one of the lucky ones who has been healthy enough to remain. Most develop respiratory illness and when they do, they are shipped out and gone forever. But you, Adam! You still play marvelously, and you are vigorous, huh? So it appears. What is happening with you?"

"I am in this room without an overseer only because I have been commanded—by none other than Rafael Schächter—to play for important visitors in two days, and I have told them that my fingers have been deprived of a keyboard for over a month, since I was first arrested in Prague. To deliver any kind of recital requires repetition and reflection. Well, they seem to want star quality, so they have told the guards to give me what I request—for now."

"I'm pleased that Schächter can still discern the difference between good and excellent, but you know that their whole display is to convince the world that they are benevolent captors. It is an affront, Adam. And we are all being used to sell a lie! But, all right, if they are asking for your best recital, please request that this Petrof be tuned twice per day for the next two days—otherwise, discriminating listeners will note the imperfection in tuning rather than the perfection of your delivery. Dieter, who is my sister's gentleman friend and my cellmate, is a fine tuner, and he has been assigned the task of maintaining the sound quality of Theresienstadt's pianos. Your request for his services will probably allow both of us to come here and meet with you."

"Wait—you say he is your sister's gentleman friend and YOUR roommate? That is convoluted, Jura. Let's put that relationship on our agenda for early discussion. Do you also have a wife and family somewhere outside the walls?"

"Ah—no. No, I have never married anyone. Having medicine as my mistress used all of my supply of affection, and I have lived alone in Prague for the entire time since we last saw one another—at least the time until September 1, 1939, when Dieter and I were attempting to cross the border into Poland and were apprehended there by the Gestapo. For the past 1,096 days we have resided here, grateful that our skills have provided a kind of elite status within the walls. Many, many others have come and gone—we don't even know to what destination or fate. Just gone! And what of you, my friend? You headed back to Posen from school to find the perfect mate and form the next generation of the Wodzinski Dynasty. Were you successful in that?"

"Well, Jura—successful for a while. But eventually the peculiarities—mine—you tolerated so easily became less tolerable to a very lovely wife seeking order and discipline within her home. She proffered an "either/or" reform, and after a very short experimental period, I opted for the "or"—which was "or else I'm leaving." She did—and took a precious daughter with her—and I set about spending the balance of my family inheritance with total lack of judgment. I'm not at all proud of the record, but it is what it is. And now I am here because my one skill—medicine—can't be practiced by a Jew in Posen. I tried going to Prague, but the same prohibition followed me there. Fortunately there are still a few concert selections I can play on the piano from memory. That should keep me from slipping further down the slope for a while, I hope. What do you think?"

"Hmm. Well, you probably wouldn't think of this on your own—yet—but even if you are performing classics from memory, tell them that you need lots of music paper plus pens, ink, and pencils to keep your performance notes. And tell them that you need a cell with an electric light bulb for study after twilight. Dieter and I will offer you space with us, so they can respond to your request without having to string a new electric line or find additional space to house you. It can be like old times at school, Adam! I think you'll find Dieter very agreeable. He's a pianist, too, although he plays popular standards like a saloon musician. He has become a favorite of the guards and officers here. They like to gather on Friday nights and sing and joke together. Dieter makes those gatherings more enjoyable. It was what he did for a living back in Berlin."

Adam regarded the suggestion quizzically. "What is the reason for music paper and pens? I missed the significance."

"Ah—of course. Three days' time isn't enough to orient you to our methods of fighting boredom and isolation. Dieter is writing a long tome for Sofie—my half sister—on the life he has experienced since they first met. He and I also hold a moot court debate nightly on ways to leave Theresienstadt, other than as a corpse. My mental health remains good, although you can probably detect the consumption that is sapping me physically. Dieter is younger and stronger than I, and he eats the best scraps from the officers' plates and exercises regularly under my urging. My final triumph as a medical doctor will be helping him to escape from here and live a long, productive life."

"And . . . your relationship with Dieter? Are you Oscar Wilde and Lord Douglas, as you once said, Juraslav? How do I fit into that lifestyle as a third occupant of the cell you share?"

For the first time, Juraslav displayed irritation. "Perhaps a thousand days of boredom could provide you with the answer better than my words can, Adam. People who are deprived of books, social contacts, decent food, and all of the gifts of personal freedom have a homeostatic mechanism of survival which leads them to whatever activity can keep their brains and bodies from rotting. Dieter and I make love in the dark, but we are not lovers. We help one another to fill the endless hours of looking at four walls containing a 'scratch' for each day spent there since September 1, 1939. Perhaps he thinks of Sofie in the dark—and perhaps I think of you. I cannot say for certain, but it has been a useful palliative for the despair we might otherwise be suffering. Does that make sense, Adam?"

The taller man held up his hand as if requesting silence. He had heard the sound of returning footsteps and immediately raised his voice to a higher level. "Thank you for your suggestion that the piano tuner attend to this instrument before my concert. Herr Schächter has requested that it be a quality performance, and I am intent upon delivering nothing less. I only wish that I had some manuscript paper on which to jot my performance notes—is there any way—oh! Guard! I did not see you there. Perhaps you can convey my requests to Herr Schächter. Or possibly I could even sit with him myself?"

The reunion meeting of two old schoolmates was officially ended, but Juraslav sensed that the persuasive Adam would be able to make his needs known, and, as a result, the coming days at Theresienstadt might become more tolerable.

CHAPTER FIFTY-SEVEN
Berlin – Early Winter 1942

AN UNEXPECTED LETTER

It arrived at his Wehrmacht office in an envelope identified as coming from Hotel do Nacimiento, Lisbon. Otto thought at first that it might be a kind of invitation from the management to repeat his enjoyable vacation of a year ago with another visit to the neutral country along the western shoreline of Europe. Perhaps they were offering special rates to former hotel guests, he thought, and his pleasant memories of the two weeks away from his command caused him to slip a letter opener through the envelope's crease rather than pitching the whole contents into his refuse bin. To his surprise, it was a personal letter, written in passably good German:

Dear General von Seigler,

When you were our guest last year I was thinking you might have recognize me behind hotel bar for you look at me curious like someone who see familiar face. Even if you sign other name on register I know you from Fischerstube Berlin before war. My friend Dieter and your daughter Sofie very close and I am thinking they leaved Germany together because both have part Jewish. Losing Dieter maked me sad for many weeks but later I understand he truly love Sofie. Now I have losed contact with both Dieter and Sofie, but imagine life is not so pleasant for them under German National Socialist government.

I see you meet with Herr Stinnes and play social with SWW lady, Branka, so maybe you thinking about some way out of Europe for you or for some other person you want to help. So, please remember you have good contact here at Hotel do Nacimiento who is not Polish spy or German business guy.

Good wishes,
Miguel do Nacimiento

Otto remembered the face of the handsome bartender who had looked familiar, but so far from the venue where he had previously seen Miguel, it might never have registered. Now he remembered: when Sofie had booked the piano player for their soirée for the Lindberghs, Otto had checked on the piano man and learned that he occupied a flat with the Portuguese tavern manager and was perceived as being a harmless homosexual musician, without any political interests. How incredible that he had become an anathema to the world's best secret police force, credited with assassinating several of their skilled personnel as well as Reichsprotektor Reinhard Heydrich!

The thought of Dieter Meister reappearing gave Otto a nervous twinge in the deepest part of his already-roiled stomach. It could deposit him right back into the smoldering Oster Conspiracy—something that the unforgiving nature of the führer would certainly revisit in time. Even more ominous was the possible consequence for Sofie, if the drama of their escape from Germany and time together at the perfidious Havlik Clinic were ever to surface. Otto knew that Dieter could not be tolerated any longer in German-occupied territory, and that he should be assisted in going far beyond the Gestapo's reach. At first, he thought of simply eliminating Dieter, but he knew that, if that were ever revealed to Sofie, she would not forgive her father. That possibility could not be entertained if there were an alternative. He resolved to explore possibilities with Klaus the next time they were alone together. He could count upon Klaus to be understanding, creative, and totally loyal.

CHAPTER FIFTY-EIGHT

Theresienstadt – December 1942

BETTER AND WORSE

Twelve hundred vertical lines creased the walls of the cubicle that now housed two excellent physicians—graduates of one of Poland's eminent medical universities—plus the nucleus musician of Friday night songfests in The Village Which Hitler Gave To The Jews. The protective cloak of Rafael Schächter seemed to shelter the three prisoners by day, and Old Jacob's coat contained their collective huddled body warmth at night. Except for one coughing spell that splattered bright red blood onto the white walls and on one of the "performance shirts" which hung on their special nails, the three had managed to live in harmony.

Their nightly game of "Escape" had concluded that it would require two helping one to make that happen—and Dieter had been designated as that one, despite his discomfort at having the only chance to leave Theresienstadt alive. It had to do mostly with his superior physical condition and younger age, but there was also recognition that he, of the three, had a special relationship possibly waiting on the outside. For the other two, there was the reality that their relationship was already realized within the walls of the old fortress. Neither physician really wanted to depart without the other.

"Escape" had also gained substance from the ongoing correspondence of weekly garbage pail mail. Draco had suggested that he could drill a small air hole near the rim of a garbage barrel and could find a short length of tubing that could serve as an air supply to someone confined inside the barrel for a few hours—under a slush of rotting fish entrails and sharp bones. He believed that he could load the overweight barrel together with the others on his Saturday morning run and transport it slowly down the river road away from the main gate to a point well removed from scrutiny by the guards. At that point, he could invert the barrel, and if the inhabitant were still breathing, he could be extracted with Draco's help and started along whatever escape route was planned. It was a beginning.

Draco's suggestion formed the basis for their next evening's "Escape" discussion. Old oil drums, which Theresienstadt used for garbage disposal barrels, held 55 gallons of fluid. The inside diameter, as nearly as they could judge, was about 60 cm, and their consensus was that the inside height was about 90 cm. Dieter was nearly twice that height, so he would literally have to be folded in half inside a barrel—and remain that way for at least three hours. It seemed unlikely, but they decided to experiment with the possibility. One evening, his two co-conspirators lay Dieter on his side and pressed his heels tightly to his rear and then forced his knees against his chest. Finally they bent his head low against the knees and used a string to "measure" Dieter's maximum dimensions. It appeared that they were only slightly greater that the maximum internal capacity of a standard oil drum, but the experiment had to be discontinued quickly because he could not breathe sufficiently and was already suffering painful muscle cramps in his thighs.

"I think I can do it!" Dieter enthused to their surprise. "Remember," he chuckled, "I held that position for nine months inside Eva Rosenberg —and Charles Lindbergh managed to survive like a sardine for twenty-seven hours. Really—with practice, I can do this! I need more flexibility in my hips and knees, and I must learn how to take very shallow breaths and not panic, but I can do this!" The other two were not so euphoric over Dieter's chances, but they decided to start him on a regimen of flexibility and give him all of the encouragement they could muster. At least this initial exercise confirmed that neither of the taller physicians could possibly be fitted into an oil drum, so the question of who should attempt the escape was settled.

On day 1204, some very bad news reached them in the auditorium. That day, December 17, 1942, the distinguished Austrian concertmaster Julius Stwertka, only recently arrived, died in Theresienstadt. None of the prisoner/musicians knew the circumstances of his death, but for all of them it signaled a watershed in their comfort and survival within the fortress. During his brief residence in Theresienstadt, he had convinced his captors that artists could not perform well without some small amenities, but now, without Stwertka to champion the cause, their circumstances were likely to deteriorate even further. Juraslav said to Dieter that evening, "You know, this escape game must soon move beyond just conversation, or it will be only folly." Dieter knew he was right, and from that night onward the three moved with deliberate haste toward executing their plan.

CHAPTER FIFTY-NINE

Salbris, France – Friday, January 1, 1943

BEING BILLIE HOLIDAY

Shortly after midnight, Sofie walked away from the small café where a hastily assembled imitation of the Quintette had played for a private party hosted by Django's patron, Luftwaffe Oberleutenant Diedrich Schulz-Kohn. She had been asked to sing "The Man I Love" by several of the German revelers and had concluded the song with trails of mascara-darkened tears running all the way to her jawline. When she ducked into the washroom to assess the damage, she saw a face that looked wretched in the mirror, and no touchup of rouge or re-application of lipstick was able to correct the appearance. Perhaps a stroll in the cold night air could revive Sophia, the fetching chanteuse from Switzerland.

She decided that the walk would require liquid fortification, so she took along her favorite cognac. But this time, she carried the entire bottle rather than risk spilling any from a delicate snifter. Before long, the brief stroll converted itself into a four-kilometer walk back along the roadway to the cottage she occupied behind Django's larger residence—and en route she drained the bottle and then threw it against a road sign pointing to *PARIS*. The smashing sound as the bottle glanced off the sign and shattered in the roadway only added to her remorse, as Sofie drunkenly observed that her world was all broken—truly, truly shattered.

Once inside the cozy little cottage, she threw her coat and scarf over a chair back and pulled her boots off as she rolled backward onto the bed. Then she began unbuttoning clothes and throwing them at nothing in particular but never quite finished the process before curling herself onto a feather-filled coverlet and slipping into a cognac-laced stupor. That was her condition when a soldier who had been dispatched to the cottage by the worried Django finally found her, two hours later.

"Is it time for my next number?" she responded when he placed his hand on her bare shoulder.

"No, ma'am—you don't have any more songs tonight, but Django and Naguine were concerned about you. You left the hotel without telling anyone where you were going."

"That's because I am depressed," was the sobbed response. "A new year is starting today—the year when I shall celebrate—no, not celebrate—observe, that's it—observe my fucking twenty-eighth birthday. So where am I? I'm tagging along with what's left of the Quintette, living off savings stolen from persecuted Jews, and sleeping alone in a loaned cottage. I drink more every time I sing, and I sing the same songs over and over and over. God gave me a really good set of pipes—everyone says that—and I can wrap myself around the best melodies being written—but always imitating someone else's style. Because I don't have my *own* unique delivery! I'm a thief there, too."

"You're not being fair to yourself, mademoiselle. You bring great happiness to your audiences, and we all love you for the energy you bring to every performance. Yes, we do! We *all* love you—so don't be so hard on yourself. Really."

"You love me? Yes? Come on—love me now! I *need* to be loved. I haven't been loved for over three stinking war years, so climb in here and love me—now!"

The lieutenant was no moralist, but he knew it was not a good idea to even consider the invitation, so he stood and announced that he must leave now. As he turned to walk away, a strong hand gripped his and pulled him backward until he fell atop the feather comforter. Through the window, a bright, full moon washed over the splendid form of the chanteuse from Switzerland, who beckoned to him as his resolve commenced to weaken. "Please Stéphane—make love to me and start my 1943 with excitement. Please, Stéphane!"

"Close enough," he thought. In the morning light he could always lie about what had happened in the cognac-infused darkness.

CHAPTER SIXTY
Theresienstadt – February 1943

SIGNIFICANT GARBAGE-PAIL MAIL
[From Dieter's Journal]

February 13 was a Saturday, and day 1262 of our seemingly endless detention and despair inside Theresienstadt. Saturdays, however, now dawned brighter in our estimation because it was on those Saturday mornings that the freshened oil drums we retrieved outside the main gate contained scraps of news from outside the walls. Since his first folded paper, adhered with chewing gum, Draco's little memos to us had become more ingenious. He had constructed a second lid which fitted exactly under the first, thus creating a hidden space where several sheets of paper could be secreted. By removing the dummy disk, we could access the slim compartment, but when the disk was realigned and pressed tightly against the real top, it was undetectable.

Draco's rambling penciled note in our February 13 pail mail informed us that Easter 1943 was to fall on the very latest possible date—April 25. (I learned later from a Theresienstadt-imprisoned mathematician that the last previous similar occurrence had been in 1886 and the next would be in 2038.) This meant that Ash Wednesday would also be at its latest extreme this year, on March 10. The importance of this trivia was lost on me, but Draco went on to say that the last Friday before Lent was traditionally an extravagant evening of seafood and celebration which left the prison guards and officers nearly comatose, so he thought that our plan should be implemented late on that Friday night, March 5, 1943, after the dining hall and kitchen had been tidied. That would allow us to take advantage of the inebriated state of our captors. It sounded like good reasoning to Jura, Adam, and me, so we agreed that day 1282 would be Freedom Day—for me, at least. My cellmates would celebrate vicariously, I was assured.

A week later, under the dummy disk there was nothing additional from Draco, but in its place a terse note from Elsa Danzig, one of Lilka's "Two Little Girls From Gdansk." She conveyed three points in her telegraphic SWW style: First, that 20,000 SWF was deposited in my Swiss name and could be accessed at any office of Bank Julius Baer. Second, my bank password was the Bösendorfer's address. And, finally, at Hotel do Nacimiento in Lisbon, there would be a contact to guide me away from trouble. Of course, this all assumed that I was free to travel around Europe, which was far from true, but I took it as an encouraging sign that Elsa believed I might soon walk outside the old fortress once again. The following Friday night, I enclosed a slip of paper confirming that Elsa's message had been understood—then destroyed—and asking who my generous patron might be. She never responded to that request.

CHAPTER SIXTY-ONE
Berlin – Early March 1943

THE INSURANCE POLICY

General von Seigler was all business on a rainy Monday morning as his trusted aide laid out the day's appointments and tasks. Otto reflected upon the long and productive relationship between Klaus Kolb and him, and he noted mentally that he must be certain that Klaus was being compensated generously for his loyalty. Otto knew that the future was certain to bring additional circumstances which could be addressed successfully only if he had Klaus constantly implementing the countless small and secret tasks which allowed Otto to remain insulated from the wrath of the country's insane leadership.

Dieter Meister now loomed as a possible threat to Otto. He was being held anonymously in one of Germany's sixty-plus detention facilities, but in one which lay outside the borders of Germany, Poland, and Austria. Theresienstadt had been singled out for Dr. Goebbels's convincing propaganda machine: It was offered to the world as "proof" that the horrors being ascribed to German detention were vastly overstated, and that Germany was as benevolent toward its detainees as the USA was to its seized Japanese-American and German-American citizens. The danger Otto von Seigler feared was predicated upon eventual correct identification of Dieter, either within the fortress or outside it, as Sofie's Jewish lover and the author of half a dozen conspiratorial murders and other anti-government attacks. That could begin a tumble of dominoes spreading toward Otto and even Reichsmarschall Göring, and he might well be precipitated again into the deadly Oster mess.

Otto addressed his aide. "Klaus, how much do you know about our national policy of detaining people who belong to certain undesirable groupings?"

"General, we all know that there are dozens of places which are off-limits, and that they house Jews, Gypsies, homosexuals, and other enemies of the State. I have been told that those places are divided into five categories which define their function."

"And what would those classifications be, in your opinion, Klaus?"

"Well, I'm told that there are formal ghettos, labor camps, transit camps, concentration camps, and ultimately—er—extermination camps. That is the spectrum, from least severe to most . . . most . . . well, most deadly, I guess."

"Mmmmm—that's a good summary, Klaus. And I trust that you have heard of Theresienstadt, near Prague? Which classification would you give to that facility, Klaus?"

"Certainly I have heard of Theresienstadt. I have even seen specialty motion pictures of it. They have been shown in the popular theatres before feature films, and they demonstrate some reasonably content people living and working together in an orderly community. It is called 'The Village That . . .'"

"Yes, yes—I know what it has been named." Otto interrupted with a hint of irritation. "But how would you, as an informed citizen, classify Theresienstadt?"

"As a transit camp," Klaus offered. "It also seems to be a showcase—Theresienstadt has housed some of the best musicians and writers among the detained, and they offer multiple performances which limited numbers of outsiders are invited to attend. While I put it into the 'transit camp' classification, I can't say that I have any idea of the ultimate destination to which the detainees are being transited. Is there a reason for your questions, General?"

"Of course there is, Klaus." He smiled for the first time that morning. "Sofie's piano-playing friend, whom I know you'll remember, is imprisoned there, and actually has been there since sometime late in 1939. His captors have identified him only as a Swiss homosexual—they have a different surname for him. He is called "Dieter Havlik." This anonymity has spared some of us embarrassment during his detention, but lately there have been rumblings—rumors—that Dieter may be planning to escape. If that were successful, I would like to do everything possible to help him move immediately beyond the range of our Gestapo. You can understand, Klaus, that linking me to a fugitive Jew criminal might be used as a weapon in any revived Oster inquiry."

"Yes, sir. But I thought you had been absolved of any possible complicity in Oster, and that your citation for directing key parts of the Polish campaign placed you into a very solid position once again. Do you think that the führer will revive Oster?"

"It is a distinct possibility, Klaus. He resented that cabal and in my opinion it sticks in his craw, and he won't be content until the plotters are punished. There are Gestapo close to him who will curry favor by turning over rocks and presenting him with alleged plotters to hang. Because Oster was within the outer boundaries of my Wehrmacht command, I could be roped in if there were a scintilla of evidence pointing to me."

"Like a Jewish spouse in the Polish SWW, and a daughter complicit with a fugitive Jewish troublemaker, correct, sir?"

"You put it too logically, Klaus. It is much too easy for a detractor to pull those elements together—so I would like to help Dieter to figuratively 'disappear.'"

"And ... why not *literally* 'disappear,' sir? People in detention camps disappear every day and are never traced. If an anonymous homosexual didn't appear for a morning shape-up in the yard, there wouldn't be a ripple of concern. Or, if he were loaded on one of those trains going to the East for 'special treatment,' who would blink an eye?"

"Klaus, you once assured Sofie that my morality would not have allowed me to plot the murder of our country's leader. Has your opinion of me changed so much that you believe I *would* conspire to dispatch my only daughter's cherished companion, who has done nothing materially wrong? I would never be able to look her in the eye again—and I love those eyes, Klaus."

"Yes, sir, I do understand. And a significant part of my respect and loyalty is rooted in my knowledge of your personal standards. So—what role would you like me to play?"

"We'll get to that later, Klaus. But, for now, I would like to ask you something not having to do with Dieter. I want to know whether you are receiving the annual stipend from Sofie's Swiss account upon which you and I agreed. Is that going well?"

"It is, sir. Two percent finds its way to me annually, and as the principal has grown larger, so also has my annual payment. I am very happy and grateful, believe me."

"Good. You have earned it. If we get Dieter safely out of harm's way, there will be a 1943 bonus—from me, not from Sofie—and not disclosed to her, either."

CHAPTER SIXTY-TWO

Theresienstadt – Friday, March 5, 1943

DAY 1282 – GRADUATION
[From Dieter's Journal]

This will be the final entry in my account of the five years since I met you, Sofie. If things go as I wish, I shall begin March 6 outside the walls of this fortress, beside the grimy river into which Theresienstadt's waste and garbage are directed. I hope that I shall be able to stand after having my legs folded closely against my body for three hours or more. I hope that, breathing through my air tube in short, shallow gulps of outside air, I shall be able to retain consciousness. I hope that the cold March night won't produce hypothermia inside my capsule. I hope that the stench of fish guts sharing my closed space won't cause me to retch and choke myself to death. I hope that, when I finally stand by the river, I shall be able to filch a cigarette and a light from whoever has extracted me from my chrysalis. If so, I shall enjoy a slow, deliberate smoke before beginning a new life.

Dr. Juraslav Havlik will not get to read this account in its final form. We both know that his consumption has advanced past hope of recovery, particularly within the dank chambers of our prison. I am pleased that he was able to listen as I read my daily entries into the story, and I thank him for insights he provided as respects many of the people and occurrences I have described. Jura will always live in my heart, and I shall try to incorporate the lessons of his kindness and generosity into my persona.

Dr. Adam Wodzinski will be wearing Old Jacob's warm coat tonight and performing my usual Friday chore of moving the stinking garbage cans to the front gate and beyond. As he and Jura unload "my" barrel outside

CHAPTER SIXTY-TWO | 349

the gate and then return to their prison cell, I know that there will be no resentment. They are both incredibly unselfish men, and, after twenty years of separation, they will again share their remaining time. I will think of them every day.

When I began this account, it was with the simple objective of making boring days pass as swiftly as possible, but as the number of those days extended beyond anything I anticipated, my labor gained additional significance. It is now intended primarily for you, Sofie, who could not otherwise know the extent to which memories of you have fortified me against the deprivations of this place. If your life has taken you down other paths, dear Sofie, please know that I understand and approve of that. You and your musical gifts should not be suspended indefinitely in a dark closet awaiting someone who has been swallowed up by this war. If my final breath is drawn in a smelly garbage barrel tonight, I expect there will still be an amused smile on my lips as I remember your flirting eyes and "Naughty Josephine" teasing. Thank you for every hour and every adventure we shared. You will always be the love against which I measure all others.

And now it is time for me to enter my time capsule. The inside has been greased, to allow me to be guided in gradually to a contorted fetal position. I have a cap on my head, which my co-conspirators will pull down over my eyes and ears to protect them, and I am wearing my best performing shirt and pants—in case I meet someone important in my dreams. I think I can do this!

Dieter

CHAPTER SIXTY-THREE

London – March 1943

MOTHERHOOD'S BURDENS

Lilka finished the final page and removed her metal-rimmed reading glasses. Then she clasped the top of her nose between her thumb and index finger and squeezed gently to soothe the overuse of her eyes. She had been reading continuously for more than three hours and now must consider the many conflicted feelings Dieter's long account had provoked. It was something a mother must absorb and weigh alone, and so she was glad that no one shared the flat with her.

First, there was the matter of Juraslav's health. Lilka had learned much about medicine and the illnesses medicines were concocted to treat during her marriage to Tovar. A person with incipient consumption should be in a dry, hot climate if possible, she remembered. So, Juraslav's cold, damp circumstances would exacerbate his suffering. So also would his inadequate diet and the constant exposure to others with ailments. But, Jura's most immediate threat was probably a decision by his captors to remove obviously ill inmates from their "display campus." She knew that those who were plucked from Theresienstadt and sent east to Auschwitz were never going to emerge again.

Her first task, she decided, must be to compose a long letter to her son, acknowledging the fact that she had once chosen service to her beliefs over normal maternal duties, but at the same time assuring Juraslav that she had always loved him totally and swelled with pride over the magnificent use he had made of his gifts. She believed that she could call upon the redoubtable Elsa to move the letter into Theresienstadt via the "garbage pail mail" which Jura and Dieter had created. But, she cautioned herself, this window of opportunity might not be open for long—and Jura might not remain in Theresienstadt for many more weeks if his health continued to deteriorate.

Reading Dieter's account of his romantic involvement with Sofie seemed to confirm Lilka's earlier judgment that Dieter had been what she would call a "homosexual by opportunity" rather than "by predisposition." Much like Juraslav, he had been relatively alone in the world from an early age, and the protection afforded by older, stronger males had undoubtedly been welcome. But, as an adult, Dieter had turned less to other men and seemed to embrace with enthusiasm a loving young woman when his and Sofie's lives intersected. Their experiences together had been driven by the severe circumstances of the times, but they had still carved out many romantic interludes and had collaborated in successful professional work. She sensed amusement and passion in their partnership, plus a healthy, open intimacy she envied.

Lilka resolved that she should call upon Otto to examine his options for helping Dieter to get to some safe harbor away from the Nazi-occupied areas of Europe. She immediately thought of neutral Portugal, where increasing numbers of refugees were moving in the wake of the war. Both she and Otto had contacts there. But first, she must learn from Elsa and her Gypsy friends that Dieter had been successful in slipping away from his captors. Dieter had already promised to send notice to London of his circumstances once he was outside.

Her final—and most difficult—choice remained the question of whether to share this fascinating, revealing story with her daughter. Of course, the author intended it for Sofie, and in time it *must* be placed in her possession. However, what kind of anxiety might the account precipitate during the hiatus between Dieter's submergence into a barrel of fish guts and the time when an "all clear" could be sounded, signaling that he was out of danger and in a safe place? Lilka concluded that there was no need to rattle Sofie's nerves with that waiting period. She could not affect the outcome in any way except possibly through prayer, and Lilka imagined that Sofie already included Dieter in her prayerful moments. No, she thought—until Dieter's escape could be celebrated, she would keep the materials herself and not reveal them to anyone.

CHAPTER SIXTY-FOUR

Theresienstadt – Saturday, March 6, 1943

DAWN OF FREEDOM

Draco positioned his tired truck as near to the five waiting barrels as possible, leaving the lights turned on and the engine idling in the chilly morning air. Although the sun had not breached the horizon, that first halo of morning light was spreading toward the gate, and he could see that the tops of the guard towers were already turning a burnished pink color as Saturday, March 6 began. If there were guards peering down on the garbage collection, he could not discern them, and he concluded that they might be sleeping off the activity of their celebratory final Friday night before Lent. Organized religion was generous in providing opportunities for celebration—it was good salesmanship, he thought.

First he unloaded five reasonably clean, empty replacement drums from the bed of his truck and directed a helper to arrange them for pickup from the concrete pier by the roadside. It might be a few hours before inmates were dispatched to move them inside the gates and back to the dining hall. He wondered who would be carrying out that assignment today, with Dieter missing from his cell.

He then signaled to his much smaller assistant to get up onto the truck bed to receive and place each full barrel as he hoisted it from the concrete slab on which all five had been deposited the previous night. Draco knew that one barrel would be heavier than the others, but he couldn't distinguish which it would be. The first, second and third were hoisted, and his helper balanced each on its rim, enabling it to be rolled to its assigned position. Number four was another matter: the large man got his hands under the bottom rim and lifted, but he could not heft it all the way into the truck, and for a moment he felt helpless and feared he might have to drop it to the ground again. He was losing his grip on the cold metal.

Draco's assistant jumped nimbly from the truck to his side and placed a shoulder under the load, immediately elevating it to the flat bed. Then the helper returned almost acrobatically into the back of the truck, gave a forceful tug to the top rim, and rolled the fourth barrel into position with the first three. The final garbage container was lifted easily, and both workers clambered back into the cab and headed east toward the now-visible sunrise on a lane marked *Prazsky*. It led to a bridge over the Ohře and a second bridge over Stara Ohře. In a few minutes they were out of sight of the guard towers and approaching a small gathering of houses at a place called Počaply, on the edge of the Labe. It was there that garbage was normally dumped and there, today, they would examine the contents of oil barrel #4—the heavy one.

Draco glanced to his right and flashed a broad, white-toothed Gypsy smile that seemed to rival the sunrise itself. "You *very* strong for woman, Elsa. How you get that way? I almost dropped barrel and waked guards until you help me. Hey—let me feel muscles, eh?"

"Maybe Sunday night—after you have a bath and a paycheck," she laughed. "Or will your wife expect you to take her for a stroll into town then? Maybe I'll ask her if you can feel my muscles when we get back to your place. OK?"

"Ja, sure. She don't care where I have appetizer—as long as I come to her for dessert. Hah! You funny, Elsa. Really—how come you so strong?"

"I use my back a lot in my work," she shot back, and then the conversation shifted abruptly to their cargo. "We must open the heavy one quickly—on the truck—to see what his condition is. Even on a Saturday morning, people begin to stir at this hour, and we can't risk being caught with an escapee. Can you pull off the road into an area that's sheltered by trees?"

"Just a couple hundred meters ahead is good place I plan for to do that. If we get him out and he can sit, he should be in seat in cab—and you have to finish in barrel. Can't have three in cab at checkpoint. At least you small enough to fit. OK—we here! Quick, let's tip barrel on side and pull fellow out." Draco crossed himself and looked upward. "Please don't be dead like fish heads!"

The oil drum had a rim-securing ratchet ring, which was pried open and set aside. That allowed Draco and Elsa to insert a screwdriver between the barrel flange and the edge of the lid and to leverage the tight-fitting cover away from the cylindrical container. Once it was off, they worked together to lay the drum on its side, and that set off a flow of fish parts and sour, pink liquid from inside onto the truck bed. The aroma was overpoweringly awful, and both coughed and gagged as they reached inside and pushed more of the mess out.

"There's his stocking hat!" Elsa shouted. "Pull it off so we can see his face." As Draco did so, Dieter's matted blonde hair and prison-pale skin were exposed, and a white tube leading from his mouth to a tiny porthole surfaced. "Draco—lift the bottom a little and I'll try to pull on his shoulders to see if we can slide him out." Once she located Dieter's shrugged shoulders, Elsa slipped a hand under each and positioned her feet on the barrel rim. Then she pushed against the rim using her leg strength and heard a sound like a plumber's plunger sucking air through standing water. The limp body moved toward her, but only slightly.

The larger Draco lifted the bottom of the barrel higher and hopped up and down, as if to shake the contents from a ketchup bottle, and finally their teamwork was successful in moving the unnaturally folded body out of its prison and onto the stained wooden bed of the truck. There was no sign of consciousness, but Elsa put her head against Dieter's and thought she detected shallow breathing. She lifted the lid of one eye and saw no focusing movement, then put her small hand tightly below the jaw and tried to detect a pulse.

"Help me move him to the cab, Draco," she said. "We must get him quickly to your house, so we can try to revive him. He'll need water, and we must massage his limbs to restore circulation. See—his hands are blue. We can't let him die after all this effort. Let's arrange him on the seat as if he's sleeping in case they look in. I'll jump into that awful barrel, and you can put the lid on, but *do not* add the retainer ring! I'm claustrophobic, and I'm afraid I'll start screaming if I think I'm locked in."

As they lifted the body, an oilcloth-wrapped package fell away from Dieter's torso, where it had been secured. Elsa retrieved it and put it back in the bottom of the barrel, then lowered her compact body inside and motioned for Draco to tap the lid into place and drive away. He did so as rapidly as possible, just as Dieter retched the contents of his stomach onto the seat, assuring his rescuer that there was life in the body.

"Where's the third faggot?" the guard asked Juraslav and Adam, as he routinely unlocked the cell's metal door. "Doesn't he do the kitchen work with you, Havlik?"

"You didn't hear last night?" Jura shot back. "He had a coughing fit and blood was going everywhere. Look at this shirt." He held up a discarded blouse which had been "inherited" months ago from a departing inmate, and which had been used since then as a cleaning rag to mop up blood spittle and to dry the insides of the lavatory bucket. It was a disgusting piece of cloth the guard had no intention of examining, and the explanation seemed credible.

"So what happened? Where is he today?" The quiz continued, and Adam decided to pick up the conversation.

"They came for him and carried him away," he offered. "It happens all the time here, and no one tells us where the sick ones go. They always say something like 'special attention,' but they don't specify what that is. We're both doctors, but no one asks us to intervene and we don't have medicine or instruments to help out, anyhow."

"You are *not* doctors. Jews cannot be physicians in the Third Reich. Everyone knows that. You are kitchen help—so get your skinny asses out to the gate and collect the garbage barrels, and clean them well. They were rank last night. This is your lucky day, ja? Now you have more room and no fights over who gets buggered. Hey—maybe you should give that up for Lent! It starts next week, you know."

As they pulled the cart across Theresienstadt's broad, open yard toward the gate, Adam raised the collar of Old Jacob's coat to conceal his face and he mumbled to Juraslav that, for now, the question of the missing inmate appeared to have been resolved. He doubted that the guard, who appeared to be lazy by nature, would want to involve himself in any kind of search or inquiry. The next hurdle would be Dieter's absence from music rehearsal, and they would have time to refine their explanation before that occurred. For now, their response to inquiries about Dieter's whereabouts would be simply, "Wherever you take the sick ones."

CHAPTER SIXTY-FIVE

Near Litoměřice In Occupied Czechoslovakia March 6, 1943

CLEAN SHEETS

It was after midday on Saturday when Dieter finally opened his eyelids voluntarily and tried to assess his condition and surroundings. He was in a room with an open hearth, and it was warm in the room because a hearty fire was crackling only a few meters from where he lay. His second realization was that he was lying on a rough flannel sheet and he was totally naked. The third was that a female was bathing his lower body with a cloth, covered with something that smelled like rubbing alcohol, and it burned uncomfortably as she cleaned sores that had formed on his legs and abdomen. When his awakening caught her attention, the woman turned her head and smiled, and he recognized her as one of Dr. Havlik's "Two Little Girls From Gdansk"—the one named Elsa.

"Does it sting too much?" was her first communication. He thought how wonderful it was after 1282 days of total neglect to awaken to a caring question. It was something that might go unnoticed all through a normal life, but his residence in Theresienstadt would forever highlight ordinary kindnesses in the future. Someone actually cared if rubbing alcohol on an open sore was painful to him! No, it actually felt good to begin attacking the damage of all those days inside the walls.

"Good morning, Elsa! I am baffled by seeing you. I'm sure you will be able to orient me, but my very first need for assurance is that I'm not dead or dreaming and that you are not some angelic missionary in the other world. I really got out of that place in an oil drum and I still have working arms, legs, and senses. Amen!"

"Actually, *all* your parts seem to be working, Dieter—if you know what I mean. I have been cleaning off layers of dirt and patches of irritated skin, but when I got to your privates, I got a very nice greeting. Don't be embarrassed; I only looked out of curiosity. You know, I live in Prague now, with Renate—the one with the huge melons whom you chose on your first day in the city. She and Ursula still tell the story of your visit, with a few twists they have added to make it even better. You are now described as having 'legendary proportions,' and I won't contradict them next time the story is told, even though I now know they may be exaggerating just a little. So—you are feeling decent? We thought you were dead this morning."

"Jura—Dr. Havlik, that is—gave me some of his morphine, and I believe that it put me into hibernation or something like that. The music director in the fortress is able to get small supplies of a few drugs, and he barters them with Dr. Havlik in return for medical attention to his musicians. Inside the walls, everyone tries to have something to trade—food, beer, information, sex, personal items—it doesn't matter much. Everything has value for someone. I had never experienced morphine before, but it is pretty amazing. I don't even remember being uncomfortable in that big tin can."

"Good—it's a memory you don't need. Three and a half years have surely provided enough things to disturb your sleep for the balance of your life without having to relive several hours in a garbage barrel. Pull these pants and shirt on, and let's have a bite to eat in the kitchen. There are several things you have to know about your movement from here to a safer place. Oh, by the way, this is Draco's house. He is making his daily rounds with the truck, and his wife is at the 'cleaning stream' nearby, doing laundry for her customers. This afternoon I must share some things with you which may come as a surprise."

CHAPTER SIXTY-SIX
Near Litoměřice – Later On Saturday, March 6

DIRTY SHEETS

"You remember my garbage-pail-mail note telling you of an account at Bank Julius Baer and a contact in Lisbon? Of course you do—you asked me to name your benefactor, and I chose not to write it where it might be found. The account was established by Sofie from funds which General von Seigler provided to her. Now the General wishes to help expedite your movement away from Theresienstadt, because you have unintentionally become a 'mystery person,' and in some quarters you and Sofie have been cited in attempts to link General von Seigler to the Oster matter. But his motives are not exclusively selfish ones. He knows you and understands your importance to his only child, and he considers it his duty to try to extend your life. As soon as you are ready to do so, his aide will arrange to transport you to Lisbon. From there, a Stinnes freighter can take you as a crew member to someplace in the Americas."

Dieter stared open-eyed at Elsa. "But, Elsa—how do you as an SWW operative have any of this knowledge or any contact with a Wehrmacht general? I don't understand. Why are you taking the risks you have today? Help me to . . ."

"Ah, Dieter—you are a flower, still. Remember the morning when we spoke together at the clinic and I recited the apocryphal tale of "Two Little Girls From Gdansk"? I told you that I was nothing more than a prostitute—a whore—who sold herself in exchange for the information which often gushed out over shared bedsheets. At that time, I was part of a very efficient SWW network that supplied information back to the Polish government, to which we were all loyal. But now that network is fragmented, and that government is a shadow housed in a foreign nation.

"Still, I must continue to provide for myself, and I have only one significant talent with which to do so. I can move without leaving footprints and gather useful information in the most benign ways. I can pick the minds of gentlemen as deftly as a good pickpocket can lift their wallets. Most never suspect what I have done—and the few who do come to that realization are embarrassed to confess their own negligence and dalliance."

"So—you have gone into business for yourself, and General von Seigler is now your employer. You are a 'double agent,' aren't you Elsa?"

"Not precisely," she corrected him. "I would be a double agent if I were stealing secrets from one employer and selling them to the other, pretending to be exclusive with each. But that's not my role. I am an 'investigator for hire.' I am at liberty to reject an assignment for whatever reason seems important to me, and the details of an accepted assignment are not shared with anyone other than the party paying me. I am like a lawyer who shares confidences only with the party he is serving and who recuses himself if he believes he might become entangled in a conflict of interests. Dieter—if that rationale is good enough guidance for a lawyer, should it not be good enough for a whore?"

"Perhaps they are related professions, Elsa. Yes—it makes sense to me, and I'm pleased that General von Seigler has retained you to help my escape. When I came out of my fog this morning and saw you there, I was totally confused, but now I am pleased. Without the help and care you and Draco provided after I was unconscious in that can, I would by now be as dead as those gutted fish. If that's a part of your services to General von Seigler, then I am totally in favor of the arrangement.

"But Elsa, emerging alive outside the walls is not my goal—it is only the first step in accomplishing many promises which I made to myself during the past 1282 days. There is one I must set into motion quickly, and what you have shared today convinces me that you can be of great assistance. You see, I devoted many of the ponderous hours in our cell composing an account that is intended for Sofie von Seigler. It is all hand-written on the reverse sides of soiled, old music sheets and bundled together for transmittal to her—wherever that may be. I hope that it, too, escaped Theresienstadt."

"Yes. It was cradled in your lap when they stuffed you into the barrel, and it fell onto the truck bed as we attempted to straighten your legs and sit you up. So you would like me to get it forwarded to General von Seigler with the request that he move it along to Sofie, correct?"

"Do you think you could ask that favor of him? I will gladly pay you for your efforts, Elsa. It is important to me that those discarded sheets on which I labored so many nights eventually find their way to Sofie. I want her to know how much she helped me to survive Theresienstadt, even though I may now be far removed from her thoughts. And I want to remind her of some wonderful shared times which we were able to create together, even as this war festered and spread."

"I'm pleased to do it for you Dieter, for free. They say that whores who give favors away are fools, but this is just one friend lending a hand to another. I know that General von Seigler will also be pleased to help. There is a very kind side to his nature which is somewhat surprising—not what I expect from military professionals, but definitely there. I'll put your opus into a diplomatic sack going to him from Prague and let him route it onward to Sofie. It may take a while; I'm not certain that they maintain contact any more. But I'm sure that the journey will be completed." She knew that the General would send the materials to Lilka, but their ongoing contact should not be revealed to anyone, especially by the General's paid agent in Prague.

Dieter placed an appreciative kiss on Elsa's forehead and then reclined back into his chair. For the first time in three and a half years, he was relaxed and happy. Theresienstadt seemed hundreds of miles away. With a few days to heal his sores, some overdue sleep, and a few good meals, he knew that he would be ready for his next adventure.

CHAPTER SIXTY-SEVEN

Lilkahaus, Near Berlin – Sunday, March 14, 1943

DIVIDED LOYALTIES

General Otto von Seigler had decided to spend a quiet mid-March weekend at Lilkahaus. The earliest perennial flowers began to appear at about this time of year, and he enjoyed walking in the pristine woods during early morning hours. After considerable reflection, Otto had extended an invitation to Branka, his attractive friend from Lisbon, to pay her first visit to his retreat. There was a Junkers Ju 52/3 passenger aircraft under his command regularly transporting classified materials between Lisbon and Berlin, and he encouraged Branka to put other things aside and spend a quiet spring weekend in the lake country. Klaus Kolb was serving as the courier for those flights, and Klaus could cover her with the necessary paperwork.

Actually, Otto was also conducting an experiment—testing whether a supernumerary passenger on a scheduled Wehrmacht document flight raised any eyebrows. He had been urged by Lilka—and he had his own reasons as well—to find a way to move Dieter Meister away from German-occupied territory without arousing suspicion. That depended first upon Dieter's success in finding a strategy to slip away from Theresienstadt, which would be no small accomplishment. *But,* Otto thought, *be ready with a plan in case the purported "master spy" gives the slip to authorities yet another time.*

Branka's initial response to his invitation had been negative, and Otto sensed that she might be hesitant because she suspected her SWW identity had been uncovered and General von Seigler might be trying to trap her. He decided to defuse that concern by acknowledging her SWW status up front and assuring Branka that his interest was purely personal. He gave his word as an officer that she would be returned safely to Lisbon at the end of the weekend. Somewhat strangely, he noted that German officers across the Continent were now fraternizing with consorts from "the other side." Eventually, the craziness of the idea won over the adventurous woman, and she reminded Otto that he was honor bound not to put her into jeopardy. There was not much of a threat in her words, but Otto knew that she should be respected. He suggested that she check with her senior associate, Lilka, in London, if there were any doubts remaining. Of course, that was not a serious suggestion.

The timing of the weekend turned out to be disastrous. On March 13, German forces in Krakow demolished the Jewish Ghetto there and inflicted heavy losses on its inhabitants. Krakow had been home to Otto through three memorable years. It was where he had met and married Lilka, and it was his daughter's birthplace. Thinking of those years, Otto again found himself conflicted over the course this war was taking. That evening, the decorated German officer and his comely Polish courtesan shared their sadness over the war and its inhumane toll, which was removing all traces of traditional Jewish communities from some of Europe's oldest and most distinguished cities.

Their quiet conversation was interrupted by a call on Otto's private line, informing him that Dieter had slipped away from his Theresienstadt captivity without being detected, and that by early April he might be recovered fully from his long ordeal and prepared to move on to Portugal. The caller was Elsa Danzig. How strange it had all become, he thought.

CHAPTER SIXTY-EIGHT
London – Saturday, March 20, 1943

A VISIT FROM BRANKA

"Lilka, I'm glad we can sit together in a restaurant and share a glass of wine. Some things can't be explored properly through exchanged messages or monitored telephone conversations. You agree? That's why I took the BOAC flight over."

"Of course I do, Branka—and I realize that you find yourself in a somewhat awkward position with respect to me and also with SWW. So, tell me what's on your mind. We have been friends and colleagues for a few years, and I value you in both roles."

"Thank you; you must know that I share those feelings. First of all, when I met Otto—General von Seigler, that is—in Lisbon eighteen months ago, I knew instinctively that he was not the German businessman he pretended to be. With a little probing, I confirmed that he was a general officer of importance. But there was no way to know back then that he had once been your husband and that he is the father of your daughter. We shared several private evenings together, and I found that it was productive to let him prattle on about the war and things bothering him. I believe I relayed most of that to you.

"But, at the same time, I also found myself attracted to the man. That was a sentiment I believed had deserted me many years before—and several men earlier. I found myself hoping that I was not endangering him by gathering small bits of information and weaving them into a fabric—but that's what I was doing. And then . . . and then his identity surfaced, and I realized how awkward it was becoming. He visited Lisbon four more times, and I knew that I had become his principal motivation for those visits.

"Then came his damned invitation to spend a weekend with him in Germany— and I never, *never* should have done it! I was in a house named for *you*, Lilka! I wanted to get out of there as soon as possible. But, even under those circumstances, I was encountering more information which I believe has value. And I was enjoying the man—not the general, but truly the man he is. So that's why I proposed this visit with you."

"I see. You have painted yourself into a corner, Branka. I suppose this is somewhat in contrast to my own actions years ago, when I chose my SWW work over the natural emotional ties to my closest family members. That has been a costly choice for me, Branka, and now, as an old lady, I am very much alone in the world. You are still young—well, young-ish—and you will have to balance your priorities for yourself. In a way, I am flattered by Otto's interest in you. My belief is that, in Otto's subconscious, you may be my proxy. You are much as I was when he and I first met, and I believe that he has missed some of those qualities. I'm jealous—but not in a resentful way. More in a nostalgic sense, Branka."

"Well, Lilka. Please accept my apologies. In a profession not notable for its ethics, I still have some, and I would *never* knowingly trespass upon the memories of a friend and colleague. There—that's my apology. I hope we can still be friends.

"There is one additional fragment of information I want to share, and I hope that it will lighten the mood of our reunion. I learned from Otto that your daughter's gentleman friend has somehow—miraculously, I suppose—recently escaped from his imprisonment in Theresienstadt. He is being cared for by people he knew near Prague, and when he is strong enough to travel, I believe that Otto—General von Seigler—is going to help him to reach Lisbon. He has asked me to help the young man if he arrives there, and I have agreed to do that. Like many of the refugees I see in Lisbon, the gentleman will probably move on from there to someplace outside Europe, but for a time he may be in my care. If that happens, I will tell you immediately."

Lilka smiled and offered her hand to Branka. "Be careful," she cautioned. "Otto is talented and interesting, but to my knowledge, the only woman who is truly special to him is our daughter Sofie—and I can't see him changing that at this time in his life. Good luck, Branka. We'll stay in contact." With that, the older woman stood, smiled, and left the room. It had not been so bad as Branka feared it might be—still, Lilka was never one to display her emotions, and she might yet harbor a measure of resentment.

CHAPTER SIXTY-NINE

London – Sunday, March 21, 1943

THE WORLD'S FINEST JAZZ VIOLINIST CALLS

"Madame Rudovska—perhaps you will remember me," the suave, French-accented voice on the telephone began. "We met in Prague at the Trocadero nightclub, where some Gypsy friends introduced us. My name is Grappelli, and I was the violinist in the little group with which your daughter made her Prague debut as a nightclub singer."

"Certainly I remember, Monsieur Grappelli—you are the royalty of the jazz violin! As a matter of fact, after watching your performance, I put my own violin on the shelf and have never played it again."

"Ah—a pity, madame. My informants told me that you were quite skilled—and equally beautiful when you first charmed their settlement in Poland. Perhaps we should sit with our violins some evening and *avoir les coudées franches*—er—let it rip! But, I know that you are too busy for this idle chit-chat. I would like to speak with you about Sofie, to whom we are both dedicated. May we do that?"

"I would like very much to do that. Are you free for dinner? There is a small, quiet French restaurant not far from my flat. Not quite the quality of Paris, but exceptional for London. Gauthier is the name—do you know it?"

"Ah, yes! A very good choice. And you must be my guest—no arguments. Can we say 7:30 p.m.? I will call and reserve."

"Until then, Mr. Grappelli."

At the restaurant, Lilka did not know quite how to greet her handsome 35-year-old dinner companion, but he relieved her of any anxiety she was feeling by grasping her shoulders firmly and planting kisses on both her cheeks. "My dear Lilka, how wonderful to see you again! What has it been? Four years, eh? They have been difficult years for all of us, but you seem to have sailed through the troubled waters well. Come—let's sit down and enjoy a glass of wine before dinner."

He had said that he wanted to speak to Lilka about Sofie, but it seemed that, as a Frenchman, he had to first navigate through a social ritual of greetings, compliments, comments on the spring weather, and observations on the city where they both now lived as foreigners. Lilka thought to herself that her many years as an intelligence gatherer had made her too impatient. She was not good at superficial conversation, and she worried that her discomfort might not be adequately disguised and her charming dinner host could be offended. So she continued to smile and nod as he talked on, and her mind wandered further and further from his words. Then she was aware of a pause and silence: she was expected to answer, and she had no idea what the question had been.

"Excuse me, Stéphane? What did you ask?"

"I asked how you would feel if I invited Sofie to join the orchestra with which I am performing at Hacketts in Picadilly. Sofie is brooding about her life in France, and she believes she should get away from Django and Naguine, who are being married next month in the little town where Sofie has been living. The "New Quintette"—that's what Django calls his group now—really doesn't make good use of Sofie's talent, and she worries that . . . "

"I understand. She finally feels all of the pressures of war, with her father and me both out of contact, and her gentleman friend—remember Dieter?—her gentleman friend wasting away in a detention camp in Czechoslovakia. It must be frightening to be cheated of all those things and not to able to see a clear path ahead. If she can leave France, then surely she should come here, but understand that I cannot allow people to know that she is my daughter. Neither of us would be well served by disclosing that she is the daughter of an SWW functionary. It might also compromise Otto—General von Seigler—to be revealed as having both a Polish spy ex-wife and a Jewish daughter in London. I'm sorry that I can't be more helpful in assisting her to move here, but she has a Swiss passport and sufficient funds, so I am confident she'll find a way.

"Incidentally—for the first time there is hope that Dieter may have been able to slip his bonds and resume life. I have no way of knowing his condition, but I have substantial hope that he will not finish his life inside a work camp. I haven't shared this with Sofie yet, because it would be unfair and even harmful to raise her hopes prematurely. But as soon as it is confirmed, I'll try to reach her with the news. That may also hasten her departure from France."

Neither had an appetite for dinner, and Lilka wanted to be alone to collect her thoughts, so Stéphane walked her to her building and they bade one another good night. Inside, Lilka poured a drink and sat by her window, watching the wartime-hooded streetlights send small circles of light downward to the roadway. So, Dieter was finally outside Theresienstadt—and Sofie was weary of France. It was time for Sofie to read Dieter's composition, but she could not risk having it with her as she departed from France. Lilka resolved to hold it until Stéphane assured her of a new opportunity in London and Sofie—Sophia Havlik from Neuchâtel—could depart from Nazi-occupied Europe.

CHAPTER SEVENTY

Near Litoměřice, Czechoslovakia, Tuesday, March 23, 1943

TIME TO MOVE ON

Elsa paid her daily visit to Dieter in the secluded little home where Draco and his wife lived. Each day since his escape nineteen days earlier, the young man had appeared stronger and more alert. Elsa had hoped he would have a month to recover before moving on, but today Draco had told her that Dieter's absence from his cell was being treated as a possible escape rather than as normal prisoner attrition. Apparently his popularity with the Friday night gatherings of singers had resulted in multiple inquiries when he failed to appear on March 12 and again on March 19. Now several officers were demanding answers regarding Dieter's disappearance.

"Good morning, Dieter!" Elsa smiled as she entered his room. "How are your sores today? And how are you feeling? Do you think you are getting strong enough to leave here and move to a safer place?"

"Not if I have to move in an oil barrel," he laughed. Then he grew more serious and added, "Elsa, I have had good food and a warm bed—and, of course your attention—for nearly three weeks. As you can see, I have gained weight, and I feel more energetic, too. If it is time to move on, I'm ready to make the effort. But you understand that they confiscated my identity papers when I entered Theresienstadt, and my only remaining 'credential' is this tattoo inside my right forearm. To leave Czechoslovakia I would probably have to swim a river, as I was ready to do on the first day we were apprehended. I'm sure that a tattoo and no papers would provide me with a quick ticket back to

Theresienstadt—or perhaps directly to Auschwitz, huh?"

"Can you drive a vehicle, Dieter?" Elsa posed the question. "The idea that is being discussed is having you drive an official Wehrmacht car over the border and back to Berlin as chauffeur for an officer in the back seat. The officer would have genuine papers—because it would be a real officer. He would direct the conversation with border guards or at any roadblock, and you would just sit and keep your mouth sealed like a good enlisted man should in such situations. So—can you?"

"Well, I drove a derelict truck from the Gypsy camp—where you and I were taken after Prague—to the border with Poland, but that is the sum of my experience. The officer would be taking a chance with me at the wheel. But I'm willing to try. It can't be too hard. Who is willing to risk that with me, Elsa?"

"I believe it is an aide to General von Seigler—Oberleutnant Klaus Kolb. Do you know him?"

"Indeed. He has been present at some pivotal times since I met Sofie. "

Elsa put her hands on his shoulders and looked directly into Dieter's eyes. She said, "Dieter, there are many people whose wellbeing may be linked to your successful departure from the Continent. Your cellmates in Theresienstadt would be punished if the details of your escape were known. So also would Draco and his family. General von Seigler's position might be jeopardized if you resurface, and, of course, Sofie would be devastated if anything happened to you or to those others. Oberleutnant Kolb and I are being paid to take the risk, but we want this to go smoothly, too. So, Dieter, it is time to organize your departure. I shall communicate the decision to my employer tonight, and I am confident that the wheels will be put into motion at once. Oh, yes—let's see if Draco will let you drive his truck around the back country roads later today, just to refresh your skills."

Dieter laughed. "My skills—of course! Except for playing piano, composing my memoirs, and cleaning dirty dishes, all of my 'skills' have been gathering rust since September of 1939. Yes, I had better try aiming Draco's heap down some back road before acting as chauffeur to a Wehrmacht officer. Otherwise, I might pose the greatest danger for both of us when I get behind the wheel."

Elsa laughed playfully and teased her dormant patient. "Of course,

Dieter, there is one neglected skill we could work on right now. I never dispense free samples, but it would be such an honor to slip under the sheets with one of the Gestapo's principal tormentors. It has been an inactive period for me, too—and I imagine that four years of abstinence has built up some powerful needs. Move over."

Dieter watched with mixed curiosity and anxiety as the rough outer clothing of the small woman was discarded unceremoniously, revealing Elsa's hard, athletic body. It reminded him of the impossibly smooth sculptures which had advertised Berlin's Olympic Games in 1936. She flashed a bright smile, almost innocent in its lack of passion or emotion, and asked, "You like? Pretty well preserved, eh? Go ahead—you can touch. They won't bite!"

Dieter held up both hands, but not to grasp the shiny skin. Rather, he positioned his hands defensively to maintain distance between Elsa and him. "Elsa," he began, "You know that when I entered the Porte Verte foolishly on my first day in Prague, it set off a series of conflicts which has brought troubles to all of us ever since that day. Jurgen Deitz and Colonel Gunther and those two Gestapo goons all died as an indirect result of my irresponsibility, and Juraslav and Adam are rotting in Theresienstadt, and Sofie and her father are in jeopardy—and you are risking yourself here. I can't imagine a more satisfying way to spend the next two hours than grappling with you on this old bed, but it has taken me four years to earn a second chance to live, and would I not be a total fool if I . . . "

"It's your decision," she interrupted. "If I were a baker, I'd offer you a cake to celebrate your escape. But I'm not a baker. I'm a prostitute, and this is the way I know to share happiness with someone. Wow! A new experience for me—being rejected when a man is only a few inches from my naked body. How do you like that!" Elsa gathered her clothing and left the room, leaving Dieter feeling that he had hurt her deeply.

CHAPTER SEVENTY-ONE

Berlin –Friday, March 26, 1943

SENSITIVE CARGO MOVEMENT

General Otto von Seigler and his aide dined together at a small café near Wehrmacht Headquarters in the heart of the city—now a target for daylight bombing runs by the U. S. Army's Eighth Air Force B-17 heavy bombers. The older officer spoke.

"Our cargo is ready to be transported from a spot near Litoměřice back to Flughafen Berlin-Tempelhof, and then onward with tomorrow's regular flight to Lisbon. As we surmised, he has no belongings and no documents, so the success of this movement will rest upon your ability to divert attention to yourself and make it apparent that this fellow is only your adjutant. I have been assured that he is reasonably healthy and able to travel.

"There are two fresh uniforms packed for your trip. His is a corporal's uniform, with the insignia of our unit. I can confirm 'Corporal Brinckerhoff's' legitimacy if *absolutely* necessary to complete the movement, but, believe me, I don't want to hear anything until it is accomplished successfully. Understood? Ja?

"The second uniform is yours. I have initiated the field promotion of Major Klaus Albert Kolb, in recognition of outstanding contributions to the Wehrmacht's successes in Poland and France, and it is effective today. No—wait—please don't thank me, Klaus. You have earned it many times over. Congratulations, Major Kolb! I foresee more successes in your future. Loyalty and competence should be recognized.

"Once at Tempelhof, you and the corporal will carry our usual diplomatic pouches to the Embassy in Lisbon. Safely in neutral Portugal, he must discard his temporary identity as a German soldier. Be certain that happens immediately—and leave no trace! You will have two days there before the return flight, and during that time there are other things to be accomplished. Herr Meister will be sheltered by Fräulein Branka, whom you know. I am entrusting you with my personal communication to her, which you are charged with delivering by hand.

"Also in your file is the address and contact number for Herr Hugo Stinnes, Jr., a German friend who resides now in Lisbon. There is a second communication from me, which I wish you to hand to Herr Stinnes at the time when you introduce Meister to him. Stinnes will be providing his transportation onward from Lisbon at the earliest possible date.

"From there, I want you to go with Meister to the office of Bank Julius Baer in Avenida do Marechal Gomes da Costa. He will be accessing an account there which will allow him to complete his journey away from Europe and hopefully into obscurity from which he will not emerge again. He knows how to access his account. I do not, so I cannot instruct you further on that part of your assignment.

"When all of the foregoing has been accomplished to your satisfaction—and not before—please call me from Lisbon and I shall give you the password information which you will need to access a second account at Bank Julius Baer. That is one in your own name, and it has been established as I promised you earlier when we first discussed the desirability of moving Dieter Meister away from areas where we are vulnerable to his capture. I believe that you will consider it a generous reward, Major Kolb—but once again, you will have earned it.

"Finally my friend, you have my instruction to assure that Dieter Meister does not fall into other hands than yours until he is in Lisbon and safely away from the possibility of capture. If anything intervenes which threatens that result, you are to put a bullet through his head without delay and to validate the action as unavoidable, because you believed that a dangerous escaped prisoner was about to escape again before he could be turned over to proper authorities. I will do my best to defend that result, but only if the circumstances appear to support your explanation. Good luck, Klaus."

The two men parted with a salute of "Heil Hitler," which in no way conveyed the profound level of trust and admiration they shared.

CHAPTER SEVENTY-TWO
March 27-28, 1943

A WEEKEND WITH MAJOR KOLB

Saturday, March 27, 1943, would be a test of the extent to which Dieter had recovered from 1282 days of deprivation. He huddled on the front seat of Draco's smelly truck with the Gypsy giant manning the steering wheel and the compact Elsa—who smelled much better than the rest of his surroundings—seated on his lap. They started before dawn and traced a pattern of the lesser-used byways to a gravel pit near the Ohře River, where they now sat with the engine idling in a chunky rhythm and the truck's one functioning light threatening to expire.

After an anxious half hour, during which the sun made its first cloud-shrouded entry over the dark river, a Mercedes staff car with two small swastika flags flying from its front fenders turned off the road and circled cautiously toward them. The car stopped about thirty meters away and blinked its lights twice. Elsa, Draco and Dieter understood that they were expected to leave the truck and walk slowly toward the staff car, making it easy for its occupant to survey them and to exit the area if he didn't feel safe there. They jumped down from the high seat onto the gravel and started the short walk. As they did so, a spotlight on the driver's side of the Mercedes snapped on and concentrated upon them. It was so bright that Dieter couldn't see the staff car any more, so he took Elsa's hand in his and walked toward the light source. Draco obligingly held her other hand and followed Dieter's example.

"Close enough. Stop there," a disembodied voice commanded. "Turn around slowly with your hands raised, then kneel, facing the light." When they had done as ordered, the voice continued. "Your names—first the girl, then the big chap, and then the other gentleman. Quickly!" They did as the voice had bade them, and suddenly the light was extinguished. Through large blue spots tormenting their eyes, they could see a German officer in the full dress uniform of a Wehrmacht major. "I am Major Klaus Kolb. It is good to see you three, but there is no time for pleasantries. Dieter and I have a full day ahead of us. And, Dieter, for the next forty-eight hours, you are Corporal Brinckerhoff, my military driver—and you do not have a working tongue for anyone but me. Please take leave of Elsa and Draco. I will drive the first ten minutes while you put your uniform on, and then you become the chauffeur."

"God save us both!" Dieter implored with a humorous look, and then he embraced the large man, nearly disappearing into his grasp. He turned to Elsa, wondering what to say or do. There were tears in her eyes, which elicited the same from him. "Damn! That spotlight was powerful," he mumbled as he dabbed at the moisture. "Elsa, you will always have a place in my heart, and I will pray for your safety every day. And don't *ever* refer to yourself as a whore again. You are a warrior." With that, he administered a kiss full upon her parted lips and released her. It was time to concentrate upon the next steps of his survival, and all other thoughts must wait their turn.

Corporal Brinckerhoff's uniform seemed too large, but Dieter reminded himself that he had lost nearly 20 kilos while in Theresienstadt, and only a portion of that had been regained during his three weeks of pampered recovery. Elsa had cut his shaggy hair to imitate a military look, and Draco had produced a sharp blade and hot soapy water to help the new corporal scrape the stubble from his neglected face. Dieter wondered whether the effect of their work was sufficient to allow him to appear the way an adjutant to an officer should look. Probably not, he concluded. Klaus was immaculate in his crisp uniform, and he appeared to be in robust physical condition. His aide should send the same message.

It was time for Dieter to move to the driver's position and for the Wehrmacht officer to assume a relaxed appearance in the rear of the precisely cleaned vehicle. That proved to be difficult, as Dieter tortured the car's gears, attempting to shift from one to the other, but after bouncing his passenger like a pogo-stick rider half a dozen times, he became passably proficient, and the black vehicle picked up speed as the roadways became smoother. They crossed the river into Litoměřice, then followed the signs toward Dresden. At the border crossing, guards spoke briefly to Major Kolb, warning him of possible aircraft activity, then waved the staff car past the candy-striped gate. Dieter was back in Germany!

"Did you hear what they said?" Major Kolb asked his interested driver. "Apparently the US Army Air Force has initiated 'strategic bombing' now that they have fighter escorts with sufficient range to cover flights into our territory. That is much different from what the RAF did. They flew at night, and their bombing was like 'pin the tail on the donkey' because they couldn't see their targets. These B-17s follow rivers and railroads during the daylight hours, and then they target the bridges and terminals. The Luftwaffe still downs some of them, but many do get to their targets. They told us to watch for formations and to get off the main road quickly if we perceive danger."

When Dieter knew that Berlin lay only two more hours ahead, he resolved to push the Mercedes as hard as possible to improve his chances of leaving Germany before a wave of Allied bombers could end his escape effort. He glanced in the mirror and was amazed to see that his passenger was gazing at the countryside much as a tourist would. There was no sign of fear or anxiety. "Do you worry about those bombers, Major?" he asked.

"I can't do much about them, so I don't concern myself," was the calm reply. "I am more preoccupied with insisting that we be allowed to depart Tempelhof on the military's runway—Runway 9 Left. It is longer, and we will have a very heavy load of fuel. It is nice to have enough insurance, in case we must circumvent active air space. Our aircraft bears neutral Portuguese markings, so I don't anticipate problems, but when there is something I *can* affect, I try to improve our odds as much as possible. Have you flown often, Dieter?"

"Never," was the apologetic reply. "I imagine it is quite exciting to watch the earth pass below and familiar objects grow smaller and smaller. Does it feel strange to be so far above the surface? And what do you do if a cloud comes between you and the ground? How do you miss the mountains and other aircraft if you can't see them?"

"Pilots get very good at reading charts before they launch into the air. And then they can do what is called 'dead reckoning,' which evaluates their air speed, the prevailing wind, and compass readings. Of course, they prefer to descend below the clouds and look for landmarks to confirm their position, but the very best ones are uncanny, and they can feel their way to destinations when most of us can't see the wingtips."

"And will we fly immediately after we arrive?"

"Our aircraft will be loaded and the three engines warmed and idling. We won't delay our departure for more than a minute or two. The fewer people who see two of us enter the plane, the less our chance of being exposed. We can drive our car onto the tarmac to the side of the aircraft, and then step up into the plane. It should take only a few seconds. I will get out of the car first and distract anyone who is there; you just leap out and climb inside as quickly as possible without creating a fuss. Please remember that you are not to speak with anyone or to let your face be seen. Pretend you are a cat burglar!"

"And then?"

"If all goes well, we will head southward, passing to the east of the high mountains, almost toward Vienna, and that will put us out over the Adriatic before long. Then we will turn toward the west and pass over the middle of Italy and continue westward along the Mediterranean coastline of France. The coastal land will eventually curve toward the south, and we will, too, as we skirt eastern Spain. At Valencia, we will turn sharply inland and go nearly straight west across Spain to Lisbon. Our aircraft is slow, and it can't operate above the highest mountains, so we always try to fly lower—over water when possible."

"So we have a pilot who does this each weekend?"

"A pilot and a co-pilot who is his navigator. The navigator is important, because non-combatant planes have to stay in 'corridors' over some countries, like Franco's Spain. If we leave the corridor, they may assume we are hostile and force us to land."

"Or shoot us down?"

"Dieter, you are thinking too negatively. Portuguese planes are neutral, and both sides in the war respect that. Once we are in the air, just sit quietly. Enjoy the scenery below us and the mountains in the distance. Oh, yes—a diplomatic pouch will be handcuffed to your left wrist. You must look like a courier until we are safely out of the aircraft and into Lisbon. Let's speed up a little and get to Tempelhof without dodging bombs, eh?"

The desultory conversation had relaxed Dieter and he was glad that Major Kolb was no longer the frozen face he had first encountered at 80 Wilhelmstrasse five years earlier. Dieter thought to himself that he actually liked the man.

From the time Dieter first saw the huge aerodrome at Tempelhof until the time when their Junkers tri-motor rumbled along the runway and left the ground, everything happened with the precision of a military campaign, and he could see Major Kolb relax visibly, with a smile of satisfaction. "Six to seven hours now, Dieter, depending upon the winds and our altitude. That was to be your next question, yes?" Dieter glanced at the profile of Berlin, which became more visible as they climbed away from the field. He wondered if he would see the city again—and, indeed, whether it would survive the relentless attack of Allied bombers sufficiently to be recognizable if he were to return one day. "Yes, that was my question, Klaus," he smiled. Theresienstadt already seemed more like a daydream than reality, and he had no idea what lay ahead for him.

CHAPTER SEVENTY-THREE
Lisbon, Portugal —Sunday, March 28, 1943

RICK'S CAFÉ AMÉRICAIN

In the early spring of 1943, across the Atlantic, American audiences were giving a first nod of approval to a new motion picture titled *Casablanca*, where subjects from all of the World War II combatants seemed to mix together in a background of charged movieland sophistication. Of course, neither Dieter nor Major Klaus Kolb had seen or heard of the production, but when they arrived in Lisbon on March 28, it was a city where reality traced those same unlikely patterns. Lisbon had survived unscathed through the war years by keeping its doors open to everyone, while allowing no interest to dominate the others. Portugal, like Switzerland and—to an extent—Sweden, had carved out the status of neutrality, which was recognized by leaders of both sides in the war.

German military officers, British bankers, and American diplomats passed one another in hotel lobbies with an ease that defied reason. Jewish families fortunate—or wealthy—enough to slip away from the German-occupied areas of Europe regrouped in Lisbon before moving on to more permanent exile. Lisbon's Portela Airport, where Dieter and Klaus landed, epitomized this unlikely ambivalence. Both the Germans and British operated regular flights into and out of Portela, and each had spies watching the aircraft of the other, trying to identify the passengers and use their movements to predict changes in war strategy. Indeed, only a few weeks after Dieter and Klaus landed safely, those alert German eyes thought they saw Britain's Prime Minister Winston Churchill board a BOAC DC-3 headed to England from Portela Airport, and they alerted the Luftwaffe, which shot the plane down over The Bay of Biscay, north of Spain. The British actor Leslie Howard was killed, along with his accountant, who unfortunately resembled Churchill.

There was nothing unusual about a German tri-motor painted in Portuguese livery landing at Portela and disgorging a uniformed major together with an enlisted courier. They transferred into an unmarked car and drove away as a normal occurrence, with only the notation *regular German document flight landed 28/3/43 at 1935 hours* in the handbook of an inconspicuous watcher near the hangar where the aircraft would be serviced.

"We are in Lisbon, Dieter," the smiling Major Kolb announced, as he unlocked the diplomatic briefcase from his companion's wrist. "Congratulations—you have officially completed your escape from Theresienstadt today!"

"And now what happens?" Dieter intoned.

"First we go to the apartment of General von Seigler's lady friend, where we can wash up and you can get into other clothes—hopefully better fitting than Corporal Brinckerhoff's uniform, eh? Then we can have a quiet dinner with Herr Hugo Stinnes, who will pick up the tab but will become considerably richer as a result of the meal, if you understand me. Do you?"

"He is being paid to help me leave Portugal? And someone is picking up that cost for me. Who?"

"That is for others to tell you, Dieter. You are better off knowing less right now. And I have no idea of your next destination, but it will surely involve a journey by steamer, because that is what Herr Stinnes does. Twenty years ago, the company—in his father's name—was one of the most powerful in Germany. Now, Hugo Jr. manages the remnants of that steamship line from here. Illicit passengers like you have breathed a little life into the corpse for now. But don't think of yourself as a pampered passenger on an ocean liner; you will undoubtedly be a deck hand and expected to do hard work. But he will tell you the details, and I will hear them for the first time when you do. Ja?"

"And . . . what of you, Klaus? Do you go back to Berlin on the return flight?"

"For now, yes. But I am not happy with the course the war is taking. You may not know that 90,000 of our troops in the East surrendered to the Russians in Stalingrad just weeks ago. They became bogged down and frozen in that miserable ice and snow. They were cold and hungry and being slaughtered. They should not have been sent there to die. This is what happens when civilians contradict the opinions of professional soldiers, and it is why some of our military commanders conspire to oust the leadership that sends them to their deaths. But . . . I am saying too much. Yes: I will be returning to Tempelhof with the return flight, and you will be in Lisbon in the care of General von Seigler's friend until your sailing date."

"Klaus—Major Kolb—I have no way to thank you adequately for shepherding me away from that gravel pit by the Ohře to a city—what? Two or three thousand kilometers away? Whatever—it is amazing to me. I think this is what Lindbergh was talking about the night I saw him at the general's residence. So much has changed while I was behind those walls. You know I couldn't be here without your help, so thank you, Major!"

"The official flight distance from Tempelhof to Portela is about 2500 kilometers—good guess, Dieter! But, of course, we flew a longer course to avoid mountains and hostile territory, so maybe as much as 3000 kilometers. That's why the heavy fuel load and the long runway. And there is no need to thank me. It is my job and I am pleased it has all gone well. But we still have a few things to do, so keep your wits about you."

Branka and Hugo Stinnes, Jr. were both as Dieter had imagined they would be. She was stylish and poised, with just enough of an accent in her German speech to convey the intrigue that went with her occupation. Her apartment overlooked the Lisbon waterfront, and it was furnished sparely but with the plush comfort one would associate with a movie personality. She greeted Dieter warmly, and he could smell her expensive French fragrance and see just the hint of a voluptuous figure—one which could undoubtedly reward a war-weary German general. Most attractive of all to him was her obvious intelligence and total self-confidence. Dieter knew instinctively that she would make good decisions on his behalf for whatever period he was destined to remain in Lisbon.

Herr Stinnes was used to the late dinners of Portugal and apparently had not missed many of them. The maitre d' at the small restaurant where he and Klaus met the shipowner knew Herr Stinnes's favorite wine and explained which of the chef's offerings that evening would be the best choice for the three diners. He had seated them in the most secluded corner of the small, ornate dining room so that they could converse without being overheard. Dieter had the impression that Hugo Stinnes, Jr. regularly dined here with strangers and that those dinners were generally very private affairs where confidences and currencies were exchanged away from prying eyes.

"I see that you are wearing a fine new suit," Stinnes observed to Dieter. "Enjoy it while you are here, because on the *Barbara* you will be wearing coveralls and a weatherproof slicker for much of the time. The Atlantic can be cold and choppy this time of year, and we move swiftly on the open water, with many course changes. That does not make for passenger comfort, but there are safety considerations which take precedence."

"You mean U-boats prowl the coastline and you avoid them," Klaus stated.

"Yes, we do that, although we fly the Portuguese colors and thus far they have watched us but never taken hostile action," replied the stout German. "There are no guarantees in wartime, but I am told that Portuguese neutrality is respected at the highest levels. Something about needing tungsten and kissing Salazar's ass to make sure the source remains accessible. *Barbara* isn't a cruise liner. She is an old workhorse with a good, reliable record but no creature comforts except in the captain's quarters, which you won't be seeing. Deckhands—there are eighteen of them—share an open dormitory, near enough to the boiler room to be comfortably warm in April, but near enough to the screws to be noisy, too. You'll get used to it in a day or two, and the salt air tends to make our sailors sleep well despite the rocking and the bump-bump-bump of the engines. Think you can do it, son?"

"I lived 1282 days in Theresienstadt, sir; I expect that the *Barbara* will be fine. Where are we going?"

"Can't tell you where or when until we sail, but you'll be at sea about fourteen days, and I will give you notice of your report the day prior to sailing. Once you get those orders, stay put and don't share the information. It's my boat, but it's your ass!"

The dinner was excellent but overly large. Dieter's stomach wasn't yet adjusted to full meals, so he laid his fork and knife aside long before Herr Stinnes was finished eating. Then he listened to the sounds of luxury in the room, as bottles were uncorked and crystal glasses were touched together amid the laughter of diners who seemed strangely detached from the world he had just left behind. An hour later, they took leave of Herr Stinnes and returned to Branka's apartment, where Dieter was all too happy to drop into the bed turned down for his use. He was aware that Branka and Klaus spoke quietly in another room but was far too tired to try to listen to the conversation. He had no idea when Klaus departed, but he awoke briefly two hours later and saw that there were no lights burning. It was his first night in a bed with springs and a mattress since he had departed from the Havlik Clinic forty-three months earlier, and he took full advantage of the comfort, knowing he would soon be sleeping in a hammock aboard a rolling freighter.

CHAPTER SEVENTY-FOUR

Lisbon, Portugal – Monday, March 29, 1943

LARGESSE

The new day was well underway when Klaus, dressed in civilian clothing, pushed the ground-floor buzzer and was admitted to the building where Branka's apartment was situated. When he reached her floor, Branka and Dieter were seated at a sun-washed window table, chatting over coffee. Klaus could see that they spoke easily with one another, and he imagined that Dieter's account of life within Theresienstadt had enlightened Branka, but that she might also have been enabled to form a better picture of General von Seigler's talented daughter. Branka had focused upon Sofie while speaking with Klaus the previous evening, after Dieter had fallen into a snoring sleep. Although it was not an interrogation and was deftly managed, Klaus understood that Sofie's importance to her father was of profound interest to Branka.

"I must tear him away from you, Branka," Klaus began. "We have an appointment with a Swiss banker, and they are notorious for timeliness, even in a country which prides itself on lateness. After the meeting, I'm going to drive Dieter along the waterfront and show him where the various companies dock their ships, and we'll do a little shopping, too. Dieter's entire belongings when he left Theresienstadt didn't fill his pants pockets, and he should have a sea bag with some suitable clothing and grooming basics. Perhaps you'll join us for dinner after that?"

At Bank Julius Baer, both men were surprised at how little the offices resembled the classic image of a bank. It was more like a private library, with bookshelves, oil paintings, and scattered wing chairs. They were seated at one grouping of chairs by a pleasant young man who spoke such flawless German that they decided he must be of another nationality. He repeated their names—carefully noted on his clipboard—and asked if they would like a cup of tea or coffee while they waited for an assistant manager to meet with them. That took only about five minutes.

"Herr Havlik? Which of you is Herr Havlik? Ah, yes! Herr Havlik, I have checked your account records, and it appears that you have never before visited Bank Julius Baer. That is very unusual for our depositors, and I can see that you have been with the bank for a period of—what?—forty-four months. No activity in so long a period of time. Military service? I am curious."

"I was informed that I needed to present only my name and a password, with no explanation for my whereabouts or activities. Was that correct information? I am prepared to write the password on a slip of paper for your eyes only—but I retain the paper. If you are not comfortable with that, I would prefer to work with the manager at his earliest convenience. What say you?"

"Here is a blank page. Please write the password." Dieter slowly traced the number and name he believed answered the question about the location of the Bösendorfer Imperial—*80 Wilhelmstrasse*—and he held it in his cupped hands near the official's face. After a quick glance at his clipboard, the official motioned to Dieter to take the paper away, and he asked pleasantly, "What may we do to be of assistance today, Herr Havlik?"

"First, I need to know the account balance. That will help me to determine the level of assistance I require."

"Of course, sir. There are two components; your original deposit, which was this number, and the interest the account has earned in forty-four months, which is this." The first figure was 20,000 Swiss francs—a breathtaking amount to Dieter—and the latter was 3,080 Swiss francs, which resulted from monthly compounding, and which likewise stunned him. He concluded immediately that the accrued interest would be more than enough for his foreseeable needs, assuming that the principal could be left with the bank and accessed at any branch of Bank Julius Baer.

Since he did not know his destination, Dieter asked the assistant manager for a written listing of the bank's offices worldwide. The man retrieved a small card containing the information from a writing desk in the corner of the room.

Dieter told the assistant manager that he would like to withdraw the equivalent of 3000 Swiss francs, half in Swiss currency and half in American dollars. The remaining 80 francs of accrued interest he would like in Portuguese escudos to cover his immediate expenses while in Lisbon. "As you wish, Herr Havlik, We can have that completed in a matter of minutes and will ask you to sign a receipt for the currencies before you leave."

Dieter's business with Bank Julius Baer had been successful. Likewise, Klaus judged that he had carried out his assignment, and his next stop would be at the German consulate, where he could direct a wire to his Wehrmacht superior, telling him that his "package" had been delivered without any breakage, and that Klaus would return to Berlin with the next regular document flight. Klaus wondered how long it would be until his instincts directed him to miss a return flight and instead to set out for the stony beaches of Almeria and the comfortable largesse he had accumulated there.

Dinner with Branka began relaxed and light. All three expressed amazement that a German Wehrmacht officer, a Polish intelligence agent, and an escaped Czech concentration camp detainee could dine together in a Lisbon restaurant with total impunity. Klaus told Branka that he and Dieter had watched the Stinnes cargo ship *Barbara* guided into its dock and learned that it was inbound from a port city in West Africa with a load of structural timbers. The estimate was that it would take a week to offload the cargo, make the *Barbara* shipshape for its next voyage, provision and load the ship, and assemble the crew. During that time, Dieter would remain as Branka's guest and restrict his movements prudently. There was no indication where the *Barbara* would be going next, so Dieter would have to wait a while longer to know his next destination.

Branka raised her hand like a schoolgirl asking permission to speak in class. "I must fill you both in on a few things. First, as Klaus knows, I flew to Berlin earlier this month to visit General von Seigler, at his invitation. You should know that, too, Dieter. He—the general—has been instrumental in assisting your escape from Czechoslovakia as well as arranging your space on the *Barbara* when she sails. Of course, this protects him from a situation where you might be used to defame him. But it is not entirely selfish; you could have been rendered silent in other ways. No, he also recognizes your importance to Sofie, so he has sponsored your safety.

"Second, I flew to England last week. It was ostensibly to attend matters related to my work here. But, in truth, I could have done that at other times. I wanted to go last week to sit with Lilka—Rudovska—Otto's former wife and Sofie's mother. You see, Otto and I began keeping company some time ago, neither of us knowing of that common denominator. It is a Lisbon kind of thing—you can see that the spectrum blends here with strange results, like the three of us being at this table tonight. I needed to assure Lilka that neither of us had intentionally slighted or betrayed her—and that is the truth.

"Third, Dieter, I learned more about Sofie's situation from Lilka. She is living comfortably and safely as Swiss citizen 'Sophia Havlik' in the center of France, and she performs occasionally with the new musical group headed by Django. However, she has initiated an effort to rejoin Mr. Grappelli with an orchestra in London. Her mother, Lilka, has received the materials you composed while in Theresienstadt, but she is retaining them for Sofie to examine *after* she is safely out of occupied territory. So Sofie doesn't yet know that you have escaped.

"And finally, I chose this restaurant because it is across the street from the Hotel do Nacimiento—right over there. See the sign? Dieter, you'll remember the name 'do Nacimiento'—it was the family name of your flat-mate, Miguel, in Berlin. This hotel has belonged to his family for three generations, and after conditions worsened in Berlin, Miguel returned to Lisbon and is part of the hotel's management. General von Seigler was a guest at Hotel do Nacimiento during the Lisbon trip when he and I met. Miguel recognized him and later contacted him. So—Dieter—before you sail, you may want to sit with Miguel and review the events of 1938. Now: Is anyone interested in dessert?"

Dieter had set his fork aside on Branka's first point, which probably avoided his choking somewhere during her unexpected briefing. He had known that General von Seigler had undertaken a personal role in his escape, and he understood the danger that he, Lilka, and Sofie potentially represented to the general if his loyalty to the führer were brought into question. Dieter had also accepted the possibility that he and Sofie might not automatically resume their relationship after so long a hiatus. People and their circumstances change radically during wartime, and they might have dissimilar priorities now. But—Miguel!!! He could be just around the corner from their table, and Dieter had never been able to adjust his feelings to the possibility that Miguel may have betrayed Sofie and him to authorities out of jealousy and resentment. Was he *really* ready to revisit that objectively? So soon after enduring the hardship of captivity? It would require some thought. He declined the invitation to order dessert; it had been a full night already.

CHAPTER SEVENTY-FIVE

Copacabana Palace Hotel - Rio De Janeiro,
Brazil Sunday, June 20, 1943

There were only a few guests in the lobby at seven a.m. Rio was a twenty-four-hour city, but even along Praia de Copacabana, the most famous beach in the country, Sunday dawned quietly over the ocean. Dieter walked out through the doorway of the handsome building and crossed Avenida Atlântica to the beautiful walkway along the beach. He savored the fresh air of early winter. It wasn't at all like winter in Germany, still, a distinctly different season for the locals. He had made some early-morning tuning adjustments to the well-kept Bechstein piano in the Bar do Copa before it opened for those guests who liked to begin Sundays with something stronger than the local coffee. Dieter's first scheduled work of the day was not until noon, when things would be bustling. In that din, only he would be aware that the piano was well tuned, but it was important for Dieter that the chords he constructed weren't adulterated by any flat tones.

Dieter had decided that enough things had now settled into place for him to write a letter to Miguel—and one of the fixed metal benches facing the broad, white beach would be ideal for that purpose. A short distance down the Avenida, he chose one and sat opposite several nets where beach volleyball would begin later in the morning. A lone bather stood waist-deep in the water a hundred meters away, and a sand artist worked diligently on an impressive model of some famous cathedral he was sculpting. When strollers along the Avenida passed, they rewarded his effort by tossing a few coins into the white sheet the artist had spread in front of his masterpiece. Theresienstadt was a long way away.

20 de junho de 1943, Rio de Janeiro

Querido Miguel,

This is an incredibly beautiful setting for a city. I am constantly reminded of how fortunate I am to be here, and I am confident that crossing the Atlantic on the Barbara *was the best possible solution for the conflicts in my life. Fifteen days on a wave-tossed ship clearly established that being a seaman is not my calling. The food on board was excellent—on the way down—but too much of it made its way back up as I looked out over those dizzying rolls of the sea. I never quite mastered sleeping in a hammock, either, and bouncing off a riveted metal floor became all too frequent an end for my slumbers. But all of that is forgotten easily in this place.*

First, please accept my heartfelt thanks for the introduction you and your father provided to the Guinle family. I have learned that they opened the Copacabana Palace twenty years ago and have owned and managed it every day since. They admire your accomplishments in Lisbon, and, in reality, their hotel is like a larger version of yours. (Although they say it copies the old Nagresco in Nice, and it does have similar architecture.) They immediately gave me an audition to perform in their Bar do Copa, and I am playing solo piano there during almoco *(you see—I am working on my Portuguese vocabulary) and again during the cocktail hour before the dinner musicians take over.*

I found a small flat in Rua Barata Ribeiro—farther back from the beach, closer to the favelas *on the mountainside. Those are amazingly rickety—just shelters made of corrugated metal and cardboard boxes. It rained hard for a few days after I arrived, and the mud washed a dozen sorry dwellings right down the hillside! I suppose the contrast between that and the people staying at the Copacabana Palace, only a short walk away, is the hardest thing for me to understand here—except for Portuguese, of course.*

Another surprise, as a Deutschbrasiliano, is the number of

Germans I am encountering here! In the south of the country—the states of Rio Grande do Sul, Paranà, and Santa Catarina—a great many Germans settled in the last century. They are said to own whole towns, large farms, and successful businesses. Here in Rio, the Germans I see are more recent arrivals. Some apparently came early in the 1930s, anticipating trouble back home. Others are obviously filtering in now for more topical reasons. I get lots of requests for songs from home—and good tips when I can play them.

One last thought, my friend. I know that it was quite difficult, and even painful, for you to speak with me about your role in linking me to Sofie and her father when you were being questioned by the Gestapo. You have convinced me that it was not motivated by any desire to injure us or destroy our relationship. You were a foreigner being interrogated by ruthless people, and you did what you had to do to save yourself. Now we should both put that chapter behind us and move on to better times as friends.

Of course, there will be one lasting consequence, Miguel, and it is this: Probably the only "celebrity status" I will ever achieve is that of having been wanted and pursued by the Gestapo!! As time passes and all things are put into perspective, I will be able to be amused more easily when I think back to those unlikely fugitive times. I only wish that Jura and Adam could enjoy the same luxury—but that is not to be.

Write to me and tell me anything you may learn from Branka or others about the people I have left behind. Please tell them I am well—and appreciative of all the consideration and courageous work it took to get me here.

Carinho, Dieter

CHAPTER SEVENTY-SIX
Hackett's-In-Picadilly, London Wednesday, June 30, 1943

THE OTHER SIDE OF THE MUSIC

Lilka was amazed at Stéphane Grappelli's lyrical solos with the orchestra but wished that more time were devoted to him in some of the arrangements. It was like covering half of the *Mona Lisa* in a gallery with fine fabric. The cloth might be beautiful, but if one had wanted to see the painting, the cloth became an annoyance. Stéphane was far and away the best violinist she had ever heard, and she thought back to that first encounter in Prague when she was doubtful over Juraslav's unbridled enthusiasm. Thinking of Jura made her nostalgic and sad—all the more reason to be certain Sofie remained safe.

As with Stéphane, Lilka wished that bandleader Arthur Young would make better use of his new featured vocalist. She—Sofie—well, *Sophia*—was able to command the elegant room with her vocals and her appearance. Even tables where lively conversations were in progress seemed to soften their chatter and listen attentively when the spotlight shifted to Sofie and she said a few words about her next carefully crafted offering. Lilka thought to herself that each of Sofie's vocals was also a short history of the songwriter, the lyricist, and the circumstances that had inspired it. She was pleased and proud to be sitting at Hackett's that evening. And . . . it was finally time to turn Dieter's writings over to her daughter, whom she judged to be emotionally ready for the contents now.

After the late set, a few people remained at their tables for a nightcap and conversation. Lilka and Sofie were among the stragglers that

Wednesday night. As everyone else did, they exchanged tidbits of information about the progress of the grinding war. Of special interest to both was Herr Himmler's recent edict against the remaining Jews in Poland and the occupied parts of the USSR. All were to be committed to death camps, and the two women could only wonder about the fates of those they had known a dozen years earlier.

"You were right to come here," Lilka asserted. "Even though France has bent enough to avoid wholesale murder, we are seeing desperate Nazi leadership adopting a scorched-earth mentality. As more Allied bombs fall on Germany—and there are huge operations every day now—they strike back blindly at the poor souls huddled in their wretched ghettoes. It is as if it were *those Jews* sending 800 bombers over Dusseldorf this week! Well, it may be only a short while until that same venom turns on people like you who assume their safety in an occupied country like France. No, Sofie—you couldn't risk remaining there longer."

"I know that you're right, Mother. But it was difficult for me to sever that last fragment of my dream of being a musical star in Paris—or even Berlin. It was so easy to imagine that outcome while I was stealing a few minutes with the Quintette and fantasizing that Dieter and Jura—and even Father—would walk through the door and applaud me. Can you understand? I know that it is selfish; it's all about me when I verbalize the dream, but truly my greatest happiness came from seeing the smiles I could elicit from my audiences. That first night at the Trocadero in Prague with all of you—and riding home together afterward—well, that is what I always hoped to recapture, and I couldn't do it by running away from possible harm."

The older woman shook her head in affirmation that she understood fully. "You know, I ran away and brought my desk full of papers with me. My whole government did that. Our army and navy did that! Only a few brave girls—like Elsa, remember Elsa? She is still somewhere in the area around Prague and selling the information she harvests to the highest bidder. Now, *that* brings me to some news that may light up your face! I have been saving it to share when it seemed that there would be no reversal."

"Yes? What . . . ?"

"Somehow, Dieter squirmed his way out of Theresienstadt—in a barrel of fish entrails—and was hidden by Elsa and Big Draco until he was recovered from his ordeal and could move on. He managed to carry a story with him—well, more an account of his life from the summer of 1938 onward. And, he sent it—or rather Elsa did—to *you*! It got to me in London, and I opened it and read it. It is dedicated to you, dear, and it is a beautiful account of shared times in bad times. I couldn't risk having it fall into German hands in France, and I didn't want to elate you and then learn that he had been recaptured or worse . . . "

"So you read what was intended for me? Before I could see it?"

"Yes; forgive me, dear. I am a professional snoop—but I am also a mother who loves her children, even though they have had to share me with Poland. My country has been my child, too—you know."

"And where is he now? Is he coming to London, too?"

"He was smuggled to Lisbon, where so many go to flee this maelstrom, and your father was able to get him aboard a boat there, leaving for someplace across the Atlantic. In time, Otto will know the destination; he paid a dear price to arrange the journey. But, the good news is that he lived through that imprisonment and can build a new life. I wish the same were true of Jura, but he became ill and diminished in the prison. I'm afraid we will never learn whether he perished there or was sent to a worse place to be put to death. So many have just disappeared . . . " Her voice trailed off, and Sofie knew that it was not the time to lecture her mother on the sin of reading others' mail.

"And where is the letter—or whatever he composed for me?"

Lilka lifted a large knitting bag from beside her chair and moved it across the table toward her daughter. "There is a letter, but the larger work is a story written on the backs of music sheets. The paper is not sturdy, so you will find a few tears and crumbled edges, but the handwriting is well preserved, and the story will hold your attention for many hours. I never put it down once I started reading, and you will probably be captured the same way."

"And when exactly did you read it, Mother?"

"Three months ago."

"*Three months???* I am learning something this important to me *three months* after it found its way to London? Please let me have it. I know I will be up very late tonight and probably unable to sleep, even then. *Three goddamned months!*"

CHAPTER SEVENTY-SEVEN

Wehrmacht Headquarters, Berlin Monday, August 2, 1943

THE SIGNIFICANCE OF OIL

General Otto von Seigler paced in front of a dozen other officers with an expression of total frustration cast over his handsome features. He looked as if he might actually explode and begin shouting as so many others did during this critical phase of the two-front war. However, the seasoned professional knew that he must resist the temptation to burst his seams, and he held his words back until he felt certain that would not happen. Then he began.

"Gentlemen, yesterday's raid on the Ploesti oil fields proved that the Luftwaffe can no longer protect *any* target our enemies are determined to attack and destroy. Yesterday, nearly two hundred American B-24s flew north from Libya to Romania—that's a thousand miles—and devastated the source of over half our crude oil. No target in Europe was protected better. We had radar, ground batteries, fighter planes, and massive camouflage to prevent such an air strike. We knew from our spies in Libya when the aircraft headed north and our scout planes tracked them for at least two hours. Still, they executed a low-level bombing which has put one of our most important resources out of business.

"We still have the best aircraft, the mightiest tanks, and the most advanced weaponry anywhere on earth—but do you know that much of our artillery is now pulled into place by horses? Do you know that many of our wonderful Messerschmitt 109s and Focke-Wulf 190s could not get into the air to protect Ploesti because they were not fueled? Do you understand that our troops in Russia are forced to march long distances because there is insufficient diesel fuel for troop carriers? And now? And now? We are scurrying about trying to concoct petroleum alternatives while our enemies grow stronger. Gentlemen, no civilian vehicle or bus should turn over an engine without multiple occupants. Everything must be done to ration the supply of oil we have so that every drop is valued. The greatest military force in the history of the world is in danger of losing because it can no longer move.

"Now, get out of here and be back with a conservation program which is totally serious—by tomorrow at this time! Dismissed. Heil Hitler."

When the room had cleared, General von Seigler turned to his aide, Major Kolb, and asked whether he believed the assembled officers had grasped the seriousness of the situation. Klaus assured him that the point had been well made, but then expressed his doubts that much could be done, even with the best of intentions and intensified rationing. The civilian population was already restive and had made massive sacrifices. Now some were beginning to whisper that the Master Plan was flawed and too ambitious. Families were seeing their 16-year old sons conscripted, and they knew the youngsters were no match for the manpower being thrown into the war by both the USA and the USSR. The General hushed him by placing a finger lightly over his own lips, then led his aide outside the building to a more secluded corner where he thought it was safe to continue.

"General, tell me—strictly off the record between two friends—can this war still be won? Or has Germany gone too far and made itself vulnerable to a repeat of 1918?"

"Klaus, your question could get you shot, so don't ask it of anyone else. Ja? But between us, my opinion is that the war cannot be won with an extrapolation of the present positions and tactics. We cannot fight a war of attrition with so vast an enemy, and our resources of coal, steel, oil, rubber, etc. are dwindling, while those of our adversaries are expanding. However, there may be other directions which could tip the balance our way.

"We are perfecting rockets which can replace manned bombers in the fight with England, and they may terrorize the populace into surrender. Also, I understand that our scientists are working on a new type of bomb incorporating deuterium, the heavy hydrogen atom used in making 'heavy water,' which could yield an atomic explosion of massive destructive force. And we hear that the Western Allies are becoming ever more suspicious and fearful of the Communist forces. They recognize that the Russians could become dominant in Europe, so they encourage them to divide their effort and put more resources into fighting Japan. This could weaken our enemies in the East.

"Having said all of that, Klaus, I must answer you that I am discouraged with the course of things and doubtful about the outcome of hostilities. If my fears are justified, I must ask whether Germany is well served by depleting its manpower and resources to a point where it could not be a viable country in the postwar world. A Pyrrhic victory is no victory, Klaus."

"I understand, sir. Will this dictate your own personal plans for the future? Will you be content to command in a cause that could prove to be disastrous to your own people? I worry that all of us may inadvertently damage our German heritage by failing to question whether we are applying yesterday's answers to today's problems."

Otto stood silently for what seemed like a long time. Klaus waited for the thought that was obviously generating within. Finally, the older man turned toward him and placed his hands on Klaus's shoulders. He looked straight into his aide's eyes and then said, "Klaus. We have both been on duty a bit too long. I want you to book yourself on a train to Spain this Friday—and to spend a quiet weekend in your spot in Almeria. Forget the world's stalemate for a few days; check your retirement account and get some summer sunshine. Things here will take care of themselves for a while. And, besides, I have decided to take the weekend diplomatic pouches to Lisbon myself. My mental health will be sounder if I indulge my body with some good food and my psyche with the company of a good woman. How does that sound to you?"

"I always try to follow your orders precisely, sir. I'll get right on this."

CHAPTER SEVENTY-EIGHT

Copacabana Palace Hotel, Rio De Janeiro Sunday - August 29, 1943

ENCORE REQUEST

The scion of a venerable Bolivian mining family had thrown a birthday party for himself in the Bar do Copa on Saturday night, and it seemed that every warm *carioca* body along the beach had drifted in, and most stayed until dawn. After the orchestra had become exhausted and signed off, someone had rousted Dieter from his flat and hurried him back to the Copa to keep the party going. A crumpled wad of American twenty-dollar bills had been pushed into his coat pocket with the promise of more rewards if the Piano Man could accompany the revelers for another two hours. At Theresienstadt, he had done much more in exchange for the scraps of food adhered to dirty plates and a centimeter of warm beer in the bottom of a glass, so there was no question in Dieter's mind about his ability to keep pace with the Rio late set. They had finally stumbled away to their rooms at seven o'clock that morning, and Dieter had taken his Sunday newspaper to a deep lobby chair rather than returning home.

Dieter regularly read the German-language weekly, which enjoyed a substantial audience in Rio. This week's featured story was focused upon the August 18 suicide of Hans Jeschonnek, the Chief of Luftwaffe Operations. It said that the sad death was motivated by Jeschonnek's profound embarrassment over the failure of his airmen to disrupt Allied bombings and the accelerating pace of those forays into the German heartland. Dieter remembered Hermann Göring's earlier assurances to Germans that his air arm was so strong that no foreign power could ever penetrate German airspace. Perhaps the greatest mystery to Dieter was his own reaction—his sadness over this disintegration of the Third Reich. After all, it *was* the entity that had pursued him relentlessly and then sent him off to perish in a disease-ridden concentration camp. How could Dieter, a continent away, have *any* feelings of regret that Germany's territorial aggression was now being countered successfully? He wished that he could again sit by the river with Miguel—or under the single lightbulb in their Theresienstadt cell with Jura—and explore his conflicted feelings.

Soon it would be the late-morning cocktail hour of a pleasant winter Sunday in Rio. Dieter was still dressed in the fashionable evening style of the myriad South American "playboys" who would return to the Bar do Copa and resume sipping Ramos Fizzes with women who never stopped smiling. Everything about them shouted privilege, and more than a little of their cash would be placed tastefully under his ashtray if he could massage some favorite melodies on request. Dieter, by now, had memorized the favorites of some of the notables and usuals, and he delighted them by greeting their entry into the Bar do Copa with a few identifying bars of "their songs." He glanced at the wall clock—he hadn't yet purchased a wristwatch—and decided to open his piano and make certain it was ready for another two hours of standards.

Before long, "As Time Goes By" wafted out of the open doorway, and like a musical magnet it seemed to pull the first members of the faithful back to the glass-top tables, fresh flowers, and attentive cocktail waiters of the Bar do Copa. Dieter recognized a famous French actress entering on the arm of a notoriously unfaithful Dominican diplomat, and he immediately transitioned to Edith Piaf's 1942 hit, "Un Monsieur Me Suit dans la Rue," which earned him an amused wave from both. It was a good beginning to a lucrative Sunday morning, he thought to himself. Again he inadvertently reflected upon the foul conditions of Theresienstadt and felt a wave of guilt, because he knew that none of his fellow prisoners would ever again sit in surroundings like these.

Within twenty minutes after the first arrivals, the room's tables were all occupied, and latecomers were being seated on barstools out of sight from the piano, or standing in the doorway, discreetly pressing folded currency into the hand of the stolid maître d'hotel. This was the place to see and be seen late on a Sunday morning, and Dieter had become a part of the Bar do Copa ambience, which was a must—together with the Ramos Fizzes. A svelte female hostess walked to the side of his piano with a sheet of paper on which she had collected half a dozen song requests, each of which was accompanied by a generous tip for the obliging Piano Man. Dieter glanced at the list and felt secure that he could give each his special treatment and earn the approval of his patrons.

The young woman bent low beside him. "I have another—a strange one," she confided. "There are three people near the door asking if you will play Joseph Haydn's composition, "Deutschland über alles." Isn't that a German national anthem or something?"

"Who are they? Do you know them?" a suddenly concerned Dieter asked. "Do they look like Nazis?"

"Nazis look like everyone else if they aren't in uniform," she shrugged. "The gentleman could be a Nazi, I don't know. The ladies are just—well—pretty ladies, like all the rest who come here. Good clothes. Nice hairdos. But—well, no jewels. Sunday morning isn't a big jewel time anyhow. Most of them go back into the hotel safe after Saturday night, you know."

"Write this on your pad and give it to them, Clelia: *Unfortunately, Haydn's wonderful anthem doesn't lend itself well to cocktail-hour music. May I offer 'Lili Marlene' instead to brighten your morning?* Sign it, *Piano Man.*"

Clelia carefully wrote the message and walked away in the direction of the crowded bar, and Dieter commenced his delivery of the tip-in-advance requests she had left behind. Two and a half songs later, Clelia again appeared by his side and put a bar napkin on the music rack. Scrawled on the blank side was a return message:

"*'Lili Marlene' would be fine if I may be permitted to sing the lyrics. Sophia.*"

Dieter entirely forgot what song he was playing, and no amount of vamping chords could take him backward in time thirty seconds to when he first saw the returned note. He stopped entirely and stood at the keyboard, searching the room, while the cocktail-hour crowd mumbled to one another. *What happened? Did someone walk in? Who could it be? Is he ill? Can you see anyone?*

Then he saw them—Branka, Otto, and Sofie—smiling in his direction from behind the mâitre d's station. Of course, he had been

Branka's guest only weeks before, so she was unchanged. But it had been four years since he last saw Sofie, and all of the promise of her young adulthood had matured into a truly breathtaking woman. Dieter suddenly remembered that he was standing in a room with two hundred hotel guests where he was the entertainment. He grasped the microphone and, in his best English, said, "Ladies and gentlemen, you must excuse me. I have just learned that one of Europe's finest vocalists is in the room, and she has consented to sing a number. Would you please join me in welcoming Sophia, who comes to us from Paris, where she appeared with the great Django Reinhardt and his famous Quintette. Here is the lovely Swiss chanteuse, Sophia !!"

There was a scattering of applause together with exchanges of questioning looks—who was this *Sophia* who had flabbergasted the suave Piano Man just by entering the room? Curiosity quieted Rio's Sunday set as the bright-eyed newcomer strode confidently to the grand piano and took the microphone from Dieter. "Thank you. I'm delighted to be at the Copacabana Palace and—after a long hiatus—again being accompanied by Dieter the Piano Man. So let's see what we can do— after four years apart—with George Gershwin's incomparable love song, 'The Man I Love.' Mr. Piano Man, give me a few bars of E-flat introduction, and we can show the Palace what this classic ballad is all about."

Four years dissolved in seconds and the two mutually supportive professionals pushed one another to the edges of the beautiful song's possibilities. The Bar do Copa erupted with applause when they had finished, and it was clear that the morning cocktail hour would spill over into the normal luncheon hour and perhaps beyond; the cariocas wanted more than just a taste of what they were listening to. Seven improvised selections later, the Piano Man finally raised his hand and announced that the luncheon string quartet was waiting to begin, so he and Sophia must take their leave for now, But he added, "I intend to ask her if she will favor us with more of her renditions during the evening cocktail hour—will you, Miss Sophia?" She nodded affirmatively and both musicians waved and even threw a kiss toward the corner where Branka and Otto had stood. Then they walked past still-applauding patrons and out the door toward Avenida Atlântica, hand in hand.

"Can we walk to an empty bench and sit facing the water?" Dieter asked. "I have so many questions that I don't know which to ask first—but, before I ask any at all, let me say that I have never been so surprised or so happy. I never thought I would see you again. Just being free once more was the gift of a lifetime, and I would have revisited my memories endlessly and counted myself fortunate to have them. But today is . . . " He couldn't complete the sentence. Her kiss punctuated it, and then they both sat with their heads resting together and watched the long, white waves carry bathers and surfers toward the shore while *gaviotas* circled above the beach in graceful, wide arcs.

"And . . . Branka and your father? I forgot about them!" Dieter suddenly spoke. "They will think we are rude. I haven't even said hello."

"They departed after four or five songs," Sofie shrugged. "Poppy always wanted to hear me perform in public, but he never got to Paris again. They aren't staying in Rio. There's some cousin of Father's in Santa Catarina—south of here. He has a huge *finca* far into the backcountry, and I don't expect Branka and Father to surface until the war is over and order returned to the world. For now, it is better that we don't know any more than that."

"And you?"

"I am hoping that you will let me stay with you here in Rio and perhaps become your musical partner again. Much as we planned to do once at the Majestic Plaza. Perhaps some day there will be a Germany to which we can return, but we may be a good bit older before that can happen. What do you say?"

"Do you have a suitcase?"

"Three of them, checked at the hotel. Herr Stinnes gave us reasonably large quarters on a freighter, so I brought my best things along."

"Then let's retrieve them and get on with life."

"Good idea! I must see whether Josephine Baker can still race your motor. And then—much later—I have many, many questions to ask about your memoir, *Über Alles*."

APPENDIX A

HISTORICAL THREADS

Über Alles has attempted to capture a finite cross section in time and to move fictional characters through an authentic landscape of the personalities, events, and attitudes of that period. These are a few of the characters and locations which may have provoked the reader's interest, with a thumbnail description of the direction each took after the time of our story.

THERESIENSTADT – From 1940, when the Nazis took control of the old fortress built by Austrian Emperor Joseph II, until mid-1945, when Germany released it to the International Red Cross, it is estimated that about 150,000 Jews, Gypsies, and homosexuals were sent there. Of those, an estimated 35,000 died within the fortress, principally from conditions there. Another 90,000 were transported on to Auschwitz from Theresienstadt after they became ill or could no longer contribute their labor. Only about 17,250 of those who were consigned to Theresienstadt were known to have survived the experience. There is a sizeable body of artistic work remaining intact from the musicians, writers, and painters who were prisoners in Theresienstadt. The fortress/camp is currently open to the public and may be visited conveniently from Prague.

REINHARD "HANGMAN" HEYDRICH, the Reichsprotektor of Bosnia and Moravia, who appears in *Über Alles*, established Theresienstadt as a "transient facility," and it remained under his general command until his death, which occurred following a car ambush in the spring of 1942. His first action as commander had been to expel the small community's approximately 7,000 existing inhabitants (who were Czech but not Jewish) and replace them with a much larger Jewish ghetto. The facility was always overcrowded except when it was put "on display" as an ideal community of Jews. Heydrich's murder was avenged by Hitler, who ordered brutal retaliation against the small Czech communities where it was claimed that Heydrich's murder had been planned.

The town of Lidice was singled out for the most brutal retaliation; its inhabitants were murdered and its buildings razed. Czech composer Bohuslav Martinů soon thereafter composed *Memorial to Lidice* while he was living in the USA, and it is still performed frequently by The Discovery Orchestra and other major symphonic groups.

THE QUINTETTE DU HOT CLUB DE FRANCE never totally regained the brilliance and singular prominence it had enjoyed in prewar Europe, although Django Reinhardt and Stéphane Grappelli did reunite briefly in Great Britain after the war, and they recorded several more excellent sides together. Each continued to acknowledge the genius of the other, but they generally followed separate professional paths after 1945.

DJANGO REINHARDT, after WWII, fulfilled his long-cherished desire to travel through America and perform with several of his most admired American jazz musicians, including Dizzy Gillespie and "Duke" Ellington. His appearances at New York's Carnegie Hall were prominently advertised and widely reported. He demanded (and was paid) exceptionally high performance fees in wartime France as well as during the period of his two-year American tour, but he gambled and spent lavishly and so never acquired permanent wealth. Django was a musical savant, but he was never trained to read music, and so his talent could not be integrated easily into the Big Band/Swing Era, which succeeded the small-combo jazz era of which Django had been a leader. The new "swing" music was built around detailed professional arrangements, which Django never learned to read. He gradually became less disciplined in his music and his personal life but was recognized by an entire generation of guitarists as the foremost creative genius of that instrument. Django had a life-long fear of medical doctors and so ignored signs of his own health hazards. He chain-smoked and drank heroically, and probably encountered some of the drugs common to musicians. In 1953, at age forty-three, Django died in France of a cerebral hemorrhage.

NAGUINE REINHARDT receives only brief mention in *Über Alles* but deserves inclusion among the historical threads of this novel. Naguine met Django when she was fourteen and he was fifteen, and she instantly fell in love with him. During the following two years, they were dedicated to one another, but then the fast-moving musician left her for Bella, an older and presumably more attractive woman who became his first wife. When Bella later went her separate way, Naguine was patiently waiting for Django, and she was with him for the rest of his life, sharing the wild and crazy adventure he fashioned for them. During WWII they decided to formalize their dedication, and they married one another in April 1943 in Salbris, France. But *Naguine* was not really the bride's name; it was a Gypsy descriptive nickname, which derived from her appearance—rich, olive skin and luxuriant, dark hair. Her real name, which surfaced on the marriage certificate, was Sophie Irma Ziegler. It is amazingly similar to the name already created for the fictional heroine of *Über Alles*, Sofie von Seigler. This was total coincidence. Perhaps it was a discreet message of approval of the project. In any event, it seemed to qualify as a historical thread worthy of noting here. Naguine bore Django a son named Babik Reinhardt, who was his father's delight and who became a competent guitar virtuoso after his father's death.

STÉPHANE GRAPPELLI enjoyed widespread popularity and demonstrated his versatility and his mastery of the violin during an exceptionally long career. He recorded extensively with two of the finest jazz pianists of all time, George Shearing and Oscar Peterson, but also "crossed the street" and teamed with some of the world's best classical musicians, including violin virtuoso Yehudi Menuhin, pianist and conductor André Previn, and cellists Julian Lloyd Webber and the celebrated Yo-Yo Ma. His fluidity and innovation never appeared to age, even as he did, and he performed regularly into his ninetieth year. Stéphane Grappelli died in 1997. Ironically, for readers of *Über Alles*, it should be noted that he appeared in a 1978 motion picture entitled *King of the Gypsies*.

REICHSMARSCHALL HERMANN GÖRING knew better than most that the war had been lost, and, as a military professional would do, he surrendered in May 1945. He was one of the principal Nazi leaders tried by a war crimes tribunal convened in Nuremberg, Germany. Göring participated actively in his own defense, attempting to present evidence that he had assisted some Jews in escaping from the wave of anti-Semitic atrocities being committed by the regime. Ultimately, his pivotal role in implementing the government's policy targeting Jews, Gypsies, and homosexuals was clearly established by the prosecutors, and he was sentenced to be put to death by hanging. Again, his military demeanor asserted itself, and Göring insisted that the death sentence be carried out by a military firing squad, as befits a soldier. That was denied by the court. Göring committed suicide on October 15, 1946, by ingesting cyanide—in effect cheating the hangman. His body was cremated and his ashes spread in a river near Munich. Hermann Göring lived only fifty-three years; EMMY GÖRING, HIS WIFE, lived on in Germany to age eighty.

REICHSFÜHRER HEINRICH HIMMLER, as head of Germany's wartime internal police activities (including the feared Gestapo), had the primary role in implementing the "ultimate solution" with respect to Jews, Gypsies, homosexuals, and others who were identified as undesirable. Estimates of the internal carnage seem to agree that at least six million Jews, half a million Romani, and another two million miscellaneous "enemies of the state" died in the camps or, indirectly, through the actions of Himmler's organizations. Himmler apparently tried to negotiate Germany's capitulation—under terms which would provide immunity from prosecution for him. The effort was unsuccessful, and he then attempted to disguise himself as a noncom to avoid identification and prosecution with the others at Nuremberg. He was captured and correctly identified by British forces near the Danish border in May 1945. Before he could be de-briefed, Himmler, like Göring, swallowed cyanide and killed himself. Heinrich Himmler was only forty-four years old at the time of his death.

LT. COL. HANS OSTER, principal author of the failed 1938 "Oster Conspiracy" on the life of Adolf Hitler, continued to regard the führer with disdain and distrust even while he functioned as an officer in the

German Office of Military Intelligence. There appear to have been several of his fellow Wehrmacht professionals who shared his viewpoint and who were horrified by the slaughter of the spreading Holocaust. Oster was a participant in multiple attempts to terminate Hitler, but he was a very clever counterintelligence operative and thus able to advance in rank to the level of Major General and to discharge key responsibilities in international counterintelligence activities. He is credited with having assisted many Jewish professionals to flee from Germany and with providing Poland and Holland with advance warnings of German invasion plans. Ultimately, he was undone when the diaries of a coconspirator, Admiral Wilhelm Canaris, were discovered; they described many of the anti-State activities of Oster, Canaris, and other plotters. Oster was arrested immediately after another failed coup, and he was sent to Flossenburg Concentration Camp, where he was accorded a death sentence on April 8, 1945. He was murdered the next day; he was fifty-six years old.

RAFAEL SCHÄCHTER – Among the many fine musicians who were imprisoned in Theresienstadt, none was more heroic than the Romanian-born Jewish composer, pianist, and conductor Rafael Schächter. For three years, from 1941 to 1944, he was the primary cultural organizer of the many talented musicians there, and his musical accomplishments and morale-building leadership almost exceed credibility. Schächter assembled both male and female choral groups into a choir of more than 200 voices, and they performed many intricate compositions, including 15 renditions of Verdi's *Requiem*, as recounted in this novel.

It should be noted that the author has taken the liberty of placing the Red Cross performance of Verdi's *Requiem* earlier in his fictional timeline to fall within the time that Dieter Meister was confined in Theresienstadt. (The actual performance probably took place in 1944.) Schächter's extraordinary accomplishments and the comfort and inspiration he brought to his fellow inmates under seemingly impossible circumstances are a stellar example of the resilience of the human spirit and the triumph of compassion in the face of evil. In this novel, which explores the effects of war on the people who are touched by it, Rafael Schächter's story begged to be borrowed, moved slightly ahead in time to accommodate this fictional treatment, and told.

Late in 1944, Schächter was sent east to the infamous Auschwitz death camp in a rail car packed with other sick prisoners. He died shortly thereafter, but a significant body of the work he accomplished at Theresienstadt has survived him. The old Petrof piano used at Theresienstadt was somehow smuggled into or found abandoned in a warehouse in the prison by Schächter—it would have been the very one tuned and played by our fictional Dieter Meister and his fictional cell mate Adam Wodzinski.

CHARLES A. LINDBERGH's early reluctance regarding the US entry into the European conflict that became WWII, plus his fascination with Germany and some German leaders, cost him popularity at home. It impeded his efforts to fly for his country as a member of the armed forces, although he ultimately made significant contributions to several phases of the country's war effort. He tested new aircraft types and ferried many to the war zones. As one of the world's most experienced fliers, he was able to help establish training and safety norms that helped his country's pilots to become the world's best. After Lindbergh's death in 1974, at the age of seventy-two years, it was disclosed that his fascination with Germany had extended beyond the field of aviation. He had launched three separate families there, fathering seven children by three women. Two of them were sisters with the surname Hesshaimer; the third was his European secretary, Valeska, who bore him two children. All of this was apparently unknown to wife Anne Morrow Lindbergh and their children during most of his life. Lindbergh continued to be a prominent figure in aviation, serving as an active board member at Pan American World Airways and consulting regularly with leaders in the airline and aircraft construction industries as well as with the military.

THE KING OF THE GYPSIES was, as described in *Über Alles*, an ancient title revived in Poland in 1898 as part of the government's effort to create a census of the itinerant people and to derive tax revenues from that source. The three generations of Kwiek "Kings" provided Gypsy leadership for three generations of subjects, and they kept their people in motion and out of trouble during much of that time. However, Nazi leadership was tireless in attacking the Romani, and they passed edicts that all Gypsy men be sterilized in an attempt to obliterate the "race." Ultimately, the Gypsy population was decimated by imprisonment in camps and reduced to a shadow of its earlier prominence, particularly in Northern Europe. However, Django Reinhardt and his brother Joseph, who were Belgian Gypsies (as were some of the other musicians who joined them from time to time), continued to live and perform without interference. There is no record of them coming under attack in German-occupied areas throughout the war. The immunity accorded them by "Doktor Jazz" (Luftwaffe Oberleutnant Dietrich Schulz-Köhn) was highly effective.

SOPHIA'S SONG SELECTIONS seem to have been unerringly good ones. Each was contemporaneously popular, and the composers and signature performers mentioned in *Über Alles* are described accurately. Deservedly, the compositions Sofie favored have survived and become standards performed by subsequent generations of musicians across the world. Unfortunately, there are no recordings of Sofie singing her favorites.

THE BÖSENDORFER IMPERIAL PIANO at 80 Wilhelmstrasse, Berlin, was the starting point for Dieter Meister's story. That particular instrument is apocryphal, but the Imperial has been the "gold standard" instrument for superb pianists and serious piano collectors since Franz Liszt first rocked his audiences. Those huge Bösendorfers have survived plagues, depressions, and wars, and they are still sought, bought, and—most important—played by the most discriminating artistes. Bösendorfer publishes an extensive list of its prominent patrons. It is much too long to include in its entirety, but these well-recognized contemporary Bösendorfer "names" may interest the readers of *Über Alles*: Vladimir Ashkenazy, Paul Anka, Tony Bennett, Placido Domingo, Roberta Flack, Marvin Hamlisch, Michael Jackson, Billy Joel, Steven Jobs, Quincy Jones, Adam Makowicz, Willie Nelson, Oscar Peterson, André Previn, Lionel Richie, George Shearing, Frank Sinatra, Sting, John Tesh, John Williams, Stevie Wonder, Frank Zappa.

Perhaps the most significant historical thread leading onward from the events described in *Über Alles* is the quintessential "perfect storm confluence" of popular discontent and opportunity that periodically catapults an iconic character to the forefront. Throughout history, ordinary citizens have embraced such charismatic leaders and followed them emotionally to extremes beyond their original intentions. When this has happened, entire nations have marched lemminglike into disaster. Because the lessons of history are not always heeded, this will probably reoccur during the twenty-first century. Our greatest danger may lie in the reality that each successive confrontation of nations is played out with ever more powerful weapons and larger numbers of people. Much like Dieter Meister and Sofie von Seigler, ordinary citizens who have minimal personal interest in the disputed national issues have almost no way to avoid being swallowed into the conflict. Too often, they become the casualties.

APPENDIX B

DRAMATIS PERSONAE OF ÜBER ALLES

(alphabetically listed by surname. The names of fictional persons are in ROMAN TYPE; those of real persons (*) are in *ITALICS*)

HEINZ BARTEL   (b. 1895)..
Assistant manager, Bank Julius Baer, Zurich

BRANKA (b. 1909)..................... ....
Polish SWW operative in Lisbon; consort of General von Seigler

ELSA DANZIG   (b. 1911) ....
Polish SWW operative in Czechoslovakia

JURGEN DEITZ (1909–1939) ....
Gestapo accountant on Prague staff of Col. Edward Gunther

BORG DONNER   (1908–1939) ....
Gestapo enforcement specialist, Prague office

DRACO (b. 1903) ....
Large Czech Gypsy laborer and bodyguard

MAGDA (b. 1912) ....
Polish SWW operative in Czechoslovakia

*EMMY GÖRING (1893–1973) ....
Second wife of Hermann Göring

*HERMANN GÖRING (1893–1946) ....
Reichsmarschall of German forces in WWII

HORST GNOFF (1910–1939) ....
Gestapo enforcement specialist, Prague office

*STÉPHANE GRAPPELLI (1908–1997) ....
French jazz violinist / Quintette du Hot Club de France principal

LT. COL. EDWARD GUNTHER (1898–1940) ....
Gestapo commander in Prague

JURASLAV HAVLIK (1898–1944) ....
Prague physician; son of Lilka Rudovska and Tovar Havlik

TOVAR HAVLIK (1874–1924) ....
Gypsy physician; first husband of Lilka Rudovska; father of Juraslav

*REINHARD HEYDRICH (1904–1942) ....
Reichsprotektor of Bosnia and Moravia, Czechoslovakia

*HEINRICH HIMMLER (1900–1945) ....
Reichsführer of German SS and Gestapo

GIESELA HOFF (b.1911) ....
Gestapo operative monitoring Humboldt University, Berlin

LT. KLAUS KOLB (b.1908) ....
Military aide to General Otto von Seigler

*GREGORY KWIEK ....
King of the Gypsies (from 1898 to 1930)

*MICHAEL KWIEK ....
son of Gregory, King of the Gypsies (from 1930 to 1937)

*JANUSZ KWIEK ....
son of Michael, King of the Gypsies (beginning 1937)

*CHARLES A. LINDBERGH (1902–1974) ....
American aviation pioneer and world hero; first to solo across the Atlantic

DIETER MEISTER (aka DIETER HAVLIK) (b. 1911) ....
German musician imprisoned at Theresienstadt

MIGUEL DO NACIMIENTO (b.1909) ....
Portuguese manager of Berlin pub; companion of Dieter Meister

*LT. COL. HANS OSTER (1887–1945) ....
*Abwehr (German military intelligence organization) German intelligence
official; plotter against Hitler*

RENATE (b. 1909) ....
Porte Verte prostitute (Prague); SWW informant

* DJANGO REINHARDT (1910–1953) ....
Gypsy jazz guitarist; Quintette du Hot Club de France principal

LILKA RUDOVSKA (b. 1875) ....
Polish SWW intelligence coordinator; mother of Sofie and Juraslav

*HUGO STINNES JR. (1891-1982) ....
Scion of German industrial and shipping family (Lisbon)

URSULA (b. 1920) ....
Porte Verte prostitute (Prague)

SOFIE VON SEIGLER (a.k.a. SOPHIA HAVLIK) (b. 1915) ....
Musician; daughter of Otto and Lilka; lover of Dieter Meister

GENERAL OTTO VON SEIGLER (b.1890) ....
Wehrmacht general; husband of Lilka Rudovska; father of Sofie

ADAM WODZINSKI (1897–1944) ....
Polish physician; companion of Juraslav Havlik

THE DAGGER

By Robert Arthur Neff

A German officer's World War II SA Dagger has been incorporated into the cover design of *Über Alles*, and a small profile of that dagger is used as the horizontal separation of text throughout the book. It is an actual dagger that came into my possession after the conclusion of the war in Europe, about the time of my fourteenth birthday, through a set of circumstances I'd like to share with readers.

The lives of all civilians on the home front were altered significantly as WWII ground along—certainly none so much as those who had loved ones serving in the military. Kids my age collected empty tin cans plus discarded rubber tires; we crafted models of enemy aircraft for "spotters"; we did some of the community maintenance tasks normally performed by absent men; and we invested our spare change in war bonds and stamps. But we were kids nonetheless, and, when time permitted, we also enjoyed normal "kid activities"—like playing baseball.

We had fashioned a lumpy, undersized baseball field in an open lot that separated my house from the next one to the west, and after school and on weekends we held noisy pickup games there. I knew the older owners of that house and also was aware that their married, schoolteacher daughter and her infant son had left their own house and moved back "while her husband was away." And, when I tracked down foul balls hit toward that house, I often saw the small boy pressed against a window, watching our pickup games.

One day, after the others had gone home to dinner, I rang the doorbell and asked if the little boy would like to walk over to the field with me and play catch. The offer was enthusiastically accepted, and from time to time that ritual was repeated. Then one day the boy's mother appeared at our door and handed me a box which had been sent from Germany and which contained a note from the boy's father to his wife, reading, "Sweetpea, this is for Bobby Neff, to thank him for playing ball with Joey." Under the note was the SA dagger.

Two years later, I left that town to go away to school, and I never returned to live there or had further contact with that family. The boy's father returned and was elected mayor of the town; his son became a respected lawyer and prosecutor in the area. As *Über Alles* neared publication, I called the son and related this story, which he heard for the first time nearly seven decades after it occurred.

ABOUT THE AUTHOR

From his early years, Robert Arthur Neff has thrived on international involvement. Military service, business responsibilities, and personal travels have familiarized him with the locations and events entwined in his historical novel, *Über Alles*, a story he describes as "either a history lesson wrapped in a love story, or the reverse of that."

Mr. Neff studied engineering, political science, and law at Cornell University, then he "entered the real world" as a JAG officer in the US Air Force. He was assigned to the 63rd Troop Carrier Wing of MATS, which aggregated squadrons deployed to overseas locations ranging from North Africa to Europe to Canada's DEW Line to New Zealand and Antarctica. These became a new kind of classroom for the itinerant lawyer.

After his military service, Mr. Neff knew that he wanted a business career that would continue expanding his knowledge of many cultures and countries. He had the good fortune to find just such a job with the Rockefeller Brothers' International Basic Economy Corporation, headquartered at "30 Rock." Initially his assignments were focused upon Western Europe and The Middle East, but later they shifted to the management of various South American businesses, and that continent became Mr. Neff's home for several years.

Prominent international businessmen were demanding more efficient, affordable air cargo services to accommodate the exploding growth of high-value international commerce. A leader in the movement was Mr. Laurance Rockefeller, whose participation in the airline industry collaterally yielded a welcome opportunity for Mr. Neff. He became an officer and director of Seaboard World Airlines, a major all-cargo airline which was pioneering international carriage innovations and also performing world-wide contract carriage for the US Department of Defense. Seaboard and the Flying Tiger Line later merged, and their combined activity eventually became an integral part of the contemporary Federal Express Corporation, from which Mr. Neff is a retiree.

Mr. Neff now resides with his wife, Julie, in Pinehurst, NC, and on Beaver Island, MI. They continue to visit other parts of the world frequently, and Mr. Neff has formalized his lifelong interest in writing, drawing extensively upon themes suggested by his work and travels. Favored leisure activities include playing jazz standards on his oversized grand piano, watching and playing tennis, and enjoying the uncomplicated attractions of Nicaragua's Pacific Coast, where he does much of his serious writing.

CPSIA information can be obtained
at www.ICGtesting.com
Printed in the USA
FFOW04n1745150916
27689FF

9 781938 462252